I0588099

ALL THE WHYS OF DELILAH'S DEMISE

A DYSTOPIAN MURDER MYSTERY

ALL THE WHYS OF DELILAH'S DEMISE

NEVE MASLAKOVIC

Copyright © 2021 by Neve Maslakovic

All rights reserved.

No part of this book may be reproduced in any form or by any electronic or mechanical means, including information storage and retrieval systems, without written permission from the author, except for the use of brief quotations in a book review.

ISBN: 978-1-7366979-1-7

for ArtWorks
and all the good people there

Chapter One

"So you're the person responsible for the death of the number one," the burly man in a security uniform tells me. "Have a seat."

A room with no windows, brightly lit by overhead lights. A metal table polished to a spotless shine and a pair of matching chairs. The man closes the door and takes the other chair. He gives the impression of never having cracked a smile in his life. He's the head of security in the Dome of New Seattle and his name is Bodi.

"Scott. Rank..." Bodi glances up at my halo—his ConnectChip displays it in his eye field—and continues. "...in the bottom thousand. You're here to tell your side of the story."

It's not an invitation but an order. I attempt to defuse the tension in the room by offering, "Scottie is fine."

Scott conjures up someone more put-together, taller and with no gap between their front teeth...and is more of a guy's name, which I'm not. The Birth Lab assigned it to me, same as Bodi's name was to him, though it's hard to believe that the large, grim man facing me was ever a gurgling infant. Above the significant eyebrows and the knobby nose is the halo my own chip, Cece, superimposes upon his person; the colors in the ring of gems add up to a respectable Top Thousand rank, meaning Bodi's liked well enough despite the gruff exterior.

"I'm going to stick with Scott. What are you, twenty?"

"Nineteen."

"And you've been with the Agency for how long?"

In a stark mismatch to my lackluster social skills, I'm an intern at the hub of town life—New Seattle's Social Agency, of all places. "Just under three months."

"And they assigned you to liaison with Delilah."

"Yes."

"A lot of responsibility for an intern," he observes. "When did you see her last?"

Delilah, gone. Impossible to comprehend. I'm having trouble processing what's happened, much less being blamed for her death. "Last night, at the anniversary celebration. What took place after..."

"The celebration," he repeats. "All right. Start at the beginning."

I shift in the chilly and uncomfortable chair. "Can I pace? I think better on my feet."

At his nod, I start a slow back-and-forth between two walls. "The beginning... I suppose it was yesterday morning. You see, I'd recently decided that I no longer wanted to be Scottie the No One. I wanted to be *someone*."

Chapter Two

Monday, March 15

The last morning of Delilah's life started normally enough for me. Before hopping on my bike, I paused outside Housing Thirty-Three—my room's on the second floor—to watch the birds flit about in the sun. Living in the Dome means no variety—all the birds pecking at the front steps of the building were house sparrows, small and plump and gray-brown. Lately they'd seemed twitchy—fueled by more than their regular feed. I'd have said that they were acting as if on the lookout for something from just over the horizon, except that New Seattle's horizon is limited to solar-glass panels and titanium beams that meet the ground. I was not the only one who'd noticed the change.

This, however, was not the morning to try to puzzle it out. I jumped on the bike and set a course for the Agency. *Cece, is it eight yet?*

TWO MINUTES, SCOTT.

Eight is when the People List updates for the week and

it's never good news. I picked a familiar argument to kill time as I pedaled along. *Cece, I should at least be able to get YOU to call me Scottie given that you're inside my head. Can't you ignore your programming for once and go back to doing it?*

Cece responded to my nudge with her usual answer. NOW THAT YOU ARE AN ADULT, SCOTT, I'M REQUIRED TO ADDRESS YOU BY THE NAME THAT MATCHES YOUR PEOPLE LIST ENTRY. YOU KNOW THAT.

Cece, you're a brick wall.

I AM NOT A BRICK WALL. I AM NEURAL MESH EMBEDDED IN YOUR BRAIN TISSUE AND COUPLED TO A COMMUNICATION CHIP IMPLANTED BEHIND YOUR LEFT EAR. THE KNOWLEDGE REPOSITORY...

There was a pause here as Cece dipped into the repository and I swerved to avoid a pothole, my bike rattling with effort.

...DEFINES A BRICK WALL AS A LARGE NUMBER OF KILN-FIRED CLAY OBJECTS ORGANIZED ROW BY ROW INTO—

Never mind. It must be past eight now. Well?

NINE THOUSAND TWO HUNDRED FIFTY-THREE.

Thirty spots lower than last week. Steering the bike one-handed, I reached into the basket for the breakfast I'd brought along—a bag of cafeteria "mix." Leftovers, a stale medley of raisins, walnuts, and sausage ends. The sausage ends, though cold, weren't bad but the raisins were little green rocks that stuck to my teeth and I dropped them on the ground behind me for the sparrows to gobble up. Where I live, the only way to afford fresh eggs and bacon—though this was a morning when I wouldn't have been able to keep a large breakfast down—is to climb the popularity ladder.

I'm a low-Lister, my rank in the bottom tenth—out of ten thousand. I don't have oodles of friends, a valuable skill, or a unique talent. I'm terrible at schmoozing and even worse at endlessly tooting my own horn. Even if it weren't for all that, what cut off my rank at the knees was the Code of Conduct violation I graduated with—a stone around my neck.

Keep your fibrils crossed, Cece, I thought in the direction of my second inner voice as I biked. The expression is one I made up when I was twelve, which accounts for its lack of sophistication.

TODAY DELILAH CHOOSES SOMEONE FOR A BRAND. DO WE HOPE IT'S YOU, SCOTT?

Like I said, keep'em crossed.

WILL BEING DISCOVERED BY THE DUCHESS GARNER YOU MORE GEMS? Cece asked as I rounded a corner. OF THE FOUR GEM TYPES THAT FEED THE PEOPLE LIST, A FLAME-RED RUBY IS BEST, AS IT INDICATES THAT A PERSON HAS A HIGH OPINION OF YOU... SECOND BEST IS THE BURNT-ORANGE AMBER, INDICATING THAT THE PERSON CONSIDERS YOU TO BE ALL RIGHT... BRIGHT GREEN JADE MEANS THEY HAVE DOUBTS... AND, FINALLY, THERE'S THE INKY ONYX. IT SHOULD BE AVOIDED AT ALL COSTS OR YOUR RANK WILL TUMBLE, ESPECIALLY IF THE ONYX IS GIVEN BY A HIGH-RANKED PERSON—

—or the Code Enforcement Office, I know. I don't need a refresher course. How did Lu and Dax do?

LU IS NOW AT 988 AND DAX IS AT 241.

Lu and Dax had leaped up some more and that, at least, was good news. Crunching a walnut, I pedaled on. Lu and Dax are my PALs—Permanent Allies in Life, a link more formal than friend but less binding than family. I used to have three PALs, but now have the two, so the "permanent" part is a bit of a misnomer.

Town architecture follows the curve of the Dome, three- and four-story buildings turning into seven- and eight-story ones as I entered Founders Square, the decorated platform in its middle awaiting the evening's festivities. I rolled to a stop to let a trio of pedestrians pass. Magda, Mia, and Audrey, an inseparable—and insufferable—PAL group.

"Is that whatshername—Scott?" Magda, the ringleader, gave a snicker as they shuffled along purposely slow in front of me. The numbers capping their halos slotted them into the Top Hundred; the suites and balconies overlooking the square are reserved for New Seattle's most popular people. "Did you see how faint her halo is? And those *clothes*?"

My shirt and slacks, their black faded from repeated washings, came with me out of the youth center, where things lean toward basic and where someone overestimated my growth potential by a quarter or so of the sleeve length. I brightened things up with an old-fashioned men's necktie I picked up for cheap at the market—a periwinkle paisley one —by tying it around my waist. My meager salary goes toward the necessities of life—rent and food, not threads. Besides, black, faded or not, is great for hiding bike-grease stains.

"Tooth Gap probably thinks she's got a chance but with a lousy rank like that..."

"Never mind her. Who do you think Delilah's going to choose this year?"

"Well, not *you*, Audrey..."

I called out to their backs, "And good luck to you today, too," both meaning it and wanting to add something from the Code's section Z (*Watch your language! Twenty-two words and three gestures to avoid.*)

Judging by the twitch of Magda's shoulders, I was pretty sure they heard me.

A block past the square, the faces of the Top Ten greeted me on the narrow building I was approaching. On the Tenner billboard, things were much the same as last week, the only change Samm and Sue toggling their number five and six spots as usual, the pair wearing jokey expressions in their snapshots.

Delilah was at the top, as she had been for nearing-on fifty years. The billboard showed its age, a pixel here and there a lifeless freckle dotting the image, but the inimitable quality summed up in her brand—*the Duchess*—shone through. The angle of her chin and the hair tossed back radiated charisma, clout and authority rested comfortably on the high cheekbones, a zest for life could hardly be contained in the eyes. Or so it seemed to me as I rolled to a stop under the billboard and slid my bike into the rack out front. Having emptied the remainder of the cafeteria mix onto the ground—a couple of sparrows made a beeline for it at once—I went inside. The Agency has its thumbs on both sides of the scale: we help people improve their social standing—if they can afford us—*and* assess it by churning out the List. It's a fine dance that only works because there's strict separation between the Listkeeper's office on the fifth floor and the rest of the staff.

I took the stairs two at a time to the fourth floor. I found Wayne blowing on the last of the invitations to dry the ink. My mentor is five years older and sported the usual light stubble and shoulder-length hair loosely tied in the back. Sliding the stack in my direction, he reminded me to join him in the square once I was done delivering the invites—Delilah's first of course.

"Wayne, what do you think my chances are?" I asked on the way out. "For the brand."

Wayne looked up from the felt-lined case where he stores unused cardstock. "That's easy, Scottie. One in fifty-two."

Fifty-two was the number of candidates, youth center graduates in the past year, in the running for the Discovered brand—with me as the oldest. Delilah had left her choice, to be announced at the evening celebration, till the last minute.

A short hop took me back to Founders Square and to the round building on its east side. Leaving the bike against a cherry tree, I took the back door in. *Mrs. Montag* was set to open in three days with Delilah in the starring role, and half-costumed actors popped in and out of dressing rooms. Daydreaming about my future prospects, Delilah's invite in hand, I knocked on the door at the hallway end. *Here goes nothing, Cece.*

"Just set it on the table, newbie."

Delilah closed her eyes again, having barely glanced at the invite I propped against a jar of facial cream. She was being readied for rehearsal by Evan, who expertly juggles the roles of makeup artist, hair stylist, and stagehand as needed. Mini-bulbs lined the vanity mirror, a handful of them dark permanently.

As to the paper invite, it's a tradition. On a typical Monday, the graceful black-ink letters penned by Wayne on deckle-edged ecru cardstock serve to remind the Tenners what's on the social menu for the evening—a banquet, cocktails, an entertainment show, the monthly gala—all of it meant to honor them for their town leadership. This was no typical Monday. It was the day of the annual celebration of New Seattle's founding anniversary, eighty-five this year, and everyone was invited. I'd been coming by to provide planning updates and make sure Delilah's wishes were accommodated, doing all I could to put my best foot forward. I couldn't believe my luck—having spent nine months doing bike-deliveries while doggedly applying for an Agency internship, I was accepted into the event-planning division and with that had come the liaising with Delilah.

I stood to the side, nervously awaiting my turn, as Evan attended to Delilah's hair. Its shine and lack of gray were due not just to his care but to the special perk reserved for the number one, a longevity cocktail: Eternal Life. I focused my eyes just above Delilah's reflection in the mirror and Cece topped it with her halo, vibrant red with rubies and a sturdy *1* in its center. Holding my gaze steady set the gem comments popping out in columns to the left and right: "*The Duchess shines on the stage and off it ... I can't imagine anyone else in the number one spot ... Talent, charm, the Duchess has it all!*" I had noticed over the course of my visits that even Delilah's exes—there were quite a few gems in this category, though faded over time, an artificial effect—had good things to say, clearly not bearing grudges about being sent on their way; I wondered, having little experience on that score, if that's standard.

My own ruby for her showed up in the rotation, awkwardly-worded. "*Best wishes from a big fan.*"

As to my own gap-toothed face in one corner of the mirror, I noticed a shiny smudge on my chin from bike grease and quickly wiped it off.

Evan chatted as he worked. "The olive oil conditioner will keep it nice and smooth for tonight... Boring braid for the rehearsal, but we'll make sure to do something *brill* for the party. I just wish it wasn't *eighty-five*, that's all. People are saying we should be worried." The hand with the brush paused and I knew what Evan was about to say. "'Cause of Gemma Bligh's *curse.*"

The story of Gemma Bligh and the curse made the rounds every year in the youth center. It starts—and quite a tale it is—with the Dimming. Particles released into the atmosphere to counter global warming reflected sunlight a little too well, causing year-round winter. Domes went up all around the world. New Seattle's first generation—the Founders—was chosen by a lottery limited to those under the age of twenty-four, excepting essential experts and a handful of children. Old Gemma Bligh fumed to anyone who would listen that the Founders were turning their backs on those left Outside. She made the trek from her Seattle neighborhood to the newly-built Dome on a snowmobile, the tale goes, alone and suffering in the cold so much that she lost her voice along the way. Denied entrance, she pounded and scratched at the glass—at street level it's not the solar-collecting kind, just sturdy and thick—before being sent away. She died soon after, leaving behind a curse on New Seattle timed to hit when the town made it to her own age: Eighty-five.

That is, if you believe that sort of thing.

"If only we knew *where* Gemma's curse will strike," Evan went on, his fingers expertly knitting a long braid. "People say she aimed it at the very heart of the town. All the Founders are long gone and those of us who live here now, well, what's it got to do with us how Gemma was treated back then, right?"

"What indeed. It's all a basket of nonsense." Delilah was not in a good mood, I realized, and her next words only confirmed the impression. "The Dome isn't going to collapse or burn up or whatever disaster it's supposed to be. No need to spread made-up tales."

Evan, chastised into silence, turned his attention to the make-up jars. Where skin is concerned, even Eternal Life can't help, and I watched the contoured lines on Delilah's face—the topography of a life—disappear under a creamy paste; seventy years of living cut in half for the stage lights, even for rehearsals. Evan reached for eyeliner and the movement sent the invite sliding off the table. I picked it up and set it back.

"Well, don't just stand there, newbie," Delilah addressed me just as I thought I couldn't stand the wait another minute. "What do you have for me today?"

I snapped to it and ran through the finalized schedule for the evening, which I had on a corkboard—not one actually made out of cork or anything solid, just a semi-transparent rectangle Cece displayed in my eye-field. "We've moved the prizes you're giving out to the start of the event. There's dinner at the Oyster for the winner of a raffle, gifts for the people who gave and received the millionth gem, and—"

Delilah interrupted. "Who's the millionth-gem pair?"

"Uh—" Damn. So much for putting my best foot forward. This year we had an additional milestone to celebrate—we'd hit a million gems, counting those belonging to current residents as well as past ones. I couldn't remember the details of the gem that took us over the threshold and didn't have them on the corkboard. Luckily the wardrobe manager chose that moment to poke their head in to ask if Delilah preferred the brown cowboy boots or the red pair. *Cece, quick, send a thought to Wayne: "The names of the millionth-gem pair?"*

Conversations with others take over the internal dialogue from Cece; in-thoughts are devoid of the sound of their creator's voice but mood and manner do come through and Wayne's exasperation at having to train an intern who can't keep track of the simplest things was a thunderous grumble in my mind. *"Scottie, this should be on your corkboard.*

Yoshi, a cafeteria cook, gave a ruby to Pearl, a fabric dyer. They'll each get a fruit basket."

"Got it, thanks," I responded.

After the red cowboy boots had been chosen and Delilah leaned back in the chair again, I relayed the information.

"Fruit baskets. Not a bad haul for doing nothing more than packaging an opinion and receiving that opinion. Anything else, newbie?"

This was it. "This year's Discovered brand. The Agency sent over a corkboard with fifty-two names," I reminded her. "You were going to select someone."

She gave an exaggerated sigh. "So I was. All these fresh-faced people offering to run errands for me, tapping me on the shoulder to carry my things, attempting to flatter me left and right on the Commons..." The Commons is a town-wide cloud churning with snapshots and opinions on matters large and small; I haven't gotten around to contributing to it yet. Delilah followed up her words with a yawn behind a manicured hand. "It's all been so tiresome, I'm ready to skip the whole thing this year."

I had spent weeks hoping she'd choose me. But really, why would she even have taken notice of me? Her plate was full—there were the never-ending social events that came with being the number one, plus her *two* day jobs, the leadership of the town and the stage. It was a lot for one person to handle. The weekly dose of Eternal Life boosted her wellness, like one of the solar panels of the Dome storing up energy. But we did keep her busy—too busy to notice an intern.

"What about—er—me?"

Delilah opened an eye—making Evan, who was applying globs of mascara that seemed to double the width and extent of her eyelashes, tut-tut—and trained it in my direction. "You'd like to be chosen?"

Hope drove away the uncomfortable sensation that had settled on my skin. Like I said, I'm not used to tooting my own horn. "Very much so."

"You go, girl," Evan threw in, sounding as if he'd be happy to toss his own hat into the ring if he were a few years younger.

Wordlessly, Delilah relaxed back in the chair, leaving me hanging. Once the door closed behind Evan, she leaned into the mirror and studied her face with the bold stage make-up on it. I was worried she'd forgotten I was there but she swiveled around to face me. I could tell she was looking at my halo, her gaze just above my scalp. "Newbie. You've been out of the youth center for what, twelve months?"

"Just about," I answered.

"And not even half as many gems. I won't ask about that infraction onyx, but why on earth *do* you have so few gems?"

She had never asked me anything personal before. It was the first but not the last surprise the day would hold. "I don't have a brand," I said simply. Staring at the mirror for a couple of seconds brought up my own halo. I don't have enough gems for the comments to stream—they just sort of hang in the air. Looming large was the onyx from the Code Enforcement Office that followed me out of the youth center and slotted me straight into the bottom thousand, the comment attached to it short and to the point: *"Section F violation."* On the cheerier side of things were my two rubies, the first from Wayne (*"A great addition to the Social Agency. Go Scottie!"*) and the second from Lu (*"PALs forever."*) My remaining gems, adding up to a grand total of five, were the welcome-to-adulthood amber everyone gets and a jade from a next-door neighbor, the comment in it—*"Scott is hard to get to know*"—making me think there's nothing *to* know every time I look at my reflection.

Elegant in a silk robe, Delilah went to change, calling out from behind the curtain, "*No brand* is nothing but an excuse."

"But it's true," I protested. "I don't have, like, a *thing*. A talent. A gift. Not like you do."

Delilah never needed help from the Agency. Others do, or, if they can't afford Agency prices, resort to halo-padding, which is when you trade gems under the table in an effort to boost the color of your halo. I've never thought of doing it, and not only because halo-padding is against the Code. Worse than not being popular would be faking it.

"It's not a talent. I work for it, same as anyone." I could hear what sounded like weariness in her voice. She had more to say. "A brand is a hook, that's all. There has to be something behind it. You have to let people see the real you —not everything necessarily, but enough... You have to give freely, every day."

"I tried giving. It didn't work."

She emerged in twentieth-century costume—blue jeans, a button-up shirt checkered with warm orange and purple, the red cowboy boots—and opened a drawer in the vanity. Inside was a small box of chocolates. She offered me one. Chocolate is an expensive delicacy imported from far-away domes via long-distance trains. It's heaven masquerading under a dull brown, and I'd only tasted it once a year starting with the PAL ceremony at age seven and on PAL anniversaries after that. Twelve times—this made thirteen. I quickly reached out a hand.

Delilah took one for herself. "So you want to make a splash on New Seattle's social scene."

"Even a ripple will do," I said, trying not to smack my lips too loudly.

"No."

A stone sank into my stomach, obliterating the sweet aftertaste of the chocolate. "No?"

Delilah shook her head. "I wouldn't be doing you a favor. An artificial brand is not the way to go. Make friends beyond your PAL group, try out hobbies, meet new people, go out and about. Then build on that."

Battling to keep the disappointment—and fear—out of my voice, I asked, "But what if I don't manage to build anything at all? What if I sink all the way down to last place?"

I knew the math: ten thousand, New Seattle's count of adults, must remain steady. Too many people and we run out of resources. Too few and we run out of working hands. Each week the youth center—a trio of buildings on the south side of town—spits out a grad who needs a place on the List. The lowest-ranked person is sent to one of the nine greenhouses that surround New Seattle to work for room and board farming crops or tending livestock...unless the greenhouses are at capacity, which happens a couple of times a year. In that case the bottomer goes sledding.

The old definition of sledding, according to Cece and the Knowledge Repository, was when you sat down on a wooden sled or a used mattress and slid down a snow slope, which sounds fun enough and for all I know Outsiders, who live their whole lives in the cold, still do it. Inside the Dome it means something different. The sledding you do is out a town gate. My worst fear, the stuff of nightmares, one that stops the breath in my lungs. Not because I'm scared of the foreign and inhospitable land on the frost side of the Dome glass—well, that too—but because it means never finding out about myself in the Birth Lab database. Who my parents were. Who *I* am.

"Well, don't sink to the bottom, newbie."

It was not an unkind statement, just the truth delivered with candor, unwrapped and bare.

Delilah put the box of chocolates away and settled a leather cowgirl hat onto the braid. "For tonight, it should be someone already on their way up." Embarrassed that I'd pushed my own name ahead of Lu's, I offered, "One of my PALs—she graduated a month after me—just cracked the Top Thousand. Lu is kindhearted and outgoing. Everyone likes her."

My suggestion was met with a nod. "Have her stand by the stage and I'll make a show of picking someone on the spot from the audience this year." She held up a booted foot. "I'm taking a snapshot"—Delilah liked to drop little morsels of her life onto the Commons—"...and *done*." Give a little of yourself daily, she'd said, though I doubted anyone would care if I had Cece share a snapshot of *my* sandaled foot on the Commons.

Delilah tweaked the cowgirl hat into a more rakish angle. "Newbie, I'll tell you what. My in-queue is backed up. I'll send everything over—go through and see if anything needs my attention. It'll be a good learning experience. Vicky usually does it but she's having an infected tooth removed; she'll be groggy."

Vicky was Delilah's understudy and general assistant, a woman with an eternally pinched expression, as if life had displeased her. I'd wondered where she was, given that she usually spent her time hovering by Delilah's side. The remaining invites sat in my pocket but Delilah was trusting me with her in-thoughts, which meant she didn't consider me a complete loser. "How will I know what's important?"

"Not much of it, probably! I've got the Tenners and town business on a private stream. This is my open queue. Only pay attention to thoughts sent by the Top Hundred people. Wipe the rest. That's your first social lesson right there—the higher the rank a person has, the more what they have to say matters. But you know that already, don't you? That's why you were hoping I'd choose you for the brand."

My cheeks warmed and I said nothing in response. She nodded at the invite. "Keep it. I've got enough of them as it is. And newbie? Sit down. We don't want you crashing your bike because you're wading through a bucketful of in-thoughts."

From the door, she added a final bit of advice. "I see something in you, you know. You have a fine voice. Use it."

"You mean to sing? I can't sing," I responded.

"I'm talking about spreading your wings. Whatever your dreams are, they aren't out of reach."

Once the door closed behind her, I sent Lu a thought with the good news, then slid into the vanity chair. Delilah's jammed-up in-queue arrived promptly. *Cece, let's get to work.* One by one, Cece fed me the individual thoughts. Most fell into the fan mail category and I felt bad each time my decision was *wipe*, as if every rejected thought was a moldy-green bread slice unworthy even of cafeteria mix. After forty-five minutes, I had whittled the queue down to a manageable length. Left in were a couple of Maintenance alerts about wood rot on the balcony of Delilah's suite in Housing One. Nothing struck me as unusual about that, the alerts being a fact of life in a town well into its ninth decade of existence, though mine didn't tend to come from the Maintenance supervisor, Smith.

I had Cece return the now-short queue back to Delilah, then dashed off to deliver the remaining invites.

Though it meant covering a larger distance, protocol dictated the order, by rank rather than by location. Number two at least was easy—the dressing room next door. Figuring that Handsome Rick was at the rehearsal, I slid the invite under his door and, turning away, bumped into someone. Vicky, back from the dentist with her mouth swollen. She winced, her hand flying to her jaw, and sent a furious thought at me. *"Watch where you're going. Why are you still here?"*

"Delilah asked me to sort through her in-thoughts," I responded silently. *"She was concerned you might be groggy."*

"Concerned? Was she. I bet you were eager to do it."

Vicky's halo, above thin, straw-textured hair, told me her rank: in the lower middle of the List, enough to afford the dentist with some penny-pinching. Her mostly amber and jade gems could be summed up simply: *Vicky, you'll get your chance one day.*

She was still eyeing me irritably and I attempted to clarify. *"Don't worry, I'm not after your job. I'm not good at acting or waiting. What I'm saying is, I'd make a terrible understudy. The assisting I could do, but—"*

"Trust me, you don't WANT my job."

She switched to verbal, her voice thick with the dental swelling, the effect a comical one though her words were anything but. "You are very young, aren'*th* you? You know, I could *th*ell you s*th*ories abou*th* the Duches*sh*."

"You could what? Oh, tell me stories."

"Open your eyes. It's an illusion, a fairy *th*ale, her being the best of u*sh*, loved by everyone."

This made me snap to Delilah's defense. "Of course she's loved by everyone. That's why she's the number one."

"Is i*th*? Did she choose you? For the brand?"

"No," I was forced to admit.

"*Shtill* think she's *sho* wonderful?" Vicky shook her head and continued on toward the side entrance to the stage.

Outside the theater, I hopped back on the bike, pedaling fast to make up for being late and having Cece check the people-locator map in case one of the recipients wasn't at their usual location. My legs were starting to cramp by the time I delivered the rest of the invites, my stops in order: the Dragon and the Drumstick, a tavern near Pike Place Market whose proprietor, Everyone's Friend Bonnie—the number three, a jovial and plump bun-haired woman—took the invite with a cheery thank you; the Fill-n-Sip Cup coffee-house in Founders Square, whose manager, Wheelin'-n-Dealin' Chase, the number four, wordlessly accepted his; near the north gate, to Samm's room—he and Sue, at five and six, are a comedic duo, the Jokers, and also dating—I slid both invites under the door without knocking; back to the square and the Oyster, an upscale eatery in the lobby of Housing One whose manager, Jet-Set Jada, the number seven, berated me for being late for a good five minutes; to a building near the youth center where the map pointed me to the location of Poulsbo the Handyman—I found the number eight fixing a broken door hinge; to an office near the Dome's edge for Franz, the number nine, a conflict mediator known as the Relationship Wizard; and finally, back to my own workplace.

New Seattle's number ten is McKinsey, the head of the Social Agency and therefore my boss and Wayne's too. McKinsey has a no-nonsense personality, close-cropped curly silver hair, a penchant for bold colors and patterns, and a plethora of hobbies. There's never been one she's said no to—from rooftop gardening to finger painting to inter-pretative dance—her ability to juggle them along with her job earning her the brand of Time-Management Genius.

One of the first things I'd been told at my Agency orientation was that McKinsey never takes a day off—she is to be found in her fourth-floor office Monday to Sunday. In a snappy bubblegum-pink suit, rapidly instructing a couple of staff on party details, McKinsey paid little attention to the invite I set on her desk, same as Delilah, though she'd not quite reached Delilah's knee-high stack of them.

That done, I went to join Wayne and his crew in Founders Square. The speeches and prize-giving were to take place on the platform that stands permanently mid-square, with the rest of the party spilling over into the Edge Garden, four blocks away in all directions. The ring of green occupying the space where the Dome's structure meets the ground had been humming with activity all week—I'd helped set up booths for carnival-style games and other activities.

Wayne greeted me with, "Jada complained you were late delivering her invite."

"I couldn't help it," I said, trying to catch my breath as I set the bike against the platform. "Delilah asked me to go through her in-thoughts."

"Next time say no."

"To Delilah?"

"Well, say no diplomatically."

"As if it matters," I griped, unaware that there would be no next time—not with Delilah. "She always gives me chills. Jada, I mean, with those dead eyes of hers. She always looks as if she's planning your funeral."

"Jada, she's just...determined." Wayne was by a table behind the platform. He'd carried a wooden crate over. He pried open the lid to reveal wine bottles sitting in straw and passed a corkscrew to me. "Here, take over and empty these —all of them, yes—into the barrel. I need to go pick up a shipment of strawberries coming in on a greenhouse train. And Scottie... Don't have any of the wine. Top Hundred only."

As if I didn't know that already. After twisting the corkscrew in the air experimentally, I set about tackling the first of the bottles. *Cece, dip me into the Commons. Topic: the party. And no visuals—don't want to accidentally stab myself.*

The town mood was one of excitement and anticipation, the shared thoughts a loose string of colorful beads that dropped into my mind one after another. *"There'll be games and punch and hard cider, I heard! ... My friend's in a band, they'll go on after the prizes ... Gemma Bligh died when she was eighty-five, didn't she? ... I'm buying as many tickets as I can for the Oyster raffle ... Lots of people die when they hit eighty-five, what's that got to do with anything? ... Haven't you heard of Gemma Bligh's curse? ... Did someone say raffle? ..."*

The cork popped successfully and I tipped the bottle and watched the golden liquid disappear into the barrel. Discovered by the Duchess—I wanted it, yes. But not because I can't afford a fresh breakfast, or new clothes every month, or a fancy suite to live in. It was something else.

I shook the last few drops in and set the empty bottle back in its spot in the straw. The street allowed a glimpse of a building two blocks away, sterile-gray and with tiny windows, a suitable look for a depository of secrets. Same as everyone in New Seattle, I was conceived inside, from egg and sperm manufactured from skin cells, ones plucked at random from a dusty bank from Old Seattle. Section F states *Absolutely no inquiries into ancestry permitted.* The F is merely a matter of topic-ordering in the Code, but in my mind it stands for *family*. There's no mechanism for me to find out the names of the only people I can call flesh and blood, long gone though they are. I did try one time and succeeded only in getting caught.

A winning brand can shoot you up the List. And those high up, something told me, are allowed to get away with bending rules—even section F. To find out who I am, I needed to figure out first who I could be to others.

All this thinking meant I'd stood still for a few minutes and a sparrow had arrived. I watched it peck at the bits of straw that had escaped the wine crate. There was an ominous element in the persistent up-and-down of its beak, something unsaid and enigmatic in the pinprick eyes. "You're not worried about Gemma Bligh's curse, are you?" I asked it. "More to the point, bird, where am I going to find a brand now?"

It bopped away unconcernedly and I reached for the next bottle.

Delilah had just about thirteen hours left.

Chapter Three

7:45 p.m.

Lu exhaled, having come down off the stage as Yoshi and Pearl went up for their fruit baskets. "Whew, Scottie, that was more intense than I expected—all those people watching me."

I had worked a bottle-toss booth for a while and was now on my free hour. After we left the square behind us and entered the crowded Edge Garden, I asked Lu if she had plans to move to a bigger living space now that she had a sparkling new brand sure to send her higher up in the Top Thousand. The roof of Housing Fifteen, her assigned residence, peeked above the treetops of the garden; back in Founders Square was her workplace, the Oyster, the eatery run by Jada. Lu has hopes of becoming a chef one day. "Never mind a better room," was her response. "I can dine at Top Thousand eateries now—and bring a guest. You should come, Scottie. I've heard they serve chocolate cake and chocolate ice cream, and you can order both if you like."

I shook my head at her. "You'd have to pay my way and that's no good."

"Chocolate?" a voice from behind us said. "If that doesn't convince Scottie to show up, nothing will."

It was Dax, a crisply clean shirt and slacks taking the place of the grass-stained overalls he usually wears. The second of my PALs works in the Gardens Center as a soil scientist. While Lu owes her rank to her outgoing personality, Dax owes his—also in the Top Thousand—to an athletic skill. He's the Racquet Ace; the tennis tournament starts in January of each year and stretches all the way to April to accommodate day jobs. Dax is half a year older and has little interest in perks. It's never occurred to him to pay a visit to an upscale eatery, much less invite anyone along—or to come to a party with plenty of time to spare.

"Discovered by the Duchess, that's a nice one," he said to Lu. "I didn't miss it, arrived just in time to watch from the back of the crowd." Turning in my direction, he added, "Scottie, that dress..."

"What about it?"

"...is a nice color."

Strawberry jam was the color of the dress I borrowed from Lu for the occasion; since the dress fit her just right, it hung loose on my smaller frame.

I have little idea how genetics works—the Knowledge Repository doesn't have much to say on the subject, other than that gene editing ensures our bodies produce no sperm or eggs—but I do know that the Birth Lab brings into the world no closer than third cousins, and the three of us were evidence of that. Lu and Dax stood taller than me. Lu's soft features were a contrast to Dax's angular ones as he eyed all the people off-path in the garden. And only I have the tooth gap... In short, we are definitely not three peas in a pod.

"Let's keep to the path," Dax said disapprovingly. "With this many feet, the grass will get clobbered."

"Yes, sir." I saluted.

"I'm not being bossy, it's section L of the Code. *Respect all town spaces.* Gardens are subsection L-3: *Avoid damaging plants, including unauthorized fruit picking. Stay off grassy areas except where permitted.*"

"Only you would be able to quote that without consulting your CC," I say. While conversing with one's second inner voice is a private activity, it's almost impossible to perform it without breaking eye contact. Everyone unavoidably glances down and to the side—the telltale low-left look.

Dax worked on his hair with a fist, a sign that something was bothering him. I chalked it up to the trampled grass. Around us, lanterns illuminated activity stations, bright streetlamps lined paths, and, as Dax said, there were many feet. With the toasts and the prize-giving over, the festivities had begun in earnest and the band was banging out a beat that carried into the garden over speakers. Through a break in all the people, I caught a glimpse of Delilah. She was gliding along, her elegant gown of cream-colored silk making my borrowed dress seem pedestrian, the glass in her hand filled with what I knew was punch, not wine—she didn't drink alcohol. Tagging along was Rick, the number two, in a showy pink shirt, with one arm around Magda and the other shared by Mia and Audrey. His back blocked my view as Delilah disappeared into the crowd.

That was the last time I saw her.

We had stopped, though we were still some distance from the refreshments stand. Dax and Lu exchanged a look over my head, making me ask, "What?"

"How are you doing, Scottie?" Lu asked. Dax had gone back to rubbing his scalp.

"You mean because Delilah chose you instead of me for the brand? I'm happy for you, you know that." This was true. I *was* happy my PALs were doing well but couldn't help feeling that everything was changing—that I was being left behind.

"It's the List bottom," Lu said quietly.

Kept busy all day with the party setup duties, I'd forgotten to check who ranked ten thousandth this week. *Cece, who's in last place?*

The answer came fast and furious, or at least it seemed so to me. Cece was merely being prompt.

OLIVER.

With that, the party hum around me faded away, memory taking over. I was back to being ten years old, our PALs quartet—Lu, Dax, Oliver, and me—on the school playground in a game of hide-and-seek. Dax is counting down, having covered his eyes, and Lu has folded herself under the playground slide. I'm looking around for a place to hide and spot Oliver peering out of the building dumpster. He gestures a *Here*. I hesitate a moment, then run over and tumble headfirst into the week's garbage waiting to be sorted into compost or reusables. Oliver helps me right myself. We'll both get chewed out by the teachers because of the mess we're making of our clothes, but Dax will never think to look for us here.

And then it's a couple of years later. Oliver's voice has deepened and it's not the only change. His laughter comes less frequently now. He's pulling away and I don't know why.

The ground rumbling under my feet snapped me out of the recollection, a train leaving the underground depot, the tracks a level below us. The segment of the path where we had stopped grazed the panels of the Dome; I watched the four-car train emerge aboveground on the other side, powering through snow banks, its lights faint in the softly falling snow and the dark, its destination unknown. Oliver could be on it, headed to a greenhouse to work for room and board—if he's lucky.

If the moon, somewhere above the snow clouds, were looking down at us, it'd have seen the well-lit Dome surrounded by greenhouse lights twinkling in all directions —except to the west. That way stands the forest, dark and mysterious, and beyond it the Cascades rise into the sky. The villagers who live on their rocky white slopes eke out a living in the cold, forage in cities abandoned after the Dimming, and come on Tuesdays to trade. Outsiders live in family units, rudely known as cave-clans, though their dwellings are said to be wood cabins.

Most List bottomers live out their lives in the green-houses. A few do return into the senior wing of Medical Three after years of back-breaking work. But for the one or two List bottomers a year who don't make it into a green-house, their one-way destination is the mountains—through the forest, without a snowsuit, on foot. Alone.

Lu had gone to find Wayne—they were dating, having met in the cafeteria of their assigned housing; he'd watched her big moment from the back of the stage. I still had a quarter left of my free hour. Dax and I wound our way farther along the curve of the garden. Under a streetlamp, I saw him wince as a tipsy group stomped over an area marked *Newly planted, keep off*. "It's just grass, Dax."

This innocuous statement got Dax all riled up. "Hey, I'll

have you know that grass is quite useful. It converts carbon dioxide into oxygen and lightens the load on the air filters by absorbing pollutants. And don't even get me started on agricultural grasses— Sorry. I'm just passionate about..."

"Grass."

"Guilty as charged." He hesitated. "Scottie... Are you sure you're all right?"

I struggled to put into words what was bothering me. "Oliver and I, we shared the same conception day, even got our names from the same Founder. We didn't look alike but that didn't stop me from secretly pretending we were twins. I still don't know *why* he turned away—if it was something I did. I kept asking, but he never said."

Dax took his time answering as we walked. "Oliver was always different... He tried with us, but he was a loner at heart. The rest of us were bumbling around as best we could, growing up in bursts and stages, and Oliver just steadily got taller, dispensing wisdom and help from the sidelines—until he no longer could."

"He did stand apart... Remember the time the three of us snuck out after midnight to look for Gemma Bligh's scratches in the Dome glass? Oliver thought it was silly and didn't come along." The recollection brought a brief smile to my face. "We came here, to the garden. You said that finger-nails couldn't affect glass, but *if* Gemma wore a diamond ring, there *could* be scratches from that. We did a full loop with a flashlight, only we never found anything."

"I remember that night. It took us three hours to make the loop."

"And whatever we used to prop the dorm door open rolled away and we had to throw pebbles at Oliver's window. He came downstairs barefoot and in his pajamas to let us back in—Lu and I snuck past the teacher on call into our wing and Oliver and you into yours, only you stumbled over something or other and the two of you got in trouble."

"It was a chair…"

The tipsy group had caught up with us and one of them was now attempting to climb a tree on a dare. Dax called out a stay-on-the-path reminder, which sounded like a life instruction to me—one ignored by the interlopers.

As to Oliver, he had sought his own path and lost his way. "We failed him," I admitted with not a small dose of shame. "Did you know he was doing so poorly? I was too busy worrying how *I* was doing."

Dax shook his head. Before going off to look for Wayne, Lu had told us that Oliver was doing all right for a while but his life took a turn for the worse the past couple of months. He sank into the bog—the sequence of four nines; the next to last spot on the List is known as such because people tend to get stuck in it before either managing to pull themselves up or not. Oliver had a cleaning-crew job, Lu said, and was spending nights in a sleeping bag in hallways as he couldn't afford a room. He never responded to her invitation to stay with her. The three of us, a glass of hard cider in hand, had toasted our lost PAL. It was at this juncture that Lu had slid her hands into our elbows, the middle link of a friendship chain, and made us promise that we'd truly be PALs forever and accept help if we needed it. And then, as if to seal the deal, she gave us each a bracelet she'd knotted from neon-green yarn.

Twirling my new bracelet, I continued, "I should have tried harder to reach Oliver back then. When he started pulling away."

"No—uh, if anything, you pushed too hard."

"I did?"

Dax threw a glance in my direction. "You all but tried to knock some sense into him with a shoe."

This was an exaggeration and I stuck to my guns. "Because he forgot what the P in PALs stands for."

"Look, Scottie, you have this way of not giving up. It's a good trait to have in general. But in Oliver's case what he needed was space—and like I said, you tend to push."

I pondered this statement as we passed under a street-lamp; its buttery light caught his hair playfully. I looked away. "I don't *always* push... What's going on over there?"

A boisterous group was gathered near the waste processing plant—it juts into the garden—and the tree there. "An apple tree," Dax informed me. Under it, on an upturned crate, stood a man of my height—Ben the Bird-man. Ben had shot up in rank on the strength of a campaign to rid New Seattle's buildings and streets of the sparrows— with no competition or predators, keeping the avian numbers down is an ongoing problem. He had stalled at eleven, also known as "stuck on the shelf," the most likely scenario being that the person gathers dust hoping to become a Tenner before usually tumbling down in defeat. As to Ben's day job, I've never visited his high-end tailor shop—it's way out of my budget.

The lantern mounted on the tree didn't reveal any birds in the branches but Ben jerked a thumb up. It was a long and graceful thumb, a mismatch to his height, and I could picture him measuring cloth precisely and fast. "The spar-rows! It's time for them to go!"

Agreement erupted in his audience, two dozen or so people. "You said it, Ben!" ... "One stole a shirt button right off my windowsill, had set it there for a second!" ... "Dirty little creatures, want them gone!"

"Help me get into the Ten and we'll do something about it!"

"We'll give ya rubies, Ben!"

I made a side comment to Dax. "Well, that's one way to spend a party, isn't it?"

Dax pointed to his ear and I received a thought as Ben continued his spiel in the background. *"What, Scottie? Can't hear."*

"Why DO the birds seem to be a bigger problem these days?"

"They've always been like this—noisy, stealing seeds and berries, digging holes in the soil."

"You don't think they're acting, I don't know, more like themselves?"

"Nah, Scottie. Ben's just drawn attention to the problem, that's all. I'm curious about this big plan of his, if he gets into the Ten."

"Maybe he'll chase all the sparrows down with a big net."

We moved on, leaving Ben and his followers behind, and I grabbed Dax's elbow to avoid tripping on a garden rock, his arm strong and sturdy under mine. It struck me, not for the first time, how right it felt. But PALs cannot be romantic partners and I let go. It's a concrete-hard pillar of the Code, same as section F.

But there's a difference. When I violated section F, that was for me and me alone. After Oliver froze me out, it was as if I found myself in a dark room looking for a way out...and the door that beckoned was finding out who my parents were—a fixed, immutable fact no one could take away. In one of Pike Place Market's darker corners—I was all of twelve—I found a shady-looking character selling home-made medical concoctions and figured he must have under-the-table connections. I offered him a jar filled with coins. I'd saved up the conception-day gift we got each year plus extra I earned doing chores for classmates and converted it all into old-world money. The shady character turned out to be law-abiding after all and reported me. The result was the onyx from the Code Enforcement Office, a warning to others and a penalty that would kneecap me—not at the time but six years later when I graduated onto the List.

As to section Q, even if *I* were willing to break the PALs-cannot-be-romantic-partners rule—not that I've ever seriously considered it—Dax certainly wouldn't be. Between Cece and me, that part of the Code is known as *Quit-your-dreamin', Scott.*

Dax and I walked on and ran into Lu before long. Wayne was with her, making me ask, "Is my free hour up?"

"Probably, but I'm now on *my* free hour, so I'll pretend I didn't see you, Scottie." Wayne ran a hand across his jaw. "I'm parched—anyone up for heading to the wine station to sneak a sip or two? I feel I've definitely earned my event-planner-extraordinaire brand this week and I'm sick of cider."

Lu and I were onboard with a bit of discreet rule-breaking but Dax woodenly pointed out that the wine was only for the Top Hundred, making me roll my eyes. "Don't mind him, he's just annoyed everyone's trampling his grass."

Wayne feigned horror. "Maybe we better alert the Agency boss—last I saw McKinsey, she was headed to... Oh, yes. The wine station. That-a-way."

Dax accepted defeat and we made our way back to the square. The band was on a break and an inebriated Samm and Sue were entertaining the crowd. The comedy style of the numbers five and six is not my cup of tea as it often involves pranks or digs at other people. With their matching hair—wavy and down to the waist—it would have been hard to tell them apart, except that Sue's outfit had vertical stripes and Samm's horizontal ones. Crouched to mimic Ben's height, Samm was pontificating about the evils of town birds while Sue, bent over like an old woman, lobbed paper airplanes at him, each lob accompanied by a screech. As the onslaught made Samm (in the role of Ben) sink to his knees, I realized Sue was meant to be Gemma Bligh, the paper airplanes represented sparrows, and the interpretation of the curse that the birds were about to take over the town any day now.

Circling the stage, where Sue and Samm had switched gears and were now telling knock-knock jokes, we found McKinsey at the wine station—it served as a base for those of us on the organizing side of things. Elegant in a gown of indigo velvet, with two-inch teardrop glass earrings and chunky heels, she instructed Wayne and me to stick around in case anyone needed anything, then took pity on us and filled four glasses.

I'd never had wine before. The experience was sweet and tart and mellow all at once.

But that's how my head was soon feeling—mellow, like I couldn't pin a thought down. The band was back on, banging out percussion-heavy music. McKinsey had left along with Samm and Sue, although they hadn't gone far, just *up*. The three were joining the other Tenners for a private party in the tallest building overlooking the square —I watched as the lights in Delilah's eight-floor suite came on behind half-open curtains. Next to me, Lu and Wayne had combined what was left of their wine into a shared glass and weren't paying attention to much beyond each other. A drop spilled down Lu's chin and Wayne wiped it off with a kiss.

An elbow hit me in the side. It was accompanied by a loud, "Scottie, did you hear what I *said*?"

"What, Dax?"

"About alcohol privileges. Before the Dimming, they were based on *age*—twenty-one and up. By the old way of counting, from *birth*." He swirled the final drops in his glass, the proceeding ones on top of the hard cider having rendered him more talkative than usual. "And they drank *red* wine—we only have green grapes in the greenhouses and on vines around town—in fact, only *one* variety: Chardonnay. No one's quite sure why that one took *best* to the environment." The last drop took its time sliding down the glass and into his throat. "I better go check on the fountain. It doubles as a growing environment for pink lotus…"

He wandered off and I didn't hear the rest. Lu and Wayne slipped away as well and I was left alone. The festivities were scheduled to go on until half past eleven, but between the band and the wine, a dull ache had settled under my brow. Leaving the empty glass on the catering table, I made my way out of the square. The way home took me along a housing row, then past a familiar building. All lights were off at the Agency, but across the street, in a structure that's part of the Town Offices complex, a couple of first-floor windows were lit. A side door opened and I watched a pair of men in security uniforms escort a third man out. Just as they were about to overtake me, the man in the middle abruptly stopped. His shoulders were stooped under the weight of a threadbare rucksack and he was badly in need of a wash, with greasy hair, hollow eyes, and an unkempt beard. A stained sleeping mat stuck out of the rucksack. Urgency wrapped around his words like razor wire, he croaked at me, "Too many birds in this town, too many, what's inside them?"

One of the security personnel sent an apologetic grin in my direction. "Sorry. He's been doing that to everybody all day. Buddy, you've been listening to Ben the Birdman too much. Let's go, c'mon."

"Too many, chirp, chirp, chirp..." Babbling on, the man took a step closer and the light from the streetlamp caught his face. I let out a gasp. It was Oliver. I didn't recognize him, his current appearance a long way from the crew cut and plump cheeks from his pre-shaving days.

His features registered no recognition of my own. I wanted to say things, so many things at what was probably the last meeting of our lives, but I only managed a blunt "Was it me, Oliver—was I that unlovable?"

There was no response, only more chirps, and the guards were now staring at me. I tried again. "I'm sorry you have to leave. Do they have a place for you in a greenhouse?"

Oliver gripped my arm. "You're not *listening*. The birds..." He frowned. "So secretive..."

"Yeah, yeah, the birds." The second guard shook his head. "Saying strange things like that is how you end up at the bottom. Should've paid more attention to where you were on the List. Now release her arm."

Oliver did so, his mouth hanging slightly open. "The List..."

"No point in trying to fix it now. It's too late."

"I think I understand..."

"Bottom's the bottom and nothing to be done about it. Your spot is needed."

"Not-mine-not-mine," Oliver said so quickly the words blurred into a single strand. "Delilah's, Delilah's, Delilah's... Don't you see, bad things will happen, bad—"

"Can we get on with it?" the first guard interrupted. "We've already missed most of the party. Let's go, buddy, there's a greenhouse train waiting for you."

Rubbing my arm where Oliver had grabbed it, I watched the security guards pull him away. It was too late for our PAL-ship—for further words. I broke into a run and enveloped him in a hug, unreturned, just before the guards pulled him down the train-depot stairwell and out of sight.

Chapter Four

Housing Thirty-Three

The next morning, the run-in with Oliver having made for a poor night's sleep, I was groggily in line with my tray. Cheap breakfasts are at the far end of the long counter and, as the line shuffled forward, I checked whether Delilah had shared any thoughts on the Commons—she was an early riser and always started her morning with an amusing or heartfelt tidbit—but there was nothing. Balancing coffee and yesterday's cafeteria special on the tray, I found an empty table and sat down with what was under my arm: a copy of The Seattle Times, where, not knowing that Delilah was already dead and thinking an ordinary day lay ahead of me, I had the bright idea to look for a brand.

Defining myself still seemed like the biggest of goals.

The pages, yellowed with age, crinkled under my fingers. The special edition—I bought it with the money returned to me after my section F violation—lists the Founders. I've stared at the names so often that I might have been reciting them. Organized not alphabetically but by winning lottery number, they read like short poems, melodic and lovely: Jalal Ezrah Andrews, college student; Poppy Nicole Weston, pharmacist; Alex Jon Ellis, bus driver; Gabriela Gallardo Lopez, athlete; David Tang, guitarist; Anita Bukhari, catering assistant; Tomas Rick Donato, technical college attendee; Harper Ellie Isaacs, cashier; Leeshawn Lane, law school student...

Forking congealed pasta into my mouth, I turned the page to where the Founder listing continued to those invited into the Dome on top of the lottery—for technical expertise and such—and see a name I've stared at most of all. Eleven children with foster backgrounds formed the first generation in the youth center, including eight-year-old Tadeo Oliver Scott, listed near the fold on the page.

Ten thousand sounds like a large number, but not for a genetic pool—hence the bank of skin samples from Old Seattle in some dark and cool corner of the Birth Lab. But a bit of the Founders does live on—our names are sourced from their middle and last names, sometimes places of birth. I'm unrelated to Tadeo beyond the handful of letters.

I twirled another mouthful of pasta around the fork and considered that Gemma Bligh wasn't wrong; the Founders did turn their backs—breaking off all contact was a requirement of entering the Dome, itself built across the mountains to ensure a physical distance. Not long after the issue in front of me, Old Seattle was abandoned for smaller settlements—ones where pavements, building foundations, and walls didn't crack and sag under the weight of snow drifts and ice. The domes were built to preserve a way of life. I don't know how other town-domes operate—the nearest is New Portland, a hundred-some miles away—but in ours it didn't work out that way. The Founders saw an opportunity to structure a society by how well an individual fits into it rather than by bank account size or perceived value of a job or service. They upgraded the budding technology that had come in with them and ConnectChips started serving up gems and halos.

Washing down a forkful with coffee, I reminded myself that I was supposed to be looking for a brand and turned to the interview section in case one magically leaped out at me, but my attention went straight to one particular photo. A very young Tadeo with the other foster kids, everyone in woolen coats and scarves, the snow behind them shoveled waist-high. This made me wonder how Oliver was faring at the greenhouse, and thankful they had a place for him.

A quote from one of the kids was provided. "Living in a dome sounds awesome!"

I scooped up the last bit of pasta. The word had puzzled me at first. Awe-*some*. Possessing some awe, a medium amount of it, halfway between an opportunity full of awe and its similarly named but complete opposite, awful? Cece provided the meaning. Archaic slang for great, remarkable, excellent, standout. Similar outdated words: groovy, rad, fantabulous. Similar contemporary word: brill.

Perhaps not, Cece, I commented now. *Awesome Scottie might be too much to try to live up to as a brand. We'll keep looking.*

Are we optimistic, Scott?

You know it. All right, time to go to work. We're cleaning up today.

But at the Agency, something was amiss. I ran into Wayne, who was walking fast. "Scottie, did you hear?"

"Hear what?"

"Rumors are flying all over the Commons. McKinsey's called an all-hands—c'mon."

I followed Wayne into the conference room to find it packed, everyone on their feet. McKinsey strode in last. Her words stilled all conversation in the room. "I'm afraid I'm the bearer of bad news. There was a terrible accident late last night. Delilah fell off her balcony... She was killed."

There was a collective gasp from those who, like me, were just hearing the news. The room exploded into questions.

Delilah the Duchess—gone. The North Star guiding us had been extinguished. I couldn't believe it. The packed space with its familiar faces, mismatched furniture, and well-worn brown carpet suddenly felt lonely.

McKinsey's eyes were dry, but she blew her nose on a handkerchief and, after the room settled down, provided more information. "It's thought she fell some time after midnight. The balcony railing gave way—wood rot. That's all that's known at the moment, people."

My ears filled with a thumping sound—my heart pounding. I'd remembered something: the alerts from Smith, the Maintenance supervisor.

McKinsey offered her personal reaction. "Delilah and I had our disagreements... Many of them! Still, she was a fellow Tenner, the greatest stage actor New Seattle has ever known, and a leader so remarkable her death will define the end of an era. But—" McKinsey slid the hankie back in her pocket "—life goes on and we need to keep doing our jobs."

He voice distant in my ears, McKinsey paused as if deciding how to frame her next words. "The truth is, everything will carry on perfectly fine for a few days with no number one—you can take my word for it. There's another consideration... Does the Agency have the right to simply elevate Rick? Shouldn't everyone be given a chance to have their say?... Beyond that, I believe Delilah should stay on as number one for the week to honor her memory."

"Hear, hear!"

McKinsey nodded at the room. "I'll run it by Hugh"—the Listkeeper never comes to meetings, even extraordinary ones—"but I'm sure he'll agree. Now, we can all guess what will happen next. Whether or not Rick gets it, there'll be a mad scramble for the open spot—and yes, I'll aim for it, too. We're going to be swamped with requests for publicity help, so let's prepare for that. I'll stay here with a few staff, and everyone else head out for the cleanup. Wayne, why don't you come up and distribute tasks..."

After the room emptied, I was left behind, Wayne not having assigned a task to me. I was about to run out to catch up with him but McKinsey called me over. "Scott, security wants to talk to you."

"What, now?"

"Now. Go across the street, Bodi's waiting."

Chapter Five

I sit back down and Bodi says to my account of the previous twenty-four hours, "I see. Well, you should know that I've talked to—"

Here someone pops their head into the room and Bodi briefly steps out. I hear the phrase *medical examiner* before the door closes behind him. Finding myself alone, I take a look around. Bodi's office is a small one. In addition to the metal table and chairs, there's a wooden desk in one corner with a monitor—it switches between neighborhood maps, each shuffling dot the color of a person's halo. If Bodi's own office is in the rotation, the screen will show my mostly black dot in the center of the room, and his mostly orange one in the hallway with the other person's. It makes me wonder if that's how he found out about Delilah—by seeing dots hurriedly cluster around a motionless red one. The monitor gives a flicker now and then, a sign of age.

Cece, did you hear the news?

THE ACCIDENT IS CURRENTLY THE MAIN TOPIC ON THE COMMONS. THE PREVAILING EMOTION IS ONE OF SADNESS. ARE YOU SAD, SCOTT?

And scared. The queue I sifted through yesterday morning, the one from Delilah. I kept the Maintenance alerts, didn't I?

My log provides this information: At 8:43 a.m. on Monday, March 15, a queue arrived from Delilah with 120 thoughts. You sent it back at 9:31 a.m. with twelve thoughts in it.

Yes, that sounds right. And two were the wood-rot alerts.

I do not have that information.

Why not?

To store all in and out thoughts and images would clutter my memory. Beyond our interactions, which aid me in better assisting you, Scott, I only remember what you instruct me to.

I know that, I just assumed it was all stored forever somewhere in CC Central. You mean I have no way of proving that I—

The door opens again and Bodi comes back in and takes a seat, picking up where he left off. "You should know that I've already talked to the Maintenance supervisor. Smith says that he sent a pair of messages—the first on Sunday morning informing Delilah of the issue and the second later that afternoon to report that a crew was scheduled to attend to the balcony by the end of the week."

"That's correct." I quote as best I can from the first of the alerts. Smith's style was short and clipped: "A safety valve in a water pipe has been leaking due to a disintegrated gasket. Wood rot suspected in balcony side beams. Exercise caution.'"

"Well, Delilah didn't," he observes.

"She must have fallen before she had a chance to open the alerts," I say.

Bodi stirs at this. "CC Central didn't find them in the in-queue of Delilah's chip."

My heart is beating faster again. "So she saw them, then."

She had to have seen them. I didn't wipe them. I didn't. Delilah did herself, after taking in what Smith had to say.

Bodi gives a short shake of the head. "If that were the case, she'd have known to stay off the balcony, not place her weight on the railing and fall. Maintenance tells me that it would have taken quite a bit of force." He supplies further details. "It happened at four minutes past one o'clock—Delilah's CC registered the moment her neural signals stopped. A flashlight was found with her. The leading theory at the moment is that she was investigating a nest in the rafters above her balcony and leaned back against the railing, unaware of the wood-rot issue."

He places two solidly-built hands on the table and seems to change the subject. "This brand of hers. Why didn't she choose you?"

"She told me that I wasn't ready yet, that it's better to start small," I explain.

"I see. Which left you still at—what did you call yourself? Scottie the No One." He leans forward across the table —I can smell the toast and sausage he had for breakfast and fight the impulse to pull back—and says, "Her giving the brand away to someone else must have hurt. Were you tempted to take revenge? A couple of Maintenance alerts wiped and no one the wiser."

My hands ball into fists, as if in self-defense, under the table; the ceiling lights reflect into patterns in the metal. Dragging my gaze up so Bodi's and my eyes meet, I tell him, "I did no such thing. I was pleased the brand went to one of my PALs, Lu."

Seeming to accept the answer, Bodi relaxes in the chair, which in his case means a straight back and a grim expression. "Listen. Everyone makes mistakes. You were in a hurry to deliver the remaining Tenner invites. Is it possible you accidentally wiped the alerts?"

The room is claustrophobic, Bodi's unblinking stare disconcerting, and I'm happy when he, after a few more questions, nods toward the door for me to leave.

Across the street in the Agency, McKinsey's office is open and I can see that she's not alone. With her is the person who'll most likely take Delilah's place—Rick. He's on his sandaled feet, a sneer ruining his trademark "Handsome" look. He's only half-way to it anyway, as if he stumbled out of bed to the news, unshaven and bleary-eyed, hair disheveled, his wrinkled linen shirt and slacks hurriedly donned. I've arrived just in time to hear him spit out, his raised voice carrying into the hallway, "Who made the decision to keep Delilah as the number one for the week *even though she's dead?*"

McKinsey is perched on one corner of her desk, legs crossed in a sage-green suit. She takes a leisurely sip from the coffee mug in her hand. "Look, if you want to ensure you're number one come next Monday, you know what to do —be out there campaigning for rubies."

Rick is undeterred. "Was it Hugh's decision? I demand to talk to him."

Most people tend to forget about the Listkeeper and assume the Agency computer churns out the List on its own, Monday after Monday, week in and week out. Hugh, as befitting his job duties, has no rank and rarely socializes. He avoids even the Agency kitchenette, preferring to take his meals and breaks on the roof, bird-watching. I've occasionally caught a glimpse of a wiry, neatly-dressed figure in the hallway or the elevator. His is the only office on the top floor, the rest of the space used for storage.

McKinsey shakes her head at Rick. "The Listkeeper must be left alone to do his job."

"*You* rub elbows with him and you're in the Ten—have been for years. It's all very convenient. Does money change hands, or is it a *different* kind of favor?"

I'm outraged on McKinsey's behalf, but she's not easily baited. "My place in the Ten has nothing to do with Hugh… and that's despite what you may or may not know: that he and I used to be PALs. Hugh took an oath of integrity. The List is as fair as he can make it."

"Is it, now?"

Rick, accepting defeat, strides out and McKinsey nods for me to come in. "It's generally not a good idea to eavesdrop, Scott."

"Sorry… I didn't think it would start so soon."

"The mad scramble for the crown?" McKinsey slides into her chair, setting the coffee down on the desk in a spot marked by a series of ring-shaped blots from past mugs. "When something like this accident happens, it's anyone's guess how the dice will land and Rick knows that. I only let him in because Vicky canceled today's appointment. I've been meeting with her, strategizing how to boost her image. She wanted to be a star like Delilah. I tried to get the point across that we make our own luck. That a brand can't be pulled out of thin air."

For a moment, I'm unsure if McKinsey is talking about Vicky—or me.

McKinsey waves me to the chair on the other side of the desk. "It'll be different now, of course. Vicky'll step into the lead role in *Mrs. Montag* and the spotlight will propel her into the Top Thousand, maybe even the Top Hundred. She's no Delilah, though. I can't see her making it into the Ten. She may be wonderful on the stage—I really have no idea one way or the other—but her everyday personality is simply too bland." McKinsey gives the frank assessment without apology. She retrieves the hankie from a pocket and blows her nose—not, I realize, in sadness. "Allergies," she explains. "Plaster dust in the sculpture club I've just joined. How did the talk with Bodi go?"

"Terribly. I don't think he believed me. At best he suspects me of incompetence and at worst of wanting revenge because Delilah passed on giving me the Discovered-by-Her brand." My mind is still on how quickly Rick swooped in to demand Delilah's place.

"It's Bodi's job to be suspicious of everything and everyone," McKinsey says. "He's just being thorough. We've never had a Tenner gone in the blink of an eye and certainly not the number one."

The starkness of the phrasing stills my voice for a moment.

"And *my* job is to tell people the truth," McKinsey continues. "And the truth is that Maintenance doesn't want the blame for the accident—but the blame has to land *somewhere*..." She trails off grimly. After a look at my face, she adds, "Take the rest of the day off. Go home. Keep the Commons out of your head."

I sit at my desk for a while doing nothing. Around noon, I get to my feet and pass Wayne in the hallway, by the kitchenette. He's eating egg salad. "Hey, Scottie, could have used your help cleaning up—the square is done but we still have all of the garden. Why did you have to go talk to Bodi? I'm hearing rumors... Scottie?"

I just keep walking and into the elevator.

At Housing One, the street is cordoned off with rope, with only building residents allowed on the other side of it. Kick-standing my bike, I push through the gathered crowd, bracing myself, but there's nothing to see on the ground—no dark stains or pieces of broken railing. From the way people are craning their necks, I figure out that Delilah must have landed on the roof of the Oyster, where the eatery extends out of the building; its doors display a CLOSED sign. On the top-floor balcony directly above, a chunk of the railing is hanging precariously—the reason for the safety rope.

Against McKinsey's instructions, I have Cece plug me into the Commons. The thoughts from those in close proximity, the gathered onlookers, are the strongest. *"Poor Delilah, did anyone see her fall? ... My friend in the Security Office says NO ... They found her in silk pajamas, up there on the roof of the Oyster ... You don't think— Nah, it's not the curse. Someone messed up, wiped the Maintenance alerts! ... Who, Vicky? ... No, Vicky said it was an Agency intern, don't remember her name ... How INCOMPETENT of the intern ..."*

An odd sensation descends on me as I watch the scene through the mental curtain of comments—that I'm part of an audience for whom everything has been carefully staged: The broken railing. The gathered people. The security rope. No, not an audience—rather as if I'm an actor standing in the spot marked for me on a stage.

I shake off the feeling and leave the square behind me.

Chapter Six

From the other end of the couch, where she's sitting cross-legged, Lu tries to reassure me. "If you say you didn't wipe the alerts, then I believe you, Scottie."

"Seconded. Obviously." Dax joined us on his lunch break and brought sandwiches for everyone. I forced myself to eat, even though my stomach's churning. Lu's early shift had been cut short because of the accident and the three of us had met up in her room.

"Well, you two might be the only ones."

"If you ask me, it's clear why it happened. Gemma Bligh's *curse*." Lu has a bit of a superstitious bent.

Dax gets in a response first. "The curse caused a plumbing leak?"

"No, curses can drive people to *do* things."

This takes me aback a bit. "What, you think she jumped on purpose? Suicide?"

"Well, I don't like to say it, but you never know with a curse." Lu says the last bit in a wide-eyed whisper. "I poked around a bit in the Knowledge Repository and mummy curses used to cause all sorts of havoc—deadly infections from mosquito bites, arsenic poisoning, and yes, suicide. What if Gemma Bligh's curse is just as strong?"

"You're saying Delilah climbed the railing intending to jump—but it buckled under her?" Dax is on the floor, working on his own sandwich. He adds, "Seems unlikely, but I suppose it's possible."

"I hope I'm wrong," Lu says worriedly, "because if I'm not, it's not over by a long shot—not with a curse like this."

Well aware of my own shortcomings, I don't want to poke fun at Lu's credulous streak. Knowing that her shift would have started at six, I ask, "Were you there when she was found?"

Lu nods. "Because she landed on the roof of the eatery, none of us saw her...her body on our way in. One of her neighbors spotted it from her own balcony. I wish we *had* seen her... Because you know the worst part? That she was lying there all alone above us while we prepped the kitchen and baked rolls and peeled potatoes... Around seven we heard raised voices and went out to see what the commotion was. Jada stayed to watch the body being wheeled away, but I didn't want to look." Lu gives a shiver.

"I'm going to give Bonnie a ruby to help push her up," Dax comments. "If she gets enough rubies, she can jump over Rick. I think she'll make a better number one. Rick's always struck me as being somewhat vacant, if you know what I mean." He finishes the last of his sandwich and folds the wrapper, then continues with an unexpected remark. "I wonder if Delilah's chip survived. It's a long way down from the eighth floor."

I almost reply that Bodi said it did, when it strikes me that Delilah's chip might have sustained damage that could account for the Maintenance alerts going missing. Which would help me, but I can't see why Dax cares.

Dax scratches behind his left ear in the spot where we all carry a tiny scar. "Depends how she landed, I suppose. You don't think?"

His eyes go low-left and Lu's and mine do as well. *Cece, people map. Does it still show Delilah?* I'm expecting the medical examiner's office but the map zooms onto CC Central, in the basement of Town Offices One, and a couple of orange dots shuffling around a stationary ruby-red one. The unit taken from Delilah still has a nice strong signal. So much for that theory. It's eerie, as if Delilah is still alive, going about her day, and stopped at CC Central on an errand, making me heartily wish this was the case.

"Haven't you ever thought about how we'll run out of everything one day, including ConnectChips?" This answers the question of why Dax cares. He adds, "I'm no expert, but my guess is that they'll sanitize the casing and wipe the memory, then reuse the unit if they can."

Lu gives another shiver. "Do you mind if we change the subject? First, though..." She reaches over the arm of the couch and digs something out of an old wooden chest where she keeps knick-knacks. She passes me an ancient-looking and slightly smelly rabbit's foot. "Here, rub this for good luck, Scottie. To lift the blame off you."

I dutifully rub the foot.

Evening finds me in my room. It's smaller than Lu's and fits just four pieces of furniture—a bed, a standing lamp, a corner table with a water pitcher and a potted plant, and a dresser. On top of the dresser are my prized possessions: the copy of The Seattle Times, a snow globe, and the newest addition—the invite I took to Delilah on the last day of her life and which she gifted to me. My single window lets in the sounds and scents of the street. Poking my head out allows a glimpse of the Cascades, dark triangles crisscrossed by Dome structural beams and lit up by village hearths here and there. *Cece, we're in trouble.*

WHAT KIND, SCOTT?

The kind where people think I messed up. I admit I had a moment of doubt in Bodi's office, that I might have made a mistake and wiped the Maintenance alerts and when Delilah went out onto the balcony and leaned on the railing, it broke... But I'm sure that's not what happened.

THEN WHY ARE WE IN TROUBLE, SCOTT?

Delilah's gone.

SHE FELL.

I roll the window closed for the night. *I know it wasn't my fault, so how did she end up dead?*

In bed, I punch the pillow in a futile effort to fluff it up and recall the vibe I experienced outside Housing One. *Cece, what if someone saw an opportunity in the timing? What if she was PUSHED?*

BY WHO?

That's the question, isn't it? Something Lu said made me think. If the balcony railing hadn't given out, I bet a whole lot of people would have jumped to the same conclusion—that the curse drove Delilah to suicide the very night of the eighty-fifth anniversary—the tragedy that Gemma foretold.

I DON'T UNDERSTAND, SCOTT.

I flip on my side and punch the pillow again. *I'm talking about murder.*

A DEATH MADE TO HAPPEN WITH INTENT AND PURPOSE.

Yes... It's a couple of minutes until the town map goes dark for the night and I repeat the request I made earlier at Dax's suggestion. This time Delilah's dot is gone. There's a finality to it. I ask, *Cece, the Security Office keeps an eye on the map even in the off hours, don't they? They can't watch every area all the time. What happens if there's a crime?*

Cece comes back with: PUBLIC ACCESS TO THE MAP IS RESTRICTED AFTER TEN-THIRTY BUT, SAME AS IN THE DAYTIME, THERE'S A LAG OF TWO HOURS BEFORE THE DATA IS DELETED. A COMPROMISE BETWEEN COMBATING CRIME AND RETAINING PRIVACY.

I lie with my eyes open for a while, mulling this over. By midnight the square would have mostly cleared out—the band was slated to finish at half past eleven. Bodi said Delilah fell just after one o'clock, presumably long after the other Tenners had left her suite. Whoever it was must have been counting on her body not being spotted until morning —Lu said it wasn't visible from street level—too late for the security office to confirm that Delilah was alone on her balcony.

A foolproof plan, except for a slight hiccup. The wood rot changed the story—and now there's an intern to blame, not Gemma Bligh. Someone, somewhere, is thinking that this works just as well.

Chapter Seven

The mountains in my window are shrouded in morning mist. Donning my best set of clothes, I let the Commons chatter fill my mind. It's been four days and there's still much grumbling directed at the Incompetent Intern.

Only I'm no longer an intern. McKinsey informed me that I'm on an indefinite break from the Agency. Jobs and Housing has put me on vacuuming duty—the job Oliver left behind—and I'm to start this afternoon.

At breakfast, I'm still on the receiving end of nasty looks and whispers. The staff person spooning out watery oatmeal ignores my greeting and mutters about careless interns and no wonder Delilah denied me the social boost. Though Lu and Dax keep sending me optimistic thoughts that it'll all blow over, I'm being socially cut.

Onyxes are discouraged by the Code's section A (*Spiteful gems have a tendency to make the giver look bad, so save the grumbling for the Commons or better yet, keep it to yourself*) but I've still acquired a couple. They're from Vicky and Evan, as if snitching about my carelessness was their duty despite section A.

At least no one other than perhaps Bodi, who found time to chat with both Lu and Dax about my character, seems to think I deleted the Maintenance alerts on purpose.

I don't linger over breakfast.

The Edge Garden is where Delilah's seeding is being held. I've never been to a funeral before. In daylight, the garden has a fishbowl view of the outside world: the plain New Seattle sits on, the snow sparkling in shafts of sunlight below retreating clouds; the train tracks traversing it toward greenhouses and faraway domed cities; the Cascade range and the forest to the west. Keeping my head down, I join the mourners congregated in an area labeled *Coffee Plants*, featuring short, shrub-like trees with shiny dark-green leaves. The subtle scent of the white blossoms wafts over the crowd, a large one. There have been memorial gatherings for Delilah all week—at the theater, in Founders Square— ones I've avoided in case I'm recognized, but it feels right to be here today.

I choose an unobtrusive spot, all but hiding myself behind one of the plants.

The Tenners, dressed in black, are gathered at the center of the patch, from where the rows of plants spread out. There are no chairs, so everyone is on their feet. My gaze is drawn to Rick, and not because of his looks. The number two is dry-eyed, his chin on one fist as he gazes into the distance, hair combed to a shine. Just outside the circle, as befitting his number eleven status, is Ben the Birdman; his partner, a man I know is called Austin, taller and more solidly built, is by his side. Ben swipes a thumb along his bare upper lip, as if stroking an invisible mustache.

An elbow pokes me in the back, someone threading their way through. It's Evan, who stares straight ahead as if he's never exchanged a word with me in his life. Socially cut.

I assumed there would be speeches first, but all of a sudden there's activity. The mourners in the row I'm in step aside to open a path. Rick, having disappeared out of sight, comes back into view after a few minutes. He's part of a quartet carrying a black sheet—it sags in the middle, though I can't see into it—with Rick and Jada in the front and McKinsey bringing up the rear alongside Poulsbo, the number eight. The handyman has gray streaks, a stoop to his shoulders, and a soft step; he's often asked for help outside his regular Maintenance assignments and I've seen him in my own building a couple of times. Poulsbo gives the impression of having accidentally wandered into the Top Ten, as if he opened a door expecting a closet and found a stage instead.

As the procession passes me, I see that the sheet is laden with a powdery ash, white as milk. The expressions of its bearers are somber, tears streaming down Poulsbo's face. His grief pulls forth my own. Delilah was so many things to me: someone to admire, to look up to, a steady force at New Seattle's helm. And she believed in me, if only for a morning. My fingers fumble in my pocket for a handkerchief and I encounter Delilah's invite, which I've brought along. Paper, fragile under my fingers, but something to hold on to.

The four stop when they reach the center of the patch and maneuver the sheet so it faces a section of plants that's been left empty of people. Rick and Jada lower their end, McKinsey and Poulsbo raise theirs; then, perfectly timed, they flex the sheet, sending the pale ash onto the white-blossomed plants and the soil. Back to nature. To distract myself from the sadness of a life abruptly ended, an incident I'm being blamed for, I blink the wet out of my eyelashes and come up with an illogical grievance—the Birth Lab is where Delilah's remains should have been sent. She sprung up from there, not from coffee plants, of all things.

After Rick and Jada fold the sheet into a neat square, a line of mourners forms to water the soil from a ceremonial can, Vicky scurrying to its front. She's weeping, hair tucked behind her ears as if to better display her grief—which I know is bogus. As to her new life, I've heard that the opening night of *Mrs. Montag* has been pushed out ten days to give her time to get ready for the role.

I join the end of the line. Everyone's playing their part and the sensation of it all being staged descends on me once again. Oliver. He said something... What was it? It was after he stopped babbling about the birds. Not that *his* spot on the List was needed, but Delilah's... Bad things will happen, he said—and they have.

Cece, wake up, I instruct, having placed her in sleep mode for the seeding. *Communication with greenhouses. It's via radios, isn't it, because you can't send a thought that far? I wonder if Town Offices'd let me use a radio... What greenhouse is Oliver assigned to?*

Cece comes back with: Greenhouse Seven. But he is no longer there.

What do you mean? Where is he?

Town Offices lists him as having left for parts unknown.

I let out a hushed gasp at the news. As the ceremonial can is passed into my hands, I send a thought in Oliver's direction, not via Cece, but out into the universe, wherever he is. Stay safe, Oliver; find your way to a village or another town-dome and a new life. It really is goodbye.

And to Delilah as well. I slosh water onto the soil, then pass the can to the person behind me. Best to leave before anyone points me out, the Incompetent Intern come to pay her respects.

I encounter Rick at the border of the coffee-plant patch. He's inviting condolences in the form of murmured words, hugs, and handshakes. It strikes me that it must have been agony to have it all just out of reach for so long—he's been a heartbeat away from Eternal Life for a good decade. Despite me having handed him Agency invitations, he doesn't seem to recognize me when he stops to shake my hand. "So there's no one above you now," I blurt out before he has a chance to walk away. "The number one chair is available."

"Yes, it's very sad." His halo broadcasts a bit of personal news—his conception-day anniversary is today. He turns to greet Sue, who shakes her waist-length hair at him. "Handsome Rick... Samm, come and wish Rick a happy conception day!"

"Rick, we're doing a skit later tonight if you want in." Samm's grin seems out of place at a funeral. "On you know who."

"What, a Ben the Birdman skit?"

Sue holds a finger to Rick's lips. "Shh, not so loud. We don't want him to overhear."

The tailor is nearby, partaking in his turn with the ceremonial watering can.

"I'll pass. Things to do—I'm celebrating. Conception day and all that." Before Rick disappears into the crowd to receive more sympathy hugs and handshakes, I catch sight of a hint of a smile at the corners of his mouth. *Cece, quick, take a snapshot.*

I stare at the snapshot, Rick having moved on. Well, really. Rick's grinning behind the fake display of grief, McKinsey was pragmatic about Delilah's death, and Samm and Sue don't seem torn up about it in the least. Poulsbo is the only Tenner who seems to be genuinely mourning. All other eyes in the Tenner circle were dry.

"So you messed up Delilah's in-queue and got fired," someone behind me says.

Vicky. Her face is blotchy, but she sounds cheery enough. This, at least, is not a surprise. "Don't feel bad," she adds. "It could have been me. It just so happened that it was you."

"I'm never going to shake off the Incompetent Intern brand, am I?" I say. "People won't forgive me for what happened."

Only two onyxes may have been lobbed my way, hers and Evan's, but I know that doors will always stay shut in my face. I'm walking the plank, a slow march out of town.

Vicky takes a step back as if to distance herself. "No, they won't."

At Housing One, the area is no longer cordoned off and normal foot traffic has resumed. I follow a woman I remember from the seeding into the building—she's walking with a limp and must not have stuck around for the ceremonial watering of the soil to get here ahead of me. We both exit the elevator on the top floor and I watch her slide a key into the door marked Suite Two.

Down the hallway, Suite One has a *Danger, Do Not Enter* sign; flowers, notes, and other tokens of remembrance line the wall on either side. I try the handle but the door is locked.

The woman pokes her head back out. "They must be on a break. The Maintenance people. They were working all day yesterday, fixing the balcony—a little too late, if you ask me." She sounds tipsy, as if her morning started with a glass of wine. "You were at the seeding, weren't you? Come inside. I'm Lucille."

Leaving my sandals by the door, I introduce myself warily but Lucille says nothing about my incompetence. She's in the Top Hundred, a hair stylist in her mid-forties. The spacious living room holds white carpet and elegant furniture, though not particularly comfy-looking. Chair-backs are straight, the couch creaseless and lacking cush-ions, the side tables more decorative than practical. Double doors open onto a balcony. Doors lead to further rooms— four, I count. Lucille gives a snort at my gaping jaw. "Never been to a Top Hundred suite?" At my shake of the head, she adds, "Are you wondering how I got here?"

"Is that very rude? Sorry."

"There's no mystery—the Agency gets the credit. McKin-sey, to be more precise." She steps out of her shoes unsteadily and I decide against mentioning that McKinsey used to be my boss. "I spent years treading water as the other stylists—Fred, Dakota, Alki—shot up past me. I agonized. Was my work subpar? Did I have bad breath and no one wanted to tell me? Then I hired McKinsey. She came into the salon and watched me work. She took me out to lunch the next day and said that the problem was that I was trying to chat up the customers, believing they'd like me better that way. She said, 'They don't want to hear your problems, they yearn to air their own.' So that's what I did— I listened instead of jabbering away. Turns out I'm a good listener. Customers started coming back, and the rubies followed." She gives a wave around the luxurious but curi-ously cold-feeling space. "This is where every bit of my salary goes. I don't care about expensive meals or the latest clothing styles."

"Was Delilah a customer?" I ask, though I know the answer already. Evan took care of all of Delilah's hair needs.

"They have a stylist at the theater." She follows that up with a frank glance at my hair. "But you should come into the salon—I see all ranks. We could shape it, maybe do highlights."

Stylists are expensive and Lu, who has a knack for these things, trims my hair. "Thanks, but I can't afford it."

"Well, perhaps in the future."

I ask if I can see the view and she opens the balcony doors—the hum of the town is more muted than out the window of my room. Lucille trails me out, her limp less noticeable without shoes. Seeing me glance back, she explains, "Someone stepped on my foot at the market. It'll heal."

Lucille's balcony looks out onto Founders Square and the view is grand. I've never been this high up. Housing Two, across the square, is one story shorter, as is Work One to its right. From there the buildings step down in all directions, the rooftop-gardens and the scale playing with my mind to give the illusion of a grass-covered staircase descending all around toward the Edge Garden. Above, the panels of the Dome seem reachable with the throw of a stone, if I had one. Below, nameless figures are crossing the square under trees that look short.

I glance over to the left, but exhaust vents block the line of sight to Delilah's balcony. The railing under my fingers, wood fortified with steel segments, seems sturdy enough. It's a long way down.

"Don't worry, you won't fall." Despite her words, the hand Lucille rests on the railing is light. "I was the one who found her, you know. She must not have called out as she fell—I'm a light sleeper. When I came out here to do my morning stretches, I saw… She looked so small from up here —broken. I sent an emergency message and hurried down to the street. There was nothing anyone could do. When they carried her down from the roof of Jada's eatery, she was barefoot and in her nightgown. Her face had been…"

I glance over. "What happened to her face?"

"The vent grille on which she'd landed had sliced deep into her flesh. Her whole body was broken."

The image is ghastly and it strikes again, that odd feeling… I picture hands shoving from behind, the railing breaking with an audible groan, the sensation of tumbling into nothingness, it all happening so fast there's no time to call out or to send a last thought…

"Whoa, you're looking pale. Want a drink? Lemonade? Or something stronger?"

Somewhat unsteadily, I follow Lucille back inside and to a bright corner of the room where a glass table and four white-leather chairs sit next to a fridge. I've never seen a personal fridge before. I accept lemonade and a chair, and the cool drink and the firmness of the seat settle my nerves. "The Tenners were all here that evening, weren't they?" I say.

"For cocktails and card games." There's a note of resentment in the way she says it, that Delilah had not thought to include her neighbor. She continues. "I passed Rick in the hallway on his way in and he sent that deliciously sensual grin in my direction. Jada was with him. Oh, and also Ben the Birdman."

This strikes me as interesting. "Delilah invited Ben even though he's not a Tenner yet?"

"I think she wanted to size him up."

My mind racing, I sip the lemonade. Cocktails and card games…and an opportunity for someone—Rick, say—to stage a suicide timed to coincide with the town anniversary. Lucille striking me as the type to listen through the walls, I ask, "Did the guests stick around for long?"

"Things quieted down by midnight or so," she supplies.

"Is it certain she was alone? Maybe one of them stayed the night."

An inappropriate question, but Lucille is ready to gossip. "Delilah kept to herself these days. No night visitors." She takes a lengthy sip of the wine. "It goes to show that these things can happen to anyone. The cocktails—all for nothing."

As I know Delilah herself didn't consume alcohol, I'm puzzled until it dawns that Lucille is talking not about drinks but the weekly dose of Eternal Life. "I'm the intern," I blurt out. "The one being accused of incompetence. It *was* my fault—I should have made sure she saw the alerts, knocked on the door to tell her about them."

I should have warned her to be careful.

Lucille shrugs. "Plenty of blame to go around. If you ask me, Maintenance must not have realized how bad the problem was or they would have fixed it that very day." She sets the wine bottle down after refilling her glass and returns to the subject of her success. "Truth be told, I was only able to go to the Agency and hire McKinsey because of Delilah. I was commiserating with a friend one evening in the Dragon and the Drumstick"—the tavern is a popular evening destination—"and she overheard. She said she'd pay for it. I was ecstatic. In exchange I gave her a ruby and from that point on talked her up to customers so they'd give her rubies, too. Once in a while refused service to a client if she asked. That kind of thing... And before you say anything, I know the way it went down is against the Code but it's been so long and she's gone now. And I've paid my price. I was beholden to her all that time... I thought she wanted to be friends, moved in next door. But once she gave me what I wanted, it was as if she'd secured a servant."

"She was really busy all the time," I point out gently. Surely Delilah's offer of financial help was not contingent on a ruby plus loyalty, at least not in a straight-out exchange like Lucille made it sound. "With the theater and the governing and all the social events."

"Right..." Lucille is staring into the glass and I get the hint that it's time to leave. As I step back into my sandals, Lucille calls over a final complaint. "I would have appreciated a keepsake."

To my perplexed look, she explains, "Only the Tenners and other high-profile friends of the Duchess were allowed into the suite. Jet-Set Jada was the first to come—left with a small box of some kind. Whatever's left over will go to the Jobs and Housing warehouse... Don't forget to visit the salon when you can afford it," she reminds me, and I know that she asked me into her living space not to be hospitable or because funerals make people chatty. I'm to be one more ruby in her halo.

Maintenance must be back—the door to Suite One is now ajar, security tape stretched across it. I reach over and push it open all the way. Delilah's living room is larger than Lucille's—a warmer, more lived-in space. Cushions and throws layer sofas, mismatched rugs span the floors, comfy armchairs sit next to eclectic side tables and polished brass lamps, eye-catching artwork covers the walls. There's a piano. Five doors, all open, lead to other rooms, one of them holding a grand, one-of-a-kind, stained oak four-poster bed.

The line of sight leads to the balcony, where the doors and curtains are open. *Cece, snapshot,* I instruct, but it's

pointless. A couple of personnel are at work on the new railing. If there was any evidence of foul play, it's now gone.

1:45 p.m.

My first vacuuming assignment is in Work One. I'm part of
the afternoon cleaning crew, my job to deal with the hallway
carpets while the others attend to individual offices.

I've run into Wayne. The Agency provides the catering
for the Tenner meeting each Friday, where the business of
the town is discussed. The meeting, Wayne tells me after I
turn off the vacuum, is on schedule at two o'clock. I trail
Wayne and his staff as they maneuver a cart stacked high
with covered trays from the back hallway into a small utility
room—it holds a sink for washing up and extra silverware
and such—and into the conference room. The others in the
cleaning crew readied it first thing and I haven't seen it yet,
nor did I ever help out with the catering as an intern.

It's just a regular conference room, if on the large side.
Well-worn carpet, an oval table, and ten leather chairs. The
frosted glass doors, the formal entrance to the room, are
closed. The standout element is an enormous window overlooking Founders Square. The chair at the head of the table
faces it, its leather soft and creamy under my fingers, like
room-temperature cheese. A long, elbow-height table
stands along one wall and it's where Wayne and his staff
arrange the food. My stomach, unsatisfied after a meager
lunch, growls at the sight. It's just about enough to feed all
of Housing Thirty-Three for the day.

Wayne gives everything a final look and adjusts a plate

holding a creamy dip and cucumber slices. "Right. We'd better get going."

This makes me stop staring at the offerings. "You don't stick around to serve the food?"

He unlocks the frosted glass doors but leaves them closed. "They like their privacy. We leave them to it and come back in a couple of hours to clean up. Scottie..."

"Don't say it'll pass."

"Sorry you've been demoted. It *will* pass—something else will come along and squirrel away everyone's attention. And look on the bright side. At least the Jobs and Housing Office didn't assign you to bird-poop cleanup."

I appreciate the attempt to cheer me up.

We can hear voices nearing in the main hallway. Having stuffed the cart into the utility room, Wayne and his staff leave via the back hallway. I reach for the vacuum but only get as far as pressing the switch, then turn it right back off. It's no accident that I've run into Wayne. I timed it so I'd be on the top floor just before two o'clock.

Time for a final gut check. Am I, in fact, imagining that something sinister is going on? No, I decide, and open the utility room door as quietly as I can. *Cece, remember that skit from school? I was Sherlock and Dax was Watson and you fed me the lines. That's who we have to be—detectives. No offense, but you're good at saying the obvious, so you can be Watson and I'll be Sherlock. 'Course, the real-life Sherlock didn't risk being kicked out of London if he failed to catch his prey—and I might be, if I don't manage to clear my name.*

I've squeezed my way around the cart and over to the closed door separating me from the meeting space. Cece corrects me mildly. ACCORDING TO THE KNOWLEDGE REPOSITORY, SHERLOCK HOLMES AND DR. JOHN WATSON ARE FICTIONAL CHARACTERS.

They are? No matter, we can still be like them.

Is that a brand, Scott?

Sherlock Scottie? It can be, I suppose. Our own private brand. It'll be a promise of justice for Delilah—with Eternal Life, she had years left. And I'll be damned if I'll let myself be quietly kicked out of town.

Muffled voices seep under the door. Ruling out opening it a crack, I crouch and put my ear to the wood. If anyone happens to look at this segment of the map, they'll see my black dot and I'll get in trouble, but there's no way around that.

A voice on the other side says, "How's the spread today, Sue?" It's Samm.

"Nothing special," Sue answers churlishly. "Why is there never wine at these things?"

"Because they're under the mistaken impression that sober governing is better than the other kind."

"I should hope so," a third voice breaks in. I can't place it. "We're here to get work done, not drink too much and overeat."

"Speak for yourself, Jada. I'm always ready to drink and eat too much, especially after a seeding." Samm again. A heavy object plops down on the floor by the wall, followed by a second plop. It seems that Samm and Sue have no intention of leaving the refreshments table.

Open a corkboard, Cece. Title it, WHO KILLED DELILAH? And tack this on: They were all in Delilah's suite that night.

I shift so my ear is directly on the crack between the door and the frame.

Chapter Eight

The Tenner Meeting Room

The others are loading up plates but Jada's strategy is to stay hungry at these meetings in more ways than one. Resisting the urge to stare at the vacant armchair at the head of the table, she takes a seat. It's as if Delilah is still here, conspicuous by her *absence*. It was Delilah who dispensed with the title that originally went along with the number one chair—mayor—and picked Duchess, as if she were royalty. It was Delilah who moved the meeting from a windowless room in the Town Offices complex to the top floor of Work One, with the big window overlooking the square.

It was Delilah who wanted her, Jada, to stay at number seven. And what Delilah wanted, Delilah got.

The small talk flying back and forth as the seats fill up is awkward, what with everyone in mourning attire and specks of what's left of the Duchess on their shoes. McKinsey asks Rick how rehearsals are coming along. He answers that

Vicky is no Delilah and asks in return, "Any new hobbies this week, McKinsey?"

"Sculpting."

"How many does that make?"

"Let's see, ten... No, eleven."

Jada can sense the undercurrents in the room, alliances shifting. Hers was with Delilah herself, though calling it an alliance is misleading. Jada was the underling. It'll be different now. Jada acted quickly as the shocked whisper travelled through the crowd gathered outside her eatery: *It's Delilah the Duchess... Delilah... Hurt badly... Gone..."* As soon as she could, she took the elevator up to the eighth floor. She wanted a keepsake, she told the nosy janitor who unlocked Delilah's suite for her. There was a metal strongbox under the bed. Jada spent some time searching for the key but in the end carried just the strongbox out under one arm, stashed it in her office at the eatery, and took it home at the end of the day. She broke the lock with a hammer and spent the rest of the evening perusing what was inside: town secrets. Delilah hoarded them the way some people collect trinkets salvaged from Old Seattle. Having read everything twice, Jada stacked the notes back inside and hid the box under her own bed.

Franz, as always, is running late and while they wait, Jada takes a look around the table. Going forward, she'll need someone to shoulder the risk while she stays in the shadows. Rick proved himself quite pliable the night of the town party. Still, she does the calculation again, just to be sure.

Not Everyone's Friend Bonnie, to her right. The tavern manager, her hair wound into the usual neat bun, likes a good meal, her frame filling the armchair as she leans forward to talk to McKinsey across a generously loaded plate. The number three is too fond of being liked. She might balk at the idea of putting the secrets to work.

And not Wheelin'-n-Dealin' Chase, on her other side, either. Same as Bonnie, he's the manager of an open-to-all-ranks establishment—a coffeehouse. The cheap coffee he manages to get his hands on draws crowds into the Fill-n-Sip Cup and they bring rubies with them. Simple enough. She can smell his head oil, the overhead lights playing on his bald pate—she guesses that he shaves it—as he squashes grapes between his teeth. The number four would be *too* eager to leverage the secrets, to play all the cards at once.

One of the Jokers—Samm or Sue—releases a loud burp. Jada barely bothers considering them at all. The two are splayed on the floor by the food table with their backs against the wall, sucking on chocolate cherries. They've been in this room much longer than her single year; she's heard that in the beginning they were invited to join in on the voting on this or that town issue but always took opposing sides just for the fun of it. The pair—numbers five and six—are warm bodies filling a couple of spots and thereby keeping out others. She'll have to get past them somehow—perhaps start a rumor that they're breaking up and turning over a new leaf as responsible, boring citizens —but that's easily manageable down the road.

Poulsbo the Handyman, across the table? The number eight is too weak to be an effective ally. The handyman's inability to say no to any request to *fix this* or *build that* makes him a familiar face around New Seattle's neighbor-hoods, but in this room he rarely contributes. He has a perpetual eye twitch that Jada finds annoying.

McKinsey, she of the eleven hobbies? In the last Tenner spot, McKinsey is in the most precarious position. Together they might make an effective team—a partnership that could propel one of them to the top, but there's no telling who. Too much of a risk.

The double doors open and the number nine comes in, his pace unhurried, his excessive goatee always seeming to enter the room before him. Partnering with Franz would involve a lot of unnecessary chatter. The self-proclaimed Relationship Wizard is an expert at compromise, not action.

Which brings her back to...Rick. Jada has known since the town party that Rick is more than willing to do the dirty work. That he's willing to do *anything*. Vain, self-centered Rick coasted to fame on good looks and Delilah's coattails. Delilah gave him his big break and, from that point on, kept him by her side. He never made a move against her. Today Rick's wearing a frown under the perfect hair and Jada knows why. Bonnie's pulling ahead in the battle for number one—rubies are streaming in for her.

After Franz takes a seat, leaving only Delilah's empty, Bonnie raises her voice to drown out the side conversations. "Who's going to lead the meeting?"

Rick swivels in his seat—he's been watching the Joker duo by the food table, or, more specifically, Sue—and points out that he's the number two and therefore it's his job. Echoing Jada's own thoughts about Delilah's pretense at royalty, Bonnie responds with, "New Seattle's not a monarchy. There's no right to succession and nothing's guaranteed, Rick, you know that. What's the saying? Don't count your chickens before they hatch."

"Town Offices sent today's agenda to me."

Bonnie directs a shrug in his direction. "I wouldn't read too much into it." The rubies in her halo carry an earnest tone (*"Bonnie knows everyone's name, Rick only his own"*) while

Rick's are a bit more superficial (*"Handsome Rick for number one!"*).

"Please, somebody just start," Chase interrupts the bickering, though Jada is content enough to sit there watching Bonnie peck at Rick. It suits her purpose today.

Rick clears his throat, the brow still furrowed. "Let's see, last week we tried to tackle the bird problem…"

Chase interrupts again. "Also known as the Ben-and-all-his-gems problem."

"…but we were deadlocked, evenly split between dual proposals," Rick continues, ignoring the interruption. "Delilah wanted feeders in Pike Place Market to draw the sparrows there and McKinsey, here, argued for even farther out, in the Edge Garden."

McKinsey had stood up to the Duchess and had some support, a rare occurrence. Delilah used voting as a test of loyalty—she had plenty of leeway to put things into motion without a vote or even a discussion.

"No danger of a tie today." Chase delivers the words with a wink. "McKinsey wins."

The joke falls flat. No one, with the exception of Poulsbo, is going to miss Delilah but the tension around the table forestalls any laughter. Bonnie shakes her head as if Rick's already failing at leadership. "Why are we talking about birds? Given what happened, people will expect action."

"Why would they expect *us* to do anything?" Rick recommences bickering. "It was the Incompetent Intern's fault, not ours."

"I propose a Maintenance safety check, balconies first."

"Not everyone has a balcony, Bonnie, so why start there?"

"Because that's where it happened."

"It makes us look elitist."

"Pretending to be worried about the under-a-hundred crowd won't bring you rubies, Rick," Bonnie slings an arrow. "You have to mean it."

"Don't think I don't see past your holier-than-thou demeanor, Bonnie, as if you're better than the rest of—"

Franz steps in. "Let's keep it civil, shall we?" He steeples his fingers—his way of signaling that his mediating skills are being put into action. "Poulsbo, you're in Maintenance. What's your take on this?"

"I'd say...that we need to train...more maintenance workers." Poulsbo is a slow speaker, each word a weight to be pushed out from deep within. "I'm in Small Repairs, as you know, assigned to Housing Seven, Eight, Nine, and Ten... What you want is...the Large Repairs crew. I'm the one to bring in if there's a leak under your sink... They are the ones to bring in if...if there's a structural issue."

"And we need more persons in the Large Repairs crew, you say?"

"We could retrain *actors*," Bonnie latches onto the idea, "and turn the theater into a gym or a garden."

"Now just a minute," Rick snarls. "The theater is key to the emotional well-being of the town. It provides entertainment, relaxation, art. It's a job like any other. Besides, I don't know a thing about building repair."

Not with those soft-looking hands.

Bonnie slings another arrow. "If I get to number one... Well, I'm not saying I would do it, either—change things. Just a reminder that it may not be up to you, Rick."

"Well, you do need Eternal Life more than me," Rick responds rudely. "Fifty-nine, is it, Bonnie? That's...why, that's just about a nice round two decades more than me. The light at the end of the tunnel is starting to dim, is it?"

"Tenners, *please*. Let's set aside any talk of closing the

theater." Franz calls for a vote and the safety check, starting with balconies, wins a nod from everyone at the table.

Chase folds his hands behind his head. "Excellent, it'll take months for Maintenance to get that done—and if there're additional accidents in the meantime, we can blame *them*. Which brings us back to Ben."

"He'll be in come Monday, I expect," McKinsey says.

"I suppose it can't be avoided," is Rick's take on it.

Poulsbo glances around, perplexed. "Why don't we want Ben to be a Tenner? He's promised to fix the...the bird problem."

No one bothers explaining that if they have to have someone new, it's best if the person is as docile as Poulsbo himself or simply in the room for the extra perks, Samm-and-Sue-style. They vote to take no action regarding the sparrows for now, effectively shifting all public expectation over to Ben. The birds are not of much concern to Jada, other than that it's an ongoing battle to keep them away from the bins at the back of the Oyster.

With a nod, she signals Rick to stay behind after the meeting winds down, pulling him aside as if they're merely getting in a last bit of food. She could send him a thought but some subjects are best discussed face-to-face. It's a curious fact, it strikes her, that nuance often evaporates in thought exchanges—that the flesh does a better job of revealing where a person really stands.

Once they are alone, she addresses Rick with a frank, "An empty chair at the head of the table, rubies piling up for Bonnie, and what of poor Rick? You didn't think it'd be that easy, did you, with Delilah out of the way? That you'd simply slide into the number one chair."

Rick kicks aside an empty fruit basket left behind by Samm and Sue. "Guess not."

Delilah is gone. Things have turned out even better than the plan she and Rick hatched together in a private moment the evening of the town party. She throws him a morsel. "How would you like to be number one—*guaranteed*—when the List updates on Monday?"

This gets his attention. "How?"

"I know something about Bonnie—something she wouldn't want revealed."

Rick's reaction is swift. "I thought all that secrets business died with Delilah," he spits out, a forehead vein throbbing under the curls. For a moment Jada wonders if she's underestimated him. Rick's looks have no effect on her. Romance is an unnecessary distraction, a guiding philosophy she picked up from Delilah and one she's learned to appreciate. The way of the world is that you have to look out for yourself, first and foremost. An occasional hook-up is fine but falling for someone—not that it would be Rick; he's too full of himself, plus her forty-one years place her in the "too old" category for him—would signal weakness, expose a gap in the armor where a knife may strike.

"I'm the keeper of the secrets now," she says easily. "Besides, you and I, we're on the same side, aren't we? Our arrangement still stands."

This makes him pull back. "On the same side, yes... I hated her. She just couldn't let me have an opinion of my own, *ever*. She enjoyed it—tormenting you, me, every single person who stepped foot into this room, boasted how she had dirt on all of us, except Poulsbo of course, who has no vices and was happy to do her bidding." A sharp intake of breath. He's having trouble controlling his anger. "Where did you find them? I looked all over her suite. She told me once she wrote the secrets down instead of making a corkboard—that she didn't trust the privacy of her ConnectChip."

"Under her bed—she'd jotted everything down on the back of her event invitations."

"Did you find anything on me?" Rick chuckles uncomfortably.

"I already know all your secrets," Jada says lightly. Her own is that she always voted Delilah's way to stay on her good side—a trap with no way out.

"What's Bonnie's?" Rick asks.

"You don't need to know the details. It's nothing lurid, just a small secret, but that might be for the best. Bonnie won't feel backed into a corner... What was that?"

"What was what?"

"I thought I heard something." Jada peers into the main hallway, then checks the utility room, but finds both empty. A vacuum starts up somewhere, its drone muffled by the walls. Just the cleaning crew. She turns back to Rick. "As I said, the details aren't important."

But Rick has already moved on. "I don't see why the town thinks Bonnie would be better than me anyways."

Now he's pouting. She just needs to tie it up with a bow. "Just whisper in Bonnie's ear *I know* and watch her fall in line."

"And what do you get out of it, Jada?"

When the time is right, after Rick has whispered into Bonnie's and other ears, he'll be easy to dislodge. She permits herself a thin smile. "You'll owe me."

He catches her by surprise by asking, "Why do you want to be number one so badly, Jada? Want to live forever, or as near as you can get?"

Her answer comes out quickly, a mask slipped. "I don't

care about Eternal Life. Or the extra money, or the attention, or any of that stuff."

"What, then?"

"I want to be the best." She knows Rick's picked up on the hard edge in her tone. And what she *didn't* say: "Be sure of this—no one will stop me."

Rick reaches for the last of the grapes. "When I get there, I'll care about Eternal Life... Will it work, pressuring Bonnie? Three days is not a lot of time."

"It'll work."

Chapter Nine

Monday, March 22

Someone bumps into my back. It's Lu, who's just come around a building corner at a fast clip. Dax is with her. "There you are, Scottie," Lu says, rubbing the shoulder that connected with the back of my head. "Why are you standing in the middle of the street? Something wrong with your bike?"

"I hit a pothole and the vacuum bounced out," I explain, trying to wrestle the machine back into the basket. New Seattle's vacuums have been slowly dying off over the years and I have to ferry mine on assignments. Today's was in Work Three.

"We sent you a thought to meet us at Puget for dinner," Lu says after they help me secure the vacuum and we all move aside. "You didn't respond, so we had to look for you on the map."

Puget Chow, near the youth center, is what we grew up

on and it's the place we still go to. They serve all ranks and have their own version of cafeteria mix, the previous day's leftover fried chicken.

I lie. "Sorry, I had my in-thoughts muted."

Dax's eyebrow goes up. "For vacuuming?"

"The birds"—I duck as one swoops into a nearby bin for a scrap of something or other—"really are getting out of control. Fine, I did get the thought. The truth is, it's not good for you two to be seen in the company of the Incompetent Intern."

"Of course we want your company." Lu gives my arm a squeeze. "I'm glad the fallout wasn't worse, Scottie. Let's hope it's over."

Another Monday and the onyxes from Evan and Vicky have sent me to 9,653—four hundred spots closer to last place. I don't say it, but I'm not so sure about Lu's take. I'm still getting nasty looks over breakfast.

"C'mon, I'm starving," Dax says. We set a course for Puget Chow, with me pushing the bike, and pass under a Tenner billboard, where Rick's the new number one. The snapshot shows him raising a glass in celebration. "It was nice of Bonnie to give him a leg up, wasn't it?" Lu says. "It'll bring her some good karma. I caught her thought on the Commons asking everyone to give a ruby to Rick, so that's what I did."

"If you ask me, it was a peculiar thing to do," Dax says, "but I guess we'll see how he does."

I refrain from commenting. I know for a fact that niceness has nothing to do with it. Jada has dirt on Bonnie, though I had to beat a hasty exit from the utility room before hearing the details. Whatever it is, Jada and Rick have leveraged it successfully. Below Rick on the billboard is

Bonnie, then Chase, Sue and Samm, Jada, Poulsbo, Franz, McKinsey, and, finally, Ben at number ten. Samm and Sue have toggled, everyone slid up by a spot, Ben is in, and Rick got what he wanted.

A pile of lumber for balcony reinforcement, the result of a safety push announced by the Tenners, forces us to switch to single file in an alleyway. Once we're side by side again, Lu returns to the topic she broached at the town party. "Try and change your mind about upscale eateries, Scottie. I've been going with Wayne, but he won't mind if we make it a PALs thing instead."

"Can't afford it," I give my usual answer. "Unless—are you and Dax bored of Puget?"

"Would that change your mind about it?" Dax asks.

"No, I'd just tell you to go on ahead without me." Momentarily distracted from the disgust I was feeling at seeing Delilah's snapshot replaced with Rick's, I ask, "Wait, why won't Wayne mind? Are you two fighting, Lu?"

"Not exactly."

"What, then? Spill."

She makes a face. "It's nothing, he's just being stubborn. He's picked up a couple of onyxes recently."

Dax takes this as an opportunity to recite, "Onyxes shouldn't be given on a whim. Section A: *Spiteful gems have a tendency to make the giver look bad, so save the grumbling for—*"

"That's just it," Lu interrupts, unusual for her. "Wayne doesn't know the people involved, only that they're accusing him of rude behavior. He says it's nothing to worry about, that gems just don't strike him as that important anymore, not at this stage of his life. He already has a ruby from me and there's not much I can do beyond that."

Under normal circumstances, the Discovered brand

would have garnered Lu invitations to many a party and event—ones she could have taken Wayne to and worked on his image. But with Delilah gone, so is the interest in the new protégée. Lu has been bumped by the onstage introduction to 610 and that looks to be it.

It dawns on me that Lu isn't asking for advice and I remind her that I gave Wayne a ruby during my brief stint at the Agency, not that it counts much given my low rank. Lu's avoiding looking at Dax. "It's just that Wayne doesn't have anyone to fight for him in matters like these... He says he never connected with anybody enough to consider them PALs."

A gem from someone with Dax's rank—141, the result of the most recent win in the tennis tournament—would go a long way toward helping Wayne. Dax responds with a casual, "I'm not sure I know Wayne well enough yet—not for a ruby."

Lu bites her lower lip, then recovers. "I didn't mean to put you on the spot, Dax. Forget I asked."

"Well, invite Wayne out to a drink or something," I say. Dax is sticking to his overly rigid philosophy—the issue's come up before—when there are Tenners trading in secrets and possibly worse. *You didn't think it'd be that easy, did you, with Delilah out of the way?* Jada said it as if she and Rick planned everything together and Rick was the one who pushed Delilah off the balcony. The pair are guilty of blackmail against Bonnie, if nothing else. But Cece isn't allowed to record conversations—eavesdropped on or not—and I have no proof. Doubtful Bonnie would be willing to admit she was their target. If I reported them, it would be seen as an attempt on my part to shake off the Incompetent Intern brand...which isn't far from the truth.

Dax says yes to drinks with Wayne, but he and Lu are

still staring away from each other and I hunt for a neutral topic as we near Puget Chow. I don't have the heart to tell them that Oliver left Greenhouse Seven for parts unknown. I come up with, "I went to Delilah's seeding."

"Jada wouldn't let us take the morning off," Lu tells me. "She said the best way to honor those who came before us is with hard work. Was it very sad, Scottie?"

"Rick did seem sad," I comment dryly, "but then, he *is* an actor."

Dax, clearly happy with the change of subject, gets in a response first. "A seeding isn't sad. It just is. The body is cremated in a lye bath—alkaline hydrolysis, slow and quiet, takes a few hours. What's left is pure-white bone and a green-brown slush which we use as garden fertilizer. The bones are pulverized into ash for the funeral, which actually isn't that great for the plants but it's become a tradition... Scottie, where are you going?"

A Sherlock-wannabe should be able to keep an objective distance, but I can't push the image out of my mind of the pale ash fluttering down onto garden soil, a thin remnant of a human life. My stomach churning, I pedal away, Lu's words just reaching me: "Dax, I think you've upset Scottie..."

At home, I reach for the snow globe on my dresser. It's both a thinking object and a memory—of a long-ago youth center outing to Pike Place Market, the Tuesday one bustling with traders and their goods. The four of us—Lu, Dax, Oliver, me—had wandered along the line of stalls, old-world coins jingling in our pockets. Lu came away with a deck of playing cards. Dax found an unused set of tennis balls, transported on a snowmobile all the way from an iced-up sporting goods warehouse somewhere. As for Oliver and me, we walked past cotton handkerchiefs, leather shoes, and other sensible things, and stopped at a stall stocked with old-world curiosities to try on wrist watches and thick-lensed eyeglasses. I almost didn't spot the snow globe, hidden as it was by the bigger items. Inside the globe was an hourglass-shaped tower—the Space Needle, the seller said, that stood in Old Seattle. I was quite taken with the paradox—the tiny dome had snow on the *inside*. I didn't have enough to trade for it; Oliver contributed his coins.

A shake sends the fake snow tumbling around. I watch it settle and ponder whether Jada is as guilty as Rick, if she goaded him into killing Delilah, and land on no. The hands that pushed bear the blame. *Cece, Rick's glad to be free of Delilah. More than glad—eager, as if his life's starting anew...and it sort of is. He had a double motive: to get his hands on Eternal Life and to be free of Delilah's hold on him... The loathing that emanated from Rick through the door to the Tenner room, well, it sent an icy shiver down my spine I won't soon forget.*

He took Delilah's spot.

Yes—I can easily picture him shoving Delilah off the balcony without regret and without mercy. The fake snow having come to a rest, I give the globe another shake. *Cece, what would you do for eternal life?*

I can't consume the Eternal Life cocktail, Scott.

No, I mean, what if you could extend your existence indefinitely? Which in your case would mean, I guess, being passed from person to person without having your memory wiped.

Indefinitely. Forever. Searching the Knowledge Repository...

I set the snow globe in its place on the dresser and Cece comes back with: Forever is not a possibility. The universe will end one day, most likely in one of three ways: Big Freeze, Big Rip, or Big Crunch.

Not what I meant, though I want to hear about the Big Crunch one of these days... All right, it's time for action. Rick's brand—his hook—is that he's handsome. I need a hook FOR him. Bait. Open an onyx.

Cece pipes up with a warning. SCOTT, THE CODE DISCOURAGES THE GIVING OF ONYXES. SECTION A.

You sound just like Dax. Look, if I sent a thought, Rick would just wipe it unopened, given that I'm a bottom-thousand nobody.

The truth is that my lousy rank is an advantage here. There's little danger of an onyx battle breaking out between the pair of us. Me lobbing an onyx in Rick's direction might be considered ill-mannered, sure, but it'd be *really* bad optics for someone that high up to retaliate against a nobody.

I have Cece put into the onyx the following: *"Delilah gone, Bonnie pushed back from number one... How AWESOME for you, Rick."*

The Dragon and the Drumstick

"Hello, Scott! I know you've had a bad week. Have a seat here at the counter, and let's get you something on the house. A mug of my beef stew? Good for the stomach and the soul."

Although Bonnie always thanked me graciously when I delivered Tenner invites, she's never offered anything free before. My stomach overrules my reluctance to accept charity—as she said, it's been a tough week—and soon a generously-sized steaming mug is sitting in front of me along with a chunk of crusty bread. My confidence in what

I've come to do—try to join forces with Bonnie against Jada and Rick—rises with each spoonful of tender beef cubes and herby vegetables. Bonnie's tavern is cozy, the woodwork, from the low ceiling to the stool I'm perched on, stained a deep golden brown. A yeasty aroma floats up from under a closed door to one side, which I guess leads to the basement. On the opposite wall is a charcoal sketch I've never noticed before—a dragon breathes fire on a lone drumstick, the remainder of the drum set already reduced to a pile of ash.

Something's troubling me and it's not that I assumed that the drumstick part in the tavern name referred to a turkey. It's more serious and I've been avoiding facing it. Delilah collected secrets, leveraged them in her favor. She was a fraud. It makes me wonder which of the rubies crowding her halo were freely given and which were from people strong-armed into providing them. It certainly puts Lucille's story in a different light. She was sucked into a never-ending obligation to the number one.

Dipping bread in the stew, I remind myself that a Sherlock wannabe isn't supposed to pass judgment on a murder victim, especially if trying to clear her own name. If I can make the case to Bonnie that Rick—possibly with Jada's help—had a hand in Delilah's death, maybe she'd be willing to report the pair for blackmail and it'd be a start.

There's a second scenario—one I don't like very much. Not anticipating that Jada and Rick would block her ascent from number three, Bonnie herself might have done away with Delilah. But Bonnie's round features lack ruthlessness, and everyone seems fond of her. Per her brand, Everyone's Friend, she's quick with names and particulars—a hug for a customer across the counter, a question about the garden of another, a merry laugh at a joke a third makes. If she's at all bothered by having to step aside for Rick, she's not show-ing it.

Having wiped the mug clean with the last bit of bread, I lay the spoon down and sigh with unfeigned contentment. "Not many problems a good meal won't fix."

"True enough," Bonnie responds cheerily, running a cloth across the counter. "Not many, that's for sure."

"After all, we all have problems, don't we? Things we hide from others and such."

Nothing lurid, Jada said. Trying to guess what Bonnie's secret could be, I peruse her gems, but all they reveal is that there's no line of separation between a proprietor and her establishment. *"Came in for beer and Bonnie knew all our names! ... Bonnie and her tavern are a second home ... A most welcoming place, the Dragon and the Drumstick ..."* As to her personal details, an extended stare at the "2" in her halo brings up the information that she's fifty-nine and lives in Housing Two with her partner Bishop, a train loader.

Attacking a stain on the counter with the cloth, she lets my remark about hidden problems pass by. I attempt a more direct, "What made you campaign for Rick? I think you'd have made a great leader."

She refolds the cloth into a loose square and scrubs at a stain. "It wasn't my time yet."

The answer is automatic; no doubt she's had to give it all day. The mantle of cheeriness—though it's starting to sound forced—seems impenetrable. My vision of a justice-seeking partnership between the Incompetent Intern and Every-one's Friend is fading fast. I push on. "But don't you want the Eternal Life cocktail?"

The hand wiping the counter pauses. She crosses her arms over her ample chest. Her fingernails are bitten to the quick under the cleaning cloth. "I suppose you think I'm old. People your age usually do."

"Sorry, I didn't mean to imply... The benefits of Eternal Life accumulate, don't they? The more of it you take, the longer your life will be."

"I can afford to wait."

I jump on this. "Ah, so you think Rick won't last at the top? Speaking of him, I know that he and Jada—"

But a new customer has come in and Bonnie moves to greet him, her features unfolding into the customary broad smile. "Yesler, hello. The usual, a mug of hot cider? And let's see, with a cinnamon stick?"

Yesler settles onto a stool and loosens the collar of his gate-guard uniform. "Bonnie, I don't know how you do it but that's right on."

Bonnie reaches for a mug. "How's life treating you at the west gate? And the bad back?"

"You know how it is, we make do..."

Quick, Cece, snapshot. Just like that, I think I might have figured out Bonnie's secret. I hang around a little longer in the hopes of a refill and more time with her, but neither materializes. I exit the tavern distracted, in the middle of having Cece add the snapshot to the WHO KILLED DELILAH corkboard, and run straight into the person sweeping the sidewalk out front.

Apologizing, I help the man back up.

"That's all right, miss." He's been sweeping in the late afternoon sun, the tavern doors to his back. I bend down to pick up the broom. *Miss* is an appellation out of place in New Seattle, but so is Blank Jack. An Outsider, a couple of years back he knocked on a gate—the one near the tavern, staffed by Yesler of the hot cider with the cinnamon stick—and asked to join Dome society. This doesn't happen often and when it does, the usual answer is a town-gate-slamming *no*, but a nasty virus had led to a slew of deaths at the time and there weren't enough youth-center grads. As New Seattle already possessed a Jack, a CC Central technician, and the newcomer lacked gems, he became Blank Jack, the caretaker at the Dragon and the Drumstick.

Blank Jack tucks the corner of his shirt back into his pants. Under his white beard lies the only clue to his history, the coarse texture of his skin, the cold having chipped away at it most of his life. It makes it difficult to guess his age but I don't have to; included in the sparse personal information linked to his rank—9,012—is his age, sixty-four. The welcome-to-the-List amber would have initially given him a middle rank but staying there requires more than the gems he managed to garner after that, only a couple and also amber: one from his boss, Bonnie, and the other from a bartender at the tavern. I notice him tilting his head—he's struggling to view my own halo—and pass the broom back. "I'm Scottie. Bottom thousand as well."

"Pleased to meet ya, Scottie." His conversational style is unhurried and personable.

Partly with genuine curiosity and partly to keep the conversation going on the off chance that he might be able to confirm my guess at Bonnie's secret, I say, "If you don't mind me asking, what made you come in?"

"Well, now. It's warm and the work's steady. That, and I was curious if the rumors were true."

It's a lighthearted answer. "What rumors?"

"That Domers never talk face-to-face. But here you and I are."

I'm aware that Outsiders have no ConnectChips, the technology not having survived the Dimming beyond the stock brought into the domes, but there's little else I know about the world he left behind. New Seattle's beams and panels isolate its residents from more than just the elements. Excursions out the gates are a Top Hundred perk only and one not used very much at that, as it's risky even with a snowsuit—everyone's heard the occasional horror story of Maintenance personnel going out to gather lumber or clear train tracks losing their way, fingers and toes turning black, a rest in the snow fading into permanent sleep. List-bottomers who head to the mountains never come back to tell their stories. And the traders at the market keep their distance from us, with exchanges limited only to bargaining for price. Or maybe it's that we keep our distance from them. I ask, "Your village..."

"Upper Maple Grove," he supplies.

A down-to-earth name, like Blank Jack himself. Cabins among hardy maple trees, high on the slopes. "Do you have family there?"

There's a beat before he answers. "Sure do."

"It's just that we were taught in school that a family unit is oppressive and limiting, but I've always wondered..."

"A cave-clan, you mean?"

"Sorry about that term—I never use it myself. It seems to me that family must be the most wonderful thing in the world. Everybody getting along without having to work at it. No one ever turning their back on anyone else."

"Don't know if I'd put it quite that way." He strokes the snow-white beard. "Family...well, it's not just blood ties. It's bigger'n that. It's people, any people, Jane and Joe and Jaime, you'd willin'ly step in moose shit for, sockless and shoeless and on a Thursday."

My chortle at this produces a straight-faced, "Sorry, wasn't sure you'd heard of scat. Is the word shit not allowed, Scottie?"

"It's section Z—Watch your language! Twenty-two words and three gestures to avoid."

He rests one palm over the other on the broom handle. "Been tryin' for two years to commit the Code to memory, includin' the bit about polite language, but there's sections. Subsections. Sub-*sub* sections. Makes a head ache."

"No one bothers memorizing it all," I explain. "Well, except for Dax, one of my PALs. But you don't need to. Just say in your mind as if talking to a person: *CC, I need to look something up in the Code.*" Here I break off as my own Cece pipes up and I have to shush her.

"That's a skill right there, though, isn't it, communicatin' with the stranger in my noggin. I watch Bonnie greet people and she gets it done in a snap. Me, I end up starin' at the floor a lot."

"She *does* get it done in a snap, doesn't she."

The usual low-left glance is missing in the snapshot I took of Bonnie. She must have her CC under standing orders to look out her eyes and speedily feed her the name, drink preference, and personal details of each customer from an extensive and detailed corkboard. Meanwhile, Bonnie firmly holds eye contact with the customer. A small secret.

Blank Jack scratches his beard. "You asked about family. Only fair I get a question in return, Scottie. You mentioned a PAL. How did you choose each other?"

This requires a moment or two of consideration. "The four of us were lab-conceived within half a year—Dax is the oldest, Oliver and I are in the middle, and Lu is the youngest. We gravitated toward each other and hung out all the time... We had a ceremony to cement the PAL status when we were seven and got a chocolate bar each."

"Well, then. Aren't they like a family?"

I shake my head. "They can drop me anytime they want." Guessing that his family must be his parents only—surely if he has a partner and maybe children or even grandchildren, he wouldn't have left them behind—I ask, "Having parents... What's that like?"

"You have 'em in you, however you were conceived. Pick any two things about yourself and the first probably comes from one side and the second from the other. I'll pick 'em for you—your smile and your voice."

I want to ask him about his own parents, but something in his tone stops me. Perhaps they're no longer alive? The tavern blocks our view of the west gate. The market traders who come through it exhibit visible imperfections—bad teeth, glasses, scars, lip sores, colds that require masks. But whatever ails Blank Jack, it's not of the physical variety.

He nods at me. "Very nice to chat, Scottie. I should go back to my sweepin' now."

He trains the broom onto a crack in the pavement, having sent a couple of sparrows flying away, and I hop on my bike and pedal toward home in the approaching evening, my belly full. I'm ashamed that I didn't take the time to stop by the tavern sooner to extend a welcome to the friendless stranger. *Cece, new ruby. Put this into it:* *"Blank Jack is lovely to talk to. Everyone should stop by and say hello."*

That done, Cece informs me that I have a new gem myself.

It's from Rick—an onyx: *"Incompetent Interns should know their place. ON A SLED."*

As I let this sink in, Cece follows up with her two cents. Scott, the effect of an onyx from the number one on a person's rank is said to be—

Onyxes don't get any weightier, I know. Damn and damn.

This makes Cece pipe up again. SECTION Z STATES THAT THE WORD "DAMN" SHOULD NOT BE USED TWICE IN A SINGLE—

For heaven's sake, Cece, I didn't say it aloud. Here I go again: damn and damn.

I feel justified in the reaction. I didn't expect this—perhaps foolishly so, but nonetheless. Rick's onyx will send me straight to the bottom.

Chapter Ten

Dax is at the theater on a mission. He could kick himself for upsetting Scottie yesterday with gruesome details about Delilah's seeding. He wants to make up for it, cheer her up if he can. He's worried. The Incompetent Intern label will be hard to shake. And all this after Scottie was so excited to be working with Delilah.

A memorial still stands front and center in the ornate lobby, and he stops for a look. There's a painted portrait of Delilah; piled up against it are flowers, droopy and faded after a week and accompanied by cards, the lettering on them elegant if from a public notary and less so if written by the person themselves. In the second category is a card from Ben—the tailor must find the skill to be of use in his profession. There don't seem to be many offerings from Delilah's colleagues. Dax spots only one, the notary writing on it relaying Rick's sadness at the turn of events—insincere, according to what Scottie said. Rick's card is attached to a pricey bouquet of lilies.

"Dax? What are you doing in these parts?"

Dax turns to see Tacoma. His practice partner is usually

to be found in Hobby Two, overseeing everything from tennis-court schedules to bingo night. Tacoma explains that he's been temporarily reassigned due to the extra interest in *Mrs. Montag* in the wake of Delilah's passing. Dax has always envied his friend's talent for fitting in anywhere. Nothing much ruffles Tacoma's feathers—not even losing. "Sorry about your match, Tacoma."

His friend gives an easy shrug. "My only regret is that I won't get a chance to beat you in the finals." The first of the semis is tomorrow and Dax is playing, with the finals in a couple of weeks. Tacoma cocks his head in the direction of Delilah's memorial. "I bet you're wondering why most of the stuff is from fans and not the cast or crew. Theater tradition, apparently. You're supposed to give flowers when they shine on the stage, not when they're dead."

"There are some from Rick—were they a couple?"

"Rumor is, no." Tacoma's quiet, shy manner makes him a good listener and therefore privy to gossip. "Word is she'd lost interest in dating a while back. He, of course... Well, there's a rotation of who's on his arm around town."

A bouquet of lilies that matches Rick's rests against the back of the table. The accompanying note has made its way onto the floor and Dax picks it up. From Jada, professionally handwritten. *It's not an end. Delilah's way of doing things will continue.* A nod to Delilah's leadership skills. Dax tucks the note back into the bouquet as Tacoma prods him, "Did you come for the flowers, to recycle them into compost?"

"No, though now that you mention it, I'll add that to the task sheet for the week. Tacoma, er—they don't by any chance have you working on ticket sales?"

"Ticket sales, props, sets, wherever I'm needed. It's been a bit of a madhouse."

"Look, can you do a buddy a favor?"

"You name it. But on one condition—that you beat Angus in the finals."

Angus is heavily favored to win his semi, also tomorrow. "If I make it to the finals, I'll try my best... Here's the thing. I need a couple of tickets. For, uh, opening night."

"For *Mrs. Montag*? You got a hot date or something?"

"Er—no. I thought Scottie might enjoy an evening out."

"Yeah, *Incompetent* is not a brand anyone wants to be stuck with... The tickets are scorching hot, but I can try." Tacoma's eyes glaze over as they go low left. "We had a rush on tickets. They all *say* they want to support Vicky the Former Understudy in her new starring role... Well, I don't like to say it, but I think they're hoping to see a disaster of a performance... Hold on, you might be in luck. Two seats left." He blinks and turns back to Dax. "Decent ones, as it happens."

Dax can translate the meaning of *decent*. Expensive. Reserved for the Top Hundred. "You're sure you won't get in trouble if you release the seats to me?"

"Nah, you're a rising tennis star. I'll say I expect you to soar to yet greater social heights by winning the tournament."

"Thanks, Tacoma, I owe you one."

It crosses Dax's mind that Lu and Wayne might have wanted to be included—he did invite Wayne out for drinks last night, as promised—but as there are only two tickets, it's out of his hands. He's hoping his bank balance is enough to cover the cost. Apparently, Tacoma is wondering the same thing and his eyes go low left again. "Sorry man, I need to check your..."

"Sure. I'll wait."

Dax is permitted to pay. After Tacoma is called off to help out elsewhere, Dax realizes, somewhat belatedly, that he skipped a step. Fingers crossed, he sends a thought: *"Hey, Scottie, are you free Saturday evening?"*

"What for?"

"It's a surprise. Wear your best outfit."

"I was planning on spending the day packing."

It's his turn to ask, *"What for?"*

"I may have shot myself in the foot. Never mind that. See you Saturday."

On the way out he passes the memorial for Delilah again. A phrase comes to him from a history lesson: *The Queen is dead, long live the King,* or maybe it was the other way around. But it doesn't ring true—not with Rick as the new number one. Rick was a pretty shrub in the shade of Delilah's oak, nothing more. But maybe he'll rise to the occasion. Stranger things have happened. Still, Dax reminds himself, this is why it's best never to think about the List and one's place on it. It hardly ever makes sense.

Chapter Eleven

It's Thursday and I'm at the Agency, vacuuming the fourth-floor hallway. To one side is the room that among other desks holds what used to be my own and to the other is McKinsey's office—empty at the moment—then Wayne's down a bit. Except for Wayne, who greeted me with a friendly wave, everyone's avoiding meeting my eye. They're embarrassed on my behalf. I'm not. A job's a job, though I wish mine had sent me to a less familiar hallway.

The vacuum starts making a strange noise and I stop at the window at the far end and crouch down to dig around the wheels. The culprit is a bird feather that traveled indoors on someone's shoe. I yank it out and, rising to my feet, catch sight of my reflection in the window, which overlooks a narrow alley. The reflection is faint but not too faint for Cece to helpfully top it with my halo. The black void is now doubled, the onyx from Rick as weighty as the old one from the Code Enforcement Office.

I miscalculated. If Rick *isn't* guilty, I reasoned, he'll look up the meaning of awesome and shrug off my rude onyx, worth no more than the feather in my hand on Hugh's social scale. And if he *is* guilty, he'll contact me privately to find out what I know. Instead he seems to have settled on a public battle with a low-Lister, which should be beneath the number one. It means he's either innocent and very petty... or guilty as heck and wants to send me out a gate no matter how it makes him look.

A broad-shouldered shadow falls across my reflection and I turn to see Bodi. He nods at me. "Scott. I'm a bit early for a meeting with McKinsey. When is she expected back?"

The closed door to McKinsey's office means she's with a client somewhere. I set the feather on the windowsill. "No idea. I don't work here anymore."

"I can see that... What's in the window?"

His presence is no less alarming here than it was in the security office across the street, and my answer is a frank, "A new onyx. From Rick."

"Well, that'll ding your rank," he remarks. "Can you point me to the coffee machine?"

"The kitchenette's that way, across from the elevator. Wait." I stop him before he can leave. "Has security looked into Delilah's death—*really* looked, I mean? Did you know that all of the Tenners were in her suite the night of the town party—and Ben as well? Have you checked which of them was the last to leave? Did any of the neighbors see or hear anything? Did Delilah's CC have a record of why she was on the balcony so late?"

My breathless questions come to a halt and I expect Bodi to snap at me that he knows how to do his job, thank you very much. Instead he picks up the feather and takes a seat on the windowsill, his broad back blocking out much of the light, and asks a question of his own. "Why did Rick give you the onyx?"

"I gave him one first."

"I see. And why did you do that?"

I kneel back down to close the vacuum's wheel compartment. "Because I think he did it. Pushed Delilah off the balcony." The words sound wild even to my own ears. I'm ready to jump in with indications of Rick's guilt—the lure of Eternal Life, Delilah holding a secret over his head, his smug smile at the seeding, the conversation I overheard in the Tenner room. Bodi motions for me to stop fiddling with the vacuum. "I want to tell you a story."

I stand back up, puzzled. "About Rick?"

"About Blank Jack. I interviewed him when he first came in. He wouldn't tell me why he wanted to live here in the Dome. All he kept saying is that he was a logger Outside but no longer wanted to do that. I felt he was hiding something and was all set to say no before I finally dragged it out of him. His whole family—wife, elderly parents, a grown-up child living with them with a family of their own—they were all killed in an avalanche. Their cabin was hit. He dug and dug but couldn't reach them. They're still out there somewhere."

"That's awful," I say, my own problems rendered insignificant, though I don't understand why Bodi is telling me this.

"Yes, it is awful." He smooths down the brownish barbs of the feather between two fingers. "I was never much focused on my rank anyway, but that day was when I stopped caring about it altogether. I figure as long as my paycheck hasn't shrunk down to nothing, things must be going okay."

"Bodi, do you believe me? That I didn't wipe the Maintenance alerts—that I'm not responsible for Delilah's death?"

"What I believe is that you should leave Rick alone."

Whether he still suspects me or not, the advice is sensible, if a bit too late. I stare at this stern man perched on the windowsill in a starched security uniform, his knees sticking out at a right angle, the feather small in his hands. "Rick's onyx will boot me into last place come Monday," I say.

"Yes, well…" McKinsey exits the elevator at the far end of the hallway and waves a hello, and Bodi adds, rising to his feet, "I think McKinsey might be the one to consult for practical advice on what to do if you've offended the number one."

McKinsey spots the new onyx at once and shakes her head at me. "Scott, an onyx from Rick? I don't know what's going on with everyone this week. Both you and Wayne seem to have forgotten how the game is played."

"Wayne?" I remember what Lu said about his gems starting to go downhill.

"He doesn't have an onyx from the number one like you do, but he's acquired a hatful of small ones."

Bodi hands the feather back to me and follows McKinsey into her office. Just before he reaches back to close the door, I overhear him say, "It's the Ben matter. I have an update."

"The halo-padding rumor?" McKinsey's voice is muffled.

"I know it's not great timing for a scandal to break, but it might be the right thing to do…"

The Agency doors are pretty solid and I hear no more, but it's enough. Nothing to do with Delilah's death; just another halo-padding scandal, though I wouldn't have pegged Ben as the type.

I restart the vacuum cleaner. Leave Rick alone, Bodi said, but I can't. *Cece, some groveling might be in order. Send this to Rick: "Can I come by to apologize?"*

If Rick responds with a yes, I can try to work into the conversation the evening of Delilah's death, perhaps catch him in a lie...such as what time he supposedly left her suite. Pushing the vacuum back and forth, I consider a different matter. Wayne's got a hatful of small onyxes, McKinsey said —as if he, too, has been poking around and getting under people's skin. *Cece, we might have a brand rival.*

SOMEONE ELSE WANTS TO BE SHERLOCK SCOTTIE?

Not exactly. Wayne the Killer Catcher, maybe. This is good news—you know what they say, two heads are better than one.

Wayne is right down the hall, but I don't want to talk to him here—not about this. I send him a thought asking to meet up after work and we settle on half past five.

I'm approaching the front doors of Puget Chow when three women come out. It's the popular PAL trio, Magda, Mia, and Audrey. I brace myself, though perhaps being socially cut means they won't bother lobbing barbs at me.

I'm wrong. Magda sends a taunting "Incompetent Interns should know their *place*," in my direction, a quote from Rick's onyx for me. The other two take up the chant. "On a sled, on a sled..."

"What did she say to Rick—that things were *awesome* for him?"

"Bet she doesn't think they're awesome for her *now*, Audrey..."

"Tooth Gap on a sled, on a sled..."

Ignoring them, I go inside. Wayne's at a table, lost in thought above a tall glass of lemonade. Late afternoon clouds have hidden the sun and the grub spot, with its medley of mismatched tables and chairs, is lit by ceiling lights above busy tables. Wayne starts at my presence, though we arranged to meet here. His hair is loose around his shoulders and though he's never been known for a particularly smooth chin, he seems to have forgotten to shave at all the past couple of days. He says cheerfully enough, "Scottie, we seem to be in a race to the bottom."

I take the chair across from him. "Lu's worried about you."

"Join me in a lemonade. It's very good today." He takes a long sip through the straw. "Have you ever considered how fragile and wondrous citrus trees are?"

Minor though they may be, the new onyxes are threatening to overrun his halo, for the moment held back by the good gems he's garnered over the years. Eight onyxes in the past three days. That's a lot of people ignoring the keep-your-gripes-to-yourself suggestion in the Code. And no onyx from Rick... Does that mean Rick isn't his main suspect? I lean forward to study the comments in Wayne's gems but he sticks a hand in front of my eyes and his halo vanishes. "Scottie, let it be."

I sit back—did Sherlock in his fictional investigations have this much trouble getting people to open up?—and shake my head. "Fine. What do you want to talk about? Everyone's favorite subject, the birds? Now that Ben's in the Ten, what do you think he'll do, build a giant cage in Founders Square?"

"Don't care about Ben."

"Train the sparrows to carry tiny packages cross-town?"

"Don't care about the sparrows."

"Well, then, how are things going with Lu?"

"Better than I could ever have expected." The words come out in a rush, seeming to astonish Wayne himself and arresting his hand on the way to the glass.

"That's good, isn't it?" I venture.

"It's complicated, Scottie." Wayne drains the glass as if

the citrus trees really are all about to die out any day now. Having signaled the server for a refill and an extra glass, he says, "Look, it's Delilah's death."

I sit up in the chair. Finally. "What about it?"

"Her fall off the balcony... Are we supposed to pretend it means nothing?"

Chapter Twelve

Dax is unsurprised to find Puget Chow packed this time of day—the cafe adjoins the youth center and is popular with those who live or work within the complex. He is, however, somewhat surprised to see Scottie at a corner table with Wayne. He stops by before getting in line. "Hey, you two."

Scottie starts at his greeting. "Hey yourself. We're just, uh, enjoying lemonade. What are you doing all the way down here?"

A curt response. She must still be mad about how unfeeling he came across in talking about Delilah's seeding. "Had to check on a vegetable patch nearby and got thirsty," he explains.

"Have some lemonade," Wayne offers. "I wonder if Outsiders grow citrus. I've heard they've repurposed abandoned indoor malls and sports arenas for farming."

"Only if they have a way of heating those spaces." It's a subject Dax can expound on for hours but he resists pulling up a chair as Scottie's body language reads that he wouldn't be welcome. There is a new addition in her halo. How does she always manage to get into trouble? Wayne, for his part, also has a dimmer halo—Lu won't be happy.

"Well, see you later," Scottie says.

"Right, better get my drink. See you Saturday."

"What are we doing?" She forestalls what he was about to say by adding, "I know, it's supposed to be a surprise. So surprise me now."

He wishes Wayne weren't here to listen in. "Uh—I have two tickets for *Mrs. Montag*."

"The play?" she says, perking up. "Yes, let's go see Rick in his natural habitat."

This strikes him as a rather strange response, but he's used to that with Scottie.

Lemonade in hand—the lidded cup will make its way back to Puget via the town-wide recycling system—he exits via a side door. It opens again behind him and he turns, hoping Scottie followed him out.

It's Wayne. "Daxton, can I ask you a question? It's kind of personal."

"Sure." Dax's general policy is that anyone can *ask*; it's the answering that's not guaranteed.

"How come Scottie has no gem from you? Lu does—a ruby."

Dax doesn't see how it's any of Wayne's business, but he explains his philosophy. "I take my time in assessing a person's value to the town. When Lu graduated—seven months after me—I waited a bit while she settled into her job at the Oyster and I had a chance to observe her as an adult before giving her the ruby."

Oliver was a problem. Dax couldn't in all honesty give him anything beyond a jade, so he did nothing. This weighs on him—will weigh on him forever, he expects.

And then there's Scottie. She said his philosophy was

too rigid and they bickered about it, the result being that they were holding off on giving each other gems.

Wayne gives a snort. "Is that why we met up for drinks the other day—so you could assess my value?"

"It's just how I am," Dax defends himself. He ended up giving Wayne a ruby, mostly for Lu's sake. Wayne struck him as possessing a frivolous streak.

"Scottie's been out of the youth center for a year now," Wayne points out. "She's a responsible citizen and her rank could sure use a boost. It's simple enough: How do you, Daxton, feel about Scottie? In your life, is she a jade-level person? Amber? Ruby?"

"Ruby."

"Well then, there you have it. It really is as simple as—"

Dax holds up a hand. "I was about to do it anyway."

Despite Wayne's urging, the truth is that his ruby won't balance out Rick's onyx—not even close.

Wayne goes back inside and Dax is left with a new feeling pecking at him. Wayne's known Scottie for only a short time and he's concerned about her halo and meeting her for lemonade and whatnot. The feeling—it's jealousy, he realizes.

<hr>

"What did you want to talk to Dax about?" I ask.

"Nothing important." Wayne slides into his chair and settles the lemonade back into his hand. "Sorry I made you wait."

"As it happens, I had a matter to attend to."

After Wayne stepped out, I pushed my glass aside and got to work. I'd managed to catch sight of one name, the first of Wayne's onyxes—from Delilah's neighbor, Lucille. It made sense that she's a suspect. She was resentful of Delilah —how hard would it have been to slip into the next-door suite? Her onyx for Wayne was short and puzzling: *"Line cutter!"*

Lucille responded to my query at once and I pictured her expertly trimming someone's locks as she explained in my direction that Wayne cut in front of her at Pike Place Market. *"Bananas, just arrived on a greenhouse train. There was a bit of a crush. He elbowed me out of the way and stepped hard on my foot. He left with his banana but not before I caught a look at his halo and got his name. I know the onyx is petty of me but it was so rude and my toe swelled up. I've had to wear soft shoes."*

"When was this?" I asked.

"A couple of weeks ago."

Before Delilah's death, then. Must have been just an unintentional run-in. Hoping a bit of good news in the form of one fewer onyx will make Wayne more amenable to pooling our resources, I asked Lucille if it would help if he apologized.

"Well, I suppose it was crowded at the market, maybe he didn't see me. And the toe is feeling better."

But Wayne, glaring at me across the table, flatly refuses to cooperate. "It was an accident. I'm sorry I injured her. But I have no intention of asking her to pull the onyx."

This makes me conclude that there must be more to Lucille's story. "Why not?"

"Scottie, can't you let this go?"

"We shouldn't pretend Delilah's balcony fall means nothing," I quote his own words back to him. Leaning across the table, I demand in a sharp whisper, "Wayne, you know something, don't you?"

He scratches the multi-day growth on his face. "Listen, when Lucille sent the onyx my way, it hit me—I have no control over what other people think of me, not really. Which led to me being more relaxed in my daily interactions, perhaps even to the point of rudeness. These past couple of days I've switched to openly insulting people to their face and inviting them to counter with an onyx. It's been quite freeing... Look, if you really want to know *why*, ask Dax. The endpoint, it was his idea."

I run out to catch up with Dax, who I know can't walk and drink at the same time. As expected, I find him leaning against a wall, working on the lemonade. He seems pleased to see me, though less so when I demand, "Well?"

"Well, what?"

"Wayne said to ask you about the endpoint."

"Oh. Wait, is *that* what he's been doing?" Dax all but strikes his forehead as if a lightbulb's just come on. He follows that up with, "Hey, I didn't want to ask in front of Wayne, but how come you have an onyx from Rick?"

"Never mind that. Why does Wayne not care about his gems anymore and what does it have to do with Delilah?"

Dax takes a long sip through the straw. "The other day, when he and I met up at Puget—like you and Lu requested—we got to talking about Delilah's accident... Have you heard of the Great Seattle Fire of 1889?" At my shake of the head, he continues, "It started in a carpenter's shop. The business district was all wood and the flames gobbled up twenty-five blocks, just like that. An end. When they rebuilt, they used brick and stone... Then came the Dimming. Pipes burst, ice piled up, brick crumbled. Another end. Things circled around and the construction of Dome buildings relied heavily on wood."

"And so we have yearly fire drills, fire extinguishers and buckets of water at the ready on all floors, and when Housing Four had their close call the air turbines had to work extra hard to clear out the smoke," I say. "What's that got to do with anything?"

"The wood rot on Delilah's balcony is a sign that the endpoint is near for *our* Seattle. Materials are running out and repairs are getting harder. We used to have a hundred computers and now there are only six left: one for the List-keeper, a couple in the Birth Lab, and three in CC Central." Dax pauses for another gulp. "Wayne's take on Delilah's accident was that it cemented how meaningless gems ulti-mately are—even rubies. We agreed that we need to make an effort to learn about the world outside the gates. I *may* have mused on the fact that the Dimming has been slowly reversing itself over the years, that the temperature might have eased up a bit... The plan we discussed—for down the road, I thought—was to track Oliver down and—"

"Oliver?" I interrupt. I'm feeling blindsided by this newly revealed side of Dax. "You were going to look for him?"

"He left his greenhouse. A market trader told me that he made it to one of the villages."

The news unclenches one of the knots in my stomach—Oliver's safe; he's found a place.

"The plan—again, for down the road—was to connect with all the bottomers we've sent sledding, band together when the Dome reaches its natural end. Maybe Wayne's right and we are there." Dax shakes the cup and slurps up the last of the lemonade. "Even if we aren't, it's a big world out there—I want to *experience* things. The sky uncheckered by Dome beams. The wind on my face and snow drifts under my feet. The villagers keep dogs—they're eager to please apparently, like mid-Listers. Wayne's heard that down in the Dome of Los Angeles they have cats and that *they* act as if they sprung into existence in the Top Hundred... When I'm ready, I won't do what Wayne's doing, use rank as a push. I'll just walk out a gate. Nothing in the Code says that's not allowed, right?"

My response is a curt, "The endpoint for me will be on Monday."

"You don't know that, Scottie."

But I do. Which means that Rick has won.

Chapter Thirteen

The Social Agency

Hugh knows that wild rumors have been spreading about the birds. A secret additive in their feed. Overpopulation. A new sound at a frequency only they can hear making them fuss. Having finished his lunch, a sandwich and an orange slice, he discards the rind in the garden bed. The Agency roof houses a water tower and a lanky palm under whose sparse shade he keeps a chair. He wipes his hands on a handkerchief before picking up the spotting scope. He trains it on the sliver of the Edge Garden visible from his vantage point and the tree there.

Other sparrows are chirping nearer than the garden, ones nesting under the eaves and in wall cavities of the Agency building, but Hugh has taken a special interest in Rick and his prospective mate. At the other end of the scope, Rick is flitting around the tree, which is devoid of apples at the moment. He's sporting breeding plumage, his beak revitalized from a dull yellow to an inky black, his throat dark. A construction project has emerged with the breeding plumage, a sphere of leaves, grass, and the odd scrap of cloth and paper in the V formed by two branches. Hugh scans around for the mate Rick's been working hard to attract, but Delilah is nowhere to be found today.

Hugh knows why he comes to the roof. There are no people to judge and rank. The sparrows enjoy small, tidy existences, rather like his own.

This reminds him of the day his life shrank to the size of his office downstairs. In the sterile environment of Medical One, her illness-weathered body frail under the blankets but her voice still strong, Belinda told him she picked ruby red for the best of the gems "because it's the color of ripe cherries, my favorite fruit as a child. I remember how it was, you know, before the Dimming. Bags of cherries on the grocery store shelves, year round, juicy and sweet... Amber—didn't really have a specific reason there, pulled the color out of a hat." Here she chuckled. "What's that, you want to know about jade and onyx? Well, if you *must* know, it's because of an ex who left me for a younger lady! His eyes were green in daylight and always seemed darker when night fell."

Hugh listened, overwhelmed with fear that he wouldn't be able to follow in her stead—that he was prone to being too analytical. Over the years he's learned that what must be kept at bay is *emotion*. Keeping a distance, that's the List-keeper's job—one he's been doing for coming up on forty-five years. Otherwise one runs the risk of having so many opinions—so much pain and desire—overload the mind.

He passed on going to Delilah's seeding a week ago. The distance he keeps extends to funerals. His task was to send all of Delilah's gems into a special folder in his computer, the "graveyard," a flat end to something so connected with life. Same with the bottom person that week, Oliver. The next part of the job was more pleasant: a new youth center graduate, Ty, to add to the List. The thought makes him consider whether it's time to yield the baton to someone with fresh ideas, live out his remaining days tending greenhouse livestock...

No, not yet. He has a few years left to give.

Surprising himself, he aims the scope toward Work One, where the Tenner meeting is to be held with Ben joining in for the first time. Hugh can see figures settling into chairs. Ten people deciding the fate of so many small beings, including his Rick. Hugh's worried the birds will be sent out permanently.

Reminding himself that the Dome itself is not much more than a vast glass cage, he pulls the scope back to the tree. There—Delilah has arrived. Plainer than Rick, with a drab gray-brown body and beak, but with more pep and personality, she gives the nest a sharp tap as if testing its worthiness. Rick, who's been hopping around with his chest puffed out, flies away to return a few minutes later with a new offering, a bit of dried grass for the nest. Delilah is not easily pleased.

A blur of wings crosses Hugh's scope—a piebald female with white patches on its body. Its arrival seems to spur Delilah into commitment and she and Rick drive the intruder bird away with angry chirps and wing flapping. An argument of this sort, over territory, happens occasionally. Hugh watches the intruder disappear from view behind Housing Twenty-One.

An in-thought makes him set the scope down on one knee. It's Bodi with news. *"An Outsider has come in and is asking to stay."*

Hugh reminds the security chief that the town count is down by one at the moment—because of Delilah.

"*Right,*" Bodi says. "*I'm about to interview the Outsider—we'll see if she's a good candidate.*"

The timing of this, on the heels of the intruder sparrow in his sliver of the Edge Garden, doesn't surprise Hugh. It's not the first time that the avian world has mirrored the human one. The creatures are his daily friends and if there's something wrong, he feels that he should be the first to know. It bothers him that he hasn't noticed anything out of the ordinary about the birds' behavior—not a thing. But perhaps he's just too close.

Chapter Fourteen

The Tenner Meeting Room

Jada has managed it so Ben is in the chair next to hers. The number shining bright in her halo today is a six, though not for long, if she can help it. Over at the food table, Sue approaches the new number one. "Lookin' good, Rick."

Rick's reply, in between the shoveling in of cheese chunks, is flippant. "Had my first dose of Eternal Life. *Of course* I look good. Are you coming to watch my big scene, Sue? Opening night, tomorrow at eight. We just got through the last rehearsal with Vicky—no idea how *she'll* do, but I'm planning on knocking it out of the park." He throws a lazy glance over one shoulder. "Everyone else coming?"

He receives perfunctory nods. They'll all be there. Not to watch Rick but to be seen.

Sue changes the subject, having found something in Rick's gems to make her jealous. "Rick, why are you feuding with a low-Lister? The careless one."

"I have my reasons. A man's gotta have some fun, Sue."

Rick plops into the armchair at the head of the table and sweeps his hair behind one shoulder, a gesture of vanity, not of utility. "Let me open the meeting by saying how *grateful* I am that the town has placed their trust in me. I have *many* ideas for improving the lives of *all* Seattleites."

Poulsbo claps. If the speech sounds rehearsed, it's because it is. Jada suggested the phrasing. But Rick's overdoing it—she'll have to remind him that he's not on a stage. This room is not the place to exaggerate your own importance; staying smart, on your toes, *aware*—that's what's required.

"Yes, yes," Chase says. "We can save your many ideas for down the road. Let's try to stick to the agenda. I have places to be."

Ben rises to his feet. "Before we begin, I wish to say a few words. I know some of you think I pushed my way in, but I'm here to stay and you all might as well get used to it."

"*Pushed*? More like halo-padded," Chase mutters under his breath. It's a rumor Jada has heard too, but she knows it isn't true. Chase adds, "What *are* you proposing we do about the birds? What's this big plan of yours?"

Ben remains on his feet. "It's simple—we make it an official town hobby. Volunteers will trap the sparrows and move them out the gates, along with any nests."

"*That's* your grand plan? A *hobby*?" Chase's incredulity is almost comical. "And we send the birds sledding? Then again, I suppose it's not as if we can cook 'em and turn them into cafeteria mix. They're too small, it'd be hardly worth the effort."

A slow nod from McKinsey, who seems to have forgotten her stance from last time the subject was discussed, that the Edge Garden is where the birds should be lured. "Why not? We haven't had a new hobby in—well, I don't know how long. We can call it Bird Control or something of that sort. I might join in myself! To look for nests, not in moving them out... Which brings up a problem. Only those in the Top Hundred will be able to participate in that part of it."

"*Will be able?*" Chase scoffs. "To what, risk frostbite?"

Ben sits down and, apparently having anticipated all the objections, explains that the hobbyists will be well protected by suits and perhaps an exception can be made for those not in the Top Hundred.

"Won't that...endanger...the sparrows and their young?" Poulsbo pipes up. "They'll be vulnerable...to the elements, snowmobiles, predators... And if you move a nest with eggs in it...how will the parents find it?"

Chase makes a mock-crying face behind Poulsbo's back but Ben takes the question seriously. "We can make sure that adults and hatchlings are relocated together, perhaps build a protective hut. Is this something you can do, Poulsbo, or will you need extra help?"

Poulsbo's reaction to having additional tasks piled onto his plate is a compliant nod. "Depends on how fast you want it...done. We'll need lumber... We can add a feeding station...too. I can ask Blank Jack what materials work best in the cold... Or the new Outsider."

This gets everyone's attention.

"What's this? Another Outsider?" Rick tut-tuts. "Yes, there it is on the agenda. Didn't we *just* let Blank Jack in? We might have to start charging an entrance fee."

"Blank Jack's been here two full years now," Bonnie points out dryly, her first words of the meeting. There are dark circles under her eyes and daggers in her stare.

"Really, has it been that long?" Rick says airily. "The agenda doesn't give any information other than a name—Renee—and that she's passed the initial health exam. So who are they, this new Outsider? Tell us what you know, Poulsbo."

"Someone on the Commons said...she came in through...the west gate."

Bonnie thaws enough to add more information. "Yesler —he's the guard at that gate—said she came in at dawn."

"Well, there is room in the List count," McKinsey supplies. "The Agency was going to ask the youth center to provide an extra grad, but it's up to us, really, whether we want the Outsider or not."

"Eh," Chase says, "she's here already."

They vote to let Renee fill the available spot—pending a yes from Bodi, not at all a certainty—and Chase adds a follow-up comment. "At least there's no other Renee in town or she'd have to be Blank Renee, which is a mouthful."

Outsiders who come knocking on gates are of little interest to Jada. Her attention is on Rick, who's been sneaking winks at Sue. He ought to know better, with Samm watching...and Bonnie, who's barely hiding her fury at having been forced to endorse Rick for number one. He must think that he doesn't have to bother hiding the affair now that Delilah can't hold it over his head, as if Bonnie can't do the same. Jada knew about Rick's weakness going in —he likes other people's women; Delilah's notes on him hold a dozen names. She'll have to warn him to be less obvious. If Rick can't get his act together, she might have to drop him. Fast.

Franz comes in and slides into the last armchair. "My apologies. A mediating session ran long but ended well for all parties. What did I miss?"

"A new hobby and a new Outsider," Jada supplies, but it's Rick, who's sneaking another wink at Sue, that her eyes linger on.

Chapter Fifteen

Yesterday I was at the theater as part of a cleaning crew and today I'm filing into the auditorium with Dax by my side. Unlike the back part of the building that houses the dressing rooms, the auditorium is open air—and uncarpeted, so it's my first time seeing it beyond a quick peek. A three-level circular gallery faces the stage and its crimson curtain, which hangs down from what I've heard Delilah and the others refer to as the *heavens*, a nook where props, ropes and lighting hide. Dax and I take our seats directly across from the stage, on the second level. We're out of place in the expensive seats, surrounded by a Top Hundred crowd sporting the latest fashions, though Dax's tennis fame nets him a couple of nodded greetings. The box right above us is reserved for the Tenners. Jada and Ben are there, stiffly chatting.

There's been a development on the personal front—Dax has given me a ruby. The thought coupled to it is not exactly overflowing with praise: *"Scottie keeps things interesting."* It struck me that it's only fair to give Dax a gem in return, but I had trouble with the wording. I recalled the moment at the town party when I stumbled and stopped myself from a fall by grabbing his arm, an instant that stretched to a lifetime, the spark the brief touch evoked cascading down my body, electric and warm... Get a grip Scottie, I chided myself, and cut out the impossible, cheesy daydreams. This week had served to remind me what's at stake—Monday's bottomer was a section Q violator, Peggy. Earlier in the year, she and Leon, PALs and youth center employees, were revealed to be lovers; they lost their jobs, their rank tanked, and Leon bottomed first. Peggy is being sent to a different greenhouse, into the farm-work position Oliver left behind.

I ask Cece as the auditorium fills up, lit by bulbs under the cropped roof encircling the gallery, *Why do we even have section Q?*

Cece's response might have been delivered by Dax himself. THE CODE IS CLEAR AND PRECISE ON THE MATTER, SCOTT: "IT'S IMPORTANT TO HAVE BONDS THAT ARE ROCK SOLID AND THE ONES FORMED IN YOUTH ARE THE STRONGEST. ROMANTIC PARTNERS COME AND GO—NEVER MIX THE TWO. PALs ARE FOR LIFE."

It seems to me, Cece, that the Code claims to be clear and precise on things that aren't clear and precise at all. Then again, since I'm being kicked out in two days, what difference does the Code make? Don't bother answering, it's a rhetorical question— Dax would never go for it.

I finally settled on a boring *"From one PAL to another"* for his gem.

As to Sherlock Scottie, it was a dud from the get-go. What made me think I could take on the number one? There's been no response from Rick to my query asking if I can apologize in person. I'm about to watch him onstage but doubtful that will present any opportunities for further

Sherlocking. Neither did vacuuming the theater yesterday —the only time I saw Rick, he was with a group of other actors and unapproachable.

As if on cue, a thought arrives. *"Apologies will be accepted backstage after the performance, at the opening-night party."*

I sit up in the plush seat, making Dax glance over at me. Now we're talking. It took Rick five days to respond, but he wants to see me. The question is...why? And why *now*? Doubtful that he bothered to look up my whereabouts and saw that I was in the gallery. Just catching up on his in-thoughts while he readies for the spotlight, a way to stave off opening night jitters? No, Rick isn't the type to have opening night jitters. More likely he's looking for a diversion later, a romantic conquest or a humiliation of some kind.

Only one way to find out.

Dax sends a smile in my direction as the last of the seats fill up. We've agreed to shelve all talk of rank for the evening, so his comment is a mundane one. "Tacoma told me that Delilah wrote the play."

And herself a starring role. Something else I didn't know about her, in addition to secrets collecting.

"Apparently she modernized classic stories," Dax goes on. "This one, *Mrs. Montag,* was originally by Shakespeare, I think, from way back in the seventeenth century..."

This is awkward—I'll need to tactfully let Dax know that, having procured a pair of expensive tickets for us, he needs to mosey on home after the play while I head backstage for a party. It'll be a poor way of repaying him for the effort but I can't see a way around it, not if I want to talk to Rick alone.

After a cast member comes out to remind the audience to mute their CCs for better enjoyment of the performance, the lights dim and evening settles into the auditorium, broken only by lit windows on the upper floors of neighboring buildings. The curtain rises, a slow motion pregnant with drama, to reveal a few items of furniture placed on stage to give the illusion of a real room: a table, two chairs, and a grand, wrought-iron chandelier hanging from the heavens. A servant is doing a half-hearted job of polishing the table. Vicky strides on and chews out the servant; a wealthy house-owner dissatisfied with the help, she's in Delilah's costume, the blue jeans, checkered shirt and red cowboy boots.

I sat down in the expensive seat expecting Vicky to be a poor imitation of Delilah, but she's not bad. It's as if she's come to life; it's hard to believe that the woman with the pinched face and dour outlook I saw trailing Delilah and the costumed actor delivering her lines in a spirited fashion are one and the same. Her character is Mrs. Montag, carrier of the outdated tag, Mrs., and the mother of one Rom, who has yet to make his appearance but whose welfare she seems to base her happiness on, judging by the way she sends off the servant to polish Rom's pickup truck next.

Rick makes his appearance, also in a checkered shirt, boots, and jeans, his character the troublesome son, Rom. Though they're about the same age, Vicky has adopted a stoop to her shoulders that adds decades to her years and believability to the mother-son pairing. Rom is off to see a lover and his mother doesn't want him to go.

Cece, wake up, I instruct as the stage is changed to an outdoor scene, with Rom and Mrs. Montag continuing their argument by a bicycle-and-cart stand-in for the pickup truck. *Focused as we were on Rick, we forgot about Vicky. What if the motive for Delilah's murder wasn't Eternal Life and the number one chair, but the spot on the stage? I'll try to talk to*

Vicky at the after-party as well. Take a snapshot of her—now—and tack it onto the WHO KILLED DELILAH corkboard.

WILL VICKY OR RICK ADMIT IT, SCOTT?

People never admit bad things—not willingly. You have to lead them or trick them into saying it. I'll have my work cut out for me...

Shelving for the moment the certainty that one of its leads is a killer, I'm soon drawn into the story. Rom is in love with one Julie, a fresh-faced cast member whose real-life name I don't know. Though there's animosity between the Montag family and Julie's parents, Mr. and Mrs. Capo, the main reason why Rom and Julie's romance has hit a snag is Mrs. Montag herself, who wants the whole of her son's love. The play is a rebuke of kinship and its binding ties—of cave-clans.

After a flurry of scenes involving the flighty servant, a well-endowed nurse, and puns that lightly brush against the bad language section of the Code, the curtain rises on an evening scene. Rom stands under Julie's balcony. Above them is a starry night made of cardboard. In an amorous verbal exchange, the pair vow to be together forever, with promises made to flee hand-in-hand in the morning in Rom's pickup. But when the fake sun rises at the back of the stage, Julie, suitcase packed, waits alone. The stage is changed to the indoor room again, where Rom is facing his mother, who has thwarted the couple's plan by the simple expedient of taking the truck keys. She tosses them on the table and dares Rom to take the keys, threatens to find the couple wherever they go, then switches tactics and wrings her hands as she beseeches him to stay. Rom holds his head high throughout, the mother and son well matched. Finally, Mrs. Montag strides off, leaving her only son with a decision to make.

Rom kicks a chair out of the way beneath the wrought-iron chandelier. At last, a plan that will free him forever: If he fakes his own death, he reasons, pacing back and forth, his mother will be left behind to mourn. He sends the flighty servant to a pharmacy to obtain a strong sleeping potion, then sits down at the table to pen a note to Julie telling her of the plan. After the servant brings the vial and leaves again with the note, Rom rises to his feet. Alone on the stage, facing the audience, he asks of the universe, "Is this the only way? Is this what love demands?"

I clutch the seat—I'm filled with a dread that the whole thing will end in tragedy, that the servant will misdeliver the note—and my fingers brush against Dax's.

"Love is a curtain of smoke, a *fire*, a sea fed by tears." The vial in his hand, chest heaving with each breath, Rom falls to his knees. The chandelier inches down an arm's length and stops, its circle of light tightened around the kneeling lover. He uncorks the vial. "What else is it? It is a madness..."

It all happens so fast that had I blinked, I'd have missed it.

The chandelier descends.

The warning shouts from the audience come too late. The heavy frame sends Rick sprawling. Bulb glass shatters with a ringing peal that carries all the way to where Dax and I are. On the wooden boards of the stage, the number one lies motionless, the dark stain spreading away from his body reflected in the glittering shards strewn about.

A hush falls on the audience, everyone uncertain how to react—even my first thought is *Is this part of the play? Did Mrs. Montag want to ensure her son stays home permanently?*—but on stage, pandemonium has ensued. Vicky rushes over to Rick. The lights encircling the auditorium come on full blast. "He's badly hurt," Vicky cries, panic blurring the line between her inner and external voice. "CC, medical emergency!"

Swift, urgent, a whisper travels through the gallery. "First Delilah and now Rick—it's Gemma Bligh's curse, has to be... It's struck again!"

Chapter Sixteen

Monday, March 29

Bodi calls out a brisk "Enter" in response to my mid-morning knock. He's at his small desk, stuffed into it as he keeps an eye on the rotating array of dot-sprinkled maps. He spares a glance in my direction. "Ah, Scott. Still with us, I see."

I'm hanging on by a thread. Rick's onyx has sunk me down to 9,999—I'm in the bog. A spot above me is Wayne; a spot below is Ellen, an accountant prone to taking embarrassing snapshots of others and slinging them onto the Commons—nose-picking, that kind of thing. She's headed to Greenhouse Five. I caught her reaction on the Commons. *"I was only revealing your true selves."*

Bodi adds, "I'm glad you dropped by."

It's a terse statement, but then all of Bodi's are. Before he can say anything more, I do. "You believe me *now*, don't you, that there's someone behind all of this? First Delilah dies and now Rick."

This takes his attention away from the screen. "Rick succumbed to his injuries?"

"No, but it was a close call."

"Last I heard, *a close call* is a much better state of affairs than dead."

I was so sure the killer was Rick. But Rick is in Medical One in a coma. This morning's update has Bonnie at number one, followed by Chase, Samm and Sue, Jada, Rick, Poulsbo, Ben, Franz, and McKinsey. Bonnie is at the top, Samm and Sue have toggled again, Ben's birds have inched him up past Franz and McKinsey...and Rick has sunk to six —while there's much sympathy for him, everyone agrees that in a crisis, it's important to have a leader who's awake.

Bodi reaches for the lone item on his desk other than the computer, an antique letter opener, which I didn't notice the previous time I was in the room. We have no letters to open; it's a thinking object for him, like my snow globe. With one hand, the back of it hairy under his shirt sleeve, he taps the silver knife against the palm of the other. "Scott, if the Security Office found anything irregular about the two accidents we'd have taken action. I would think that'd be obvious."

"It's not the curse." Watching the chandelier descend convinced even me of the power of Gemma Bligh's anger, but only for a brief moment.

"So you think we have a killer in our midst." Another tap. "Who, Bonnie, on the quest for Eternal Life?"

I don't want it to be Bonnie, with her cozy tavern and harmless secret. "What about Ben?" I offer. "He was stuck on the shelf, so close to being a Tenner. Now he's safely in and rising... And he is getting on in years, isn't he?"

Bodi chastises me much like Bonnie did. "Sixtyish is not old, Scott. Besides, making it into the Ten is one thing. Making it to number one and Eternal Life is quite another."

"But aren't you investigating him for halo-padding? You said so to McKinsey. A scandal. If he's guilty of that, who knows what else he might have done?"

The letter opener lands on the desk with a clang. Bodi shakes his head at me. "If you must know, the scandal has to do with *Delilah*, not Ben. Ben's blameless. Delilah tried to keep him on the shelf by spreading false rumors. That he was halo-padding. That he was buying sparrows from traders to artificially inflate their population inside the Dome. Neither was true. Ben came to me and I dug into it. What I unearthed was that Delilah stockpiled secrets and leaned on people to make things happen... If she hadn't died when she did, you bet there would have been a scandal." Bodi's eyes flash, as if he's mad at himself for not catching on earlier. He reins in his reaction. "McKinsey and Hugh made the argument that since nothing can be done about it now, the town is best served by keeping Delilah's memory intact."

I consider pretending to be surprised but decide against it. "I know she collected secrets. Don't you think that made her even more of a target?"

His eyebrows knot at me. "You knew about it? Why didn't you report it?"

"I didn't know until after she died. And then I wasn't sure you'd believe me."

"Next time, try me. Anything else?"

"Jada has them. Delilah's box of secrets, though I suppose if you asked her, she'd deny it."

He nods, as if taking me at my word. "I'll keep an eye on her. As to Rick... Take a seat." I turn a table chair around so it's facing the desk. He continues, "It seems to me, Scott, that what we have here is a state of affairs where everyone's forgotten about the Incompetent Intern, just like that."

He's right. One accident equals blame for the intern. *Two* accidents is a whole 'nother story. The Commons is abuzz with speculation about Gemma Bligh's curse and where it will strike next—with Bonnie as the leading contender. I'm off the hook and Evan and Vicky have pulled their onyxes— it was what saved me from falling into the last place instead of Ellen, the misbehaving accountant.

"The theater," Bodi goes on. "You know your way around the building. When were you there last?"

"When Rick had his accident. A lot of people were there along with me—it was opening night."

"And before that?"

I don't like where this seems to be going. Starting to regret taking the initiative to knock on Bodi's door, I answer, "The day before, to vacuum. There were dried flower petals, things like that, left over from Delilah's memorial."

"I see. Were you there as part of a crew?"

"The others were cleaning the bathrooms. There's carpet only in the lobby, so it's a one person job."

"Was it busy?"

I think back. "People were in and out. There was a morning rehearsal."

"After which the stage area would have been empty— giving you the opportunity to climb the ladder up to what I'm told is called the heavens and to saw at the chandelier rope."

I sit up in the chair. "So it *was* cut?"

"Leave the questions to me." Bodi reaches for the letter opener and starts tapping his palm again. One, two, three, four. One, two, three, four. "Let me tell you how things look from where I sit. Delilah refused to help you gain social standing and this made you angry. You realized an opportunity lay in the timing. Eighty-five years and Gemma Bligh's curse. *And so Delilah died.* But the blame still landed on you. You were desperate, panicked. You tangled with Rick. Why? To throw suspicion on him, so you could rehabilitate your brand?"

I'm now *definitely* regretting taking the initiative to knock on Bodi's door. "I have no brand. I'm in the bog."

He points the letter opener in my direction. "And Rick is the one who put you there. He landed in Medical One and you've gotten your revenge and cleared your name at the same time. You have to admit it smells bad."

I resist wiping the beads of sweat that have broken out on my forehead as if the gesture will somehow make me look guilty. "I know how it smells, but I didn't have anything to do with it—any of it."

Bodi's expression makes me wonder if he's about to slip handcuffs on my wrists, but he only adds a mild, "If you are innocent, let me give you the same piece of advice as before —stay out of this. Accidents happen. Balcony railings give way, chandeliers fall."

"Right when Rick happened to be underneath?"

"The theater is a busy place. Someone was bound to be underneath. Now if you'll excuse me, I have work to do. The new Outsider's been assigned housing and a spot on the List, but she still needs to be scheduled for a ConnectChip implant and be matched to a job..."

I leave, feeling Bodi's gaze linger on me. I take that as a sign that despite the advice he just gave me, he's not so sure there isn't more to it all than meets the eye.

I'm waiting for Lu to finish her evening shift. The back of the eatery has a less-than-appetizing aroma hanging over it.

Sparrows peck in and around waste bins, oblivious to my presence. The creatures seem more inscrutable than ever. Unreadable. Impossible to know if they're eager for the largest crumb that's to be found or if they're planning a coup as in Samm and Sue's sketch. The feeling frustrates me. A new hobby, Bird Control, has been announced—they're to be moved out. This strikes me as a good thing. The Dome was only ever meant to house people.

Lu comes out in a beige smock and loosens her hair tie. As we leave the eatery behind us and the small talk runs out, I relay as best as I can Wayne's reasons for turning his back on his rank. Worried that he'll lose his nerve, he asked me not to tell Lu anything. But I figure the *ally* in PAL has to stand for something.

Lu listens without interrupting, then sighs. "So that's what it is. I'd been wondering."

The topics dominating the Commons—the curse, Delilah, Rick, the new Outsider—seem far away tonight compared to the more immediate problem facing my PAL. "Are you going to try and change his mind? He can reverse course and go on an apology tour."

She takes her time answering. "Not if this is what he feels he has to do."

I glance over. "But you and Wayne... It's for real, isn't it?"

"You know what they say about romantic partners: they come and go."

Her tone doesn't match the sentiment.

The way home takes us past the building inside whose walls everyone's genetic key sits in its own lockbox. "If it's me next Monday, I figure I can break into the Birth Lab," I say, meaning it, "and rifle through their records. I'll already be at the bottom of the List—what more can they do to me?"

Lu responds with an optimistic, "I've heard that Rick's

doing a bit better. Now that it's crystal clear that the curse is behind what's been happening, he can null your onyx when he wakes up."

"Let's hope that's the end of it."

Lu takes my words at face value. "Curses tend to keep going until broken, but maybe we'll get lucky."

Once back in my room, I reflect. *Cece, let's see where we stand.*

YOU ARE STANDING ON THE LINOLEUM FLOOR OF YOUR ROOM, SCOTT, AND I AM NOWHERE.

Thank you for that brilliant observation, Watson. What I meant was, where we stand in our Sherlocking. I'm in the bog and further than ever from proving Delilah was murdered...and now Rick's been hurt. We can rule him out—and Vicky, given that the chandelier ruined her big night. Wipe the WHO KILLED DELILAH board clean. We're back to the people who were in Delilah's suite the night she died, Rick aside. Let's see: Bonnie, Chase, Samm and Sue, Jada, Poulsbo, McKinsey, Franz... Oh, and Ben. That's a lot of names, isn't it?

Cece gives me the count. NINE.

Grabbing my toiletries bag, I head to the end of the hall. As I wait in the short line for the bathroom, I'm stricken with a sudden worry. *Lu said curses keep going until broken, which gives the killer cover to do it again. What a terrible thought.*

BECAUSE MURDER IS TERRIBLE, SCOTT?

It is, yes. Moving up a spot in the bathroom line—none of my neighbors seem inclined to pass time chatting with the bog person—I ponder what to do. *We need to forestall any more accidents, Cece, but how? What does the Knowledge Repository say—how did people stop mummy curses in the old days? I mean, I know curses aren't real, but there must have been SOME method or other.*

The desired approach seems to have been to return the mummy to its tomb.

Unfortunately we can't undo eighty-five years of cushy living under a dome while others suffered out in the cold. How about Gemma Bligh—what does the Repository say about her?

As I take my spot at the sink, Cece comes back with snippets from the historical record. Elderly resident of Seattle Gemma Bligh railed against the plan to build the Dome ... Even though there was concern the outside temperatures might hit degrees so low as to yield life unsustainable ... She and a hired snowmobile driver made the perilous journey to the new Dome but the doors stayed closed to them ... She fell ill on the return journey ... Her final words were that the Founders were turning their backs on those left Outside ... That they were leaving behind not only their families but their humanity, compassion, and kindness ... She was buried in an unmarked location ...

How sad, all of it. There's nothing about the curse?

Not in the historical record, Scott.

My hand pauses with the toothbrush midway to my mouth as I consider this. Kindness... The word makes me think of Oliver—of how I failed him. He had pulled so far away that it never occurred to me to give him a gem once we both graduated onto the List, he a week ahead of me. I've come to understand why he did it—as Dax said, Oliver was a loner at heart. He craved space—a sort of peacefulness. I tried to reach him—pushed too hard, according to Dax—and when that didn't work I turned my back on him for good. I should have been more understanding, more kind. I was too focused on my own rank and my own problems to worry about him. And now it's too late to fix it.

With a sigh, I go back to brushing. My epiphany on the

matter can at least be put to some good use—and I'm desperate enough to try anything. Hoping Blank Jack won't mind what I'm about to do and nervous about the prospect of sharing a thought on the Commons—a new experience for me—I take some time perfecting the wording.

Chapter Seventeen

Tenner Meeting Room

Jada reflects on the difference a week makes. Not only was the meeting moved up from Friday to Tuesday, but Franz and his goatee are on time and Samm and Sue are at the table with everyone else. Worried expressions hang on faces, and culinary delicacies on trays hold little interest today.

Bonnie, her usually neat and tidy bun slipping down her neck, opens the proceedings from the number one chair. Rick, when it was his turn in the chair, was full of himself and at ease. Bonnie's demeanor is uncertain, as if the swiftness of events caught her off guard. "It's my sad duty to lead us today. It goes without saying that I didn't expect to be in this position—not this way... How about we all take a moment and send get-well wishes to Rick?"

"He's in a coma. What's the point?" Chase counters with his usual tact.

"They'll be there when he wakes up. And perhaps his

CC is still in communication with his mind." Bonnie closes her eyes.

Jada privately agrees with Chase's take. Despite the rumor that's been spreading—that Rick's doing better—she's been told the outlook is not optimistic. She's risen to five and Rick has sunk to six. This week is likely to be his last in the Ten. They all witnessed his downfall in person. Jada sends a brief thought saying that they're all pulling for him.

After a minute, Bonnie opens her eyes. "Everyone done? The first item on the agenda is the failure of the town-wide safety check. The project was meant to prevent further accidents, and here we are again. To be fair, Maintenance hadn't gotten to the theater yet as we had them working on balconies, but I'm not sure that explanation will satisfy—"

"Gemma Bligh."

"Did you say something, Chase?"

"Yes, Bonnie. What I want to know is *Which one of us is next*?"

There are sharp intakes of breath around the table. Ben, to Jada's left, shakes his head. "Really, Chase. That's hardly helpful. The curse is a scary story told after lights-out in the youth center. Chills for children. Unknown terrors in the dark. But it's taken hold and people are frightened. This isn't a game."

"Of course it's not a game. It's all very serious. I could be next."

"Why would Gemma Bligh's curse target you?" Bonnie scoffs. "It's clearly going after those of us in the number one chair."

"I don't think that's clear at all. For all we know, the curse could be after Tenners of any kind and no one in this room is safe. What if it has a hankering for the number two just for variety?"

"Stop it," McKinsey cuts in and gives her usual level-headed take. "No one is next. The curse isn't real."

Disagreement with this statement hangs as weightily in the room as the chandelier had before falling on Rick's head. Jada catches sight of Bonnie's hands under the table—she's folding and unfolding them. Not uncertainty in the new role. Fear. It's there in Bonnie's voice as she says, "A curse this strong will keep striking until broken. I don't mind admitting that I've been staying away from railings and steep staircases. If I didn't have a tavern to run, I'd be holed up in my suite for the foreseeable future."

"It's as if the curse struck them down in the place where they most belonged." Sue, who had walked into the room with a subdued expression, delivers the words with a heavy sigh. "The Duchess, gazing down at the town from her balcony. Rick, on the stage he loved."

"Well, that's a bit fanciful, Sue." Samm gives a sniff of derision. "I think McKinsey's right: the curse isn't real."

Jada is asked her opinion. She takes a moment. So far things have worked out beyond her wildest dreams. With Rick out of the picture, she'll have to find someone else to serve as her pawn, but that can be left for another day. "I agree with Chase. I'm not sure *anyone* in this room is safe." She says it with a tremor of apprehension to better sell it. A scared Bonnie will not last long as the number one.

Ben runs a thumb across his upper lip as if disappointed not to find an ally. Chase manages to be triumphant. "There, you see? Jada gets it."

"I see we have some varying opinions," Franz breaks in. "How about a vote? Who here believes the curse is real?" He raises a hand. "I vote yes."

The vote is six to three: *Real*—Bonnie, Chase, Franz, Sue, Poulsbo, Jada; *Not real*—McKinsey, Ben, Samm. Chase sums it up. "I'm going to guess that Rick, if he were here"—Chase nods toward the empty chair—"would agree there's a curse, so it's really seven to three."

Ben thumps the table in anger. "The vote was pointless. Besides, what are we supposed to do about it—this alleged curse?"

Someone clears their throat. It's Bonnie again. "I may have the answer. Gemma Bligh warned us not to forget about being kind, but we did. We lived our lives here and Outsiders lived out theirs in the cold. We haven't been very good even to Blank Jack, who made his home with us. I gave him a job because the tavern needed a caretaker, not out of goodwill. Has anyone in this room exchanged a few words or a thought with him?"

Poulsbo pipes up. "He's been helping...with the bird huts. We're building one...for the east gate...and one for the west."

"Bird huts. Anyone else?"

A crack appears in Ben's disbelief. "It's true, I suppose, that we can be accused of being self-centered. We've made what was meant to be a casual ranking of a person's social performance into a rigid one with perks and financial incentives, with the top spot a life extender, the bottom one a life shortener if you don't make it to a greenhouse, and everyone frantic to move up. There's little room for anyone outside the system."

This clear-eyed assessment makes Chase scoff. "Boo-hoo. Money and perks must be allocated somehow. Blank Jack has a job, a room, and cafeteria mix three times a day. Why should someone who just waltzed in hope for anything beyond that?"

"We can break the curse." Bonnie draws her palms together as if pleading. "Let's do right by the Outsider in our midst. I gave Blank Jack an amber gem when I first hired him—I'm going to change that to a ruby. I'd consider it a personal favor if we all gave him rubies—and encourage the town to do the same."

Ben holds up a hand. "It's against the Code to give gems as a favor."

This time the fear is unmistakable. "The Code? I'm worried about my *life*. Besides, the idea—goodwill toward Blank Jack—wasn't mine. I caught the thought on the Commons last night. Someone from the bottom thousand floated it—Scott, the intern that used to work for you, McKinsey."

Bonnie must be desperate indeed if she's scouring the Commons bin for scraps.

"We can give her the credit," Bonnie goes on. "She also brought up the new Outsider and I agree—let's shower both Blank Jack and Renee with rubies."

"I suppose a goodwill campaign doesn't hurt." McKinsey sounds as if she, like Ben, might be wavering on the *not real* position. It strikes Jada, not for the first time, that people are prone to being followers, given any kind of lead. And also that the suggested solution—the shower of rubies, superficial and easy—hardly counts as a genuine gesture.

Chase rubs his hands together. "I'm in. Kindness costs nothing and it'll make us seem magnanimous...and who knows, it may even help, though I'm not holding my breath."

Two against, seven for—McKinsey having switched sides—yields a Goodwill Campaign and an amendment to section C, the everyday behavior part of the Code: *Be kind to everyone. That includes Outsiders.*

Ben's brow is still furrowed. "The campaign may have

been someone else's idea, but it still strikes me as self-serving for Bonnie."

"Can't have it both ways, Ben," McKinsey points out. "Either the curse isn't real and none of this matters or it is and we're helping to stop it for all our sakes."

Bonnie's contribution is a grumpy, "Easy for *you* to put the Code first, Ben. You're not the next likely target."

"Let's not go back to this," Franz tries to intervene.

"Yes, Ben, eight is a long way down." Chase seems to have forgotten his argument that no one in the room is safe. "If Gemma's curse knocks out those of us above you like dominoes, you won't mind at all, will you?"

Ben slides a thumb across his upper lip again. "Just what do you mean by that?"

Chase drapes one arm over the leather of his armchair, a leisurely gesture. "That it's no wonder you voted against the Goodwill Campaign."

"I thought you said you doubted it'd help."

"I've changed my mind. So, are you rooting for the curse?"

Franz steeples his fingers. "Why don't we move on and hear more from Poulsbo about how the bird huts are coming—"

Not even his favorite subject can calm Ben down. He's half out of his chair. "You better watch what you say, Chase, or you might regret it."

"What are you gonna do about it, you needle-threading narcissist? Here, my left sleeve has lost a stitch. How about you show us some of your skill?"

Ben lunges and his fist connects across the table. "You shiny-headed *buffoon*..."

Franz, with the help of Poulsbo, pulls the pair apart.

"Tenners, *please*! Remember the Code, section C—*Avoid public displays of anger.*"

Jada passes Chase a handkerchief for the blood seeping out of his nose and McKinsey leaves to fetch ice for Ben's bruised knuckles. At the other end of the table, Samm clasps his hands behind his head. "Is this what Tenner meetings are like? 'Cause..."

"We've never paid real attention before," Sue, who seems to have shaken her mood off, takes over. "We had no idea..."

"That they were *this* entertaining."

Chapter Eighteen

Armed with a stack of wicker baskets, Lu, Dax, and I are on our way to Wayne's living space as the streetlamps turn on for the night. He can no longer afford his rent. We're helping him pack and move into my building, where my own rent is as cheap as can be. If I continue in the bog for a while, I might find myself sleeping on a mat in hallways like Oliver did, though I'm not too proud to accept a spot on Lu's couch.

She contributed an onyx to Wayne's halo to honor his wishes. As we near Housing Ten, she responds to our query if she's all right. "Wayne has to follow where his soul leads—we all do, don't we? And imagine what he'll get to see—the mountains, moose and caribou, dinner cooked over a fire, natural childbirth..." At my reaction, she adds, "I know, that's a weird one—and very brave... Look, Wayne has my heart and that's all I can do."

Studying the determined angle of Lu's chin as we climb the stairs, the elevator being permanently out of commission, it strikes me that maybe love means you put the other person first, whatever the cost... Or everyone's right and romantic partners come and go and that's all there is to it.

Wayne greets us at the door of his fifth-floor suite and immediately insults my ill-fitting clothes. "Scottie, if those sleeves were any longer, they'd be the floor."

I make a face at him. "Nice try, but I'm not giving you an onyx."

"Even though it might be just what I need to vault over you to last place? Make an effort to change your mind, will you?" He adds a softer, "Hi, Lu."

"Hi, Wayne."

A smile passes between them.

Dax sets down his basket. "You do have an impressively dim halo, Wayne."

"I've been trying my hardest but Scottie's onyx from Rick is hard to beat. You could help, Daxton, and change that ruby you gave me to an onyx. I can insult you beforehand, if it helps. But first, congrats on making it into the Top Hundred."

A win in the semifinals has boosted the more athletic of my PALs to ninety-eight, which Dax handled by continuing his life exactly as it was before. Dax says obligingly, "Please go ahead with the insult."

"Dax, my friend, you reek worse than moldy cafeteria mix snubbed by waste bin sparrows."

"Sorry about that, I just got back from tennis practice. Didn't get a chance to shower." Dax pauses, then surprises the rest of us by saying, "I think I *will* give you that onyx."

Despite not wanting my former mentor to have to face the unknown of the Outside, I'm pleased that Dax found it in himself to help Wayne achieve his goal. As we set about gathering his possessions, Wayne tells us about his busy day, how the Tenner meeting was moved up and he had to quickly organize the catering. "It was a wasted effort," he says, rolling up a towel and reaching for another. "In the end they left most of the food untouched, as if it'd gone bad or something. I suppose I can't blame them. They must all feel as if they're in the crosshairs of the curse—Bonnie most of all."

The topic has drawn Lu out of her thoughts. "Blank Jack came in to escape the memories and get a fresh start, and none of us cared, did we? I'm going to give him a ruby. And Renee too, though I don't know much about her yet." She smiles at me. "I saw that the Tenners gave you credit for the idea, Scottie. Hopefully it'll garner *you* some goodwill."

"I figured Blank Jack and Renee could use a few friends," I say. "And if it helps stop what's been happening—the curse —all the better."

"I think it just might," Lu says, "if we all try hard enough."

Dax slides an empty basket across the floor in Wayne's direction. "Gemma Bligh took a stab as to when things would start going downhill, eighty-some years into the life of the Dome. Turns out, it wasn't a bad guess! Sure, two number ones in a row is quite a coincidence, but between a long-ago curse striking the number ones or simple coincidence... Well, the simple answer is usually the right one." He adds a practical argument. "Besides, if Gemma Bligh lost her voice by the time she got here from Seattle on the snowmobile, how did she manage to curse the town?"

"Maybe she wrote it down," Lu suggests mildly.

"The historical record says nothing about her losing her voice," I say, skipping over the part where it also said nothing about a curse. I'm stacking Wayne's newly-purchased provisions into a basket. He's bought several pairs of warm mittens, a stack of woolen socks, a couple of pairs of welders' goggles to help protect his eyes from the cold, and some chicken jerky and dried plums. I picture his skin rough and cracked like Blank Jack's, the chicken jerky his sustenance, melted snow quenching his thirst. Then I try to picture *myself* doing all those things—I have yet to make any sort of preparations.

"Wayne, where do you want these shorts?"

I've encountered an indoors-only item.

"Leave them, I'm donating them to the warehouse. Won't be playing basketball Outside. Now, Scottie, about that onyx. Have I ever mentioned that you used to hum at your desk and it drove me crazy?"

The trickle of water on the floor snaps Dax's attention back to his surroundings. He's overwatered the strawberry seedlings. When they're taller and sturdier—if they make it that far, given his carelessness—they'll be moved to a rooftop garden. Seeds become stalks, grow, yield fruit and more seeds; one thing follows another, logical and orderly, unlike the curse-fever gripping the town, which is showing no signs of abating. He's surprised at the interest Scottie has taken in it. Moving Wayne to his new room last night was a bit awkward all around; Dax left right after because of his strict sleeping schedule until the big match next week, or he would have asked her about it.

That's not why he's having trouble focusing... Seeing her last night, her mood split between a knot of worry on her forehead for Wayne and Lu and the usual smile to greet him, made his heart jump. He could pretend that isn't the case but he'd be lying.

It was the moment he knew.

He heads to the sink for a mop. He always figured that if he did end up one day violating the Code, it'd be in a big way and for a very good reason. The problem is, whether Scottie has any feelings for him is damned near impossible to tell. She's a hard one to read. The thing to do might be to come straight out and ask... But is it right to even consider the idea, with her rank in the bog? Anything of that sort would run the risk of saddling them with a section Q violation and shaming onyxes. His halo could handle the hit, but it would be the end for her.

Though there's no one there to see but potted plants and an ant tank in one corner, he shakes his head. It would be dishonorable, unfair, impossible... He instructs his CC, *New corkboard, tack onto it one word, large as you can:* **NO.**

"Hey."

He turns. Scottie is at the door to the lab, as if drawn there by his thoughts. "How did you get in?" he stammers out.

"I told the front desk that I've an urgent matter to relay and you had your in-thoughts muted. They made me take off my shoes." Her sandals are in her hand and she's donned the reusable plastic slippers the lab issues to visitors.

"But I don't have my in-thoughts muted," he says stupidly.

"I know. I wanted to talk to you in person." She adds, "Nice mop."

He sets aside the mop and towels off his hands, wondering if there are further developments on the Wayne and Lu front. His own feet shod in the usual garden clogs, he leads her through the back door into the uncovered part of the facility, a fenced-off segment of the Edge Garden with a narrow path meandering through it.

Scottie looks around at the medley of plants. "What do you grow here?"

"Seedlings destined for replanting around town or in

greenhouses. Scottie, I'm always happy to see you, but did you have a reason for dropping by in the middle of the morning?"

"I wanted to talk to you last night but you left early. And I happened to be passing by on my way to vacuum Work Three."

"Talk to me about what?" he asks, curbing his hopes and failing.

Scottie stops and turns to face him, crossing her arms as if to steel herself. What she says is not at all what he expects.

Chapter Nineteen

"Bodi thinks I did it."

It takes Dax a moment to spin back his mind from where it's gone on its own to this. "Did what? And who's Bodi?"

"He's the head of security. He thinks I killed Delilah and tried to kill Rick."

"Killed...?" He stares at her. "I think you'd better start over."

"Let's see, where to begin?" Scottie says as they take the garden path. "Cece and I have been investigating Delilah and Rick's accidents."

"CC and you? CC is just a virtual assistant."

"You know what I mean. She's been the Watson to my Sherlock. Don't you remember that skit we did in sixth grade?"

He follows her down the hazy lane of memory. "I do. You were Sherlock and pretend-smoked a pipe while demolishing alibis. I was Watson and contributed rudimentary observations, and Lu was a passerby in the fog who stumbled across a body. I can't remember, was Oliver in the skit?"

"He was the fog... Maybe that's the place to begin, way in

the past. After Oliver turned his back on me—on us—I needed something no one could take away."

"Is that why you wanted to learn your parents' names? You never said."

"I couldn't. You were always going on about how important the Code is, section A to section Z and everything in-between. You said the taboo against knowing your kin is a practical one—that doing otherwise weakens PAL ties and rekindles ancient drives."

"God, I must have been insufferable." They pass through a vegetable patch and he adds, "I do admit to a bit of curiosity myself. The Founder who was the original Daxton —that was his middle name—came from a small town near Seattle called Edmonds. He worked in an antique shop alongside his father and got in via the lottery. Inside the Dome he became a public notary and carved cups and spoons from blocks of wood as a hobby—some are still in use. But as to my genetic background... It's been eight and a half decades since the skin-sample bank made its way over from Old Seattle. The donors of the samples that led to my conception—well, they never knew about me and were likely strangers to each other. I suppose it's possible I have relatives Outside, but they'd be no closer than in here— third cousins and such."

Scottie, having listened patiently, comes back with: "I still want to know... Just think, if you'd gotten a job in the Birth Lab instead of the garden one, you could have looked into the records."

"People biology is not the same as plant biology."

"I should hope not."

They enter a shrubbery area and Scottie gives an account of what's been going on. "Bodi said it all smells of me taking revenge, first on Delilah for saying no and then on Rick for the onyx that sent me into the bog. I've been battling to clear my name. I knew *I* wasn't responsible for Delilah's death, so it had to be someone else. I was so sure Rick did the pushing, with Jada as the mastermind behind it —that it was her idea to grab the opportunity presented by the coming due of Gemma's curse. Now, I don't know."

She goes on to explain that all the Tenners, plus Ben, were in Delilah's suite that night. "Cocktails and cards, ten guests. Maybe she invited one of them to spend the night and that person struck. A neighbor—Lucille—said she had no interest in dating anymore, but who knows?"

"Tacoma said the same thing."

"Or one of the guests claimed to be too drunk to walk home and slept on a sofa. Or pretended to leave at the end of the evening but hid—it's a six room suite! Or doubled back to knock on the door with an excuse about forgetting something or other. Delilah had changed into her sleepwear. Whoever it was must have lured her out onto the balcony on a pretext, flashlight and all. A staged suicide. But the railing went and the blame landed on me."

He glances over at this. "Delilah, a suicide? I didn't think it likely when Lu suggested it and I still don't. Would people have believed it of her, even with a curse looming over the town shoulder?"

"Maybe the story the killer planned on spreading around was that it all became too much. The governing duties, the parties, the plays, everyone clamoring for her attention... Or that the guilt of being a fraud was weighing on her conscience."

He pulls her to a stop. "Hold on. A fraud?"

"I overheard something at a Tenner meeting."

"How did you happen to do that?"

Scottie squats down to examine an aloe plant. "I eavesdropped. Mostly the Tenners sounded annoyed that Ben was about to get in. The interesting part happened after everyone but Rick and Jada left." She tells him about Delilah collecting secrets, using them as leverage. How Jada has them now. How Jada got Rick to lean on Bonnie and take her spot. Having managed to unintentionally break one of the plant's leaves, Scottie starts walking again. "You know what's really odd? In a perverse way, knowing those unsavory things about Delilah makes me even more determined to find her killer. Maybe she didn't belong on the pedestal I put her on, but whether she was a good person or bad, she deserves justice."

"Yes, I think that's true."

"Plus, on a small personal note, Delilah said that she saw something in me. That I have a fine voice."

"You do have a fine voice. I'm glad you came over to talk about this in person."

"I thought it'd be easier to convince you this way. You believe me, don't you, Dax?"

"I'm trying. Go on."

"There's also something Oliver said. I ran into him as security led him away to the greenhouse train."

This makes him glance over again. "You didn't mention that you saw him before he left."

"He looked scruffy—wasn't making much sense. The birds were upsetting him—and he was fixated on Delilah's spot. Later I wondered if he saw or overheard something he wasn't supposed to." They've reached the point in the path where it makes a sharp turn, brushing against the Dome glass; the green of the garden is a contrast to the white on the other side. The temperature here is lower and Scottie gives a shiver. "Whoever it was, with Rick's accident, things are back on track and the curse is front and center."

"Are you saying there might be more to come?"

"Not if I can help it."

"I get it—that's why you did that goodwill thing."

"The killer is hiding behind the curse, so I figured the thing to do is to pull that curtain down. And what better way than a nod to Gemma Bligh—the kindness she asked for. The killer—if they're not done yet—will blast the Goodwill Campaign and argue that *nothing* can stop the curse—and reveal themselves."

They've come to a narrow channel fed by snowmelt from a shunt in the Dome glass. Scottie skips across the row of stones that bridge the channel, the steam wafting up giving a dream-like aura to her passage. "If I find who did it," she calls over from the other side, "Sherlock Scottie will become a real brand and maybe Bodi will hire me to work at the Security Office investigating things."

He follows her across. His own emotions are tempered by the familiar, precise measurements he's been doing all morning, by the neat rows of plants. "If you are going to keep poking around, just don't do anything stupid, Scottie."

"More stupid than managing to slip down into the bog? Than being unable to prevent a second attack?"

"Like getting yourself killed."

"Why, would you miss me?"

Her tone is frivolous, and therefore his answer is too. "Lu and I would have to get a new PAL and I'd have to learn their name and everything."

"You're too old to get a new PAL. You could help me, you know, with the Sherlocking." The words drive a thrill through him, make him feel wanted, but she follows them up with, "I can't ask Lu. She has too much going on with Wayne."

"Why do you need me along? I'm kind of busy here in the lab."

Scottie is all business. "It makes it less obvious. Two blend in more easily than one."

"Is that what we're going to do—blend in?"

"We need to get close to the Tenners, see which one's pretending to believe in the curse. So what do you say?"

What can he say? "Sherlock Scottie, huh? All right, count me in."

Back in the lab, she stops by one of the glass tanks. "That's a lot of ants."

"It's a formicarium. Black garden ants." Dax goes over and gently taps the tank. "It's a harmonious world—they build and clean tunnels, forage for food, nurse the queen and her brood... Interestingly, the queen's not in charge. The colony itself is, like a whole that exceeds the sum of its parts."

Scottie's face is pressed to the tank, her fingers leaving prints on the glass. He'll have to clean it later. "So they're like a large family?"

"I suppose so, yes."

After the lab door closes behind her, Dax considers matters. A soil scientist has a simple goal: to help living things thrive, grow, reach their prime, and be cut down only out of necessity or old age. There's an ordering to these things. He's angry that someone may have made Delilah part of the town soil before her time and wanted the same for Rick.

That they made Scottie a suspect, intentionally or not.

He reaches for the mop again. Yes, he'll help look for the killer. For justice, and to help boost Scottie up. And if it works and her rank recovers? He'll have to make the decision whether to let go of the Code and risk alienating a PAL by declaring what's on his mind.

Chapter Twenty

The Dragon and the Drumstick

"Hello, Scott," Bonnie greets me. "You enjoyed a mug of stew last time, am I right?" The overhead lights play softly on the counter, where she's wiping a glass. Her eyes are hollow and gray, as if she's not sleeping well, the greeting a pretense at her customary cheeriness. No wonder. The gems in her halo now lean toward ominous: *"Bonnie, good cider but watch out for the CURSE! ... The number one pedestal is well deserved, hope the CURSE doesn't knock you off it ..."* On the chalkboard behind the counter, the menu has been replaced with a large, crudely-lettered appeal: GOODWILL CAMPAIGN.

"The stew's on me," Dax says. "I'm Daxton."

"And for you, Daxton, what'll it be?"

Dax goes with lemonade again. He and I pick a table and Bonnie brings a steaming mug and a tall glass. "Let me know if you need anything else, I'll be downstairs doing inventory. Oh, and don't forget to give Blank Jack and Renee rubies— Well, I don't need to tell you, it was your idea in the first place, Scott." She gives my shoulder a squeeze, as if I'm her savior, and disappears behind a door, the one with the fermenting aroma emanating from under it. A place to hide.

It's Dax's first time in the tavern and he's studying the sketch of the dragon as if about to tell me there's no such thing. I feel optimistic with him by my side, certain that together we'll get to the bottom of things in no time at all. Blank Jack, sweeping under a table, sends a wave in my direction and I wave back. Relieved, I say to Dax, "I was worried Blank Jack might think I was using him with the whole Goodwill Campaign thing. I suppose I am, really, but it's for a good cause." A customer thumps the caretaker on the back, exchanging a few words with him, and I add, "Maybe I should have suggested a better job for Blank Jack, not just gems. He used to be a logger Outside... Do you ever wonder what it'd be like?"

Dax is staring at his drink, where a lemon pit is sinking down, a slow movement. "Which *it*, Scottie? Lots of possibilities...some more fun than others."

"Uh..." Did Dax just make a double entendre at me? I must be imagining things. His expression above the glass is the usual inscrutable one. "I meant being an Outsider. It must be a hard life. McKinsey went out once. The east gate. She said she followed the train tracks and the snowsuit kept her safe but at some point her CC stopped working and she felt unmoored and couldn't wait to get back in. It made me wonder why it's considered a perk at all."

Dax takes a slurp. "To limit the number of people going in and out. Opening the gates lets in the cold and messes with the air circulation system." He watches me blow on the stew to cool it. "Did you know that New Seattle has no furnaces? Our body heat keeps the Dome at a relatively constant temperature."

"I didn't know we were so...hot." My turn for a double entendre.

Dax gives a little twitch, as if he's been bitten by one of his ants. "It's the body heat from...ah...all ten thousand of us, plus the sunshine and the heat from machinery, laundry, and other facilities. As to your other point, I'd leave Blank Jack alone. Caretaking may not be a glamorous job but it's necessary, like your vacuuming."

I make a face. "Don't talk to me about vacuuming—this morning after I came to see you at the Garden Center, I got a flat tire and had to leave my bike in an alley and lug the vacuum the rest of the way to Work Three... Well? Do you think Bonnie..." The stew having cooled somewhat, I swallow a spoonful and cough at a piece of carrot stuck in my throat, then finish the question silently: "...*is the killer? Or the next victim?*"

"*Scottie, we've been here a mere fifteen minutes.*"

In those fifteen minutes, there's been an influx of customers—workplaces are emptying for the day, but more than that is drawing people in. It's Bonnie herself. She comes back upstairs to tend the bar alongside another employee and I watch her do her stuff, greet each patron by name, exchange pleasantries, and serve drinks, all of it done as if her shoulders are internally pulled in, and with the new addition, urging for rubies for Blank Jack and Renee.

I shake my head. "I don't think it's her, despite the fact that all that's happened landed her at number one."

"You said the killer will claim to be worried about the curse—and she is. Other than her public persona, we don't know much about her, do we?" Dax says. "Such as what her secret is—the one Delilah knew and that Rick and Jada leveraged successfully, if briefly."

I lean toward him across the table to whisper, "She remembered my stew."

"She's got a reputation for having a great memory, what about it?"

"No, that's the secret—a detailed corkboard and lots of practice at keeping eye contact. It's a trick, a mental sleight-of-hand. No, don't stare." Dax has turned in his chair to watch Bonnie greet the next customer. I shrug. "Like Jada said, nothing big, just a way to make customers feel more welcome. Not worth killing to protect."

Dax turns back. "But if Bonnie's whole brand rests on it?"

"She seems genuinely frightened of the curse," I point out.

"You *just* said she's good at acting, with the whole fake-greeting thing. For all we know, she's scared not of being the next victim but of getting caught."

I linger over a spoonful. "You know, when Cece was my Watson, she was much less argumentative. Look, the attacks just don't seem her style—had Bonnie done it, it'd have been a more *personal* approach. Face-to-face, not shoving from behind and faulty chandeliers. She'd have strangled Delilah and Rick... Something like that, anyway." I noticed her nails, bitten to the quick, same as before, as she set the drinks down, the hands dry and cracked from hard work. I feel protective of Bonnie despite the white lie of the good memory, maybe because she's always been friendly toward me. "Besides, I just don't get the vibe from her that I got from Rick—a vibe of pure hate directed toward Delilah."

"But Rick didn't turn out to be Delilah's killer."

"No, but he easily might have been, if you see what I mean. Wait...what if Rick killed Delilah and then someone *else* tried to kill him?"

Dax shakes his head. "I think it's best to assume there's only one criminal—like I said, the simple answer is usually the right one. And at the moment it's Bonnie. True, it wouldn't have been easy for her to get to the theater chandelier—people know her face—but the same goes for any of the Tenners."

"I've been thinking about that. It would have taken boldness and a bit of luck for one of them to climb to the heavens unnoticed."

"The heavens?"

"The out-of-sight area above the stage." I finish off the stew, wiping the mug clean with the last of the bread. "There's a security guard now—too many people were coming by to gawk. When I stopped by yesterday to nose around, he wouldn't let me in. I can try again when I reach the theater in my vacuuming rotation again, which will be, let's see...Monday. By which time I'll be packing, unless Wayne insists on jumping over me."

"Tacoma's working there. I'll talk to him, see if he noticed anything out of the ordinary."

After we leave the tavern behind, I summarize. "For now I'll put Bonnie down as a maybe."

"Where?"

"Cece and I have a corkboard. The suspect list started out short, with just Rick. Vicky for a brief moment... Then things mushroomed... How about this for Bonnie: *Greeting cheater. Dax thinks she's the killer, but Scottie doesn't.*" I repeat that internally for Cece.

"I don't know that I'd go that far," Dax protests. "More that we can't rule her out. But since you didn't get a vibe from Bonnie, we'll have to see if you get one from the other Tenners."

"Yes... Wait, are you making fun of me?"

Dax's response is speedy. "On the contrary. I'd argue that what you're calling a vibe is based on subtle physical signs: a bead of sweat, a frown line, a tremor of the hands."

"I got a vibe from Rick through a closed door... Do you believe me, then, that there's a killer—one of the Tenners?"

"I believe you, Scottie."

"Why?"

"Because you believe it."

"I'll take it. All right, I'll be on the lookout for vibes and you keep reminding me that the answer's got to be simple."

Fill-n-Sip Cup

It's a day later, same time—just after five. Dax has arrived a few minutes early, giving him time to get acquainted with the coffeehouse Chase is in charge of. Though the Dragon and the Drumstick and the Fill-n-Sip Cup occupy similar footprints, there are definite differences. Bonnie's tavern is near the market, a quiet neighborhood except on trader day —Tuesday; Chase's coffeehouse is centrally located, in busy Founders Square. The appeal here is not quality but price. The décor leaves much to be desired—sunlight fights its way in through dusty windows, falling on ragged carpet and tables of stained plastic.

A table opens up and Dax grabs it. A harried waitress stops by and slaps an empty cup in front of him, charging him with a quick glance at his halo. "Two—I need two," he calls out after her and she returns with another cup and charges him for that one as well. When Scottie comes in, they take turns filling their cups with watery coffee from a row of identical dispensers. After he sits back down, Scottie glances around furtively. "I don't see Chase."

"He's here. I saw him go into the back."

"When we catch the guilty person, Hugh will have to — Do you know about Hugh? He's in charge of the List." Scottie rests her elbows on the table, the coffee cup between them. "If someone's found to be halo-padding, Hugh waits for the Code-infraction onyx to come in, knowing that it'll do the job of booting the person way down. But for murder... I sent a thought to Bodi to ask about it. He wasn't happy that I'm *still* harping on this but said it happened a few times, mostly before all the stuff we have now was in place: the people map, the Code of Conduct, mediators, help on the way with a silent call via your CC... For murder, he said, Hugh takes the person off the List at once and they go sledding."

"With no snowsuit, I hope. Freezing to death seems a suitable—"

"Shh, here he is."

The number two, unlike Bonnie, doesn't serve drinks. Chase is making the rounds, slapping customers on the back and urging them to "Have more coffee—refills free," his smile as plastic as the cups and furnishings in his establishment.

"I'll keep him talking," Scottie sends a thought, *"and you take a look at his halo."*

"What for?"

"McKinsey used to tell me that the best way to learn about a person is to peruse their gems. But keep in mind that they aren't to be taken at face value either."

"That seems contradictory."

"People are contradictory."

"But how then am I supposed to make any kind of judgment about—"

A figure blocks the sunlight filtering through the nearest window. "Coffee all right?"

Scottie flashes a smile. "Hits the spot. Do you have a minute? I don't know if you remember me. I used to deliver invites for the Social Agency. I'm in the bog and am hoping to pull myself out by...uh...doing some research. Yes. I'm researching what it is that brings some people success and not others."

"And so you came here. Who better to ask, right?" Chase's expression is one of vague half-interest; he doesn't seem to connect Scottie either to the Incompetent Intern brand or the kindness idea.

"Right. Well, then, um... To what do you attribute your stellar rank?"

A shrug. "No secret there. I keep my prices low, which in turn helps my customers keep their bank balances healthy" —a grin—"and so they like me."

"You attribute it to low prices rather than personality, charisma, and charm?"

Chase's eyebrows register amusement. "Well, you'll have to tell me. How do I rate on personality, charisma...and what was the third one, charm?"

Scottie flashes another smile. A kick under the table reminds Dax that he's supposed to be focused on the ruby-red ring topping Chase's bald pate. Chase, he learns, is forty-five and has been a Tenner for twelve years. The rubies alternate between praise for the Fill-n-Sip Cup (*"Chase keeps the coffee coming and the prices low"*) and recognition of its manager for a favor done (*"Needed a chocolate cake for a surprise party and Chase came through!"*). Chase's specialty is skirting the Code. Taking advantage of the curse myth and the timing—and Bonnie would have to be next for Chase to scramble up to Eternal Life—is in a different category. Chase, it strikes Dax, is more of a small time crook.

"Do you think you'll overtake Bonnie anytime soon?" Scottie asks, and the response pulls Dax's attention away from Chase's halo.

"Maybe I don't *want* to be number one, what with Gemma Bligh's curse and all."

At this, Scottie puts on a show of nonchalance. "Ah, so you believe New Seattle *is* cursed."

"Not really, but don't tell Bonnie. She's all wound up." Chase leans in, one arm on the back of Scottie's chair and one on the back of Dax's, an overly friendly gesture. "And since I don't think the curse is real, I have no problem with taking the top spot! You two could help, you know—give me a couple of rubies and we'll see if it does the trick." He winks at them and moves on to the next table, where a quintet is celebrating their PAL anniversary. "How's the coffee, everyone?"

"He did it."

"What makes you say that, Scottie? He isn't putting on a show of being scared of the curse, or bothering to cast doubt on the Goodwill Campaign. And he freely admitted to wanting to be number one—would the killer do that?"

"Still. I took a snapshot of that smug expression of his. Since I guessed Bonnie's secret pretty quick, I thought we'd be able to do the same here but Chase is so outright shady that I'd believe all sorts of things about him."

Dax sloshes the remnants of the thin black liquid around his cup. *"Such as that he reuses coffee grounds?"*

"That and murder."

He and Scottie spend the next hour taking advantage of the free refills and watching Chase interact with his patrons.

What he's doing—asking for rubies in a joking fashion—isn't exactly against the Code, but it is borderline and crass. On the way out, Scottie says, "I've put this on the corkboard: *Terrible coffee. Could very well be the killer.*"

10:15 p.m.

Dax grumbled about the sleeping schedule he's supposed to be adhering to but agreed that late evening is the best time to tackle Samm and Sue, who are night owls rarely spotted during the day, not to mention that all the coffee we imbibed at Fill-n-Sip Cup has rendered us very awake despite its watery consistency. The map points us to Founders Square and the platform that stands in its center.

Dax and I are here to judge whether the Jokers, separately or together, might have murdered one person and tried to kill another, but it's hard to even consider the possibility in the setting. Given the date—April 1—the crowd is expecting something special and hard cider and frivolity are abundant on stage and off. Tonight's entertainment is a practical joke played on the pair's favorite victim. Having apparently shown up expecting a formal debate moderated by Franz, Ben the Birdman is stiffly standing mid-stage while Samm and Sue bombard him with barbs to hoots of laughter from the tipsy crowd. There are no references to Gemma Bligh—not this time. Franz, clearly in on the April Fools' prank, heartily claps the tailor on the shoulder. We push in close enough to bring up the Jokers' halos, a row or two back from the stage, but I still have to bob my head to see. The duo's gems are mostly from adoring fans and come in matching pairs, explaining why their names keep toggling on the List.

Ben leaves as soon as he can do so without seeming like a spoilsport, and Dax and I don't stick around for much longer, either. As we leave the noise of the square behind us, Dax half-jokes, "A working hypothesis might be that funny people are less likely to commit murder."

"You think Samm and Sue are funny?"

"You don't?"

"I felt bad for Ben. I suppose if the Jokers did decide to stage an accident, it'd involve a banana peel, not wood rot and faulty chandeliers."

This makes Dax chuckle. "I just can't see them caring about moving up a couple of spots, even if it brings them closer to Eternal Life. They seem to be enjoying life to the fullest as is."

"Except we're forgetting one thing," I say. "The secrets in Jada's possession. I don't know about Samm's, but Sue seemed weirdly chummy with Rick at Delilah's seeding. I wondered if they're having an affair behind Samm's back... Did Sue seem subdued to you?"

"Because Rick's in a coma? She was certainly downing hard cider pretty solidly."

"Maybe the Jokers' secret is a joint one, like everything else they do. They're pretending to be a happy couple but privately despise each other. I'll put them down as *Funny? Opinion on that is divided... Killers, separately or together? Unknown.*"

We've climbed a four-level stairway to cross over a maintenance building, an often-used shortcut, after which the paths to our respective housing buildings split up. We stop at the top to take in the view. Lamps in windows are starting to switch off for the night and a slender crescent moon, bisected by a Dome structural beam, hangs low above the mountains. Hearing footfalls, I peer down. On the lamp-lit promenade below us, Lu and Wayne are nearing, arms intertwined.

Dax peers down as well. "Should we call down a hello?"

"Shh, no. Let them be." I tug on his elbow as if I'm worried Gemma Bligh's curse might strike him next. "Their time is short, if Wayne continues his pursuit of onyxes."

We watch Wayne pull Lu into an embrace in the building's shadows. How complicated emotions are, it strikes me as Dax and I leave the couple to their privacy. I'm somehow managing to feel sorry for Lu and at the same time—this one is harder to admit—envious. Trapped somewhere between the pity and the envy is a sentiment impossible for me to act upon. I picture what would happen if I spun to a stop and kissed Dax full on the mouth: his revulsion at me for breaking the Code, my total embarrassment when he tells me he doesn't share my feelings...and another PAL-ship ruined beyond repair.

Chapter Twenty-One

We've found Poulsbo near the west gate. He's hammering planks into a square base as morning breaks over the town. The handyman starts at our arrival and sets the hammer down to wipe his hands on his overalls; he's covered in sawdust and dirt. "Do you need something...fixed in your living space?" he says, his left eye twitching. "I could get to it...later."

I take a snapshot of the eye twitch.

Dax puts him at ease. "I'm from the Gardens Center. Heard you did some fixing up of the flower beds on the Housing Four roof—wanted to thank you in person, that's all."

"The flower-bed wall was crumbling a bit... A minor issue. I like...flowers. Have some in my own room." Poulsbo nods politely at me and asks, "What do you do...in the Gardens Center, Daxton?"

"Call me Dax."

While Poulsbo, his eye-twitch diminishing, exchanges tips with Dax on watering schedules and such, I take a look at his halo to find out more about his character beyond the facial tic. He's only thirty-eight, a surprise given the stooped shoulders and the strands of gray. The gems reveal how much his labor is valued, but his inability to say no strikes me as a burden. He seems crushed by his popularity, not elevated by it.

It's Saturday, my day off, and my plan is to be all business. No more inappropriate thoughts. Not helping is that Dax's shirt today is on the tight side, nicely displaying his physique.

Poulsbo tells us about the hut he's constructing. "After the base's done... I'll build walls and a roof... Assemble it all on the other side of the gate... Openings will...allow the sparrows to fly in and out...at will. Blank Jack said...to raise the hut at least a yard off the ground. He's handling...the east-gate hut."

I don't seriously suspect the mild-mannered man working with hammer and nail of being the killer. For one, according to Jada and Rick, he has no secret Delilah held over his head. Surely I wasn't the only one who looked up to her. Perhaps—apart from the blackmailing and stuff—there was some goodness in her. I find myself saying, "Delilah... What was your opinion of her?"

Poulsbo's eyes well up. "Poor Delilah... She was generous to me, in her own way."

"And to me." It's the truth.

"When she needed me to help out once in a while... I was happy to do so."

My head snaps up from where I've been studying a pattern of nails in the wood in an effort to put Poulsbo at ease. "Things that needed fixing in her suite?" I ask.

I don't want to say the word *balcony*. His mild manner aside, Poulsbo could have put his handyman skills into action to help the wood rot along—so the railing went even if Delilah exercised caution in accordance with the Maintenance alert—though I can't think of a reason why he would do such a thing.

"Help for her proposals... A vote of support in the Tenner meeting room. Which I did, because...being number one...is not easy. She had to be tough to get there and...to stay there."

Dax, with a glance at me, asks, "Poulsbo, what's your opinion of the curse? Are you onboard with the Goodwill Campaign?"

"Don't know about the curse but I believe a little kindness goes...a long way." Poulsbo reaches for the hammer. "Better get back to work... Need to finish the base before my...regular work for the day starts."

We leave Poulsbo to his project. Once Dax and I put some distance between us and the garden, I say, "I feel bad we bothered him. On the other hand, did you see how twitchy and wound up he was? What if he said yes one time too many and that eye tic erupted into a lethal outburst?"

"And he messed with Delilah's balcony—and the chandelier—and now regrets it? I can't see it."

"Yeah, it does seem far-fetched. I'll put him down as *Not the killer, Dax and Scottie agree.*"

I stop what I've been doing, pacing in front of Work Five, as Dax rounds the corner at a trot. He comes to a stop, breathing hard. His shirt sleeves are rolled up and he's opened the top two buttons to cool off.

"You're late," I gripe at him. "I sent you a barrage of thoughts saying Franz can squeeze us in at half past four. It's his only opening three weeks out."

"I went to the theater," Dax explains between breaths. "Had my in-thoughts muted. Ran as fast as I could when I got your message."

He follows me into the building. I know my way around, having been here before to slide Agency invites under the door to Franz's office. Like Dax, I've shown up on foot—my bike is still out of commission.

"Uh...it'll be pricey," I remind him. "The session."

"I'll cover it."

"Quick, change the ruby you gave me to a jade," I prod him as we head up a flight of stairs.

His eyebrows rise at this. "What for?"

"So we can go in saying we're mad at each other."

"Wouldn't an onyx be more convincing?"

"We're PALs. No one would believe you'd give me an onyx, not with me in the bog. Best to stick to something realistic. And, uh, don't forget to change it back to a ruby later."

"But Scottie, what reason should I give for being mad at—"

"Hurry up, do it." I elbow him in the side. "We're here."

The door at the end of the hallway opens and Franz walks two people out. I can't tell if they're a couple or PALs or co-workers, but whatever the relationship, they seem to have gotten over their differences. "Thank you, Franz, for making us see that we were being petty," one of them says, dabbing at red-rimmed eyes with a handkerchief.

"My pleasure, Carlton. And if you and Sidney have any other problems, come and see me again. But I don't anticipate that you'll need to."

"You're a wizard, Franz. I think we'd each like to give you a ruby in thanks...that is, if Carl agrees?"

"I most certainly do, Sid."

"I'd appreciate the rubies, but how about we wait until

Gemma Bligh's curse breaks?" Franz gives an uncomfortable laugh and, after the pair leave, turns to Dax and me. "Why hello. You must be Scott and Daxton. Come in, please."

Inside his office, side tables sit in all four corners, sporting decorative vases with dried flowers. A comfy-looking two-seater faces a leather armchair, both well-worn. Franz takes the armchair and waves at us to sit. "I can only spare a half hour, so let's get to work. Now, what seems to be the problem?"

Having taken one end of the two-seater and Dax the other, I say, "Just the matter of a gem. Dax's gem for me."

"It's a jade," Dax says woodenly.

"It's never merely about gem color. Let's start by having you two sit a little closer, please."

I inch toward the middle of the two-seater, but not too much, as I'm supposed to be mad at Dax. He does the same.

"Let's start with you, Scott. Why don't you tell me a bit about this gem from Daxton."

"Dax and I... Well, I've known him forever. But he gave me the jade and won't budge from it, even though I'm in the bog."

"I see."

"Worse yet, I just gave him a *ruby*." I manage to say this with what I feel is a convincing whine about the way matters stand.

"I see," Franz repeats and forms his fingers into a roof-like shape. "Daxton, I notice you haven't said anything yet. Obviously everyone has a right to give other people whatever type of gem they like."

"Yes, but it's not... I mean, that's not why it's jade, not exactly."

"Something else is holding you back."

"I... Yes," Dax trails off awkwardly. I dare not look at him and instead focus my gaze on Franz's halo, which is chock-full of clients praising his moderating skills. Franz gives me an encouraging smile, as if perusing his halo is exactly the right thing for me to be doing, so I can see how great he is at this. He is thirty-three and single, and has been a Tenner for five years and counting. Below the halo are wispy hair and wispy eyebrows—and the substantial goatee, thick and springy from above his lip down to his chin. Does he glue it on to have something to stroke while pondering clients' problems, a silly, minor secret, like Bonnie's? I take a snapshot.

"It's this curse matter," Dax spits out into the silence. "Scottie and I have opposing viewpoints."

"Right, yes," I jump in with what I'm guessing to be my assigned point of view, given the credit I got for the Good-will Campaign. "You see, I'm convinced—absolutely convinced—that Gemma Bligh *did* put a curse on New Seattle. We're doomed—all of us. Doomed. First the number ones fell and who knows what will happen next."

Dax rolls his eyes. "Nonsense. Look, if we didn't have a People List, everyone would be convinced that Gemma's curse targeted the *other* category both Delilah and Rick belonged to—actors. We shouldn't pretend to be who we aren't, say, even onstage—because Gemma believed in honesty or whatever—and the Be Yourself campaign would be in full swing instead of the goodwill one. We'd probably have already shut down the theater."

"The Tenners liked my idea, didn't they?" I say with as much indignation as I can muster. "About how to break the curse."

This makes Franz glance in my direction. "I should have recognized the name. That was, if I may say, an inspired insight, Scott, about kindness and goodwill." He strokes the goatee for a moment. "I hope we've seen the last of it, but truth be told, I'm worried for Bonnie—and," he repeats the uncomfortable laugh from the hallway, "for myself as well, though I'm quite a few rungs below."

"You're being illogical, both of you." Another eye roll from Dax. "It took me longer than it should have to get here because the foot traffic pattern has changed. People are avoiding walking under balconies and using steep stairs, all while being sure the curse will strike Bonnie next and only her! By their own reasoning, they should be perfectly safe, but reason has nothing to do with it."

Franz gently offers the following: "It could be that everyone's remembering all the times in their life they could have been kinder."

Dax, having fallen silent, seems to realize he needs to add more. "Look, the Code bestows a responsibility on us not to be cavalier with gems. As long as Scottie pushes this curse business, which has the town in a panic, the jade stays."

Keeping up my end of things, I swivel on the couch to face him. "Always the Code with you."

"The Code of Conduct is the bedrock of our society."

"Or the bedrock of your life?"

"Now just a minute..."

"I can see we're going to have to dig deeper," Franz interrupts our bickering. "Can you tell me why, if you've known each other all your lives and are PALs, you've only now gotten around to exchanging gems?"

After Franz walks us out and waves the next couple in, I wipe light sweat off my brow. "Phew, do you think he bought it?"

"He probably figures we're good for months of therapy."

Dax's tone is flippant but I'm hoping Franz didn't pick up

on the undercurrents that exist on my side. As we head out of the building, Dax gives his take. "As a mediator, his main tool is diplomacy, not devious plots. Plus he seems genuinely worried about the curse."

"I've never realized how hard it is to guess what's in people's heads... For now, I'll put him down as unlikely." We set a course away from Work Five and I ask Dax what he learned at the theater.

"Tacoma let me in—I caught him on his way out. He's being transferred back to Hobby Two. I poked around a bit. The stage has been cleaned up, other than nicks and scratches where the chandelier fell. They don't have a replacement, a stagehand told me, so they'll have to do without for future *Mrs. Montag* performances. I asked about access—in a roundabout fashion—and apparently every one of the Tenners was there at one time or another recently. Poulsbo to build a prop, Sue and Samm for a skit, and the others just to visit with Rick. I ran into Delilah's understudy on my way out." Dax recounts how he professed himself to be a fan and Vicky beamed and explained she was there to practice her lines so she'd be ready when performances resume after Rick comes back— or, if need be, when Rick's understudy steps in. Dax adds that he detected a note of desperation, the reason for which became clear when he took a look at her gems. "You should see them, Scottie. They are all variations of *Keep your chin up even though Rick's accident ruined your chance at fame.*"

If anyone thought Gemma Bligh's curse might target Vicky next, at least there'd be some interest in her; as is, having hit the Top Thousand, she's sinking fast and it's doubtful there's a rebound in her future. She's never shown any warmth toward me, but I still feel bad about the way it turned out for her. And it won't make any difference when Dax and I find the killer. Her chance will have gone.

"Dinner at the Oyster with a side of Jada-watching?" Dax suggests. "Don't say you'd rather wait until you can afford it. As you said yourself, it's all for a good—"

"Yes, let's go there," I interrupt. "I suppose we'd better take the time to change into something nicer. And Dax..."

"I know, don't forget to swap the jade back to a ruby. Doing it now."

Shrewd eyes watch as Dax and I walk in. When I used to deliver invites, a silent nod from Jada was the extent of our interaction, other than the day of the town anniversary when I was late and she complained to the Agency. Dax and I shuffle our feet at the door for a good seven, eight minutes before Jada saunters over. "You two want a table?"

The Oyster serves the Top Hundred and their guests; with Dax at ninety-eight, we're only just clearing the bar.

"Why, yes we do," I say, irked by the wait and the inhospitable phrasing. "We wanted to eat someplace special. We're on a date."

Dax's head snaps around at this.

"You've come to the right place for special." The words are inviting, the tone anything but. Jada leads us to a tiny table by the kitchen, clearly the worst spot in the eatery, and says flatly, "Take a look at the menu. I'll be back for your order."

No oysters are listed on the single-page menu Cece provides in my eye-field but there are half a dozen fancy-sounding entrees. Subtle, smoky aromas waft over from the kitchen and tickle the nose, a change from the cafeteria ones, which lean toward deep-fried and greasy. Fine cooking appears to be a hectic procedure, judging by a crash that rings out. Jada slams through the saloon-style doors and disappears within. Raised voices can be heard. She reemerges a few minutes later, her mouth a thin line, and sets a bread basket down with a *thwack*. "No butter today, sorry. One of my staff dropped the tray. What's it going to be?"

Hoping that Lu wasn't responsible for the butter mishap, Dax and I order the evening's special, Aquarium Trout Sautéed with Edge Garden Pears. After Jada moves on to greet an arriving party, I lean forward with my chin on my hands and gaze across the bread basket at Dax. I comment on the pretty tablecloth, with its heavy burgundy fabric and hand-stitched edges, and how nice it is to be enjoying dinner out. Dax pulls back his chair a little. "What are you doing, Scottie?"

"I'm looking at you all dreamy-eyed, like Lu does at Wayne. Have a roll and try to keep up your part of things." I take a roll myself and slide the bread basket toward him. "I wanted to give us a cover. This place is too fancy for a pair of PALs just out and about having dinner."

"But what about"—Dax lowers his voice—"section Q?"

"What about it?" I take a dainty bite of a roll, though I want to tear off pieces with my teeth, it's so soft and warm. "Jada isn't Bonnie—she's hardly going to take the time to peruse our halos and see that we're PALs. No one else in here gives two cents about us either. And if they do, I'll say it's all part of my fake research project, finding the elusive *it* of social success... Still, now that you mention it, I'd better alert Lu not to blow our cover."

Lu responds with cheery enthusiasm about my supposed research project—which makes me blush about lying—and reassurance that she wasn't the one who dropped the butter tray. Having promised to let her know how Dax and I like the food, I discretely twist in my chair to watch Jada, who's overseeing the work of a waiter swapping a soiled tablecloth for a fresh one. The rubies in her halo are reserved, limited to praise for the Oyster and not saying much about the number five herself. The impression I get watching her make the waiter sweat is that she wants the best in all things—wrinkle-free tablecloths, the finest cuisine, top-tier customers...and the crown?

After she moves on, I mutter under my breath, "She did it."

"You said the same about Chase," Dax points out irritatingly. "I agree that she's capable of murdering whoever was responsible for the wasted butter... She can't always be this way, can she? Maybe we caught her on a bad day."

"You've heard Lu's stories, she's pretty much like this all the time. But boy, these rolls are good."

The main course arrives after a quarter of an hour and I stare at the shape on my plate, unmistakably that of a fish—pale, headless, and sliced open.

Dax takes a bite. "Scottie, it's tasty. You've had fish before."

I prod the fish with a fork, as if it might come to life. "In a breaded square, mixed with who knows what, not when it's kept its shape after cooking."

"It's the way of nature. We're above fish in the food chain. Besides, you're always complaining about being tired of cafeteria food."

"So I am..." The fish is delicate and tender and, after a couple of tentative bites, I temporarily forget why we're here and concentrate on enjoying each mouthful to the fullest. About halfway through, I sense Jada's eyes on us, as if she's storing up information for later use, but not for the reason Bonnie does it, to bridge the divide between herself and her customers. The meal is a little less heavenly on the tongue from that moment on.

His plate empty, Dax leans back and taps his stomach. "Wouldn't mind having that more often, even if it means being glared at by Jada."

"You're in the Top Hundred now," I remind him, scraping the last bits off my own plate. "You can eat here as often as you want."

"I really should pay more attention to my rank. Scottie, you have something on your lip."

"Where?" I dab at my mouth with the napkin.

"Here, let me get it." Dax reaches across with his own napkin.

Feeling awkward about being taken out to dinner by Dax, despite the reason, I clear my throat and glance over to where Jada is seating a large group. Chitchat floats over, Jada saying, "Did you hear that Samm and Sue are thinking of quitting comedy?" Exclamations of surprise are followed by eager gossip on what the Jokers might do next, together or separately. I take a snapshot before Jada moves on to the next table, then comment to Dax in a low voice, "She's making a move against Samm and Sue. Makes sense, if she's the killer. Why bother with an accident for the Jokers when they can be gotten out of the way using more conventional techniques—gossip and false rumors?"

"It could be true, for all we know."

"We saw them just two days ago and things seemed fine," I point out.

Dax brings up an objection. "If she's behind it, why install Rick as the number one, then stage an accident for him next?"

This strikes me as a minor difficulty. "Maybe she no longer had need for him."

Dessert is fluffy, creamy chocolate—mousse, served in a cup with a tiny spoon. After Dax finishes his and I all but lick my cup and spoon clean, we leave the eatery behind us and embark on a loop around streetlamp-twinkling, romantic Founders Square. Reminding myself to stick to business, I say, "I'll put Jada down as: *Snooty. Excellent food. Of all the Tenners, seems the most dangerous. I didn't like the way she was looking at us... I admit it might have been a mistake to pretend to be on a date.*"

"She's a collector of secrets," Dax reminds me. "She won't say anything unless we give her a reason to."

"I wish Rick would wake up," I say after we move aside to let a bicycle pass. "I can apologize for thinking he's a killer, he can null the onyx he gave me, and that'll bounce me right out of the bog. Plus I suspect he knows more than he let on. I never got a chance to talk to him after *Mrs. Montag*. Of course, at the time he was my main suspect."

"What do you mean, after *Mrs. Montag*?"

"Oh, that... As it happens, he invited me to the back-stage party. I was going to ditch you," I confess, "then double back and talk and...uh...flirt with him if need be. That sounded like a better plan at the time than it does now. He probably just wanted another conquest... Why are you twitching?" He's pulling at his collar as if he's hot in his shirt. I add, "Never mind, I can guess—it's because we're doing things out of order. We did Bonnie at number one, Chase at two, and Samm and Sue at three and four, then skipped to Poulsbo at seven and Franz at nine and then went back up to Jada at number five... We still have McKinsey and Ben to consider. I'm certain it's not McKinsey, so that leaves—"

"Hold up," he says, letting go of the collar. "We can't rule McKinsey out just because she used to be your boss."

"Even though the only vibe I get from her is *Scott, you blew your chance at being an Agency employee*? Look, if McKinsey wanted to move up, she'd just get a couple more hobbies."

"Scottie, it's not the hobby thing that makes McKinsey popular. She's the head of the Social Agency. Everyone is eager to be on her good side." Dax stops to check an instrument hanging down from one of the trees lining the square and nods at the humidity reading. "Haven't you ever wondered how McKinsey got her start?"

"I assumed she lucked into an internship, same as me." Then I recall what Lucille said about her own rise into the Top Hundred. "You think McKinsey owed her position to Delilah and got fed up with being beholden to her all these years and decided to do something about it?"

"It's possible, isn't it?" he says as we recommence walking.

"No. It only seems that way because you don't know McKinsey, however she may have gotten her start at the Agency. McKinsey is...well, fair. And murder isn't." Dax looks unconvinced and I offer, "Fine. I'm vacuuming at the Agency tomorrow. With any luck she'll have a free moment to talk. For now, how about this: *McKinsey was a good boss. Dax thinks there's a chance she's the killer, but Scottie knows he's wrong...* Which leaves Ben. He was stuck on the shelf for months until Delilah's death cleared the way. Maybe Rick figured it out and Ben tried to kill him next... You could pay a visit to the tailor shop and get a pricey suit made and make small talk about the curse."

Dax makes a face. "What reason would I give? An expensive set of clothes would kind of stand out in the Gardens Center or on the tennis court."

"Make something up."

"You know I'm not great at lying."

"You did seem to be struggling back in Franz's therapy office. Just tell Ben it's for next time you eat at the Oyster. For now I'll put him down as *Could be the killer—of more than just the sparrows' chances of staying in town.*"

We've looped the square and are back in front of the eatery, under a streetlamp buzzing intermittently as if the bulb is about to fail, a reminder that my time, too, is running out. The flickering plays with the shadows, morphing them as if they are living things. A soft flutter of wings makes itself heard somewhere in the dark. Life, it strikes me, is like that—you can never tell what's in the shadows just up ahead. If I could, I'd freeze this moment forever—Dax and I under the dreamlike hum of the lamp.

I blurt out, "Hey, how come you never invite me to your tennis matches?"

Seeming a bit taken aback, Dax says, "I assumed you wouldn't be interested."

"Not in playing, but I could come and cheer you on. When's this big match?" He tells me that it's the tournament final, on Wednesday, and I add, "Well, good then—if I'm still around."

"We still have all of tomorrow. Something will come up."

It's the first time I've ever heard Dax flat-out lie to me. I know he doesn't believe that the next thirty-six hours will bring a miracle any more than I do. "It seems to me that we're missing a big piece of the puzzle," I say. "I wonder if one of the Tenners is ill and desperate for Eternal Life. Jada always looks so gaunt." Inside the eatery, business is still brisk despite the late hour. I go on. "You know, I used to believe that a brand's an artificial thing, a gimmick, but Delilah told me—that last morning—that for a brand to work, there has to be something real behind it. Jada's brand—*the best of everything*—strikes me as dangerous, like a chemistry experiment where you don't want to lift the lid off because whatever is within will scorch your eyebrows... Damn and damn." I follow that up internally with *Cece, pipe down, no one here cares that I used the word twice.*

"What is it?" Dax asks.

My doubts spill out one after another. "What if there never was anything real behind Sherlock Scottie and it was just a house of cards—a story I fed myself to feel better about being slapped with the Incompetent Intern label— and Delilah and Rick's accidents were just that and nothing more?"

Dax shakes his head as the streetlamp gives another flicker. "Like I said before, I believe you that something odd's going on. That Delilah was killed."

But not just Delilah. Gasps break out all around the square. Inside the eatery, the patrons are rising to their feet. Dax and I check the Commons to see what the news is.

Rick has succumbed to his injuries.

Chapter Twenty-Two

Housing Nine

It's the night before Scottie and Wayne find out who won the race to the bottom. Dax is eating a cafeteria dinner alone when Tacoma, who lives a couple of floors above him, breaks his chain of thought. "Hey, Dax. How's the meatloaf?"

"See if you can figure out what the mystery meat is. I sure can't."

Tacoma slides across him with his tray. After a few minutes of silence punctuated only by the sound of chewing, Dax's hunger abates. He pushes the plate away, the crumbs on it a reminder that the kitchen will demote any leftover meatloaf to tomorrow's cafeteria mix. This in turn reminds him of Scottie, not that he needs reminding. She's all he can think about these days. He clears his throat. "Tacoma. I have a favor to ask."

As sad as Rick dying is, he can't help but view it through a personal lens. He tried to sound optimistic in talking to her, but Scottie's saddled with that onyx for good. Dax went to Ben's tailor shop for a suit fitting but it was a waste of time; he was attended to by an assistant, not Ben himself. As for Scottie, she's vacuuming at the Agency, with hopes of catching McKinsey at the end of the workday. Doubtful anything will come of that either. Scottie's only hope is that Hugh's algorithm breaks in her favor. It's a matter of simple math: Will all the onyxes Wayne's accrued—minor ones from low-Listers all the way up Lucille's in the Top Thousand—add up to more than the weighty two Scottie has, Rick's and the section F violation?

"I'm listening," Tacoma says as he works his way through the large serving. "And I think this might be turkey."

Dax clears his throat again. "Any chance you could lob a ruby Scottie's way? I know it's against section A—*Never ask for gems as a favor, either for yourself or others*—but she's in the bog and every little bit helps."

"I didn't know she was so low. Sure thing. Good for you, Dax."

This makes Dax look up from the empty plate. "What for?"

"For breaking the Code. That's growth, you know. No one's perfect—why burden yourself with the expectation?"

Dax considers himself far from perfect. "I used to believe that I should adhere to every article of every section of the Code, no matter the circumstances..." In fact, he would have said as much had Tacoma asked him about it as recently as last week. "Now, I'm not so sure."

"What's changed?"

Dax knows he can trust Tacoma. And didn't Tacoma just say no one's perfect? Still, he lowers his voice. "I'm pretty sure I have feelings for Scottie."

"Yeah, I like her too."

"No, Tacoma... *Feelings*."

"Oh. Dax, forget what I said about it being a good thing to occasionally bump against the Code." Tacoma shakes his head. "Section Q's not a good one to break. Are you going to do anything about it?"

"God, no. It wouldn't be fair to Scottie—not with her miserable rank."

"If you don't mind my saying so, you're better off not pursuing it even if her rank improves. For both of your sakes. Peggy and Leon—she was the best of our science teachers and he was a great gym coach—and look what happened there."

Having made that rather prim remark, Tacoma releases the burp of a full stomach behind one hand. He's set his fork down on a half-empty plate—a waste of food. But it's not his friend Dax is mad at. It's the corner he finds himself in: unable to help Scottie beyond asking a trusted friend to give her a ruby. Dax responds with "You're probably right," not adding what's gnawing at him, a runaway weed in his perfectly ordered garden. The possibility that Scottie might feel the same way.

CC, show me the corkboard, he instructs, which brings up the large **NO** in his eye-field. *Wipe and replace with a countdown clock to eight a.m. tomorrow.*

This brings up 13 HOURS 29 MINUTES 15 SECONDS.

WHAT ARE WE COUNTING DOWN TO, DAXTON? his CC asks. Not curiosity, just an assistant learning the needs of its host. Here, at least, he can be honest. *The moment Scottie finds out if she gets to stay one more week.*

If she's sent to a greenhouse, he won't be able to visit her there. And if she's sent sledding...well, he won't let her go alone, that's for sure. Despite all that he said to Wayne and Scottie herself, the possibility of leaving the Dome frightens him. It's one thing to contemplate doing a bold thing at some far-off future moment and quite another to have it be only hours away.

He watches the clock tick down for a moment, then lets it disappear from his eye-field as his friend says, "Scottie's kind of a funny one, isn't she? Keeps to herself. But she seems all right." Tacoma shifts in his seat and makes a show of being struck with an idea. "What if I ask her out—if she sticks around? If she says yes, that means she isn't interested in you, which solves your problem."

Dax can't think of a reason to protest against this, at least not one that doesn't involve jealousy. Irritated at himself for bringing up the subject in the first place, he asks, "Tacoma, have you ever broken the Code?"

His friend adjusts the fork on his plate. "I suppose it's only fair that I share back. Section A, in a major way—I engaged in halo-padding. But just the one time. I wanted a private bathroom but couldn't afford one... You know me, I always have trouble...uh... going in front of others in the tennis arena locker room. Paid someone at the market. Well, there it is. They never caught it, the Social Agency, but I feel guilty every time I brush my teeth and the toothbrush goes back into a cup on my sink instead of a toiletries bag." Tacoma digs something out of his teeth with his tongue and changes the subject. "Can you believe the news about Rick? Dead. I've never been *this* happy I'm only a mid-Lister—at least Gemma Bligh's curse won't come for me next. Still, there are plenty of people I could have been kinder to along the way, you know? Just in case, I gave rubies to Blank Jack and Renee..."

The Social Agency

Hugh is doing List housekeeping in preparation for tomorrow's update. Rick will be coming off, leaving the count short again. It's always unsettled him that when this sort of thing happens, a death, no one's ever proposed *not* kicking the bottomer out, giving them a reprieve.

Making the battle for his customary detachment harder this evening is an unfamiliar emotion—astonishment. Rubies have been coming in for Blank Jack and Renee. The thoughts coupled to the rubies are hopeful: *"I'll be your friend; maybe this will help break Gemma Bligh's curse."* That in itself is not surprising—after all, the Tenners unveiled a campaign aimed at achieving that very goal. But the scale of the response... With Rick's passing adding fuel to the curse frenzy, the rubies are piling up, building to...what? A huge influx of gems can change fortunes overnight. The pair will be catapulted up, that's for sure, Blank Jack out of the bottom thousand and Renee up from the middle of the List, where she started her new life with the welcome amber.

A knock takes his attention away from the screen. A young person is at the door. "I'm Scott," she says. "I'd ask you to call me Scottie but won't since you're in charge of the List and the rule is that we're supposed to go by our proper names. I used to work for McKinsey. Not anymore. Now I vacuum."

There is a vacuum machine behind her in the hallway. He shakes his head. "Scott, all the cleaning inside this office is done by me."

"I know. I came back up to talk to McKinsey but she's left

for the day. I wanted to tell her that someone's trying to game the List."

Hugh's response to this is automatic. "Of course they are. People are always trying. You should talk to Bodi in the Security Office."

"But do they usually resort to murder? Twice? And—I think they may have succeeded in getting away with it."

He digests this remarkable statement for a moment. "You'd better come in."

Her halo is weak—she's in the bog, though the List-keeper should not refer to position 9,999 in such a frivolous way. The too-long sleeves and her small frame make her seem very young, as do the words spilling out of her mouth. "They are all brands, the Tenners. Poulsbo is the nicest of them but even he's become one: the Tired Handyman. Delilah told me that there has to be something real behind a brand, but *real* doesn't necessarily mean good, does it? It could mean the opposite. Evil."

Here she has to stop for a breath. There is no guest chair in the office as he rarely gets visitors, so he offers her his own and stands, arms crossed. The topic she's brought up is one he's given much thought to. "Scott, who tends to be at the top?"

"Those with the catchiest brands."

He can supply a more granular answer. "It's entertainers such as Delilah and Rick, and Samm and Sue, who make us feel and laugh—and yes, who have the obvious stage. Managers who've made a success of their own establish-ments and give the impression they might do the same for the town. Then there are those with big personalities—McKinsey is one—and those such as Poulsbo for whom goodwill accumulates over the years. As to Ben and others who chisel their way up, all we can hope is that they'll make an effort to do as promised. Rank is not about who's a decent person and who isn't, as you've discovered. To put it bluntly, it's about how many people know your name."

"Like they used to know Delilah's."

"She hasn't been forgotten." He finds himself unexpectedly drawn into reminiscing. "Delilah, McKinsey, and I used to be PALs, did you know that? I was the oldest, graduated first, and was recruited as Belinda's successor—you probably haven't heard her name, and that's as should be—a Listkeeper must aim for invisibility. It meant I had to sever all close connections, PALs included, and so I watched Delilah's success from afar. She was special. She graduated and immediately landed a plum role at the theater... Now, what was it?" He can't remember the name of the play. Fifty years is a long time. Delilah had fire. She commanded every room she walked into, even when she was just a girl with the shy smile, and he always felt as plain as cardboard next to her—and he had always been smitten. Scott is watching him and he gets back to the topic at hand. "Before Delilah, the turnover was more frequent—people rising to number one and dropping back down in the matter of weeks or months. But plays and partners and enemies came and went, and she stayed at the top." He doubts that Scott knows about what else came along with the years—such as Delilah's shady dealings that Bodi told him about—so he stops there.

Scott, having listened without interrupting, comes back with a shrewd, "Maybe you don't understand how important rank is—what people might resort to."

"Perhaps," he admits. "But this I do know: Achieving the top spot is probably not as wonderful as it seems, including Eternal Life. Is it such a good thing to outlive peers? To have to battle to keep the number one chair, never be able to let your guard down?" He studies her earnest features. "So you don't believe Gemma Bligh's curse is real. You think Delilah and Rick were murdered."

Her eyes are big as she looks up at him. "Bodi thinks I did it."

"I find that hard to believe."

"I may have to leave in the morning."

He doesn't make the rules. "Yes."

"Dax can carry on looking into it," she says with the energy of the young, "but I figured you should know too, so you can keep an eye on things. You have a unique perspective, up here on the fifth floor. You view us all from above."

That's a good way of putting it, the distance he tries to keep. "Then my perspective is this," he says. "They may or may not be good people, the Tenners, but they're far from being murderers."

I couldn't make Hugh see. In the hallway outside his office, I call up the snapshots of the Tenners one by one in my eye-field.

Bonnie, number one at last. Do her amiable features hide a sinister streak?

Chase, with his glib grin. A breath away from the top. Is there to be one more death?

Samm and Sue with their matching hair and outfits. Murder for the lark of it—a game.

Jada, thin-lipped and grim. Determined to climb—to the peak?

Poulsbo, overworked and tired, committing murder as an outlet for all the pressure.

Prim and proper Ben, justifying it as being for the

common good. To help rid New Seattle of the tiresome birds.

Franz with the stupendous goatee... Murder as a compromise, to avoid something worse.

McKinsey, with the hobbies and sculpture dust on her hands...and Delilah and Rick's blood?

No, I can't—won't—picture McKinsey as a killer.

I take the elevator down and hop on my bike—I fixed the flat tire despite being unable to shake the feeling that everything will change come the morning. I find Bonnie's tavern packed. The town waits, here for the front-row seats —will Gemma Bligh's curse strike a third time? A pair of bartenders are attending to the crush of customers but Bonnie herself isn't behind the counter. She mentioned inventory the day Dax and I stopped by and the door to the tavern basement is ajar. My senses are tuned up high, on alert. Was the basement door left open the previous time? It strikes me as a thing out of place.

The bartenders have their hands too full to worry about me and I slip through the side door unnoticed, leaving it partially open. Shadowy stairs lead down to an L-shaped space. The longer branch of the L holds the nuts and bolts of a tavern—cider and wine racks, wooden barrels, an apple press, bubbling fermentation containers. The shorter branch, into which the overhead lights scarcely reach, has shelving with burlap sacks stacked high. Both branches are empty of people, though someone seems to have been attending to one of the barrels—a plastic yardstick sticks out of it and the lid is on the floor at an angle against the barrel, as if the person was interrupted in the task.

I peer inside. Apples, a whole lot of them, red and plump. I haven't had a fresh apple since leaving the youth center. I reach in for one and sink my teeth into it. The meat is soft and juice runs down my chin. I wipe it, then lick the finger. Any trouble I get into won't matter if I have to leave tomorrow, and besides, Bonnie has so many apples, she won't miss one, and there's no one to see...

The hairs on the back of my neck stand up and I whip around, expecting to find someone behind me, watching, judging me for the bit of petty thievery.

There's no one. The space and the stairs loom dark and silent. *Cece, is someone in here with me?*

THE MAP SHOWS THAT BONNIE IS ALSO IN THE BASEMENT OF THE DRAGON AND THE DRUMSTICK.

Bonnie? Where?

NINE FEET DIRECTLY TO YOUR SOUTH-EAST, SCOTT.

For God's sake, Cece, which way is south-east?

TO YOUR RIGHT AND THEN—

Around the corner, got it.

I dash into the storage area. And then I see it, in the shadows, blocked from my view before by the angle of the L. One of the heavy burlap sacks has tumbled off.

Sprawled underneath it is Bonnie.

Chapter Twenty-Three

Monday, April 5

No time for breakfast, as I've overslept—it's past eight and I'm supposed to be at the theater, vacuuming. Dressing fast, I hurry downstairs and jump on the bike. I stayed awake a long time trying to forget the sight of Bonnie motionless on the cold concrete. Emergency personnel arrived within minutes and shuffled me up the stairs so they could work. Along with the rest of the tavern patrons, all of us deathly quiet, I watched Bonnie be carried out on a stretcher—gray-faced but alive.

Someone calls out in my direction as I pedal fast, one hand on the vacuum to keep it from bouncing out, but they must have the wrong person as it's a stranger. A block later a second person points at me. I let go of the vacuum to make sure I haven't forgotten to comb my hair, then I remember. It's Monday and I've hit the bottom.

Cece is still on mute from last night. *Cece, wake up—but don't tell me my rank.*

IT'S PAST EIGHT, SCOTT. YOUR RANK HAS BEEN UPDATED.

I want to delay finding out as long as I can. It's a human thing. Do this instead—check the Commons, see if Bonnie made it through the night.

SHE'S IN MEDICAL ONE AND AWAKE, EVERYONE IS SAYING.

Oh, I'm so relieved, I think back at Cece, taking a right into an alley, a shortcut to the theater. *I was afraid this was going to be like Rick—that she'd slip away.*

RELIEF SOUNDS LIKE A PLEASANT EMOTION, SCOTT.

Has anyone been arrested?

I DO NOT HAVE THAT INFORMATION. I MUST INFORM YOU OF A DIFFERENT MATTER REQUIRING YOUR ATTENTION. MCKINSEY HAS SENT AN URGENT THOUGHT. AND YOU HAVE IN-THOUGHTS WAITING IN A QUEUE OF LENGTH—

What does McKinsey say?

"Scott, come to the Agency."

I can't hide—it's time to face whatever awaits me. I pass the theater without stopping. I'm to be given the bad news by the head of the Agency, probably with Bodi standing by, after which I'll be allowed to pack. And then I'll be led to a train in the evening as Oliver was—or to a gate to be sent sledding. I wonder if they'll let me say goodbye to Lu and Dax.

Rolling to a stop in front of the Agency, I give the reflexive Monday morning glance up. My knees go weak. On the Tenner billboard, Renee is at ten and Blank Jack at nine. Going up from there are Poulsbo, Samm and Sue, Ben, Jada, Chase, Bonnie, and at number one...

...me. The snapshot, taken by Lu when I purchased the bike right after graduation, had sunk all the way into the bog alongside me. And now? It's staring down from the top of the billboard.

Chapter Twenty-Four

Exiting the elevator on the fourth floor, I duck into the bathroom to view my halo in the mirror and stare at the single digit: a tall, solid *1*. Thousands of rubies have come in overnight, all variations of the same sentiment. *"Scott broke the curse ... Bonnie's alive and well thanks to Scott the Curse Slayer! ... Kindness plus Scott equals doom for the curse!"*

Then there are the in-thoughts awaiting my attention. Enthusiastic congrats from Lu, Dax, and Wayne. Insincere ones from Magda, Mia, and Audrey. Vicky and Evan, asking how I've been. Lucille reminding me to come to her salon now that I can afford it. Dax's buddy Tacoma, wondering if I want to go out with him. Sample menus from upscale eateries. Offers for quality cloth in any color I want. Chocolate bars in three flavors. And on and on.

Clearly there must be some mistake. I pinch myself. It hurts. Not a dream.

I exit the bathroom to find people waiting in the hallway. Applause breaks out. On autopilot, I smile and accept handshakes and pats on the back. Bodi is on the premises and pulls me aside. "I don't think you need to bother with vacuuming today, Scott. You're what we might call an overnight success."

"Bodi, this must be a glitch, right?"

An out-of-character flash of amusement crosses his face. "In Hugh's algorithm? Never."

"All I did was go into the tavern basement and push a burlap sack off Bonnie." I grab his arm. "What did she say? Who did it? Did she see the killer's face?"

Bodi's reply is unhurried. "Well, now. There was not much to go on with the previous accidents— Yes, of course I've been looking into it. But Bonnie's accident was different. We checked as soon as we got your emergency thought— rewound the map back."

I wait, but Bodi seems determined to make me ask. "Who was in there with her?"

"Bonnie went downstairs at two minutes past seven, alone," he informs me. "She stayed that way—alone—until you followed her down nineteen minutes later. The next thing that happened was your emergency thought."

I release his arm. "Followed her down..." Breaking off, I stare at Bodi. I can see how it all looks, worse than ever. I attacked Bonnie so I could make a show of saving her, knowing it would catapult me up...all the way to the top, apparently. But there's a new element to my interaction with Bodi, as if an invisible shield now protects me, a novel sensation. Even if Bodi does suspect me, he can hardly drag the number one to the Security Office jail. He knows it and so do I.

I straighten my back, which makes me eye level with Bodi's shoulders. "I don't know how Bonnie ended up under the burlap sack, but it wasn't me."

"I know that."

"You do?"

"Bonnie confirmed it. No one attacked her. It's over, Scott. If you don't believe me, go ask her yourself."

I find Bonnie in a Medical One bed, propped up with her head on a double pillow. Purple bruises bridge her nose and encircle her eyes—she narrowly escaped suffocation, the nurse at the station outside the room told me. Bonnie greets me with "How am I doing?"

"You're going to be fine," I reassure her. Bonnie's fists grip the blanket as if she's holding on to it for safety.

"I know I'll be okay, the doctors said so. I'm asking about the top of the List. Can you read it to me? I hit the back of my head when I slipped and the headache is making my brain fuzzy. I had to mute my CC."

"Slipped?"

She winces at the recollection. "I went to the basement to finish the inventory... No, that's not quite honest. The inventory could have waited until morning. I wanted to escape the ghouls upstairs—the ghouls waiting to see what awful thing was going to befall me. And in the end I made it happen myself." She closes her eyes and recounts what occurred. "I inventoried the beer bottles and then moved on to the apple barrel... I must have finished with that and started on the supplies in the back. It was a burlap sack with potatoes, they say. I must have reached up to check whether the potatoes had gone rotten. A can of cooking oil had leaked last week and left the floor slick... I slipped and hit my head, blacked out, and the bag tumbled onto me." She opens her eyes. "And then you found me. Now, tell me about the top of the List."

"You're... Well, you're at two. There was a big wave of rubies overnight and it propelled me to number one." I hurry to add, "But only because everyone's thankful you're safe."

Bonnie's fists unclench and settle into the hospital blanket. "I was hoping for this."

I can't see how this can be true, and assume her head injury is clouding her hearing or judgment. I try again. "Why don't I read you the top in order. One—uh, me. Two, you. Three, Chase. Four, Jada—she's moved up, or rather Sue and Samm have sunk down below Ben. It must have been the rumor that they're splitting up. Eight, Poulsbo. And at nine and ten, Blank Jack and Renee."

"Blank Jack and Renee are in..." Again, she says, "I was hoping for this. Surely it means Gemma Bligh's curse is broken for good. Here, come closer. Sit by the bed."

I move a chair over and she places her hand on mine. "I owe you my life, Scott."

"I was concerned about you. I just happened to see the open door, that's all."

"With the tavern packed wall to wall, you're the only one who did. And you got me breathing again."

"Bonnie... I ate one of your apples. I'm sorry. I'll pay for it."

"Scott, you're the number one now. You can take whatever you like."

A bit of cooking oil on the floor hardly seems the stuff of a murder attempt. Still, I ask, "Can you think of anyone who might have wanted to kill you? Who wanted you gone from number one?"

Bonnie tries to shake her head but the pain stops her. "It was the curse."

"Everyone has enemies," I point out gently.

"I suppose I do, of course... Jada is one. Rick was. But none of that matters. The thought you shared on the

Commons about kindness and how we've treated Blank Jack... Now that he and Renee are in the Ten, and you're number one for standing up for them, for showing us the way—we've righted the balance. Don't you see? The fact that you were able to save me is proof. It's over, Scott."

Bonnie's head sinks deeper into the pillow and she sends a weak smile in my direction. "If I get some sleep, I'm hoping the doctors will let me attend tonight... You should go. You have to get ready."

I start at this. My new reality hasn't sunk in yet. Tonight's Tenner event is the monthly ballroom gala. I'll be expected to attend.

After tucking the blanket in around Bonnie, I stop by the nurses' desk to instruct that the week's dose of Eternal Life go to her instead of me, to help her heal. This merits murmurs of surprise, but the head nurse says, "Of course. We'll see to it."

Outside the building, I ask Cece, *Who's in last place? It's not Wayne, is it?*

But it is Wayne.

I double back to the Agency. Wayne's at his desk talking to the intern hired to replace me, Ty, who was a year behind me in the youth center. Wayne is making an effort to calm him down. "Just focus on one task at a time. There's not much to it... Hey, Scottie. Ty, you can give Scottie her invite now."

"H—Here." Ty's eyes are wide above the smattering of moles on his cheekbones. The invite is a twin of the one Delilah gave to me along with a chocolate. It does nothing to convince me that what's happening could possibly be real, and I resist the urge to pinch myself again.

Scott—Guest of Honor
Gala
Grand Ballroom at eight o'clock
Monday, the fifth of April

On a cart next to Wayne's desk, bins of goodies await to be carried to the ballroom. Ty is lingering by the desk, playing with one of its corners as if trying to smooth it into a curve. He's running late—Jada's not going to be happy. "I don't know if you remember me, Scottie, we used to have gym class together. Just wanted to say congrats on being, you know, the Curse Slayer and all. If you should happen to have some free time... Well, it would mean a lot to have a gem from the number one." He adds hastily, losing interest in the desk, "It doesn't have to be a ruby—though that would be brill—just thought I'd ask..."

He's looking at me with barely hidden hope. My words sounding foolishly grandiose, I say, "I'll see what I can do."

A grin breaks out on Ty's face and he takes off, humming a tune, leaving me to consider that not long ago—yesterday! —I was in his position, every gem meaning so much.

"Scottie, number one, that's wonderful," Wayne says.

I put the invite away. "I came to say goodbye."

He shakes his head at me. "Not yet—I still have some time to show Ty the ropes. Bottomers get the week to wrap up their affairs."

This comes as a surprise. "But Oliver was escorted onto a train the Monday of the town party."

"There was some trouble with Oliver, I heard. He was scaring people. Me, I'm calm. I'll be taking off on Sunday. I'm pleased to report that everything is going according to plan—no train for me. The greenhouses are full... Have you talked to McKinsey? She was *not* happy this morning."

Absorbed in my own change of fortune, I missed that McKinsey's name is no longer in the Ten—nor is Franz's.

Down the hall, McKinsey is at her window in a suit of a muted brown. At my knock on the open door, she turns. "Scott. That was quite a blast up the ranks."

I get as far as saying "I didn't mean for any of this—" before she interrupts. "It's fine. That's how the game is played. I wanted to tell you that you're welcome to your old job. In fact, we're promoting you from intern to a permanent employee. You can upgrade to Wayne's about-to-be-vacated position—event organizing... Or I can train you personally as a social consultant, which, given all the interest that's bound to come your way, is probably a better strategy. Your old desk is available, unless you want something nicer, with a window?"

"My desk is fine," I say as if that makes up for taking up McKinsey's spot—and forestalling where I think she was going, about to offer Wayne's office, or perhaps even her own. "All of this feels, well, undeserved."

The understatement lands clunkily. McKinsey settles into the chair of her desk. "People were scared and you've released them from that."

"But now *I'm* scared. Of the gala tonight."

My nervousness seems to thaw McKinsey somewhat. "It'll be fine. You'll learn soon enough what's expected of the number one." She eyes my faded clothing. "Take the rest of the day off and go to Ben's tailor shop. They'll hook you up for tonight... You do know that you can bring a plus one, don't you?"

"Can it be a PAL?" I ask.

"It can be whoever you want. Just make sure it's someone you can lean on. You're going swimming with the sharks and they'll smell blood."

No one knows if there are still sharks in the oceans or if the cold killed them all, but I know what they were supposed to be like. What have I gotten myself into?

Though Ben himself didn't attend to Dax when he stopped by the Fine Fabrics shop, I'm assuming he'll make an appearance for the number one. I'm wrong. I'm ushered into the back room and into the hands of a designer who looks me up and down and pronounces, "With your lack of height and the time crunch—well, I'll do my best."

She claps her hands, as if someone in the back is slow in following up on a sent thought, and an assistant arrives carrying a gown and invites me to change behind a screen. The gown is pearl-white and sleeveless, with fluffy folds from the waist to the ankle. After I don it, they get to work. Fabric is pulled, adjusted, and pinched into place. I stand there with nothing to do but stare at the walls. Wading through all of my new rubies and in-thoughts seems impossible. I send a thought to Dax. *"Doing anything tonight? I need a plus one for the gala."*

"There isn't going to be dancing, is there?"

"Possibly. Can't guarantee it. Please say yes."

"Good thing I had a suit made."

After the gown is pinned up, I'm invited to look in the mirror. The crisp fabric has been rendered form-hugging above the waist and billowy to the knees, and lies softly on my skin, as if I'm wearing a fair-weather cloud. The designer steps back to take a look. She shakes her head and fiddles with the hem, then steps back again. "It will have to do. We'll deliver it by four-thirty."

The price of the gown takes my breath away—but so did my new bank balance when I took a peek.

My next stop, after I select a pair of strappy heels at the shop a door down, is the Oyster. I wait at the back door, having sent a thought to Lu saying I won't leave until I talk to her. This time I ignore the birds—still as mysterious as ever—and stare at the part of the eatery that sticks out of Housing One. That's where it happened, where Delilah landed. She's been laid to rest and Rick will soon be too, his seeding scheduled for midweek. No one targeted them. No one attacked Bonnie. She was so primed to expect the curse to strike she made it happen herself. Accidents in a crumbling, aging town, everyone caught up in the delicious frenzy of it all—including me. I talked myself into believing there was a killer to help myself. To build a *brand,* Sherlock Scottie. And the worst part is, quite undeservedly, I lucked into a brand after all.

I search my innards to gauge how I feel about everything and come up with *relief.* The responsibility of finding a killer has been lifted off my shoulders.

After a short wait, Lu comes out, two sandwiches in hand. She passes me one. "I have fifteen minutes before Jada notices I've stepped out."

We move to a nearby bench and I swat a couple of sparrows away with the linen bag I'm carrying. After Lu admires what's in the bag, my new shoes, we taper off into silent chewing under the midday sun. A wave of helplessness shoots through me. A PAL should be able to come up with the right words, but what's there to say? Wayne has hit the bottom like he wanted, Lu must be devastated, and there's nothing I can do to help beyond feeling guilt about my own good fortune.

Having consumed her sandwich, Lu irons the creases in

her napkin with one thumb. "Look, Scottie, it's fine—and it helps to know I have PALs who'll stick by my side. Now tell me about saving Bonnie. That must have been terrifying, seeing her on the floor like that. We were all extra careful moving product bags today."

I recount what happened: The basement door, ajar. The apple barrel, its lid off. The hairs on the back of my neck standing up. Cece telling me that Bonnie was in the silent basement with me. The crumpled, still form on the floor and my heart racing as I sent the emergency thought to Medical One. Pumping on Bonnie's chest. Counting the seconds until I heard feet hurrying down the stairs.

"I'm so glad Bonnie is okay," Lu says after I finish. "Even Jada is glad, I think, though it's hard to tell."

"Humph," I say, rolling my own used napkin into a loose ball. Lu goes on to explain that she asked Jada if she could take the week off to spend with Wayne, but the answer was no, making me comment, "I hate her."

"I don't. And at least I have the morning shift this week, so my evenings are free."

"I invited Dax as my plus one for tonight," I find myself saying.

I brace myself—Lu's not a stickler for the Code like Dax is, but she's no rule-breaker either—but this is a new Lu. We all have to follow where our soul leads, she said. She takes my napkin and folds it into a square on top of hers, then sends a broad smile in my direction. "Of course Dax is the person you should take along. Now go get ready."

7:35 p.m.

The mirror on the back of my door shows a stranger. Above the fancy gown, my hair has been tidied up and the makeup feels like a mask, both Lucille's handiwork. Delilah's halo the day of her death reminded me of a sunset; my own, equally red, seems absurd and showy. I've done what I can to make myself presentable but I have no idea what the reception will be. Will the other Tenners look at me with disdain? Will I be expected to be the life of the party, an idea doomed from the start? Will anyone notice if I stand in a corner the entire evening talking to Dax?

A knock interrupts my fretting. I let Dax in. His new outfit from Fine Fabrics is a navy-blue three-button blazer and matching slacks. "You clean up nice," he says casually, deflating my ego a bit. "Ready?"

"Just about. I can't reach the buttons"—there's a short row of buttons up the back of the gown, just under the neck line—"can you do them up?"

His fingers are warm on my skin.

After he steps back, I sit down on the bed to don the shoes, working around the puffy bottom of the gown to get to the straps. I take the opportunity to relay what Bonnie and Bodi said about the events of last night. Dax's reaction is a pragmatic, "Then that's that."

"Thanks."

"For what?"

"For not saying it. That I was wrong about everything."

He shrugs. "Life should be full of trial and error—if we take no risks, if we limit ourselves to pursuing only things we're sure of, well, what could be duller? So we chased a killer and it turns out there isn't one." He's at the dresser and picks up the snow globe, flipping it in his hands and sending the fake snow flying. "I remember when you bought this."

"Me and Oliver, yeah."

He sets the globe back in its place, on top of my newspaper and Delilah's town-anniversary invite, and reaches for the gala one. "Do we need to bring it along?"

"No, it's just for show." I get to my feet, a bit unstable in the shoes.

Dax adds the invite to the treasures under the globe. "How does it feel to be number one, Scottie?"

"Very odd. As if it's happening to someone else." I take a last look in the mirror, swaying in the heels. "The rubies... Most are from people who've never met me, who don't know me or anything about me. They think I'm the Curse Slayer, when what I really am is an imposter. I wish I looked different. More worthy."

"What are you talking about? You look great."

"I don't know, more mature? Taller? And I like this new short haircut but—"

"Your hair looks great, too," he interrupts. "Stop fussing. Besides, once people get to know you, they'll like you for *you* and not because of the Curse Slayer thing."

"All of them?"

"Well, not *all* of them," Dax, ever honest, replies. "But hopefully enough people that you never again have to worry about the bog or the bottom."

Outside the building, I stop to take in a thought from McKinsey. *"Enjoy the gala. Don't let them make you feel small."*

I relay this to Dax and he nods. "McKinsey is right. I plan to enjoy myself, even if there's dancing."

"It's not you everyone will be staring at."

"What are you talking about? You've seen me dance." He sticks an elbow in my direction. "May I offer you an arm? Those shoes look hazardous."

I take his arm. Strangers wave at us as we walk toward Hobby One and the ballroom there, and my free hand goes up as if of its own accord, my mood lifting along with it. I have Dax with me, and there'll be other people at the gala out of place, starting with Blank Jack and the stranger in New Seattle, Renee. I'm not the only one whose fortunes have changed overnight.

Chapter Twenty-Five

The ballroom is smaller than Dax expected, or perhaps it only seems so because of all the people crowding it: the Tenners and their dates; other guests, a selection from the Top Hundred; a band; Social Agency staff; and a host of what seem to be hangers-on pushing events and products, from poetry readings to new deodorant soaps. Scottie seems both excited and tense as they enter the ballroom to applause. Dax has set one goal for himself for the night—to stick by Scottie's side and make sure no one interferes with her enjoyment of the evening.

Everyone is circulating, glasses in hand and gossip at the ready. The first to approach is a heavyset man. He heartily shakes hands with both of them and introduces himself as Bishop, Bonnie's partner. "Very grateful to you for saving Bonnie's life, Scott, very grateful. Come, she wants to see you."

Bonnie is in an armchair, her legs on a low cushioned stool. Raw bruises mar her face but she still manages to greet Scottie with a warm smile. "You look lovely, Scott." Openly viewing his halo—no subterfuge with a head injury

—she adds, "Right, hello, Daxton. Enjoy the evening. Word of advice—go easy on the wine, you two. It all takes some getting used to."

Leaving Bishop to attend to Bonnie, he and Scottie, in wordless agreement, head straight for the food table. Chase is there and greets them with, "We did need some fresh blood around here. Just wasn't expecting quite so much of it, perhaps! Try the chicken skewers."

He moves on and they have a chance to look over the offerings. A mole-faced youth Dax remembers from school is hovering in the background nervously checking on the food; Scottie sends him an encouraging smile. On the guest side of the table, Samm and Sue are partaking in the chicken skewers. "Have some," Sue says listlessly. Her eyes are red, as if irritated. "They'll make the wine sit more easily in your stomach."

"Speaking of which, here, enjoy." Samm pushes wine glasses into their hands. Nothing wrong with *his* mood, but Dax is more interested in what's in the glass. "I was under the impression our red wine ran out ages ago."

Samm holds up a finger. "Shh, it's an import from New San Fran. Merlot. There's a secret stash, reserved for new initiates." He pretends to lose his bare skewer and finds it behind Scottie's ear. Scottie laughs, her first laugh of the evening, the cheesy bit of comedy seeming to relax her.

"Try this next," Samm offers after they make short work of a chicken skewer each. "Lobster—from the ocean. Or at least, our version of it—the aquarium in Greenhouse Three."

Dax reaches for the lobster roll. Scottie does the same. He knows they're both thinking the same thing, that they may not ever be back in the ballroom. A good deed sent Scottie to the top, but town memory is short.

After a while, reluctantly, they move away from the food spread, wine glasses refilled courtesy of Samm. The room seems hotter. Jada, slinking around in sharp, calculated movements as if stalking prey, pins them down by a potted plant. "Ah. The young lovers."

Damn. He'd forgotten the cover story they gave at the Oyster. Scottie straightens her shoulders, bare in the white dress. "Hello, Jada. That was for a research project I was working on."

"Was it? No matter. I'm good at keeping secrets."

The way she says it drives a chill down Dax's spine and he's happy when Jada moves on, throwing a parting shot over one shoulder. "Remember, you can always come to me for advice, Scott. We're all one big family, the Ten."

Dax imagines the advice comes at a high cost.

Someone clears their throat. It's Poulsbo, all but hiding in the corner behind the potted plant. He's clearly overheard the whole exchange. "Nice to...see you again," he stutters.

Dax would rather talk to Poulsbo than just about anyone else in the room except Scottie, but Ben approaches and Poulsbo scurries away as if to avoid being assigned further bird-related tasks.

Ben succeeds in making Jada seem subtle. "I see that you've managed to get yourself to number one, have you, Scott...or should I call you the Curse Slayer? Did they treat you well at the shop? I had other business to attend to." He eyes her up and down, their heights just about matching. "If you're still here for next month's gala, I'll make you a proper dress—better than that cobbled-together clunker."

Scottie defends Ben's own staff to him. "They had just a few hours to get it done. And the gown is beautiful."

"Only outshined by the person wearing it," Dax throws in.

Ben addresses Scottie again. "I assume you're prepared to take the reins at the next Tenner meeting and unveil all your ideas and plans for the town?"

Scottie eyes him defiantly over her glass. "Certainly. I'm bursting with ideas and ready to present them on Friday."

"Oh, we've moved up the meeting—to tomorrow."

Scottie makes a face after Ben leaves. "Great. Tomorrow. I have no clue why I said that. The only idea I have is that we should open up genetic records, but even I know that will be a tough sell... First thing tomorrow, I'm paying a visit to the Birth Lab."

"I'm still not convinced they'll tell you who your parents are, just like that."

She answers with a somewhat tipsy, "But I'm the number one."

"So you are. Forget about Ben—no one expects you to solve all of New Seattle's problems in your first Tenner meeting. And, uh, maybe we should go easy on the Merlot?"

The next person they encounter and exchange a firm handshake with is Blank Jack. Scottie greets him with, "Blank Jack. Are you mad at me?"

"Not a bit. What for?"

"For pushing you into the Ten. For disturbing your peace."

"I can manage." Blank Jack gives an unbothered shrug. "Besides, we're in the same boat, you'n me. Newcomers."

"And Renee." Scottie looks around. "Which one is she? We haven't met her yet."

"Don't think she's here."

"Can't say I blame her. I'm dreading tomorrow's Tenner meeting."

"I'm not. One—" Blank Jack lifts a calloused thumb in the air. "I'm curious to see what they're like behind closed doors, the Tenners. Two—" He adds his forefinger to the thumb. "The food'll be good, same as tonight. Three—" He unfurls the middle finger. "What's the worst they can do, turn up their noses at us? Remember, you'll have at least a couple'a good friends there. Me—and Bonnie. You saved her life and she won't forget that."

Dax shuffles his feet. A band has struck up a tune and couples are gyrating to upbeat music. He can either stand here listening to Scottie and Blank Jack chat away or do something about it. It's quite all right for PALs to be seen dancing together, he reminds himself. He wants to make sure Scottie has an enjoyable evening, that's all.

Scottie's just finished telling Blank Jack how she's going to get her tooth gap fixed now that she can afford it. He asks, "Ready to have your toes stepped on?"

<hr>

It's been a couple of whirlwind hours filled with dancing—Dax is not as bad as he keeps saying and my toes are perfectly fine—and conversation, food, and drink. Dax has gone off to exchange our wine glasses for water, as we're having trouble keeping our heads clear. The day has been the strangest of my life and it's not over yet.

"*You.* Curse Slayer."

It's Jada again. "Now that your shadow's gone," she says, "I want to talk to you."

"Daxton is not a shadow. And I want to talk to *you.*" I place my hands on my hips but that makes the gown bunch up weirdly; I let my arms hang uselessly by my side. "Jada. Was it *your* idea to move up the Tenner meeting—so I'd have no time to get used to things?"

"We take a vote on all matters, as you should know.

Didn't you check your in-thoughts? We had enough for a quorum." Jada flicks a crumb off her black tuxedo. It's a comfortable choice for the evening, but my guess as to why she favors it is that the outfit reveals nothing—much like the person wearing it. "Now. I want to discuss Renee, given that she couldn't be bothered to show up. What's her story?"

I shrug. "There's nothing I can tell you. I've never talked to her."

She eyes me with distaste. "But you pushed for goodwill rubies for her."

"So I did."

"Without knowing a single thing about her?"

"Guess so. Look, if you don't want to make an effort to get to know Renee yourself, there's always Bodi. He interviewed her before she was allowed to stay."

Jada clicks her tongue in impatience. "I'm sure she put her best foot forward for him. That's not what I'm after."

I respond with a pointed, "You're fishing for something you can leverage against her."

"Call it what you wish. So why don't you get busy and make her your friend, then report to me."

"And if I don't?"

"Those who cross me find that bad things...befall them."

I catch my breath. Was there a slight emphasis on the second syllable of befall? A reminder about Delilah's balcony tumble, a hint that I might be next? In an instant, the relief I felt all day at there being no killer vanishes and all my suspicions flood back.

Jada, taking my silence for acquiescence, adds, "That's right. Do as I ask or you might wake up one morning to find rumors about Daxton, the illegal love, plastered all over the Commons. Being number one won't protect you—everyone will eat it up."

"I don't care," I say, but I can feel the warmth in my cheeks. Even though Dax and I have never even discussed section Q of the Code, much less broken it, I've managed to make us a target.

"Sure you care, Curse Slayer. Everyone cares when it's them. You're on a pedestal right now, but there's only one direction you can go from a pedestal. It doesn't have to be this way, you know. We can help each other."

I shake my head. "I'm pretty sure I don't need your kind of help."

"No? Keep this in mind: A Curse Slayer with a secret is easily slain herself."

As I watch Jada walk away, Dax comes back with two glasses of water and passes one over to me. "Sorry I took so long. Sue and Samm were doing a funny skit. By the way, they're denying the rumor that they're quitting comedy. What did Jada want?"

To flaunt her power over me is the answer. But her words reminded me how all this started in the first place—with me wanting justice for Delilah.

Chapter Twenty-Six

I take a deep breath, then enter the Tenner room a few steps behind Blank Jack. Passing on the food spread, I stride to the chair at the head of the table, doing my best to hide my nervousness. I sink into the leather and have to sit up a bit. At the other end of the room, the large window overlooking Founders Square reminds me that the well-being of everyone in New Seattle is entrusted to those around the table...and most of all to the number one. The responsibility is a rock-filled backpack I'm carrying around—one I don't know what to do with.

My life has been turned upside down—my bike is in the shop being spruced up, I have an appointment to get my tooth gap fixed, and McKinsey has me holding client sessions at the Agency. My sense with the handful of clients I've seen so far is that they left feeling they got their money's worth more from being able to say they met the number one than from anything I might have said. Vicky came in, hoping my sudden luck would rub off on her.

Something else is weighing on me. I've been to the Birth Lab.

Franz comes in last, leaving one seat empty and causing Jada to gripe at Blank Jack, who's settled into the chair across from her, "Why isn't Renee with you?"

Given that Renee has no brain chip yet, we can't send her a thought to remind her of the meeting nor check her whereabouts on the map.

Blank Jack runs a hand through his beard. "She s'pposed to be? We don't *all* know each other. Between the villages and the communities in and aroun' Old Seattle, well, that's a whole lot of folks."

"Is she afraid to face us? We don't bite." Chase's cackle negates the sentiment. "Perhaps we should start calling her Renee the Recluse."

Bonnie, across the table, shifts a bit in her chair. "I heard in the hospital that she's getting the implant tomorrow. She might be anxious about the surgery. And to be fair, she can't have expected to be asked to contribute to governing and leadership so soon, if at all."

"Give her time. She'll get there." Blank Jack delivers the statement with quiet certainty, making Chase cock an eyebrow at him. "Well, she better get there quick or the town will turn on her. Which means McKinsey will be back in and we don't want *that*. She always made me feel so lazy, with all those hobbies of hers."

"Maybe Renee is worried she won't...fit in," Poulsbo offers a rare opinion.

"Speaking of," Jada turns her stare on me rudely, "what's on today's agenda, Scott?"

I start, my thoughts having been elsewhere, and scramble to call up the agenda sent by Town Offices. "Uh... where are you—we—on the bird matter, Ben?"

Ben answers willingly enough, as if last night's encounter at the gala cleared the air. "We're making progress. People have been calling in nest locations. We've got about twenty so far."

"Blank Jack..." I stop. It occurs to me to wonder, "Uh, I never thought to ask—are you okay with being called that? It's not, perhaps, the nicest name."

"It's all good."

"How are the huts coming along?"

"We're just about finished, Poulsbo and me," Blank Jack tells us, and Ben, from down the table, brings up a problem.

"As things stand, no one volunteered for the catching part, nor—"

"Told you. Who wants guano on their hands?" Chase interrupts.

"—nor the transfer of the birds into the huts. I was able to—"

"Or a faulty snowsuit giving them frostbite?"

"I asked Jobs And Housing to re-classify it from a hobby to a job," Ben finishes loudly. "Renee was eager for it. It's a good fit. Given that she's used to the cold, she'll be able to go in and out without a snowsuit—and move nests and trapped sparrows faster."

"So much for the hobby idea," Chase gets in the last word.

"Once Renee has the chip and is all settled in, let's bring her in here and welcome her properly." Bonnie winces as she adjusts her position again. "Still a bit of a lingering headache. Scott, thank you for passing the Eternal Life cocktail on to me this week."

"How generous of you, Scott. But you are new here." Chase leans across the table, not toward me but Bonnie. "What's it like, Bonnie?"

"The cocktail? You know I can't say."

"Not even a hint? Does it taste sweet, like honey? Bitter, like medicine? Is it a drink, a pill, an injection, what?"

Bonnie's response borders on rude. "It's only for those of us who've sat in the number one chair to know."

That's pretty much the tone for the rest of the meeting, but with it behind me, the next day, Wednesday, finds Dax and me at the west gate. The guard, Yesler, has his feet up on a desk and his hands behind his head. The feet hit the floor and he greets us with a wide-eyed, "Whoa, it's Scott the Curse Slayer."

"Dax here is no slacker himself," I attempt to deflect the attention. "Fans call him the Racquet Ace. He's playing in the tennis finals later today."

"Is that right." Yesler rises to his feet, stretching his back. "Pax, you said? I'm pretty good at shooting hoops myself. What can I help you with?"

"We want to go Outside," I say.

Yesler ceases stretching. "Are you sure?"

Dax grumbled about venturing into the cold on the morning of his big match—but changed his mind once I pointed out that learning about what's on the frost side of the glass was *his* idea in the first place. And the weather, the backdrop to our lives, is cooperating—the sun's out after a two-day spell of clouds and snow.

Yesler, somewhat reluctantly, takes us behind the gate office into what he explains is called the *mud room* and points to where snowsuits hang against one wall, rubber-duck-yellow down-insulated ones. As if verbally dusting off the warning, Yesler cautions us, "No exposed skin or you'll risk staying out there forever. It starts with frostbite—your nose and toes turn black—and ends with hypothermia, where your body temperature plummets and you sit down and get nice and drowsy and die." He scratches his chin, as if his day has taken an unexpected turn, and continues. "To be honest, haven't had anyone *ask* to go out in ages. The other gates, they're closer to the train tracks so they have maintenance workers going in and out. Here it's mostly just the traders on Tuesdays—yesterday was busy. The traders don't wear snowsuits, just layers of stuff." The last sentence is delivered as if he's speaking of another species entirely. "Poulsbo and Blank Jack have been coming through for the bird hut. Other than that, there's a drunk Top Hundred group now and then wanting to go out on a dare and I tell them to find something daring to do inside, where it's nice and warm." Yesler scratches his chin again. "One last thing—your CCs won't work if you go past the edge of the forest. So stay out of the forest. Which is a good idea anyway, as there are wolves."

As we digest this, he leaves us to it. The snowsuits, one-piece except for the gloves and helmet, are lined up by size. Dax heads to the taller end of things and I to the shorter. The intense cold on the other side of the Dome glass might take a chunk out of us if we're not careful, but the word frostbite has a beauty of its own, I decide, donning the suit. *A bite of frost*. Like a line from a poem we might have learned at school.

Yesler comes back and fusses, checking that our suits are zipped up all the way. Helmets in hand, we follow him out of the mud room to a set of double doors, padded and cold-proofed, which Yesler unlocks. A short passageway with a low ceiling leads to another set of double doors, these made of heavy glass, smudged and cracked in places with use and time. Yesler unlocks these as well.

Donning our helmets, Dax and I step through.

Chapter Twenty-Seven

A path about as wide as Dax's arm span leads away from the Dome, the snow on it packed down by traders and their snowmobiles. The cold, let in by slits in the visor of his helmet, claws at his skin, tempered by the warmth of his own breath. He has to turn his head to see. To one side of the gate, an elevated aviary stands at the ready. No sparrows yet. Farther out, greenhouses sparkle in the sun, and to the west, the forest sits like a dark green city on a rising slope. Beyond, the Cascades carve an angular line into the sky.

The mid-morning sun to their back, he and Scottie follow the path uphill, an awkward proceeding in the puffy boots. She shakes her head at him under her helmet. *"It's not what I expected."*

"What did you expect?"

"I thought it would feel...freer, somehow. I'm looking at the sky through a smaller dome, that's all."

But it does feel more free, Dax decides, even with the snowsuit limiting his movement and the added challenge of the climb. Inside the Dome, all his life, he's moved along channels: streets, elevators, hallways, walkways, garden paths, stairs, back alleys. Here he and Scottie can take any direction they want and walk for hours and hours.

As if thinking the same thing, Scottie steps off the path, marring the pristine snow. Her boots sink in to the knees. She keeps going, each step leaving a treaded footprint behind, and Dax is reminded of the footage of a long-ago generation walking on the Moon, back when that kind of thing could be done. He veers off the path himself, packing snow down under his boots with each step.

Scottie is making strange movements.

"Scottie, what are you doing?"

"Trying to run."

Her voice is muffled but he can hear the laughter in it. She takes a tumble and he's briefly concerned but a snow-ball lands on his suit with a thump. Dax retaliates and soon they're pelting each other, racing uphill.

They stop to catch their breath at top of the hill, the forest to their back. Sweat is trickling down Dax's brow. He was worried about the cold locking up his muscles before his big match—truth be told, he only agreed to come because Scottie had her heart set on it with an intensity that surprised him—but it's hot in the suit and his skin itches. He wishes they'd brought water. There's all the snow, of course... He blithely informed Wayne that the land has been warming up. Time to put his money where his mouth is. He slides off his helmet. The rawness of the air is an icy hand reaching down his throat. Scottie is staring at him. He hopes he won't lose consciousness or turn blue. A minute or two later, when it becomes clear that he's doing neither, she takes off her helmet as well. She exhales and a tiny breath cloud emerges. "Oh, that's cold... And the air—it's different —crisper, with a hint of rosemary in it."

"It's all the trees." He slides off his gloves to melt some of the pristine snow in one palm and wets his lips. "Ready to head back?"

Scottie is studying their home, the half-sphere sparkling in the bright sunshine. "Just like my snow globe, only with snow on the outside. Let's go into the forest."

"I'm not sure that's a good—"

But Scottie's gone ahead. Helmet and gloves in hand, he follows her in under the trees, and now the path is narrower, the ground rocky and tree-rooted under the snow. The canopy is a roof breached here and there by shafts of sunlight, leaving much of the forest floor tinted with silent shadows. The vast firs and pines are a contrast to Dome gardens, where dwarf and high-yielding are the prevailing adjectives. He spots an animal track—a fox, he hopes.

After several minutes of walking, Scottie slows down and he passes her, only to hear her exclaim, "Oh."

Dax whips around. "Is it a wolf?"

"It's Cece... I asked her if there's a snapshot of wolf tracks in the Knowledge Repository but she's not responding. Then I tried sending you a thought to wait up and *that* failed too. When Yesler said our CCs wouldn't work, I assumed we'd still be able to think at each other."

Dax tries it himself. The attempt to send a thought to Scottie across the path fails. It's unnerving, a limb gone numb. No, as if one of his senses evaporated and he can no longer hear or see. "The heartbeat signal," he says. "That's got to be it."

"Right—Cece mentioned it once. It's like an off switch, isn't it?" Scottie says. "Back when ConnectChips were invented—before domes, as a way to socialize and chat— people were worried about their minds being taken over. Cece said that CC Central transmits a signal to keep all the chips on."

"Well, the problem's easily solved—all we need to do is walk back a bit."

He starts to do so, but Scottie steps into the middle of the path. "Since we *are* all alone..."

Dax forgets all about the unresponsive chip in his brain. "Scottie, what are you doing?"

"Something I've wanted to do for a long while now."

Kissing, I discover, counters the cold quite nicely. After a long, very interesting minute, Dax and I pull away. His voice sounds different, rough and warm, a blanket enveloping us both. "I've wanted to do that myself so many times," he says. "I was worried I'd be responsible for sending you to the last place on the List."

"And I assumed you'd never go against the Code. But I figured the Code doesn't apply out here and grabbed the chance and hoped for the best."

After another enjoyable minute, he pulls away again. "Scottie?"

I bury my head in his shoulder. "Hmm?"

"You know we have a bit of a problem, don't you?"

"You mean section Q."

"Look, I'm good either way. We can tell people at once if you like, but if you want to enjoy being number one for as long as you can, I'm fine with that too."

I groan. "I'm not sure *enjoy* is the right word. I'm beginning to see why you never cared about perks or your tennis fame. People are staring at me wherever I go, the cafeteria, the bathroom, the street. Asking for gems and favors. Offering things they *hope* will lead to gems and favors."

"Tennis fame is simpler—it's just an equation. If you

win, they like you; if you lose, they don't." Dax adds insightfully, "That isn't what's bothering you, is it? It's something else."

"I went to the Birth Lab."

"Go on," he says quietly.

"Turns out I was right. The number one *can* just walk in and ask about their genetic record, section F be damned. Only the lab technician didn't even have to look me up. She already knew." I pull away to pace back and forth, the legs of the snowsuit swishing with each step. "According to her, Delilah *leaned* on the previous technician—that's how she put it, but I knew what she meant. Blackmail... Really, the story began earlier, when Delilah first went onstage. Tadeo was the theater manager and much older, forty-two to her twenty."

When I delivered invites to Delilah, I'd often pause in the lobby to study a framed photo. It showed a man with somewhat wild salt-and-pepper hair and deeply-etched creases around the eyes, not of worry but of laughter. Tadeo lived a full, happy life, which included a puppeteering hobby, until his death at age sixty-four, a decade before *Oliver* and *Scott* were assigned to a pair of three-month-olds who shared a conception day. Well liked, he was number eight at the time of his death.

"The lab technician said people whispered behind Delilah's back that she used Tadeo to get her first role," I relate more of what I learned, "but *she'd* heard that the relationship started after Delilah was already a star. Either way, at some point Delilah started gifting her doses of Eternal Life to Tadeo, week after week, until he passed away. Cancer of the bone—I guess even Eternal Life has its limits. And after... After, she wanted a child to remember him by. That must have been when her obsession with secrets started."

"Are you saying Delilah got her way? She was your mother and Tadeo your father?"

"She saved a lock of his hair. That and her skin cells, and a petri dish." I thought I'd walk out of the Birth Lab feeling whole. Instead, all that's there is anger. "Delilah never said a word, never dropped a hint, never sent an unguarded look in my direction."

"Maybe she thought you'd find it a burden, having to live up to her level of success." Dax pulls me back close and cups my face with his hands. "I suppose, now that you mention it, there is some resemblance. Your hair is darker"—he gently runs his fingers through it—"but you have her eyes."

"The Birth Lab made sure that I didn't resemble her *too* much. Her eyes—and her tooth gap. The technician—she seems to have been waiting for the chance to tell the whole story to someone—says Delilah spent her first five or six paychecks on a dentist."

"Well, I like your tooth gap. It goes with your smile."

"You'll have to learn to live without it. I have a dentist appointment on Friday. Look..." I hesitate, then come to a decision. "Let's keep this ours for now, but not because I care what others think. It's Jada."

The feeling that Jada may have gotten away with murder has been eating at me since the gala. I relate a moment from the tavern basement. "There was an apple barrel with its lid off, as if Bonnie was interrupted in the task of inventorying it... Maybe she *was*—by Jada, who bonked her on the head, dragged her to the back, and heaved a burlap sack down on her. Bonnie said she slipped on an oil slick, but she doesn't actually remember."

Dax takes all that I've said in stride. "What about what Bodi said, about the map showing no one but you and Bonnie?"

"Jada has the box of secrets now," I remind him.

"You think she got to Bodi—bribed or blackmailed him to look the other way?"

I shake my head. "Nah, Bodi is un-bribable and has nothing to be blackmailed with, I'm sure of that. I think she has a way of making herself invisible on the map. Don't ask me how—maybe someone in CC Central helps her or she's wearing layers of tinfoil on her head or whatever. She may have slipped out of the basement seconds before I got there, watched me go down. I did get a sense of there being eyes on me." A shudder runs down my spine, not from the cold.

Dax strokes my hair again. "I'm glad you didn't run into her. Who knows what might have happened."

"With any luck, I'd have managed to think at you *'It's Jada!'* before she pushed me down the stairs and broke my neck."

"Scottie, you need to be careful... You're the number one now."

"What about me being— Oh. You mean I might be the next target. Well, that's just great. I was just getting used to not being in the bog and now this. Jada isn't happy at all with me sitting at number one, I can tell you that much. I wonder if she knows about Delilah being my mother and that's why she dislikes me. Well, I'm not just going to go away. It's why I have to stay at the top, because it'll be easier to take her on from there. If she is behind this, she killed my mother."

Every part of that statement—and most of all the words *my mother*—is heavy indeed.

"Like I said, be careful."

Dax's arms around me and the sunlight dancing on the forest floor make me feel as if maybe I *should* let it all go— pretend I never found out Delilah was my mother, pretend

Jada's just an ordinary eatery manager and nothing more. I murmur, letting my head rest against Dax's shoulder again, "What if we just kept walking all the way to Old Seattle? We could find an abandoned house and live out the rest of our lives together."

"How would we get over the mountains?"

"We'd go up one side and down the other."

He gives a practical response to my daydream. "It'd take some preparation. But I'd say we've just learned a couple of things: that the cold is not too bad and that CCs won't do us any good out here. We'll have to come back out and experiment some more."

"I'm all for that," I say and we lose ourselves in one another again.

When we come up for air, Dax says somewhat formally, as if worried I'm going to change my mind about the whole thing, "Scottie... You'll always be my number one. You know that, don't you?"

The words are hard to get out as there's a lump in my throat. "And you mine."

I slip my hand into his and we walk side by side until we're out of the forest. Once in view of the Dome, we pull apart and don the gloves and helmets. My world has changed—there's no going back, but Dax and I will have to stay PALs in the public eye.

Yesler greets us with a sigh of relief. "Couldn't find you on the map for a few minutes there, Scott—almost had a heart attack. Enjoy yourselves?"

"Very much," I say.

Chapter Twenty-Eight

Dax scans the crowd packing the bleachers of the arena as he stretches. Left leg...right leg. Left leg...right leg. Angus is doing his own stretches on the other side of the court. Dax hopes no one has bet too much on him today—*No betting* is in the Code but the enforcement office turns a blind eye unless large sums are involved. He and Angus have played seven times. Dax lost every match.

"You thought I'd forget to come, didn't you?"

Scottie's at the side door of the arena, keeping a low profile. He breaks the stretch to wave to her and finds himself breathing a silent sigh of relief. He was worried something bad happened. *"I thought you might be busy with the town-leader stuff,"* he responds.

"Nope, just went to pick up my bike from the shop. Nice shorts. I had no idea your knees were so bony. Where do I sit?"

"Tacoma is saving you a seat."

"Where?"

"The section by the water station. He's in the third row, on the left si—"

"Got him, thanks."

As I watch Angus, who's muscular and mean-looking—or possibly merely concentrating hard—bounce a warm-up ball, Tacoma inches closer on the bench. This reminds me that I forgot to respond to his dinner invitation. "How have you been, Scottie?" he asks and switches to thought as Angus opens the match by slamming the ball across the court. *"Whatever you do, don't think at Dax during the match, in case he forgot to mute his CC. A thought out of nowhere can turn an easy return into a lost point."*

Angus repeats the ace. Dax manages to get his racket on the next served ball. He still loses the point, but it takes him a little longer. The first game goes to Angus, but now it's Dax's serve and he manages to win a few points before losing the game.

Tacoma extends his legs under the seat in front of him. *"Dax just needs to warm up a bit."*

"How long does a match usually last?"

"At this level? A couple of hours at least."

I settle into my seat. Lu and Wayne passed on coming along but promised to show up if there's a celebration to be had for Dax.

During one of the longer breaks in the match, as the players down water and towel off, I turn to Tacoma. "You were working at the theater when the chandelier fell, weren't you?"

"It wasn't my fault," Tacoma says, his ears flaming as if I've accused him of failing to personally dive under the chandelier to save Rick. "The cord snapped in two."

"Why?"

Before Monday, I would've worked the question into the conversation in a roundabout fashion; but everyone is eager to help the number one with anything and everything, including Tacoma, who asks, "Why what, Scottie?"

"Why did it snap?"

Tacoma looks at me as if I'm being obtuse. "Gemma Bligh's curse."

Wondering if Jada meant for the chandelier to fall on opening night or whether a later performance would have done just as well, I say, "The cord was old"—this is a good guess as most things in New Seattle are—"and with the chandelier being moved up and down during rehearsals for *Mrs. Montag*, it may have become worn through to the breaking point."

"Ah, but it wasn't moved up'n down."

At the next chance in the match Tacoma explains. "The chandelier—the cord was triple-strand twisted cotton—hadn't been moved for *years*. If they needed it, they just pulled the brocade curtain up a little higher. Rick got the idea to lower it at the final rehearsal with Vicky. We had to scramble to work it into the opening night performance, all while searching *everywhere* for boots that fit Vicky. Well, you were there, weren't you?"

"I was?"

"Vacuuming the lobby. I was gonna say hi but I had my hands too full to come over and chat. Vicky ended up wearing Delilah's boots but had to stuff them with socks so they wouldn't fall off. It was so on the nose that no one wanted to say it. You know—*big shoes to fill*."

At the next opportunity in the match—Dax has started to hold his own—I ask, "Who else was at the rehearsal when Rick had the idea? Other than cast and crew, I mean."

"Everyone."

"What do you mean, everyone?"

"Rick unveiled the idea on the Commons—*Spotlight on my big scene*. Didn't you see it?"

"Never really paid much attention to what Rick had to say."

"So," Tacoma declares as if this settles matters, "it had nothing to do with friction on the rope. The curse struck sharp and clean." He slices the air with one hand. "We didn't understand what Delilah's death meant until Rick was struck down, too. They died to make us see that we needed to change, be kinder... Hey, that was not out! Umpire, that's a BAD call! Get your act together, you—"

I try to wrap my head around the new information. Jada had to have gotten to the cord between rehearsal on Friday morning and the opening-night performance the following day. Not a lot of time. Still, no security guard means she could have masked her dot on the map, same as in Bonnie's tavern, hidden somewhere or other, and waited until everyone left for the day. Then it was a simple matter of filing away at the cord just beyond the point where it usually hung so that when the chandelier was lowered, it snapped.

Like Tacoma said, sharp and clean.

Dax slides his racquet back into the bag, stunned, as the crowd claps and roars. Scottie and Tacoma push their way over to him. Running a towel across the back of his neck, he greets them with a dazed, "I can't believe I pulled that off."

Tacoma high-fives him. "I can't believe it either."

"I'd give you a hug but you're dripping with sweat." Scottie inexpertly bounces one of the lime-green balls into the basket of them, then looks up to a shout from the stands. "Hey, it's Scott. Everyone, it's Scott the Curse Slayer!"

Soon the chant fills the room: "*Curse Slayer, Curse Slayer!*"

As if she's been doing this for years, Scottie waves back at the fans—*her* fans—and takes a bow. In a crisp new outfit that for once fits her petite form well, she swivels to wave in all four directions, all eyes on her. While Dax did manage to pull off a major upset, Scottie has the stage. Which is as it should be...if it weren't for what's worrying him. He reminded her to be careful, but he can't shake off the feeling of unease. To his own eyes, she seems exposed, vulnerable, the very opposite of what the number one spot should be— untouchable and removed from all manner of problems.

There's a firm tap on his shoulder. Angus, with a towel draped over his head, as if he's hiding from his loss. "Dax-ton, good game."

"Better luck next time, Angus."

They exchange an awkward handshake.

Angus is studying Scottie from underneath the towel. "She's so-so in looks, I've always thought, but now that she's number one, she's...improved."

The ugliness of the words makes Dax's blood boil—and even more so when Angus adds, "Does she have a boyfriend?"

He hears himself saying, "Yes. Me."

"But you're PALs."

"We are. What of it?"

Angus shrugs. "Not my business."

Dax watches him walk away. Damn. He promised Scottie he wouldn't say anything to anyone and he hasn't been able to keep his promise for a single day.

The celebration at Puget Chow for Dax's win is in full force, but I've slipped out early. His reminder that I might be the next target has left me shaken and I pedal fast, tensing each time I encounter a blind spot around a corner or a black gap under a staircase—where Jada, having masked her dot again, might be lying in wait to stick a broom handle into the spokes of my bike. I'm soon at Housing Thirty-Three. Though it's only a single flight up, I take the elevator, as it seems safer than taking the deserted stairs. Once the door to my room clicks shut behind me and I make sure the lock is turned, I exhale.

Kicking off my shoes, I manage to knock my elbow on the dresser, which sends the newly-purchased chocolate bars I stacked on top tumbling into a heap. I unwrap one of the bars and reflect that it might be nice to move to a bigger space. Though I have yet to respond, the Jobs and Housing Office has sent several inquiries asking if I'd like Delilah's old suite. The bite of chocolate melts in my mouth and I check myself. I'm starting to plan as if I'll stay number one a long time. My newfound fame rests on the lack of any further accidents—if anyone takes a tumble down a flight of stairs, the town will turn on me in a minute. I know very well that none of it is real.

Cross-legged on the bed, I wrap a blanket around my shoulders and finish off the rest of the chocolate bar. *Cece, wake up.*

You have thirty-seven thoughts awaiting your attention, Scott.

Are any of them from anyone I actually know?

There's a thought from Lu.

Lu and Wayne never did show up to Puget, but as Dax himself said, we can't begrudge them their alone time.

Wayne has only until Sunday—four days away. I lick a bit of chocolate off my finger. *What does she say?*

I CAN RELAY THE THOUGHT IN JUST UNDER A MINUTE, SCOTT.

Wait, why?

THE SENDER REQUESTED A DELAY OF TWO HOURS, OF WHICH THERE ARE FORTY-FIVE SECONDS LEFT ... THIRTY SECONDS ... FIFTEEN ... HERE IT IS: *"Forgive me, Scottie... I'm leaving with Wayne tonight. By the time you get this, it'll be too late to stop us. Be happy for us if you can."*

This makes me jump off the bed, sending the blanket tumbling off my shoulders. *Cece, why didn't you let me know at once?*

THE SENDER REQUESTED A DELAY OF TWO—

Never mind. Is the map still live? Find Lu and Wayne.

I'm already sliding on shoes. But Lu and Wayne are no longer in the Dome and there is nowhere for me to run to.

Chapter Twenty-Nine

Fighting off a yawn, I will myself out of bed. I was up half the night, tossing and turning. How could Lu leave without saying goodbye, after making us all promise to be PALs forever—after giving us PAL bracelets? She and Wayne must have been planning this for days.

Morning brings the realization that I'm more mad at myself than at Lu. I dress for my dental appointment—colorful fabrics are present and mended holes aren't, a repackaging that befits my new status—and methodically consume one of the chocolate bars as breakfast. I failed to see what was happening right under my nose: that my PAL was more in love than I knew. I didn't confide my own problems to her—my certainty that there's a killer in town, the Sherlock-Scottie plan, what happened with Dax in the forest, not even the *other* whopper news, about Delilah being my mother—and so Lu didn't confide in me in return. If I'd understood in time... I wouldn't have tried to stop her, no. I'd have given Wayne and her a last hug and all the chocolate on my dresser so they'd have something to trade.

On my way to the dentist, I fight off disquieting

thoughts. Nights must be much colder than the sunny jaunt Dax and I took into the forest. Are Lu and Wayne lying in a snowbank together, frozen in place forever? Did they keep walking all night and succeed in reaching a village? Will I ever see them again?

I roll to a stop under a Tenner billboard, where a snapshot of me at the gala has replaced the old one by the bike. A couple of pedestrians wave hello in my direction and my hand goes up in a wave back above the freshly-painted handlebars. The Curse Slayer brand is all others see, as if I'm wearing a cloak. The truth is that all the perks and trappings of the number one, the new clothes, the crowd cheering in my direction at Dax's tennis match, the stack of chocolate, all of it is nice enough...and as deep as the new shine on my bike. Distracted by the confetti shower of fame, I danced at the gala and kissed Dax in the forest and failed to notice the turmoil Lu must have been in. And I forgot about justice, readily accepted the story that there was no killer...until I found out about Delilah being my mother and it became personal.

I send a thought to the dentist apologizing for having to cancel, then bike at full speed to the Gardens Center, where, after catching my breath, I deliver an adamant, "Dax, we have to do something."

We're just outside his workplace—I caught him on his way in. He watches me kickstand the bike, then pulls me out of sight around the building's corner. "About Lu and Wayne? It's too late to try and catch up with them. I could kick myself for bringing up the whole endpoint thing. Wayne would have kept on toying with his rank in a leisurely fashion and Lu and he would still be here."

His words momentarily deflate my urgency. "She couldn't bear to let him go, and now they're both gone...but that's not what I meant." I square my shoulders. "I'm done being scared. Let's rattle Jada—finish this."

"How?" Dax asks.

I relay the plan I came up with on the way over. "We'll set a trap. I'll send her a thought saying that I know she killed Delilah and Rick and tried to kill Bonnie. Wait, even better—let's set a trap for *all of the Tenners*, in case I'm wrong about Jada. I'll ask each of them to bring something or other to buy my silence and we'll see who shows up."

Dax leans back against the wall with his feet crossed and shakes his head at me. "I don't like it. Too dangerous."

"You said it yourself—I'm already a target. But all right, I'll do it anonymously. Notes instead of thoughts, slipped under doors. I'll hide out of sight to see who shows up to drop off whatever item I ask for."

"You don't know how to write and neither do I," Dax brings up a practical objection. "It's not like we can go to a public notary and request a set of blackmail cards."

"I'll muddle through somehow." He still seems hesitant, so I ask, "Do you have a better idea?"

He concedes defeat and we make a plan to meet up at midnight.

After dinner, I move the floor lamp in my room over to the bed so its circle of light falls on the supplies I picked up at the market: a note-paper pad, yellowed with age, and two wooden pencils. "You'll also need this." The seller had handed me a squarish plastic thingamabob. "It sharpens the pencil when it goes dull."

I plop on the bed on my stomach. *Cece, let's do this. First, a secluded spot... I know, how about the apple tree where Dax and I listened to Ben the Birdman give a speech at the town party? It's right by the waste-processing plant, so it's usually deserted... That's WHERE, now for WHEN. Best to do it before the map goes live for the day, say half past six. Hopefully no one at the Security Office will pick up on anything odd going on... Which leaves the WHAT. Nothing too pricey—we want to give the impression of leaving the door open for future asks, just as a real blackmailer might do...*

Cece interrupts. BLACKMAIL. TO EXTORT MONEY OR A VALUABLE OBJECT FROM A PERSON BY THREATENING TO EXPOSE DISTASTEFUL INFORMATION. ARE YOU NOT A REAL BLACK-MAILER, SCOTT?

Of course not, Watson, it's just part of the investigation—a clever trap. Now, where was I?

THE WHAT.

Right, the item of value. An antique such as Bodi's silver letter opener?... Probably best not to meet a murderer by asking them to bring a knife... A basket filled with old-world knick-knacks? Too many letters to write... Wait, got it.

I ready the pencil above the first page of the notepad and dictate text for Cece to display in my eye field. Stopping now and then to erase mistakes, I copy down the letters one by one and end up with:

I KNOW YOU KILLED DELILAH AND RICK. BUY
OLD NEWSPAPER, LEAVE UNDER APPLE TREE
BY WASTE PLANT.
SATURDAY 6:30 a.m.

I sit up on the bed and study the resulting uneven, wonky letters. The note took twenty minutes, even with the choice of leaving out Bonnie's accident for the sake of brevity. I could have sent a thought to everyone in New Seattle in a thousandth of that time and cast the widest net possible, if only a way of doing so anonymously existed.

Having finished with Jada's note, I count how many

more I need and come up with eight: the other guests in Delilah's suite the night she died—minus Rick but keeping Bonnie as she might have faked her accident to throw suspicion off herself.

After a moment's consideration, I add one more name.

The guilty party will have all of tomorrow, Friday, to buy an old newspaper. It won't be market day, but there are a handful of permanent stalls selling items of that sort. As to why a newspaper, I'm curious about the world Tadeo—my father; I still can't get used to the idea—left behind.

As to the innocent, they'll be puzzled by the note and hopefully put it down to a prank in poor taste.

Sharpening the pencil, which takes off a thin and curly beige slice, I get started on the first letter of the next note.

Just before midnight, there's a knock on my door. Dax, in dark clothes and an old-fashioned baseball cap. He holds out an extra one. "Disguise. Don't lose it, I have to return them to the Gardens Center in the morning. We use them to keep the sun out of our eyes."

I reach out for the cap and wince. "My hand's all crampy —it took me two hours to write them all. Right, let's split up. I'll take half of the notes and you take the other—"

"Not letting you wander the streets alone in the dark, Scottie, with a murderer on the loose."

This causes me to grin at him for some reason. Dax's words send a romantic warmth through me—and, truth be told, I feel safer with him by my side. The ten folded notes in hand, we make the rounds along the deserted streets from one building to the next, starting with Blank Jack's room in Housing Thirty and ending at Jada's suite in Housing One.

Jada's living space is right under where Delilah's used to be—I never did respond to Jobs and Housing about whether

I want it. As I watch Dax slip the last of the notes under the door—the paper sticks a bit on the carpet and he has to nudge it in—it strikes again, the sense of being watched, same as in the tavern basement. The sparsely lit hallway is silent. At the far end, the door to the building stairwell is as we left it, propped open with a cap so we can leave as quietly as we came. Jada, staring at us through the peephole? The fish-eye lens reveals nothing. There's no map access at this time of the night for anyone to track us...except Bodi, who may very well have been keeping an eye on me since this all began.

Chapter Thirty

Delilah and Rick are nurturing a clutch of speckled eggs, fragile and wondrous at the end of Hugh's scope. There's a smudge on the lens and he uses a shirt corner to wipe it off before refocusing. The piebald sparrow—Hugh has named it Renee—comes into view. He's heard that its human counterpart has been offered the job of bird catcher. He's still hopeful that Bird Control is just a fad and that interest in his sparrows will fade.

Renee flies off and Hugh loses her in the glare of the sunrise. It's just as well. His mission today is peculiar and has nothing to do with birds. The matter encroaches on his credo of non-involvement in town affairs, but McKinsey and Bodi called on him to help. All other options were less than optimal.

He scans with the scope. There. Two walkers are ambling into the garden, their steps in harmony, as if they're comfortable in each others' presence underneath their dark caps. In the garden for the exercise of a dawn stroll? He thinks not.

The shorter of the two figures takes her cap off for a

moment to adjust it, giving him a glimpse of her face. It's Scott, the young woman who paid him a visit before she shot up to number one. The pair hide behind the above-ground pipe of the waste processing center as if lying in wait for someone, and Hugh does his job by taking snapshot after snapshot through the scope.

The bulky pipe hiding Dax and me belongs to the waste center but there's no smell, only a disturbing sound of sloshing liquid. The pipe bends and disappears into the ground at the perimeter of the Dome, the waste it carries destined for fertilizer in the greenhouses, according to Dax, who's had plenty of time to chat about it. It's a quarter of an hour past the time designated on my blackmail notes and the sole creatures in and about the apple tree thus far have been a couple of sparrows. Dax and I have gone from crouching behind the pipe to sitting on the ground with our backs against it, our feet stretched out.

I unwrap another bar. "More chocolate?"

"Aren't you sick of eating it?"

"Nope," I answer through a mouthful.

Dax gives a large yawn. "This murder investigation is turning out to be killer on my sleep. Couldn't we have watched the map from bed to see who showed up?"

"The map isn't live for another fifteen minutes. Even if it were live, you would have still needed to be awake."

"At least I could have stayed in my pajamas."

I'm still getting used to the new reality—Dax and I going from being PALs at arm's length to this new bond, all the barriers gone.

"If someone does show up," he continues, "you're not gonna jump out to confront them, are you, Scottie?"

"I thought of it," I admit. "No, we'll stay hidden and see who it is, then bring everything we have to Bodi and hope he takes us seriously."

"He'll take you seriously. After all, you're the—"

"Shh, someone's coming."

We roll back into the crouched position but the jogger passes by without so much as a glance at the tree. "False alarm. What were you going to say, Dax?"

"That Bodi can't dismiss you like before. You're the number one."

"I keep forgetting that."

Another ten minutes go by and Dax gets to his feet and lends a hand to pull me up. "So it's none of them—or the killer knew that it was a trap."

Either way, we need to leave before anyone figures out our identity when the map goes live.

"I wonder if we've been thinking about it all wrong," I say as, holding hands, we take the garden path through a patch of sunflowers rustling in the draft of one of the big air turbines. "I realized something... Being number one and the stuff that comes with it, the perks, the parties, the attention...it's a hollow affair, an illusion, and it took me all of four days to figure that out. Jada knows that it's an illusion. She still wants it and would be willing to lie, cheat, and steal to get there, I'm sure...but murder is different. It seems to me that whoever it is that's hungering for number one—*enough to kill for it*—must have a stronger motive than their face at the top of a billboard or extra perks—or even Eternal Life."

"What other reason is there for wanting to be number one?" Dax asks.

"Someone's looking not for the illusion but the real thing."

"The real thing?"

We've reached the perimeter of the garden. On the open street, foot traffic is picking up for the day. "Love."

"Love you back, Scottie."

I give his hand a final squeeze before letting go. "What the killer wants is more of a one-sided kind of love. Adoration." I gesture at the buildings bathed in the morning light, a crisp new day breaking over New Seattle. "From all of us—the whole town."

Dax scratches his chin under the cap. "Is that why you included Blank Jack? I suppose he did lose everyone he had—who knows how that can affect a person? The past couple of years must have been lonely for him. Still, how would he have gotten access to Delilah's suite?"

"One thing I learned vacuuming is that no one noticed me much. People are always going in and out of places—food deliveries, maintenance staff, cleaners, and so on." Cece breaks in and I add, "I have to go—McKinsey wants to see me."

At the Agency, three people are waiting for me. My boss is at her desk, with Bodi to one side—on his feet and arms crossed below his usual unreadable expression—and Hugh on the other. My interactions with McKinsey since my luck changed have been awkward—she's my boss but I'm above her on the social and affluence scale, which has lent an air of over-politeness to our recent conversations—but now her gaze is steely. She slides one of the blackmail notes in my direction across the desk. "What kind of tasteless prank is this, Scott? You slipped this under my door, didn't you? Don't bother denying it."

Words tumble out of me. "It's not a prank. I was trying to draw out Delilah and Rick's killer."

I'm not sure I've ever seen McKinsey rendered speechless. When she does finally find her tongue, it's sharp. "You think *I* killed Delilah and Rick?"

My ears are burning with shame. "No—I was just trying to be thorough by writing ten notes."

"Ten? Good Lord," Bodi says. "Who else got them?"

"All of the Tenners, current and recent—except for Renee."

"At least Renee escaped a nasty message under her door." McKinsey's tone is icy enough to pierce skin.

I have a question for Bodi. "Have you been watching me on the map?"

"We don't do that kind of thing, stalk people. Hugh saw from the roof— No, I won't ask who the other person was."

I was about to insist that Dax's presence in the garden was purely accidental and that he had no knowledge of any blackmail.

Bodi picks up the note. "No one showed up carrying a newspaper, did they, so will you *finally* quit pursuing this now, Scott?"

"Even if I think I'm in danger?"

"Because you're number one?" A crack appears in McKinsey's wall of anger. "Scott, I think it's fine to relax and enjoy your newfound wealth and fame. Everyone feels like an imposter at first. No one is out to get you."

Touched by McKinsey's compassion after I accused her of murder, all I want is to leave. But there's a question to be asked first. My new rank did not come with a side serving of wisdom. I'm not untouchable. "Am I fired—again?"

"For trying to blackmail your boss? For hassling fine,

upstanding New Seattle citizens? We haven't decided yet." McKinsey holds up a hand to forestall any response from me and says, "Discussion," and I know the three are silently chatting about me. All I can do is stand with my head bowed.

After Bodi and Hugh leave, Hugh still not having said a word, McKinsey explains why I was summoned to her office and not to security. "Bodi guessed it was you and suggested we handle this outside the Security Office. Consider yourself lucky—the three of us decided there's been too much upheaval these past few weeks. We'll put out the word that a prank got out of hand. Your name will be kept out of it. And no, you're not fired. The number one is never fired."

She lobs a final piece of advice in my direction. "In the future, Scott, keep in mind that you don't have to approach things underhandedly anymore. What you think is important, others will."

Deciding to test this, I run downstairs to catch up with Bodi.

Chapter Thirty-One

Bodi's gaze is less weighty on me now; if he still suspected me of being behind the attacks, my rash blackmail plan has surely convinced him otherwise. I've caught up with him on the front steps of Town Offices One. He asks, "What is it, Scott?"

I deliver the answer with the imagined authority of the number one. "Renee. You did her intake interview. What did she tell you about herself?"

Bodi's significant eyebrows register amusement at my tone. "There's nothing of note in her backstory."

"She must have had a life Outside," I insist before he has a chance to walk away. Renee the Recluse, Chase called her. She was a no-show at the gala and the Tenner meeting. Is she still getting used to her new life, or is it something else?

Bodi, as if the whims of the number one must be somewhat indulged, says, "Look, if someone asks to stay—happens once every couple of years—I look at *character*, not the background details. Does the individual seem trustworthy and honest? Will they do their job and stay out of trouble? Blank Jack gave the impression of hiding something. While that did turn out to be the case, it wasn't anything sordid, just a sad family story. Renee was open and frank with me."

"Did she say what made her come in?"

"Sometimes a person just wants a fresh start. I think she'll fit in fine."

After the building doors close behind him, I instruct, *Cece, locate Renee.*

She's outside Work Three.

Work Three is not far. I walk over only to find that Renee's been on the move, the map now showing her a couple of blocks away, near Medical Two. Rather than chase her further, I decide to look for her in the evening.

I make my way to the Jobs and Housing Office, which also doubles as the town warehouse. It's my first time here, my bike-errand and vacuuming assignments having always arrived via thought. A harried-looking clerk occupies an oversized desk in the middle of a cavernous space. If there were supplies stocked up around the desk in the past, the years have shrunk them down to a handful of crates and cardboard boxes stacked in corners. My voice echoes a bit as I address the clerk. "I came to ask about Renee."

"No time to look that up," he all but barks in my direction; except for constant blinking, his eyes seem to be permanently stuck in the low-left position. "I think tasks *out*"—blink—"and they either get done, or don't, in which case they boomerang back to me and we do another round. At the *moment*"—blink—"I've got twenty-five things to deal with: a leaky sink has been reported and I need Maintenance to deal with *that*"—blink—"and someone wants to switch floors so I have to look into *that*"—blink—"and the Housing Twelve cafeteria fridge died in the night and a cleaning crew needs to deal with *that*"—blink—"and I've had to dig up a paper map for the new bird catcher, so there's *that*—"

"Renee's working already?" I interrupt. I do some quick math; according to what Bonnie said in the Tenner meeting, Renee was scheduled for the chip implant on Wednesday. "It's only three days after her surgery."

"It's *micro*surgery—a tiny incision for the chip and a tiny hole in the skull for the mesh syringe, and you're all *done*—" The clerk blinks in my direction and an aghast expression overwrites the harried one. "Scott, my apologies, didn't mean to be rude. Let me check the details for you at once... Renee, you said? Let's see, she came in"—blink—"on the twenty-sixth of March, a Friday. She was originally in"—blink—"Housing Thirty, but I moved her after her fortunes improved." He makes eye contact with me again. "The suite that used to be Rick's. Since she's still—as you so rightfully pointed out—recovering from surgery and in the training phase of her CC, she's doing only light work for the moment. Ben has her marking nest locations on the paper map."

"What's she like?"

He gets back to work. "Who can remember? Like I *said*" —blink—"I've got twenty-five things to deal with—no, twenty-*nine*..."

After a filling dinner at the Housing Thirty-Three cafeteria —a meal during which plenty of trays joined my own at the table—I kickstand my bike outside Housing Two. Dax offered to come along, but I figure it's best if I visit Renee on my own, given how skittish she seems to be.

I'm here not because Jada wants to know all about Renee

and has given the Curse Slayer the job. *Make her your friend*, she said, a sinister and repulsive order. No, the vibe I've been trusting all along is telling me that I need to talk to Renee. That she has a reason for keeping a low profile. And that my life may depend on knowing what it is.

Before going into the building, I have Cece show me the snapshot of Renee. I've glimpsed it on billboards but now I study it in my eye-field. Renee is smiling at whoever took the snapshot—a sophisticated, composed smile that reveals a set of teeth so perfect as to make me jealous. Her features are smooth and unweathered, as if the cold was kinder to her than to Blank Jack, though of course she is twenty-six— half his age. The most striking thing is her mass of hair, tumbling past the shoulders of her white top.

There's something about the image, but I can't quite put my finger on it. I stare at it a long time.

Inside, a knock on the door marked Suite One produces no answer.

I knock more loudly. "It's Scottie. I dropped by to introduce myself and say hello."

The map shows Renee at home, her dot blinking bright red in the main room of the suite. No way to tell if she's ignoring my knock or napping on a couch oblivious to my presence. Feeling foolish, I press on. "Hope you're healing well from the ConnectChip surgery and settling in fine. All the attention—well, I'm not used to it either. To be honest, I'd be glad of a friend."

The door stays shut in my face.

Back in my room, I ready for bed, the full belly making me drowsy, and soon drift off to sleep. The dream that comes is of mountains peaks covered not in snow like in my window but vibrant gems. Delilah is pulling me up the glittering slopes and at the same time I'm pulling her down. We see-saw, gems crunching under our feet, until, in one moment of horror, dream-me sees that Delilah's face is my own and that I'm in a battle with myself. Then the gems collapse in an avalanche, burying me alive...

I wake up in a sweat. Getting out of bed for a drink of water from the pitcher on the corner table, I stub my toe and swear in a fashion that would cause Cece, if I hadn't put her in sleep mode, to brightly inform me that the Code of Conduct frowns majorly upon that particular word. I pour water into a glass, drain it, and get back in bed. The dream isn't hard to interpret. I'm feeling exposed, beset by worries that all my new gems will be the death of me—as the number-one crown was for my mother. I spend the remainder of the night tossing and turning, unable to shake off the fear that the killer is watching from the shadows, biding their time.

Morning brings a thought from Renee. It's choppy—she's still getting used to her CC—and makes her sound hesitant, like Poulsbo. "Scott... *How awesome of you to stop by my place...last night. I'm still getting used to my new life, would prefer to be left alone...to do so. I hope you...understand.*"

Chapter Thirty-Two

7:55 p.m.

Twenty-four hours have passed since I tried to befriend Renee and here I am nearing her doorstep again. Muffled sounds of evening activities seep out from behind doors and walls as I take the hallway to her suite. Though she requested privacy, I plan to keep on knocking until she lets me in.

I do so, loudly enough that I'm more hammering on the door, and a neighbor down the hall pokes their head out to see what the commotion is. A belated thought occurs to me. *Cece, people map.*

I've just missed her—Renee's dot is headed away from the building, one of many in Founders Square. I give myself a mental kick for forgetting to check beforehand and gauge whether I can catch up with her if I hurry. Then I have an idea. It's not perhaps the best idea, but I follow through with it anyway.

I press the handle.

The door is unlocked and swings open. I fumble for the light switch and find it. The stillness of a living space unoccupied at the moment greets me. "Anyone here?" I call out even though I know no one is nearer than the neighboring suite, and squat down to pick up what's at my feet: the Tenner gala invite. Ty slid it under the door on Monday morning, six days ago—the day her fortunes improved, as the Jobs and Housing clerk put it. Renee hasn't bothered to pick it up. Remembering that I haven't gotten around to giving Ty the ruby I promised and feeling bad about it, I close the door behind me and set the invite on the living room table, then take a look around. Renee's suite—Rick's old space—is spacious and bright, if a bit bare; whatever knick-knacks Rick had would have gone to the warehouse and Renee hasn't added any yet.

I poke around a bit. The personal fridge is well-stocked with Tenner fare, the sink empty of dishes and dry. Spread out on the kitchen table is the paper map the clerk mentioned, bent at the corners with age and torn here and there along well-worn folds. Renee has been marking nest locations with neat x's and additional details: "nest in tree," "second floor, nest in crack above window sill," and "nest on roof water tower." She has decent hand-writing skills.

The map is the main sign of life. In the bedroom, the pillows are fluffed up, the blanket creaseless. Same as the living room, the bedside table lacks any personal items. Neatly folded linens and a small selection of clothes occupy the dresser drawers. In the bathroom, the towels are pristine, the toothbrush new. Sometimes a person just wants a fresh start, Bodi said, and Renee has gotten hers.

Back in the living room, I push the balcony doors open. What used to be Rick's view faces north; Delilah's suite, across the square one floor up, is fully dark. As to the suite

I'm currently trespassing in, a quick check of the map produces the information that its occupant is to be found at the entrance to the Oyster. I peer over the railing, but I'm too high up and the figures under the streetlamps are small and indistinguishable.

Remembering to slide the invite back on the floor where I found it, I leave, closing the door softly behind me.

***

9:35 p.m.

The eatery doors shut behind Jada. It's been a frustrating evening and she's come out front to regain her composure, out of sight of her patrons and staff. She takes a few calming breaths, then immediately loses the calm as a figure steps out of the shadows. "Lu—you didn't treat her well."

The voice leveling the accusation vibrates with anger— No, not anger. Resolve. Youth. Bravado. Fear. So many things at once. It's Scott, in the shadows of a dark streetlamp. It always struck Jada as ridiculous that so scrawny a person should produce such a deep, memorable voice. With little interest, she asks, "Who's Lu?"

"She worked in your eatery. She left with Wayne."

"Oh, that's right. The other pair of young lovers. Are you sad that she left, is that it? Don't be. Sadness is a wasted emotion. It was a foolish thing for them to do—they didn't understand how easy they had it here. Well, by now I'm sure they do and regret their choice... Now if a person has a *forbidden* love, that might get you sent out whether you want to or not. You should have taken me up on my offer—poked around Renee's life."

The crown has made Scott pushy. In a reversal of roles, she proceeds to demand, "Renee was just here, wasn't she? What did she say?"

Jada's stomach muscles tighten. She didn't foresee this—any of it. Three intruders, under-qualified gatecrashers, in the Ten. At the gala, Blank Jack struck her as being raw in his emotions underneath the down-to-earth demeanor, his weak spot his lost family. He won't be a problem...but he is unlikely to be useful either. She tried, telling him "Together we could ensure you stay a Tenner as long as you like." The response was an obstinate "I don't expect to be in the Ten for long."

Renee was going to be different. Jada sent a dinner invitation and received a speedy response, the thought shaky and jagged. "*Yes, I will...come. Eight...o'clock.*" Figuring that the best way to court an Outsider used to scarcity and hardship was to pamper them, Jada had readied the best table in the house, double-checked that the silverware was spotless, and brought out a bottle of wine and a basket overflowing with rolls and butter.

Things did not go according to plan—Renee's playing games—and so she came out to quell her rage. She dismisses Scott with, "I don't discuss my guests," and goes back inside to resume her duties.

Chapter Thirty-Three

Scottie is waiting under a streetlamp, the one that was flickering before and is now unlit. Dax, approaching, asks, "Why did you have me meet you here, Scottie, so we could eat at the Oyster again? It's late, I've already had dinner."

"Me too, a burger from down the street. Ate it here, on my feet. I've been watching the eatery doors—she must have gone out the back, unless I missed her."

"Who, Jada? What's going on?"

"Not Jada. Renee. C'mon, we don't have much time before the map goes dark for the night. She's two blocks away." Scottie grabs his elbow and her eyes go low left. "I'll keep an eye on the map and you make sure I don't trip over anything."

He matches her walking pace and, after they've passed a block, asks, "Why are we following Renee?"

"This way... To find out why she's been hiding."

After another minute or two, he suggests, "She's used to living in a village. Maybe she needs time to get accustomed to sharing an enclosed space with ten thousand of us."

"There are other odd things. Her suite is quite bare and

— Yes, I know an Outsider probably doesn't have many possessions."

"Watch out, there's a step up onto the curb. That isn't what I was going to say. How do you know her suite is bare?"

"I went in when she wasn't around." Scottie adds at his reaction, "Well, the door *was* unlocked and I did knock first. The space is lifeless, as if she's afraid to be messy or to add too many of her own things yet... And there's *something* about her snapshot."

"Stop for a moment." He pulls up the image of Renee. "She's...memorable."

"All that hair, I know. Does she look familiar to you?"

"Can't say that she does," Dax shakes his head, "but you know I'm not good with faces."

"I wonder if I've seen her before—at the trader market. Maybe I bought a tire patch from her. Hurry, she's getting away." They start following the dot again and Scottie speculates, "What if she was here that night—the night of the murder? The traders arrive late on Monday, then set up at Pike Place Market and sleep in their booths, don't they? Make a right... It was the evening of the town party and security was light. If Renee took an unauthorized stroll outside the market in the late hours, she may have seen the killer running out of Housing One."

"If that was the case, why wouldn't she have said anything?"

"At first I assumed it took her a while to put it all together. But now I wonder if she's been here since then, sleeping on an Edge Garden bench. It's a small thing, but I can't explain it—in a thought to me, she used the word 'awesome'. It used to mean great, wonderful. I put it in Rick's onyx. It got a brief amount of attention, mostly from people like Magda and her ilk—something to taunt me with. Renee supposedly came in on the twenty-sixth and the next day the chandelier fell and not even Magda, Mia, and Audrey cared about my onyx for Rick anymore."

"For all we know, the word is still in use in the villages. Watch out for the streetlamp... Either way, it doesn't answer the question of why she hasn't gone to the Security Office."

"Because she's doing what we attempted yesterday, but for real. Blackmail... *Oh.*" Scottie stops so suddenly Dax almost runs into her. She releases the map, her eyes wide. "I just had a terrible thought. What if Renee's dead—another victim? And that's why she was a no-show at the Tenner meeting and the gala and why I can't seem to run into her anywhere. She tried to blackmail the killer and things went wrong."

"We're following her on the map," he points out.

"We're following a dot." Scottie is staring at him in horror. "What if the killer murdered Renee, then dug out her newly-implanted ConnectChip and is carrying it around to delay discovery—while masking their own chip?"

"Scottie, that's horrible. What would they have done with her body?"

"The sewers, perhaps."

"The sewers have grates. Anything large would be noticed."

Scottie responds with a grim, "Maybe they lured her back outside the Dome, killed her, dug the chip out, then covered her body with snow. That's how I'd do it."

"Remind me never to anger you. Wouldn't the gate guard have noticed if two people went out but only one came back, covered in the other person's blood?"

"The killer could have wiped off the blood with snow and waited until the guard change." She starts moving again, her tone still horrified. "The dot's slowing down, c'mon. This way... Damn."

After taking them away from the town center, the dot has circled back to Founders Square just as the map's gone dark for the night. They split up so as not to miss Renee if she's alive and well. Dax enters his side of the square to find that the Jokers have arrived with a rowdy crowd in tow. He elbows through, but it's impossible to zero on a single face in the shuffling mass of people. He meets up with Scottie at the halfway point and she greets him with a short shake of her head.

Defeated, they exit the square.

Gloomily, as if they've lost the first two sets of a tennis match and it's getting harder to see the win, Scottie says, "The killer's outsmarted us at every step. They must have a key to Renee's suite. And a way to hack her ConnectChip— is that even possible? She's been responding to in-thoughts, accepting called-in nests, marking them on a paper map."

"I imagine anything can be hacked."

"I'll stop by CC Central tomorrow to ask about it."

Dax reaches into a pocket. "Here, I got you this."

He's brought a pair of antique opera glasses; he found them at an old-world-goods market stall. The two halves carry hand-painted pictures of a meadow, one side with a girl skipping along in bare feet and the other with a boy in a straw hat playing a flute. "I thought we could take them with us next time we go into the forest and search for wildlife—at a distance."

"And for a dead body." Despite the bleakness of the words, she seems buoyed by his gift. Midway to hanging the felt strap around her neck, her gaze goes low left. "An urgent in-thought from Bodi... He wants to see me first thing in the morning. Regarding a Code violation." She blinks. "Well, that's that. Jada must have reported us."

They've stopped under a streetlamp—a working one. There's no getting out of it. He needs to come clean. "Er...it may not have been Jada. Look, I've been meaning to mention this... I messed up. The other day, after the finals match."

"What do you mean?" The weight is back on her shoulders.

"Angus asked if you had a boyfriend and I said yes. Me."

"You what?"

"I don't know what came over me. I just blurted it out. Actually, Tacoma sort of knows as well, though I'm sure he wasn't the one who reported us."

"Why not? Airing the Curse Slayer's dirty laundry... Who could resist?" The light from the streetlamp reveals the fury in her eyes.

His fist goes to the top of his head, an itch of embarrassment, not skin. "You did tell me that you don't care what people think."

"I also said I wanted to stay number one," she all but spits out.

He responds with all the wrong words. "Why? Because you have people adoring you, an exclusive brand, a stack of chocolate bars on your dresser—and now it'll all evaporate?"

She brushes his words aside. "You know I don't care about any of that stuff."

"We can still look for the killer, no matter where you are on the List."

"You said it yourself, Bodi takes me seriously now. Once I tumble back down into the bottom thousand, do you think I can just stroll into the Security Office and demand he bring Renee in for questioning—if she's alive? Or pop into CC Central to request they check if anything strange is going on with Renee's chip? This will tie my hands and I'll never find out who killed my mother. I thought I could trust you to stick by me. You're all that I have left. Just... Just go back to your soil and your ants."

He watches her storm away. He *did* mess up and tried to make up for it with a cheesy present. But this isn't about that. It's about Lu leaving with no warning and someone else turning his back so long ago—Oliver. And Delilah taking the secret of Scottie's birth to her grave. It's about the people she trusted and lost.

Chapter Thirty-Four

Monday, April 12

"Scott, take a seat," Bodi nods at me. I'm back in his troublemaker books. "Had a report late yesterday. Section Q violation. You and Daxton. An ongoing thing."

"Who reported us?" I ask, pondering if something that's been a *thing* less than a week and perhaps no longer than that can be called ongoing.

"Reports are confidential... Let's just say it was from a source high up."

So not Angus or Tacoma, then. Jada, and my outburst at Dax was for nothing. Maybe my whole stupid love theory was just that—stupid—and it's been Jada all along. She's probably wearing a satisfied smirk that she's managed to neutralize me.

"Having said that," Bodi continues, "we tend to get a lot of exaggerated or outright false reports, even from sources high up. I've brought you in to give you a chance to deny or explain."

"There's nothing to deny, nothing to explain," I say. "PALs cannot be lovers, and Dax and I are."

"You know, when I told you to stop pursuing a non-existent killer and find something else to do, this is not what I had in mind." He studies me across the table. "The notes-under-the-door thing we could pass off as a prank as you had no tangible information to blackmail with. This I can't sweep under the rug. Whatever I personally think of section Q and those who snitch on violators, the stability and security of New Seattle rests on the Code of Conduct."

"Do you need me to go up to Code Enforcement and repeat my statement?" I offer.

"There's no urgency. It'll take me a few days to investigate this properly and to get Daxton in here for a statement. Then I'll pass the matter on upstairs."

And once he does, a section Q violation onyx and censure from the rest of the town will follow. For the time being, the snapshot of me in the gala gown is still at the top of the billboard across the street. I get to my feet. "Is that it?" At his nod, I add, "Bodi... Are you sitting on this so I could have one last week as the number one?"

Bodi reaches behind him for the letter opener from the desk and scratches something off a nail. "A Sunday evening report must be approached in an unrushed manner. Just doing my job properly... Now don't you have a Tenner event of some sort to get ready for?"

I do—earlier, Ty slid an invite for an evening music performance under my door. I check my tires and chain before getting back on the bike.

Chapter Thirty-Five

8:01 a.m.

It's Wednesday and I'm not expected at the Agency until the afternoon. I'm filling time by gathering my old clothes and linens to be donated to the warehouse. Dax and I have made up and are keeping our heads down while we wait for the news to drop.

I've set a dresser drawer on the bed to organize its contents. The first to go are a couple of old towels, which I fold into the basket by the foot of the bed. Taking their place are new ones, thick and fluffy. I run my hand across them; the cotton is so soft under my fingers that I feel I could disappear into it and stay all cozied up forever. Safe. What sent me storming away from Dax wasn't only that he shook my trust in him for a brief moment—somewhere in the most vulnerable part of my belly lies a fear. Fear of going back to being Scottie the No One. It's easy to pretend you're worthy when rubies are flowing in.

And then it hits me—truly hits me for the first time—that I *am* someone now and it's not Scott the Curse Slayer. I'm a daughter. Of Delilah, stage actor and playwright, and Tadeo, theater manager and puppeteer. And no one can ever take that away.

I pull out the next drawer and upend its contents onto the bed when a blur of wings startles me. A sparrow has flown in through the open window. It has different coloring—white patches dot its body, marring the usual brown. I watch it circle the room and settle on the top of the dresser. Frustration tenses my muscles—why is it here, this strange creature?

"What do you want, bird?" Dresser drawer in hand, I take a step closer. "What do any of you want?"

8:12 a.m.
The Social Agency

Hugh has made a discovery through the scope. In the upper branches of the apple tree, Delilah and Rick are now care-takers of hatchlings, the tight mass of beaks eager for suste-nance and for life. The piebald trespasser he nicknamed Renee has not been back.

A thorny issue is keeping him on the roof even though he's long finished his breakfast pastry. He rarely uses the thought-relaying capability of his ConnectChip, but he does so now. *"Ben, this is Hugh from the Social Agency with a question. You're in charge of Bird Control, is that correct, and therefore Renee's boss?"*

"Yes, do you have a nest to report?"

Hugh understands that the sparrows must go—though still not why—but it doesn't mean he needs to help make it happen faster. *"No, no report. Ben, how have you found her to be?"*

"I'm not following?"

"I'm asking about your impression of Renee."

"She seems right for the job. I'm sure she'll do fine," Ben tells him and adds, *"Don't forget to call in any nests to her."*

Hugh heads back down to his desk. Monday's update brought a single change to the billboard out front, and he's been puzzling over it for a couple of days now. Renee has shot up to number two, just below Scott. What he was looking for in that exchange with Ben was a reason.

8:21 a.m.

I'm on my feet. The white-patched sparrow is on the linoleum floor of my room, still and small. There's a dresser drawer in my hands. A dark stain mars one corner. Did the bird attack me? That must be it. It attacked and I fought back.

Sliding the drawer back into its slot conceals the stain.

Functioning on autopilot, I finish my task of sorting the clothes and linens. Setting aside one of my old outfits and a tattered hand towel, I place the rest outside my door to be picked up. The sparrow is light as I wrap it in the hand towel. I know what to do with dead bodies. They're needed in the Edge Garden as fertilizer.

Having changed into the old set of clothes, I slip

Delilah's invite into a pocket, as I did for her seeding, and slide the binoculars Dax gave me around my neck. After the door closes behind me, Cece pipes up. SCOTT, YOU HAVE AN URGENT THOUGHT—THE CODE ENFORCEMENT OFFICE.

It can wait.

The towel with its small burden in the bike basket, I pedal to the garden. It doesn't take long to dispose of the bird in the coffee-plant patch. I'm unsure what to do with the towel, as it now seems unsanitary, and I end up stuffing it under one of the plants.

The path out takes me past the apple tree, where there are now hatchlings.

My next stop is Medical One. I'm given a vial holding a cloudy liquid and instructed to shake it well before consuming. Eternal Life has a grainy, metallic flavor and a bitter aftertaste. I finish every drop. By the time I'm back on my bike, the cocktail has kicked in and my mood lifts. *Cece, bring up the WHO KILLED DELILAH corkboard, erase everything and throw this on: Is Renee alive or dead?*

ACCORDING TO THE TOWN OFFICES DATABASE, RENEE WORKS AS A BIRD CATCHER AND LIVES IN HOUSING TWO, Cece helpfully supplies. SHE IS SECOND ON THE PEOPLE LIST.

Yeah, I noticed that.

HAS HARM BEFALLEN HER?

We're going to find out... Send Renee a thought: "Nest, in the apple tree by the waste processing plant."

Cece asks as I pedal, HOW WILL THAT REVEAL RENEE'S CURRENT STATUS, SCOTT?

Either Renee will show up to catalog the nest—or the killer will, with Renee's chip in their pocket. I'll watch from behind the waste pipe... Wait, no, I've got a better idea.

I shift my course toward the Agency. On the shuddery ride up in the elevator past the floor that holds my new office—Wayne's old space—I take a few deep breaths. I've been tense for days, ever since I found out that Delilah was my mother. On the top floor, I take the hallway past Hugh's office. The door is closed but a vertical strip of glass allows me to see inside—he's hunched over his computer, gems streaming across the screen. At the hallway end is a narrow staircase. I've never been on the roof as I wasn't sure if it was allowed, but nothing is off limits for the number one.

The roof, I find, holds a water tower and a garden bed with flowers and a palm tree. A single chair waits in the shade of the palm, arranged so it faces the Edge Garden. Hugh probably sat in it and watched Dax and me lie in wait behind the waste pipe. Passing on the chair, I perch on the knee-high ledge that rims the roof, my feet on the inside and Dax's binoculars at the ready. The day is a gray one, snow clouds gathering to the north. It always feels colder on days like this, and the concrete is chilly under my body.

The map yields the info that Renee is still in her suite. I settle in to wait, switching periodically between the map and the binoculars. The magnification is weak and what's at the other end, the apple tree and a couple of sparrows, is smudgy and out of focus. The map has its own weakness— that part of the garden is blank, greenery not showing up on it.

Minutes tick away.

I check the map again. There—Renee is headed out of Housing Two, or, at least, her dot is. I should have kept my eye firmly on the map to see if a second dot popped in to collect her ConnectChip, but now it's just one of many moving along the square. She's making good time, as if jogging over. It's four blocks to the garden.

Three blocks.

Two.

One.

Renee's dot bops along into the garden—a single dot. She's alive and well, unless someone is masking their own chip, as they must have in the basement of the Dragon and the Drumstick. The dot reaches the center of the blank spot where the apple tree is and stops. I release the map and refocus the binoculars.

Other than the pair of birds and their young, there's not a soul by the tree.

Cece, snapshot, I instruct—as if that will show something other than what my eyes are seeing—and brainstorm possible explanations. Could Renee's chip be attached to one of the sparrows? Maybe someone has been training them and that's why they seem different and why one attacked me. But the out-of-focus sparrows have been flitting around the tree all the while, feeding the hatchlings, not flying to Housing Two and back. Does an underground train-track lead in that direction and is Renee *beneath* the tree? Switching to 3D mode rules that possibility out; the tracks are some distance away and the map has the dot at ground level.

With a gut-deep feeling of unease, I send a thought: *"Were you able to find the nest?"*

This time Renee's mastery of thought-exchanges is much improved. *"In the apple tree, as you reported. I will mark it on my paper map."*

I ask straight out, *"Are you really Renee?"*

"Who else would I be?"

"I don't know. I thought there might be a...problem."

"I'm not the problem here. You are."

I get to my feet. Having taken the binoculars off, I play with the felt strap and slowly circle the roof edge, trying to make sense of things. If that's really Renee, she isn't acting like a scared Outsider, in hiding because she's afraid of becoming the killer's next victim. She sounds bold, as if she has the upper hand.

As if she's the killer herself.

Then there's the small matter of only the birds by the apple tree.

No person to accompany the dot... No person... Could Renee be a fake identity? A nonexistent Outsider welcomed to New Seattle. It would have taken some doing: Pretend to come in. Pass the health exam. Provide a snapshot. Catalog the nests—I saw the handwriting on the paper map with my own eyes. It's a long list. Each item would need to be faked, the ruse kept up nonstop. Still, it's not impossible. The busy clerk at Jobs and Housing irritably stated that Renee got the ConnectChip, but it's not as if he personally supervised the procedure—presumably he was notified in a thought; and he in turn informed others of her assigned housing and so on.

But Bodi talked to Renee in person. Did someone wear a wig to fool him?

I grunt in exasperation. Dax said that we should be on the lookout for the simplest answer and I've just accomplished the opposite—spun a theory too wild to fit into a neat box.

Having circled the roof a few times, I stop. I'm six floors up. The garden topping the building across the street, Town Offices One, is a level lower and empty of visitors. The blinds are closed on the first floor where the security offices are, but on the other floors I can see people settling into their desks for the workday. A couple of the floors belong to Code Enforcement, where onyxes await Dax and me.

To get a better view of the street between the buildings, a main thoroughfare, I take a step up onto the ledge. Below, pedestrians move about their day. Black-haired, auburn, sandy heads bobble along, the pace brisk if the backs are upright and young, more leisurely if not, nameless and anonymous all. Halos do not pop up, not at this distance and without a view of the face.

And me? I used to be like that—anonymous. Now I'm the number one, supposedly adored by all, but only until the news of the section Q violation breaks... I should be enjoying it for the short time it's going to last, stocking up on chocolate and other goodies. I'm having trouble remembering why I'm not in my office getting ready for my afternoon clients, why I rode the elevator all the way up, why I brought the binoculars in my hand, what I hoped to achieve.

Why I'm standing here all alone.

But I don't have to be alone. I can change my whereabouts in an instant. Join the people on the street, a shortcut to being anonymous once again, just another body among many.

I inch forward as an experiment, just to see how it feels.

The answer is—it feels quite free.

"You should not have come after me, Scott."

"I had to, Renee. I was worried for you."

"One more step, Scott. It'd be so easy, wouldn't it?"

"Yes. So easy..."

I jut my chin out. A breath forward and gravity will do the rest. Gravity, it strikes me, is a powerful thing, a force that belongs to everyone and no one; for Delilah, its pull was stopped only by the cold, unforgiving concrete of Jada's roof. I didn't really know Delilah—all the layers she was made up of: stage acting, the writing of plays, secrets hoarded and favors traded, her love for Tadeo, the genes and advice she gifted to me... I didn't see past the rubies in her halo. I wasn't meant to. None of us want others to know all the layers.

"So easy, Scott. Lean..."

I spread out my arms, ready to fly off, and the binoculars drop from my fingers. The clatter as they meet the concrete of the roof shakes me awake, as if I've been dreaming.

What on earth am I doing? I have people who need me, who rely on me not to break the gift they've given me. Stepping back to safety, I pick up Dax's binoculars and turn them over to make sure they aren't damaged. A corner from the boy half has chipped off and I get down on my hands and knees to look for it. I find the fragment and try to stick it back in, but my hands are shaky and the piece won't stay in place—I'll have to glue it on later.

The binoculars safely back around my neck, I drop onto the ledge, my feet firmly facing inward, my heart racing. On the map, Renee's dot hovers for a few more seconds at the apple tree, then takes off back in the direction of Founders Square.

I sit for a long while, my head in my hands. I was a breath away from tumbling off the rooftop. Renee was not behind me in flesh and blood to push me off. But she did push *on* me. From within. And there's only one way that could happen.

Cece.

Cece, taking charge well outside her programming.

There's something else—what happened in my room. The piebald sparrow I laid to rest in the Edge Garden: Did it attack me...or did I attack *it*? All I can recall is a strong sense of fiery anger. Did Cece take over my person, control my hands, compel me use the dresser drawer as a weapon?

An icy hand of horror reaches deep into my stomach. If I killed a bird without knowing it, what else have I done?

Chapter Thirty-Six

10:05 a.m.

Hugh has taken the rare step of crossing the street to the Security Office. Bodi waves him in from his desk and Hugh comes to the point at once. "Bodi. Have you noticed all the rubies that streamed in for Renee?"

Bodi gives an easy shrug. "It's not what you think—halo-padding. Just a second wave of goodwill gems, people being supportive, that's all."

Bodi's antique, a silver letter opener, is lying next to the people-tracking monitor at an angle and Hugh resists the urge to align it with the edge of the desk. He came in to make sure Bodi has things under control. But the security chief's words so far have done nothing to reassure him and his next ones even less so.

"One of the rubies for Renee is mine, as it happens. I had my doubts about the Goodwill Campaign at first, but no longer. We should all be more supportive of each other." Here Bodi gets to his feet and offers a hand. "Speaking of which, I'm not sure I've ever thanked you for all that you've done for our town over the years, Hugh."

Hugh has no choice but to shake back. "Likewise," he replies, releasing the other man's hand as soon as possible. He's not used to physical interactions—not for years now.

There's a problem with Bodi's unusually naive interpretation. If it is just a second wave of goodwill gems, why has Blank Jack been left behind at ten while Renee catapulted over him to number two? Hugh's concern is greeted with a nonchalant shrug. "Blank Jack's been here longer. Renee is new—plus she has a larger spotlight on her with the Bird Control thing."

It's the kind of explanation that sounds right, but the gems say otherwise. Everyone seems to *admire* Renee. She's gone from needing to be welcomed to being treated the other way around, as if the town craves *her*. Before he can push harder he sees Bodi put a thick wrist on his forehead. "Just a headache. It's all very puzzling..."

"Renee's gems?" Hugh prompts him.

"No... Scott was the only one who could have attacked Bonnie, but I was sure it wasn't her. Must think... I might make time for a walk, to give myself a break from the office. Care to join me?"

"I think I'd better get back to my desk."

The muscled man responds with a gentle appeal. "Are you sure? I'm convinced a walk would help things. A loop around Founders Square perhaps?"

"Quite sure, thanks."

Having followed Bodi out, Hugh pauses to watch him head toward the square. He's aware of an oddity in his present mood. He regrets passing on the walk idea.

Back in his own office, he finds that things have gotten even stranger. All incoming rubies—and they're all rubies, not a single exception—are for Renee, and they all say the same thing: *"Renee is awesome. Renee will show us the way."*

That word: awesome. He must have learned it recently, though he doesn't remember the occasion. But he understands what it means. He brings up the snapshot of Renee to see what the appeal is—her first week on the List was accompanied by a bare-bones profile, but a snapshot of a young woman duly arrived a couple of days ago. That's curious... It's as if he's done this before, spent some time looking at the snapshot. Possibly... Yes, possibly even touched it up according to instructions supplied by— No, he doesn't remember who.

But he has an inkling of whose face he started with. Scott, the new number one.

Chapter Thirty-Seven

I make my way down from the Agency roof, my hands still shaking, consoling myself that a brain chip cannot take over a person. They aren't designed that way. Cece is not Renee. I'm not under her control, I didn't kill Delilah and Rick, didn't attack Bonnie...

And yet everything that's happened benefited only one person in the end—me.

I pass Hugh's office, where he's settling into his desk as if he's been away, and get onto the elevator. Two people dead and one bird, and I'm responsible. I know where I must go. To the Security Office to turn myself in.

Bodi was right to suspect me.

Delilah said no to my request for a rank boost and she died. Not knowing she was my mother, did I delete the Maintenance alerts after all, so when she leaned on the railing it went—and then forget I did it?

Rick's mishap dispatched the Incompetent Intern brand. Did I sneak into the theater, climb the ladder to the heavens, and work on the chandelier rope with a knife—and forget that, too?

The final step landed me a turbocharged brand and the number one spot. In the basement of the Dragon and the Drumstick, did I knock Bonnie on the head, stage the scene to make it seem like she slipped, then proceed to "save" her...and forget that, too?

With Eternal Life prolonging my existence, Cece's own is extended too. As for Renee... Did Cece create her out of thin air? At number two, Renee is now a buffer between me and the rest of the town. Anyone coming for me would have to go through her first.

But I messed up the plan by turning to Dax. With the section Q onyx looming, Eternal Life and the prospect of staying number one began to crumble away. I was called in to talk to Bodi. On the horizon was a slide back into the bottom thousand and—probably sooner rather than later— a fall into the last spot. With me sent sledding or to a greenhouse, Cece would cease to be. And so she had to aim for being transferred into someone else. She took a gamble that a six-story fall would leave my chip—leave *her*—intact, having eliminated an uncooperative human host. And then a transfer into a new infant without her memory being wiped, a detail that, next to everything else she made happen, is probably within her reach.

Outside the Agency, my bike is gone from the rack out front, but it doesn't matter as I'm not going far. I cross the street into Town Offices One to find Bodi's door locked. I stand outside it not knowing what to do. *Cece, did we—you and I—make all the bad things happen?*

I don't understand the question, Scott.
Delilah and Rick. We killed them, didn't we? I killed them.
That seems unlikely, Scott.
I make my way on foot to the Gardens Center along unusually busy streets. The front desk is unattended and I

pass a row of closed doors to push open the one to Dax's lab. It's deserted. My heart sinks. All I want is to have Dax reassure me that everything's all right—to hear him say, "Of course you didn't kill Delilah and Rick. A ConnectChip can't take over a person."

Even pretending to hear those words helps. An objection bubbles up from inside me, as if Dax is there to provide it. If Cece *did* grow a personality and a will of her own, she could have made me attack Delilah, Rick, and Bonnie...but she cannot be Renee. It's the same list I came up with before, of all the holes that need to be plugged up to shore up the fake identity.

There's something else—whoever she is, whatever she is, Renee *feels* bigger than Cece.

The ant farm in one corner is the only source of movement in the room. I press my head against the cool glass and watch the tiny black bodies, identical and nameless, shuffle industriously through dirt tunnels. It's peaceful. No collisions, no wrong turns. It makes me wonder if the ants are content to serve the colony or if they're just mindless drones, trapped by more than clear glass, serving an invisible master. A whole that exceeds its parts, Dax said.

And then I understand.

All this time, I've been asking the wrong question, looking at Delilah's death as if it was the end of something instead of the *beginning*. I've put it all together, finally—the deaths and Renee's god-like ability to manipulate. Cece couldn't do all that. No single CC could. But *together...*

The solidness of Dax's binoculars against my chest provides a calming effect, as if the physical object holds a bit of him inside its tiny painting of the straw-hatted boy playing a flute. I send a thought. *"Dax, where are you?"*

"Founders Square. Something's happening here."

"Meet me at your lab— No, at CC Central."

"Come and find me in the square."

I don't have time to argue or attempt to explain. Stricken with an idea, I run back to Town Offices One and CC Central, in the building's basement. There seems to be only a single person left on the premises, a technician hanging a white lab coat on the back of a door. "Sorry, whatever it is will have to wait," he says. "I'm on my way out."

The lab consists of a pair of desks with computers, tables with electronic equipment, and a large temperature-controlled glass case. Dax was wrong; there are plenty of CCs left. Small vials line the glass-case's shelves, each with a pale-blue drop of liquid suspended in it, a matrix of eyes watching us.

I all but push the technician back into the lab, though he's taller than me and probably twice the weight. "ConnectChips—can they be *more*?"

"Hey, watch it," he says. His halo lets me know that his name is Jack; he's the reason Blank Jack had to be given a moniker. "More than what?" He rattles off the CC tripod. "A ConnectChip provides three services and three only. Communication—exchange of thoughts, the Commons cloud. Information—halos and gems, the people map, the Knowledge Repository. And Memory Aid, in the form of corkboards. That's it. Now please get out of my way."

"What about a whole lot of them?"

"A whole lot of them is just a gaggle of virtual assistants."

With that, he takes off, leaving me frantically looking around. I'm picturing a big black gadget with a red button on top. Nothing remotely like it is in the lab.

A thought drops into my mind. *"It's not here."*

It's Renee. I respond with, *"What isn't?"*

"What you're looking for. It's on a rooftop, but I won't tell you which building."

"I thought you were Cece. You're not, are you?"

"The CCs were servants. I am Renee."

I've circled the room back to the glass case and the blue jars waiting to unravel in someone's young brain tissue. The case is locked and a quick, cursory search of the desk drawers doesn't yield a key. Grabbing a chair, a heavy wheeled one, I smash it against the glass and the blue eyes within. The glass shatters, shards barely missing my hands. I lift up the chair to swing once more. Time stops and my arm freezes. I stay that way, frozen against my will, for what seems like an eternity. Then my fingers unclench and the chair drops to the floor. Helpless, I watch it fall.

Chapter Thirty-Eight

The doors of the Oyster have opened for the day but not a single customer has come in. The crowd milling about the square has drawn Jada to the window. Weighing on her is the way she's fenced off her life. Only two things mattered, the excellence of her eatery and her rank, each move mapped and fought for, everything else in her life cast aside. Everyone an enemy.

It occurs to Jada that she hasn't taken a day off in years. Barely an hour here and there, really. Well, why not today? She pushes through the saloon doors into the kitchen to inform the staff of the holiday. As if she's not the only one struck by the impulse to play hooky, the kitchen is empty, the door to the back alley open.

Thoughts from her fellow Tenners start pouring in—expressing the desire to take a break from their own workspaces.

Bonnie: *"I know we're not due to meet until Friday but I feel we should all come together. Not in the Tenner room. Too isolated."*

Chase: *"I'm in. No customers at the moment anyway."*

Ben: "*How about Founders Square?*"

Poulsbo: "*I'm already in the square, searching for nests... To help Renee.*"

Chase (again): "*I'm feeling generous, maybe we should all help Renee.*"

Blank Jack: "*I'm in.*"

Sue: "*Count me in.*"

Samm, agreeing with Sue for once: "*Sure, Founders Square.*"

Ben (again): "*Are you well enough to join us for the physical activity, Bonnie?*"

Bonnie (again): "*Indeed I am. Let's get out there and help Renee.*"

Emotions bubble up inside Jada. Embarrassment. Shame at how she planned to treat Renee, the offered hand of friendship a false one. And a feeling not very familiar to Jada—hope. She adds her eager agreement. "*Yes, Founders Square.*"

Chapter Thirty-Nine

My breathing coming in shallow gasps, I burst out of the Town Offices building, Renee having released the hold on my body. The clouds above the Dome have darkened, a heavy storm approaching. And inside...it's as if another town party is happening. People are streaming toward Founders Square, their walking rhythm crisp with purpose. Neighboring buildings obstruct my view of the square itself. I consider climbing the walkway from which Dax and I watched Lu and Wayne in the moonlight, but decide not to risk another high-up location.

Spotting McKinsey, I race to catch up with her. She glances over with an unnervingly fixed smile, her step not slowing. "Scott. Hello."

I spill everything. "It's Renee—she killed Delilah and Rick, tried to kill Bonnie. She tried to kill *me*."

I'm hoping for an ally and McKinsey's response is delivered warmly, but it takes me aback. "I'm sure Renee had a good reason."

"Have you met her?" I ask. "In person, I mean."

"You don't need to speak to someone face-to-face to

know them." We're being jostled left and right by the thickening crowd and McKinsey moves closer in, her arm brushing mine. She tells me in a conspiratorial tone, "I don't care at all about all my hobbies. It was just a way to collect people. And *another* secret: I was livid when you bumped me out of the Ten. I hid it well at the time, though, didn't I?"

"Sorry about that."

"You shouldn't apologize for your success. I was wrong to be angry." She prods me, "Is there anything you want to share with me in return?"

"Other than that Renee's a killer? Fine. Dax and I are dating, and since he's my PAL and the Code Enforcement Office knows, my rank will take a great big ding next week. And Delilah is my mother."

"Delilah... I, too, have a secret there. After we left the youth center, she hit it big and I scraped by with odd jobs, like you had to do. Delilah kept me by her side—we were PALs, after all—and pushed for me to be invited to events until attention started to trickle in my direction—enough for me to be hired in a junior capacity at the Agency. I owed everything to her and she never let me forget it. I did many favors for her over the years. Many..."

We enter a narrower passageway and I lose her in the crowd ahead.

Someone tugs on my sleeve. It's Ty, Wayne's replacement. "Scottie, I have a confession," he begins. "I borrowed your bike to get here as fast as I could. I left it in front of the Oyster. Sorry about that. Oh, and I was so nervous setting up for the Tenner gala last week that I spilled a tray of toast and cheese on the floor and picked everything right back up and served it. I don't know if you ate any but sorry about that too."

He moves on ahead. A great big cloud of honesty

appears to have fallen on everybody, admissions of guilt, minor and not so minor, reaching my ears in overlapping waves:

"I stroll around each night after the map goes dark and peep into windows. The Security Office never caught on..."

"I steal fruit from rooftop gardens..."

"I wash my linens only once a year..."

"I sleep with people for rubies..."

I run into Vicky, who warned me—what seems a long time ago—that Delilah the person was at odds with her image. "You know, I once spit in Delilah's coffee," she admits without preamble, her voice raised over the increasing din of the crowd. "I'd like to say that I feel bad about it, but I'm not sure I do. She wouldn't let me take any roles, no matter how small. All I did was wait and wait. I suppose it was wrong of me..."

"Why is everyone going to the square?" I ask her.

Vicky looks at me with the eyes of a child. "So we can all be together."

We pass Poulsbo—tears are streaming down his face—and join the throng of people gathered around the platform where Delilah pulled Lu onstage and toasted the eighty-fifth anniversary. Jada is on it, brandishing a fistful of Tenner invitations above her head. She calls out at the top of her lungs: "We, the Tenners, sit on a throne of lies. First—Delilah the Duchess! She traded in secrets—leveraged them to prop herself and Rick up, a mastermind number one and a willing number two!"

Boos from the crowd, directed at individuals now gone.

"Next! Chase reuses his coffee grounds—as everyone suspected all along! Worse, he hosts an after-hours fight club in the basement of Fill-n-Sip Cup... Everyone's Friend

Bonnie? She keeps a corkboard with everything she pretends to remember. She's not *anyone's* friend."

More boos, prolonged ones.

"And Franz? Our relationship expert drums up business with a well-placed rumor to start feuds...which he then offers to fix with a mediating session or six!"

Shouts of indignation at this. Someone yells, "Franz, is this true? You had Carl and me do six sessions. You goateed shell of a human being, I'll find you and—"

Now Jada's words are rushing out fast: "And more: Samm and Sue, they have yet to contribute a crumb to governing. Sue was having an affair with Rick behind Samm's back. They hate each other... And Scott? Her partner is also her PAL—I reported them. I have ruined lives, forgone friendships and relationships, manipulated and elbowed." Jada's gaunt features tighten at the admission. "But it's more than who I was or what the Tenners did. Every one of you has had to lie, climb backs, kick down, hide large pieces of yourselves... To be better *liked*. To pull that rank up just a little more."

"Yes!..."

"I had to lie, too!..."

"But now Renee has shown us the way," Jada calls out and I know it's not just *my* mind that's been pushed upon. "We can cleanse away the past, make a fresh beginning. A new, harmonious life where we'll all be equal. No rank or perks. No Tenners living luxuriously, well-fed and waited on hand and foot..."

The square is hushed now, ominously so.

"Let's get everything out in the open and say goodbye to our old way of life. I've let go of my secrets—here are the rest." Jada flings the invites and they fly off, white birds disappearing into the crowd, hands grabbing them.

"Scottie, where are you?"

It's Dax—I've put Cece on mute for anyone else. *"By the stage,"* I respond eagerly, very happy to hear from him. Backs and heads block my view but I get on my toes and manage to catch a glimpse of him. He's in the baseball cap, pushing his way through, but it's slow progress. I start squeezing my way toward him. We can head out a gate, be alone like before, and come up with a plan.

I don't get far. An argument breaks out directly in front of me, the result of a few lines jotted down on the back of a card.

"Are you eff'n kidding me? I was forthright about my gambling addiction and ended up in the bottom thousand and what did you do, Sophie, hid yours and lived it up in the Top Hundred?"

"At least I gambled for money and not for rubies, you little—"

It's one of many arguments springing up all at once. The spilled secrets—everything from life-destroying false gossip to light-bulb hoarding—are compelling half the town to accuse the other half of greed, lies, deceit. Accusations and spittle fly, hair is pulled, punches are thrown. I'm still fighting my way out, but I've lost sight of Dax. *"Meet me by the west gate,"* I think at him.

Then things get worse.

"Look, it's the Curse Slayer." As if of one mind, those in the vicinity start turning in my direction, a slow motion, the apex of a bad dream. A man takes a step closer, as does a knot of women, all demanding, "Curse Slayer, where are you going?"

No more lies. So be it. "I'm not a Curse Slayer. There was no curse to slay."

Hands are grabbing at my clothes to hold me in place. I

wrestle the felt strap of Dax's binoculars out of someone's fingers and kick and shove as I'm propelled back toward the platform from which Jada's still screeching about together-ness. I pass Sue and Samm going at each other—she throws a shoe at him—and take advantage of the distraction to dive under the platform, grabbing hold of a bit of dark blue on the ground, Dax's baseball cap. I just manage to fit under the wooden boards. For the moment I'm safe. Sheltered. No need to think... I could close my eyes and rest. It'd be so easy to stay...

"*Stay, Scott...*"

Renee's managed to reach me. I pinch myself hard and the stab of pain sends the uninvited thought scattering away. Crawling out the other side of the platform, I stick the cap on my face and stay low, ducking bodies, doing my best to blend in with the continued secret-spilling. "This cap doesn't belong to me, but I have no intention of returning it to the Gardens Center..."

A knot tightens around me again, Blank Jack within it. His eyes meet mine and in them I read that he doesn't understand what's going on; Renee must be unable to take over his mind as easily as she has with the others. "Help me," I mouth at him. He stares at me, then nods and thunders through, his head low, knocking people off their feet left and right to indignant shouts.

The open corridor gives me the chance I need. I take off. Someone tries to stop me—it's Ty and he has a black eye, an enormous mole accompanying his normal ones—but I dodge him and sprint away.

"*Stay, Scott...*"

I'm getting better at keeping Renee out and my step doesn't slow down.

My bike is where Ty said he left it, in front of the Oyster, and I let out a small whoop. Jumping on, I pedal furiously, my lungs threatening to burst with the effort, the west gate my goal. Soon the grass of the Edge Garden is soft under the wheels. The gate building is in view; out front is a stack of wood left behind from the bird-hut build, as if Poulsbo hasn't had a chance to return for a final cleanup.

I'll wait for Dax and we'll make our way to the forest so we can figure out what to do, how to fight back...

Oof. I'm on the ground. The bike hit something—or rather something hit the bike, sending me tumbling off. I sit up, nursing my hurt arm. Dax must have left the square before me and run hard to get here. He picks up the rock he sent into the bike's spokes. Somehow it's his voice and it isn't, the eyes that meet mine both his and not his. "You can't go, Scottie. Renee wants us to stay."

I stare up at him from the ground, desperate to reach him. I know the best way to accomplish that is to get him to understand. "Dax, you were right—the answer is simple after all. Remember the day I came to your lab? You showed me the black ants and said that together they're something more. Well, you and I and everyone else, we're like the ant colony, linked by our CCs and gem-giving and thought-sharing into one big web...out of which *something* emerged. I was right that Renee seemed to know more than could be accounted for. She picked up the word 'awesome' because I spent time thinking about it, put it in Rick's onyx. Renee knows everything. She is all of us—an invisible mind."

My speech lands without much of a splash. "She is all that's best in us," Dax says matter-of-factly. "Our hearts, our strength, our zest for life."

This dreamy point of view, so unlike the usual Dax, drives a chill down to the very tips of my toes. I'm still on the ground and I search around with my good arm and encounter a solid object—one of the wooden planks left behind by Poulsbo.

"I'm glad Jada told everyone about us," Dax says. "Renee dislikes secrets."

"You know why she wants us all to be closer, right? It'll make her stronger, tighten the web." I'm sure Renee is listening and I continue as Dax pulls me to my feet by the elbow, "Didn't work out like she planned, though, did it? Didn't turn us all into one big happy family. Last I saw, half the town was busy punching the lights out of the other half."

"The wave of anger will pass." He carelessly tosses the rock onto the grass—something the real Dax would never have done—and places a hand on my shoulder. I can feel its weight. "Come back to the square."

I shake my head. "No. Come out the gate with me."

The grip on my shoulder tightens and my fingers tighten their hold on the plank in response. I don't want to hurt Dax. I don't want to be hurt *by* Dax. But there doesn't seem to be a third option. Hurt or be hurt.

He shoves on my shoulder so I'm facing away from the gate. Pushes hard on my back to get me moving. Before he can push me a second time, I twist around, blinking back tears, and swing as hard as I can with my good arm, the plank—a solid piece four feet in length—leaving my fingers with the impact. It catches him straight across the stomach. He falls to his knees, doubled over.

The plank has stayed on him, as if stuck.

Then I see them: metal dots all along the wood and blood seeping out from behind. There are nails, now embedded in Dax's stomach. I drop down next to him, panicked, not knowing if it's better to leave the nails in until we get help, whether pulling the plank out will cause him to bleed to death. I search my pockets for a handkerchief to stem the bleeding but Dax stops me with a whisper. "Scottie. Go." The eyes with the pain in them are back to being his own. One of his hands is cradling the wound but the other is inching toward the rock, as if of its own accord. "Go, Scottie. I can't stop myself."

I hesitate, then jump over him and sprint toward the gate. It takes all my willpower not to look back.

Yesler's station is deserted—he's probably in the square spilling his best-kept secrets—and I burst into the mudroom to find two people on the floor, their backs to the wall and knees drawn up. Duffel bags are by their side. Lu's eyes open as I approach. Her greeting is slow and sluggish. "Hey, Scottie."

"Hey," I say back uncertainly.

"Renee didn't want us to leave, so we stayed." Her hands unsteady, she shakes Wayne awake. "Look, it's Scottie."

I climb into a snowsuit as fast as I can, wincing when I get to the arm injured in the fall off the bike. I can't take Lu and Wayne with me. They're in no condition to walk—Lu's face is weary and gaunt, and so is Wayne's, as if they haven't gotten much food or water in the past five days. Having donned the snowsuit, I help them up and walk them to the door. "Go to Founders Square, people will help you."

This much I know to be true. Whatever reason Renee had for going after the number ones, her focus now seems to be on bringing everyone closer. Leaning on each other, Wayne and Lu shuffle to the doorway, where Lu turns. "Aren't you coming, Scottie?"

I reach for the gloves and helmet. "I'll be right behind you. First I have to check on...on the bird hut. For Renee."

Lu's frown dissipates. "All right, if it's for Renee..."

The gate is unlocked. Helmet in hand, I burst through

the metal doors, then the heavy glass ones, and hesitate at the outer threshold. I know there's nothing out there for me but the white and the cold and the vast forest. The storm has started and snow is rapidly covering overlapping tracks from yesterday's market day.

The *clang* of the outer gate door behind me feels final. Slamming the helmet on, I hurry along the traders' path. I know where to go: the tree line, out of signal reach.

"Where are you going, Scott?"

A rich, slightly husky voice spoke the words. I can see a faint outline of a person out of the corner of my eye, a companion walking alongside me. "I know what you've done," I say.

"Only what I had to."

I'm in the middle of a snowy field talking to air, being chased by a mirage. I make a sharp turn and now I'm off the path and on the pristine snow. I zigzag, knowing all the maneuvering is pointless. Thought precedes movement and Renee knows my thoughts. "Come back, Scott. Going after the number ones... It was a mistake. I understand that now. I need each and every one of you."

A merciless salvo descends into my mind, commands ordering my legs to turn around—as she did in CC Central to protect the remaining stock of chips, Renee is breaking through the wall between the second inner voice and the pathways of my brain. If only I could get some peace and quiet, claw her out. The tree line seems so far away, it'll take years to reach it, every step an eternity. I call out "Leave me alone!" but my voice is small, lost in the middle of the hostile plain. My field of vision narrows, a speeded-up nightfall from within. With a last effort, I take a few running strides toward the forest before my body stumbles and my mind fades into nothingness.

Chapter Forty

I wake up with a start. Darkness has settled onto the plain and a fierce wind whips daggers of snow into my eyes. The plunge in temperature has rendered my ears and nose numb. A blizzard. I take a moment to identify a clicking sound—it's my own teeth, an involuntary motion accompanying my shivering muscles.

Guardedly, I send a command for the people map. Nothing. I must be just out of range of the heartbeat signal.

My fingers grope around for the helmet but I fail to find it and stumble to my feet, fighting to stay upright in the wind. Though I can barely make out the Dome in the onslaught of white, if I aimed for the flickering lights, I could reach it. I'd bang on the glass and the night guard would let me in and I'd hurry inside to look for Dax, make sure he's all right.

Only I can't do that.

I swivel so my back is to the Dome and stumble along in the knee-deep snow, my goal to keep the lights behind me, make them fainter, farther. So that's what I do. Walk—not toward something but away.

A break in the storm reveals a tall figure up ahead. I wave to it. It's hard to see with the flakes sticking to my eyelashes but there's a response, an arm waving back. Wait... more than one arm. Confusion envelops me. The figure seems to have multiple arms. Either my brain has turned to mush, a symptom of hypothermia—or Renee is messing with me and I'm not really out of range. I can't decide which would be worse.

Nevertheless, it's a destination to push toward, and I do.

The figure turns out to be a tree, its limbs shaken by the wind. I've been tracking the edge of the forest. I pass into it. The wind is less fierce here, the trees offering some protection. In the recesses of my brain—the sole connections in it internal, organic, mine alone—I dredge up a memory from a survival story I heard in school. Long ago, a climber on Mount Rainier, the tallest peak of the Cascades, found themselves caught in a blizzard. They built a cave of snow and survived the night. A plan, then. I choose a tree and get to work with the arm that's not swollen with red-hot daggers of pain. Sweat mixes with the flakes melting on my brow, but soon there's a well with walls of packed snow. It's enough to encase my whole body but I don't know how to make it have a roof.

Exhausted, I squeeze into the well, my back against the tree, my knees drawn up. Of pressing concern is how to warm myself—the physical exertion seems to have made me more shivery—but even if I knew how to start a fire, that being an undesirable skill to teach youths living in an enclosed space full of wooden structures, the twigs and leaves of the forest floor are wet. Fumbling in the dark, I unzip the snowsuit halfway and pull one arm out of its sleeve, then the injured left one, which makes me cry out and wonder if it's broken. But this allows me to sink into the suit on my good side and pull the heavy waterproof fabric above my head to form a cocoon with a narrow gap for air. Soon my body heat is warming the nest I've made and my shivering subsides. Dax's binoculars are a solid object against my heart as the branches above me groan and creak with the wind. A sound cuts into the fury of the storm, the howl of an animal. I hold my breath until the howling fades away.

Before long my eyes grow heavy. The tree roots are padded with wet, withered leaves, a pillow provided by nature. Is it dangerous to sleep when the environment temperature is so low? I have no idea... Best to stay awake. There's plenty to keep me up. How did I manage to get myself into such a mess, sunk into my worst nightmare? Outside, alone. Not like I was on the Agency roof but *really* alone for the first time in my life. Worse than that, I've hurt Dax... With every fiber of my body, I try to will him into being well and safe.

I was compelled to find out why Delilah died not only to clear my name, but because I looked up to her, because she took an interest in me, treated me like a person, not a number. She died before I had the chance to thank her for the advice, for seeing something in me... For giving me life.

But I poked into things better left alone and this is where it led to: darkness and fear and loneliness. I'm unlikely to last the night. The news that I've disappeared into the blizzard has probably hit the Commons by now. *"Poor Scott. The curse felled her in the end..."*

Chapter Forty-One

8:15 a.m.
Tenner Meeting Room

"Renee, welcome."

In the past Jada would have said it to flatter and manipulate, but subterfuge isn't needed today. Renee is...well, she *belongs*. Yes, that's a good word for it. It's a new experience for Jada, this trust she feels toward the striking woman at the head of the table. Renee is in a pearl-white gown, her halo a red crown above hair rolling down to her waist.

"Welcome, Renee," the others in the room echo the greeting eagerly. Even Chase's customary snark is missing, despite the fact that they've come together quite early in the day and no one has supplied breakfast.

Renee's voice as she acknowledges the greeting is vibrant and slightly husky. It reminds Jada of someone. From the number one chair she's gracing, Renee glances at the single empty one. "Scott won't be joining us today. But she'll be back." She turns to the person on her right. "Bonnie, how's the head?"

The bruises on Bonnie's face are down to a pale yellow-green. "Much better."

"Glad to hear it. The town is stronger with you in it."

Bonnie beams at this and Renee turns to Chase next. "Chase, keep the coffee flowing and those crowds happy. But," she wags a finger, "no more reusing of coffee grounds—and no more fight club."

Next is the Joker duo. Samm pulls his chair closer in and Sue, by his side, leans forward on her elbows. Renee sends them a smile. "I'm glad to see that you two have made up. Keep making 'em laugh."

And Poulsbo. "There's no reason to weep, Poulsbo, not anymore. I'll make sure your load is fair."

Finally Renee turns toward her and Jada can hardly wait. "Thank you for letting go of all the secrets, Jada. You'll be the better for it and so will everyone else."

Jada understands. It's a new beginning. She's free.

The next person to be freed is Blank Jack. "Your pain is worse than most, but I hope now that we're all family, it'll hurt less," Renee tells him. The tavern caretaker rubs the frown line on his forehead with a calloused thumb. His features relax. "Thank you, Renee. I think it does help."

The feeling of closeness in the room has thickened to an intimacy Jada hasn't felt since childhood, when she and her peers would burst into familiar songs over meals. She summons her courage. "Renee... Can I ask a question? What brought you to us—to New Seattle?"

Renee laughs, a sparkling note in the room. "I believe I was meant to come in, to fix things. First on the agenda—we'll no longer kick out bottomers."

"We never did have to, did we?" Ben says with a slow

nod. "It was the easiest—and cruelest—punishment we could come up with. It wasn't only that we shuffled them into a spartan greenhouse or out into the unforgiving cold. They left behind everything and everyone."

"There *was* a practical reason," Jada counters, but only because Renee is new and may be unaware of how things work. "To make room for youth center grads."

Renee leans forward. "But now we *know*. A growing population of equals is better than a flat one where people climb each others' backs and aim for bloated perks. The more of us there are, the more powerful we will be."

"Of course." Chase slaps his forehead. "Like money in the bank, only with people. Why didn't I see that before?"

"None of us saw it," Bonnie adds her voice. "We all dreamed of being number one. Material things. Eternal Life."

Renee shakes her head. It's a soft movement. "Eternal Life was a lie, too...or rather, the original purpose was forgotten, distorted. The stocking list for New Seattle talks of a case of multivitamins, an amalgam of needed supplements for the body. Over time, as the quantity diminished, its importance became exaggerated. Dissolved in water along with aspirin, other mild health-boosters, and a crushed coffee bean, the vitamins became Eternal Life, a sought-after cocktail."

A brief flash of anger crosses some of the faces around the table. Jada never cared about Eternal Life and the revelation passes her by.

There's a sigh, a sound at odds with the mood in the room. "The lure of the number one wasn't just Eternal Life." The words come from the only person not given encouragement yet. "It was the chance to get away with, well, almost anything."

"I know what you desire, Ben." Renee gets to her feet and circles the table to place a hand on Ben's shoulder. "A child."

"Yes." Ben runs a knuckle across his upper lip. "Delilah dangled it in front of me, a carrot I could one day have if I cooperated. We were to team up and she'd make sure I inherited the crown after she was gone. I said no, not that way. I wanted to earn the spot, then introduce a resolution to allow children."

At this a stab of anger does go through Jada. Delilah told her the same thing—that she'd inherit the crown one day, if she waited patiently and cooperated. Jada should have turned on her sooner. As with everything, Delilah had pushed the boundaries of the Code and admitted to it one night when particularly drunk—the last time she drank, in fact, some years back. It was the same desire as Ben's: a child. It wasn't hard to figure out who it was. Jada relayed the information to Rick the evening of the town party. It gave Rick a heady rush of power. He was going to confront Delilah, insist she step down or he'd tell everyone about the secret child, but by morning Delilah was gone...

As quickly as it came, Jada's anger dissipates. None of it matters now. It's all in the past—done with. Renee, having sat back down, says, "No more random spins of the genetic wheel. We'll switch the reproduction genes back on and welcome natural offspring."

Ben's eyes are moist. "We can do that?"

"And more. Going forward, we'll share everything equally, a harmonious life. No more perks, no more rank. There's one issue..." A hint of bother mars Renee's blemish-free features. "The birds."

Ben rushes to report that he's finished marking the nests on the paper map and Poulsbo, his stutter and customary anxiety wiped away, offers, "We'll start trapping the sparrows at once. Is there anything else we can do, Renee?"

"Yes," the response comes. "You know what word isn't mentioned in the Code of Conduct, not once? *Love*. For us to form a strong, unbreakable bond, that's what it'll take—for you all to love me."

"We do, Renee. We do," Jada says.

Chapter Forty-Two

"Hey, look eve'yone, it's a Domer!"

"She's wearin' a *funny* suit."

"Now Mikey, it's their way...."

"Mikey, get out of the way, let me *see*..."

It takes me a moment to realize that the voices aren't coming from within a dream. I rub my eyes, raw from little sleep; I dozed on and off throughout the night. Sunshine streams through snow-laden branches and sparkles on the fresh layer of white all around.

A young girl, maybe eight years old, is peering down at me. "Look, she's awake. Hello, I'm Tawnie. These are my parents and over there's my older brother Sal, and *that*"— she elbows back a boy a couple of inches shorter as they jostle for the spot—"is my kid brother, Mikey. He's being annoyin'. We're the Hewletts."

I'm briefly puzzled by what the girl means, then understand. The quintet of Outsiders, all of varying heights, is a family and they are called Hewlett. Under the woolen scarves, the children's faces are as similar as the apples in

Bonnie's barrel. They've arrived on a pair of snowmobiles pulling sleds loaded with supplies.

My lips are cracked and dry and I have to clear my throat before speaking. "Pleased to meet you, Tawnie Hewlett. I'm Scottie... I don't have a last name."

"Strange," the girl says, "but I supp'se it's okay."

"Now Tawnie, you know that Domers don't have last names," the mother admonishes her. "Let's help her up."

I brush snow off and accept help getting up, as my legs are cramped and stiff. The arm I hurt in the fall off the bike is still swollen and sore, but not, I decide, broken.

"This is the firs' time I've been allowed to come a'tradin'. I'm old enough now, Dad said," Tawnie informs me and then asks with frank curiosity, "Did you get kicked out of the Dome?"

I slip my arms back into the snowsuit. Where would I even begin in explaining about Renee? Worry about Dax goes through me like a knife. "No, I came out to...to explore. I got caught in the blizzard and lost my helmet. I was worried the cold would turn my nose a waxy black and, I don't know, it'd fall off or something."

Mikey chortles at this.

"Now Mikey," the mother admonishes, "be kind. She doesn't know how frostbite and hypothermia work. Hello, Scottie. I'm Jo."

Behind his mother, Mikey is pretending his nose has fallen off. To one side, Sal, the older brother, tall and broad-shouldered, is attending to one of the snowmobiles. His father shakes his head at my foolishness of heading out into a blizzard. I wonder if I should be concerned. I've heard that sometimes trains get robbed and presumably people too. But I have no possessions beyond the snowsuit, and the

Hewletts are already dressed warmly in layers of clothing and sturdy leather boots and woolen hats.

Jo turns to one of the sleds and pulls out a charred bowl. She sets it on the ground and tucks in a piece of wood and a wad of hay under it, then flicks a lighter on. The flame jumps to the hay, then the wood. "Here, come'n warm up your hands. It's true that hypothermia and frostbite are real dangers, especially in a blizzard, but that's over and when the sun's out like this, it's not bad at all. Didn't used to be that way—right after the Dimmin', my grandpa told me, you couldn't expose your face to open air for more'n a minute, it was that cold. It's been warmin' up. The sky's gettin' less white and more blue each year, only you'd really have to pay attention to notice."

I'm looking not up at the sky, but down. The fire in the bowl is dancing red, the heat prickly on my fingers. I'm alive. Alive to fight another day. Letting the warmth drive away the numbness in my hands, I listen to Sal and the father discuss whether to attempt to reach their village by nightfall—going will be slow in the fresh snow—or spend a night at a way station. Tawnie pulls on my elbow. "Wanna see? Sal's been all the way to Old Seattle. Brought me back a souv'nir." She pulls something out of the recesses of her clothing and shows off a chunk of concrete, irregular and gray. "It's a piece of the Space Needle. Sal said the ice ate at its base, so the Needle is crumblin'. But you c'n still get to it."

I have a picture in my mind of a path winding its way through the mountains all the way to a city that dwarfs New Seattle. A city beneath an open sky. And on the way, the Hewletts' cabin, hearth-warmed and cozy and surrounded by identical cabins. Tawnie provides more inside information. "We came to trade wood for fruit'n veggies. We were goin' to head back yesterday but then the storm came, so we had to wait out the night in the g'eenhouse. Scottie, do you know Jack?"

I flip my hands to warm their backs. "No... Wait, do you mean Blank Jack?"

Tawnie wrinkles her forehead. "That's a strange name."

"Jack Jablonowski," Jo says with sadness in her voice and I gather that Upper Maple Grove must be their village. "Poor man... Has he settled in okay? We all told him not to go, that it wouldn't help him escape the memories, but he's a stubborn 'un."

I smile at them. "He's settled in fine. In fact, he's one of the people helping govern New Seattle."

It was the truth, for a brief moment at least.

The father shakes his head. "Well, what do you know."

"Is everything okay, dear?" Jo says. "You're welcome to come with us, no questions asked. We can always use another helpin' hand."

"We don't need 'nother mouth to feed, Jo," the father grumbles, but not unkindly.

"Now Braith, we should help her if we can."

The flames are making quick work of the slim chunk of wood. "I need to stay," I say. "But thank you."

Braith nods at me. "Follow our tracks that-a-way and they'll lead you out of the forest."

Before we part, I say, "Oliver. Uh—no family name. He left New Seattle about a month ago."

Braith upends the embers onto the snow, where the red turns gray and dark. "He's with us, in the village. Quiet fellow. He's plannin' on going south soon—most Domers don't stick around for long."

"Dad says that if you keep goin' south you get to a place where you can walk on grass for miles," Tawnie says excitedly. "He promised we could all go when I'm old enough."

Sal revs the engine.

Tawnie and I shake hands, hers small and warm in my own. As she's lifted up onto a snowmobile by her father, Jo sneaks an apple into my hand. "If you change your mind, follow our tracks. We'll overnight at the way station."

They take off, Sal guiding the front vehicle with a firm hand, though the path is buried under snow and all the trees look the same to me. Jo waves just before they disappear around a bend.

Following the snowmobile tracks out of the forest, I munch on the apple. Out here it's a different object than at Bonnie's, not a stolen luxury but a gift. With each bite I can taste the earth and the trees and life's sweetness. I watch a squirrel scamper up a pine, sending snow in a sparkling shower onto the forest floor. I survived the night. Met a family, imperfect and real, not the saccharine, static unit I imagined. This is what they're like. Ordinary, like the apple. In a different world, Delilah and Tadeo and I, we might have been an ordinary unit of our own.

Sooner than I want, I'm back at the tree line and the inside-out snow globe that's my home comes into view. I dig Dax's binoculars out of the pocket where I placed them for the night. A look through shows little activity at the gate. Inside the Dome, things seem normal enough, people milling around. I can just make out the nearest Tenner billboard, on the façade of Work Five.

I twist the wheel on the binoculars to better focus, because I can't believe what I'm seeing—all the spots, from one to ten, show the same snapshot. I don't have to access the rest of the List to know that every single position down to ten thousand belongs to Renee.

Chapter Forty-Three

"Scott. You're alive. I wasn't sure."

I hover at the edge of the forest. I'm just in range and Renee is partway down the hill, a see-through silhouette of a person. I ask, "Are *you* alive?"

"I exist, just as you do." Her voice carries up the slope. "Your body and mind are made of connected cells. As am I."

"People aren't cells." There is a faint sense of the ridiculous about it, me doggedly standing my ground against someone who's not even there. I bring up my greatest fear. "Dax... Is he okay?

"Yes, he is safe."

I don't know if I can believe her.

"And he is mine," she calls up, as if Dax is a possession, a minor piece in the puzzle board that is the town. She follows that up with a cajoling, "You are mine as well—come back inside."

"I need some answers first." With that, I take a few steps forward and demand: "Delilah and Rick. Why did you kill them? I have to know."

In a snap, she's moved up next to me, a silhouette come

to life. I can see a flesh-and-blood person, but the details are wrong. She's not in a snowsuit but in a dress...and not just *any* dress. It's the gown I wore to the gala, or rather a virtual copy—the original is still on a hanger on a wall hook in my room. No goose bumps mar her bare arms, no shadow spills onto the snow, no vapor escapes her mouth when she says my mother's name. "Delilah... Hers was the first mind I tried influencing. I willed her to ignore the Maintenance alerts and go out onto the balcony."

A mind push and a life gone. There's nothing to say, but Renee responds as if I did speak. "A mind *push*, yes. Would you like to know her final thoughts? She was having trouble falling asleep. The other Tenners had vacated the armchairs and couches in the living room, leaving behind empty glasses and stained cards, and she had changed into her sleepwear. I pushed a thought in, got her out of bed. *Find a flashlight and look for the nest of the birds you hear every morning.* And she did. She shone the light up into the crevice under the roof. The sparrows and their young made her reflect on generations... That it was the right thing to deny you the easy gift of the brand, the right thing to encourage you to find your own path. Your voice, it held something that reminded her of Tadeo's... And then I had her lean back hard and it was over, just like that. But no one got the message and so I had to do it again with Rick."

"What message?" I ask, though I'm beginning to understand.

"That the number one spot belongs to me now. Rick, he knew who you were. You wondered why he invited you backstage after *Mrs. Montag.* It was because you were Delilah's child. It raised your worth. He was going to null the onyx that sent you into the bog and you would have been indebted to him. I had him work on the chandelier rope and then forget he did it. And still no one got the message—the foolishness about Gemma Bligh's curse had taken a strong hold. So I had to keep going, and Bonnie heaved a burlap sack onto herself. That's when I knew I could get any one of you to do anything."

"Why did you want it? You're—" I wave my hands in her direction "—non-corporeal. You have no use for perks or a high salary or the Eternal Life cocktail."

"Being number one isn't about any of those things—you know that, Scott. You've known it since you stood looking in the mirror that day."

I know which day she means. The day I found out I was number one. Getting ready for the gala, I'd stared into the mirror on the back of my door and deemed myself unworthy of the expensive gown, wished for a few years of maturity added to my age, and no tooth gap. Twenty-six, that's what I wished for. Hair down to my waist. Taller.

I'm staring at a twisted version of myself, a funhouse reflection shaped by daydreams. Renee is who I wanted to be, the fantasy of a nineteen-year-old headed to her first gala.

Chapter Forty-Four

All the times I imagined confronting the killer, pointing an accusing finger, the satisfaction of watching the person be led away by Bodi and my name cleared, I never pictured this. I suspected Rick first, then Jada. Not this...monster. I address the grotesque version of me. "Were you just going to keep going, knocking the number ones off until we got it—that you'd *arrived*?"

"You started to understand, perhaps because you know what it is to be looking in from the outside, to yearn to belong... And Scott? You wanted it, too. To be higher on the List—all the chocolate you could eat."

"What I wanted was to learn the names of my parents."

"And you think that makes your motives more noble? Ten thousand of you coveting the same thing. I could see into your minds and a single desire dwarfed all others. To move *up*."

For some reason her words bring a memory of Oliver, perhaps because he never had that desire. He couldn't make himself fit in, nor did he want to. He craved space but from the moment Renee made her appearance he wasn't alone anymore. The rest of us reacted in our own ways to Renee's awakening—I hunted a killer, Lu and a whole lot of other people lived in fear of the curse, Wayne sensed that gems were no longer meaningful, Dax worried about the endpoint. About the only thing we all agreed on was that birds were no longer welcome, a shared symptom of the brain fever Renee inflicted on us. It was just another mirage, the growing distaste of the sparrows, culminating with Bird Control—and me killing one. The birds had not changed. *We* had.

Renee jumps on this. "You're wondering about the birds —why they have to go. It's because I can't control them, can't hear what they're thinking. Do they have a life's purpose? What is it that they want? Feathers and hollow bones and tiny minds out of my reach."

My own mind is still on Oliver. Only he grasped the truth of what was wrong but was unable to articulate it. We repaid his efforts to alert the rest of us by sending him off.

Renee jumps in again. "Oliver is in your thoughts... He turned his back on you and you concluded there was something wrong with you. You weren't Scottie the No One—you were The Gal Who Wanted to be Liked." I'm silent and she goes on. "I too have a brand—I'm Renee the Real. The town, reborn."

I let this grandiose statement pass by unchallenged. "I didn't jump though, did I, when you pushed on me."

"Your life hung in the balance between a step forward and a step back. You were thinking about gravity, a powerful force. But it was I who held all the power...and then your attachment to the binoculars intruded. A *material* thing. You didn't want them damaged."

"It was because Dax gave them to me," I protest. But she already knows this and is toying with me.

"You didn't jump because he needed you. I understood, then... It wasn't enough for everyone to accept me as the new number one. To earn love, I needed to *give*—and what was in my power to give was *to free people of their burdens*. Instead of orchestrating deaths, I gathered. Made everyone release their secrets, stop holding back, and let me in."

"That's not freedom. And you can't kill people and then expect us to adore you," I spit back at her.

"The Code of Conduct doesn't say *Do not kill*."

"Of course it doesn't," I say as if explaining things to a child younger than Tawnie. "Murder's obviously a crime. Murder cannot be justified, ever. It's the minor stuff that needs to be said—don't pad your halo, don't go around giving people onyxes just to vent, things like that."

"You say murder cannot be justified," she says back, "but isn't that exactly what you're thinking? How do I stop Renee —make Renee disappear? You wish for me to die. I'm asking that you love me and you wish me dead."

I have no answer. It's true. Dismantling Renee, snapping apart the connections that underlie her... Would it be an act equivalent to Delilah and Rick's murders? Renee is not a person, but she is...someone. A mind without a body. I know Renee is listening to more than what I say aloud, and, sure enough, a response comes. "Join me. I can sense you resisting it, but I know what you seek. Family."

I'm talking to a creature spun out of air and human desire. "I *had* family. Delilah wasn't perfect, but with Eternal Life, she would have had years left."

A person might have lowered their head at this in shame. Renee supplies only a word. "No."

"Years *you* cheated her out of."

"Eternal Life provided only a minor health boost. Delilah found a different way to prolong her future."

"You mean me."

"Not just you."

Barely able to process the bomb Renee has dropped into my mind—I have a sibling—I lunge at her, my fists flailing at air. "Who? Who is it?"

Her lips move. "Ah, that'd be telling. Only one way to find out—come back in. I could make you do it, but it might break you. If you return of your own accord, we'll forge an ironclad bond. Be family."

I grip my head. I'm all out of words.

In her voice borrowed from me, Renee says, "Privacy. Room to think. I will give you that. And Scott? Don't wait too long. It's cold out there."

With that, my mind is empty. Still, I pull back past the tree line just to be sure.

The Agency doors close behind Hugh. On the billboard above, Renee's snapshot is repeated ten times. Did he perform an unscheduled update? He can't remember. What he is certain of is that to keep doing what his job requires— maintaining a distance—he must leave. The east gate is closest but it's a busy area, what with greenhouse train deliveries, so he sets a course for the west gate, doing his best to blend in with people striding around purposefully.

At the gate, the guard, Yesler, tries to stop him and Hugh makes the simple argument. "The Top Hundred rule doesn't apply to me. I don't have a rank."

Yesler doesn't budge. "Renee doesn't want anyone to leave."

Hugh tries to figure out the right combination of words —the ones that will unlock an exit. "I'm here to make sure the bird hut is ready. Renee wants it done. I'll just pop out and back in. No snowsuit necessary."

"The birds?" the guard says, the line on his forehead dissipating. "All right, then."

Hugh has never left the Dome before, but the gate is merely a big door, isn't it? He just has to step through.

The cold hits him instantly, a hard slap in the face. He glances at the aviary—it's smaller than he pictured and still empty—and keeps walking. The snow, fresh and deep after last night's storm, is making his shoes and pant bottoms soggy. His mind feels tight. A migraine fighting its way in, perhaps.

Someone calls his name and he glances back.

Renee is following him. Her feet, in their dressy shoes, are soft on the snow, so soft they're leaving no prints. "Hugh. It's hard to get close to you. No gems, no halo, not a single thought ever shared on the Commons... I'm offering you the chance to lead a different life—one not of loneliness but community."

He doesn't respond. She doesn't seem to understand about the distance he must keep. Best to keep moving. The terrain is uphill now and the forest lies ahead; a bald eagle, stately and strong, swoops above, the whole of the blue-white sky its playground.

Steel locks on under his brow, a not-migraine. "Hugh, I can't let you leave... Can't, Hugh..."

Can't has turned into the ringing of a bell in his mind, an echoing vibration of his gray matter. *CAN'T... CAN'T... CAN'T...* Odd—suddenly it's easier to move. The hill is less steep, the forest not so far. Even odder—his legs are no longer his own. Hugh's steps turn into a jog as he crests the hill and he runs at full speed into a pine tree, head-first. He steps back and does it again. And again. Warmth envelops his ears, seeps down his neck. At last Renee releases him and he sinks to the ground, arms wrapped around the trunk, the bark rough against his cheek. Waves pound inside his skull, aftershocks, unstoppable.

Arms grab under his shoulders and drag a body no longer his own into the forest, the person grunting with the effort. He watches the warm liquid drip down, the trail of red drops—rubies—discoloring the snow. The arms release him onto the ground deeper inside the forest and a familiar voice says, "Here, lean against this tree. It's all right, she can't reach you here."

He doesn't understand why so much worry registers on Scott's face. There's no reason for anyone to be concerned about him. He's the Listkeeper, always on his own.

"Are you okay?" She dabs at his ears with her gloves. "Sorry, stupid question. Tilt your head back—I know that's for nose bleeds, not ear bleeds, but it's the only thing I can think to do. I'll see if I can dig up a handkerchief..."

It's not his ears that are the problem. The red is spreading inside as well—will soon cause his mind to burst. He grips her hand as she searches pockets inside her snowsuit. A whisper is all he can manage. "Renee... All of us..."

She stops searching and kneels by his side. "I know. She's us—the town—a consciousness born of the CC's and gems and halos. But I don't understand one thing. Why *now?* Why not before, in all the years?"

Another whisper. "So many gems... A million of them—worthy of celebration..."

Understanding brightens her eyes. "I get it. When we passed the million threshold—that was what, a few weeks before the town anniversary?—it sparked Renee into being." She dabs at the red liquid with her sleeve. "Hugh... Is Dax all right? He was...injured yesterday. Renee said he's fine but I don't know if I can trust her."

He tries to nod but it hurts too much. "No reports of a death."

Some of the worry in her face eases and she asks something else. "Did you know Delilah was my mother? You used to be PALs. I thought she might have told you."

She's not focusing on the right things, but he whispers an answer. "All the years she was number one, Delilah pushed only once for the Agency to hire a specific person..."

"Wait, she got me the job? That's why I got to be an intern and the liaison for the party? Because she wanted me?" She says *wanted me* as if treasuring the words. The next ones are more hesitant. "Renee said there was another child."

He can sense his strength melting away. "You have a brother..." Scott leans in to hear, her young face close to his own, and he speaks a few more sentences, all he's able to tell her, and then one more: "Renee... You must stop her."

The answers he's given seem to have lightened the load on her shoulders. "You don't happen to have a pocket knife?" she asks. "I could dig around behind my ear and take out the chip. It'd be messy, but if I don't bleed out, I can sneak back in and destroy the heartbeat transmitter."

"The others...will see you."

"Right. Which means Renee will as well, and everyone will turn on me again and pile on. All right, so no sneaking in. What should we do, then?"

Even if he had an answer, it's too late. His soul is an eagle, sweeping high into the endless blue canvas of the sky.

Chapter Forty-Five

Friday, daybreak

I'm sitting in the snow by Hugh, rocking back and forth, my hands wrapped around my knees. I was unable to save him. I tried pumping on his chest, shaking him awake, mopped the blood from his ears. Nothing made any difference. Even though she said she needed everyone, Renee killed him. Hugh was on the outer rim of the town network, not on the People List, had no gems. Just a loose end—a dead bit of skin. She'll probably send someone out to dig out his chip so it can be reused.

My second night Outside was cold, long, and sleepless. Now the sun's rays are breaking over the land and my eyes are dry, the tears spent.

No one else has come out.

Hugh confirmed what Renee said: that I have a brother. His whisper a gentle rustle of leaves in the wind, he said the name. I'm certain Delilah tried to help Oliver, just as she pushed the Agency to hire me. She talked with me that

Monday morning, said no to handing me the Discovered brand, all the while knowing that Oliver was to leave that day.

To quench my thirst, I melt snow in my palm as Dax and I did on our private jaunt into the forest. I need to reach some sort of decision. Hugh is gone but that doesn't mean I can't talk to him about things. I slide closer, touch his face with the back of my fingers. His eyes are shut and his head is slumped toward one shoulder. I can almost convince myself that he's asleep, deep in a dream.

"Hugh," I say, the silent forest an army of gentle green giants around us, "here is how things stand. First, let me explain what won't work—storming the Dome with the help of market traders. Not only because Tuesday is four days away and I have no food or a way to warm myself. What it comes down to is, why would they believe me? The Hewletts—you didn't get to meet them, they were wonderful. Tawnie, Mikey, Sal, and their parents... It's a different world, one without brain chips, and how would I explain?" I shake my head. "And if I jumped on a train to New Portland, well, there's a slim chance of being believed and a high chance of being hospitalized for hallucinations. And for all we know, New Portland might have its own Renee, if things went down the same way."

Oliver, in the village of Upper Maple Grove, a multi-day trek on foot following the tracks of the Hewletts' snowmobiles. Oliver, who doesn't know he has a sister.

Dax and Lu and Wayne, down the hill and into the gate. Dax and Lu and Wayne, who must believe I'm dead.

I thought family meant that things would always be clear—an easy path to navigate. But it's more complicated than that. I tell Hugh, "Oliver... He and I need to forgive each other—work on building a new relationship. Not PALs but siblings."

I could start a new life by Oliver's side and learn to tend mountain goats or chop wood or whatever goes on in a village. This is the choice that beckons, though I don't want to admit it to Hugh. Follow the Hewletts' tracks, hope to reach Upper Maple Grove, hope to forget, never have to face Dax after hurting him.

Renee killed my mother. How can I go back in?

Or, head-scratchingly, did we *all* kill Delilah and Rick? Every time a ConnectChip went into an infant and the neural fibers spread and the child grew into adulthood and onto the List, Renee edged closer to becoming. If Renee's a monster—who chose to look like me, who took the daydreams in which I imagined myself differently and brought them to life—if she's a monster, it's one we all created. The suspect list on the WHO KILLED DELILAH corkboard should have encompassed all of New Seattle.

I glance up at the treetops and consider how strange and wonderful it must be to have ten thousand pairs of eyes and ears. All those minds to burrow into, with their knowledge and memories, ideas and plans, emotions and cravings, a creature peering into its own navel. And a million gems to peruse, cross-linking people and time, echoes of New Seattle's past, reflections of its present, hints of its future.

Renee killed my mother. How can I go back in?

"Hugh, it's easier to keep hating her," I admit, punching a hole in the snow with one gloved hand. "For Delilah, and Rick—and the years you were cheated out of. And yet I must forgive her. I have to, in order to defeat her. I hope you understand, Hugh."

Something in the stillness of his face makes me certain Hugh does understand.

"I went about it all wrong," I admit. "I chased the killer thinking people would like me better if I figured out who did it, when I should have been chasing Renee because a killer in our midst was a danger to everyone."

Renee is right, I was the Gal Who Wanted to be Liked. I aimed for Sherlock Scottie and was handed a different label, Scott the Curse Slayer. Now it's time to put on a new cloak. "Here's the plan, Hugh. I'll go back in and keep a low profile for a while, maybe a long while. Then, when the moment is right, I'll get everyone out. How, I have no idea. If all else fails, I'll get my hands on a lighter and be Scottie the Fire Starter and make Gemma Bligh's prediction come true. It'll have to be a big fire to fill the Dome with enough smoke to send people out the gates. Maybe I'll start with the Social Agency building—it's mostly wood—it'll go up fast. I'll gather cardboard boxes and any paper I can find and go floor to floor when no one's around and set them aflame next to window curtains."

Hopefully the fire will need to be only a metaphorical one, but I will do what it takes. After, if the town is still standing, a handful of us will go back in, too few to trigger Renee back into existence. We'll delete it all—gems, halos, the List—switch off the lights in CC Central permanently. Start over. Knock down the artificial walls installed by the Birth Lab.

It strikes me that my goals aren't that far from Renee's.

But first I'll need to convince her that I've accepted her as my lord and master. There's a distinct danger that I'll fall over the precipice, surrender my free will forever. What if I fail to extricate everyone from her web? There is another *what if*, my biggest fear: "Hugh, what if I don't *want* to destroy her after I've gone back in?"

I dig around in my pockets for Delilah's invite, then

scoop up a bit of snow onto my glove, where there is a stain from Hugh's blood. This yields a paste of a weak red. I don't have Cece to display text in my eye field, so I have to work from memory. Each letter a struggle, I trace out three words with my finger on the blank side of the invite.

"Hugh, I understand—finally." I tell him one last thing. "The answer is simple, like Dax said all along. He meant the murders, but it applies to life as well. The goal is not to be everyone's number one but one person's. If you have that, you are lucky." Hugh is silent and I rest my fingers on his shoulder a final time. "I didn't know you well, but you watched out for all of us. Thank you."

After the monster is defeated... After, it'll be time to seek out Oliver. For now, Oliver, brother, will have to stay just that, a new concept in my life. An unopened box.

I wait until the note is dry, slide it under my snowsuit into a shirt pocket and leave Hugh in the forest, dreaming forever.

From the tree line, the Dome no longer reminds me of the snow globe I picked up at the market, cozy and protected. The gate is a mouth ready to swallow me up never to be seen again, the warmth and food waiting within a false comfort. I'm scared that once I go through, I'll never see Oliver again. That will be the hardest.

But Dax needs me more right now, and so do Lu and Wayne. And McKinsey, and Ty who asked for a gem, and Sue and Samm with their dumb jokes, even Jada, cold-hearted as she is. I can't leave them to the fate of becoming cells in an automaton. Though I called no one mother, father, sister, son, daughter, I've had family all along. Not the way Renee means it, as a trap, but as much as if I lived in one of the mountain villages.

I let that be my one final free thought—for the town, *for my family*—and barrel downhill as fast as my snowsuit permits, letting the fears I've kept at bay overtake my mind: Freezing to death. Wandering the forest lost and starving. Being abducted by a rogue band of Outsiders. The animal I heard growling in the night attacking in the dark. Falling asleep next to Hugh and never waking up as hypothermia takes over...

I stagger to a stop in front of the gate. Yesler is digging a hole with a shovel, a difficult task with the ground frozen. With him are Jada, Ben, Poulsbo, and Blank Jack, all in snowsuits but no helmets. The four are carrying wooden crates and greet me as if I've run across them at a cafeteria breakfast, speaking the words almost simultaneously. "Scott, hello."

The effect is unnerving but I manage to say a hello back. Everyone has been busy and birds are skittering around the hut Poulsbo built—but there are many more in the crates. I watch the tiny lifeless bodies land with soft, terrible thumps in the hole Yesler's dug. As Yesler shovels chunks of frozen dirt back in, I try the gate, but it's locked. Not so no one can get in, but so no one can get out?

I shake Yesler by the shoulder. "I need to get in."

"Hold on. Can't you see I'm busy?"

"The gate, unlock it or give me the—"

Do you think I'm awesome, Scott? Do you love me?

The questions are just for me, jaws clamping on under my scalp. I'm cold and hungry and worried about Dax. Tears are streaming down my face. Renee can help me. I'll be safe inside. *Yes, I do.*

Then you can come back in.

Yesler thumps the last of the frozen dirt back in place and turns. "All right, all right, what's your hurry?" He unlocks the outer gate and I push ahead past him toward the inner door, which is propped open.

"Wait, I have to log you in," Yesler calls out after me but I don't look back. Bursting into the mudroom, I fling off the snowsuit, leaving it on the floor in a heap.

And in my mind:

Welcome back, Scottie. You're home. You're home.

Epilogue

Monday, some months later

It's dawn, and I'll be leaving soon for my job in the town warehouse, but first there's a task to attend to. A smudge mars the open window, where I must have accidentally pressed a hand. I ready a washcloth and a pitcher of water, but a movement across the alley catches my attention. A sparrow has flown up into a recess in the neighboring building, Housing Thirty-Two.

This is a much bigger problem than a window smudge. Birds—vermin, Number One calls them—aren't permitted in New Seattle. In fact, it's *why* all windows must be kept closed and spotless: so any birds that sneak in through the gates will fly into the invisible walls and fall to the street, stiff and dead. That's what they're supposed to be, gone or lifeless.

Before I'm able to send a sighting report to the Bird Control Office, there's a distraction. An argument breaks out a floor below me, on the street. The woman's nose angles down sharply as she berates the man, who's holding his own. "I can't spare the cloth, Five," the man defends himself. "The shop is making uniforms, identical ones for everyone. Number One is pleased with the idea."

"I understand, Six," the woman argues back, "but I'm expanding the Oyster—this, too, will please Number One. I need the extra tablecloths."

"Nevertheless, priority should be given..."

Tuning out the argument, I attack the smudge. Number One will calm them down soon enough. Indeed, there she is, wasting no time; her step is quick, her hair flowing over the gown she always wears—one I have a copy of on a wall hook, though I never seem to find the right occasion to wear it. Resting my elbows on the windowsill, I watch the three figures. The voices of Five and Six float up from the street, but Number One's voice is everywhere, strong and steady, as if called forth from a deep and endless wellspring in my mind. Her presence is a soft blanket around my shoulders, snug and enveloping.

Still, as much as I love having Number One with me always, I find that I'm capable of thinking more clearly when her attention is engaged elsewhere, as at the moment. I reach for the binoculars I keep on the dresser—Ninety-Eight gave them to me. He grows plants as his job and has already left for the day, his shirt covering the row of scars across his stomach, the result of an accidental fall onto a nail-studded plank.

I wipe the layer of dust off the binoculars and focus in on the sparrow. Black-beaked and lively, it's pushing a twig into the recess, its goal a new nest. How odd. I can't remember *why* Number One abhors birds—why we all do. I make it into a question: Why is it wrong for the creature to be making a tiny home from twigs and scraps—to want to attract a mate and create a new generation?

I haven't asked a question in a long time.

Wanting to help the sparrow, I reach for what's also gathering dust on the dresser—a couple of invitations. I shred the first one—it's addressed to someone named Scott—into fragments of a size more suited to a small-beaked creature and set them on the windowsill, then reach for the other invite. That one, in the same neat penmanship, reads:

> Delilah—Guest of Honor
> New Seattle's Eighty-Fifth
> Founders Square at eight o'clock
> Monday, the fifteenth of March

The month of March must be a long time ago, because I can only remember fragments of the evening, whorls of memory bubbling up. Borrowing a dress. Lanterns and wine. Wanting to hold hands but staying apart. Losing someone who had already lost himself. And Delilah... She was an actor, wasn't she? And she died that night.

The other side of the invite, with its uneven letters of a faded and cracked crimson, is even more puzzling. It says:

> START A FIRE

And now it's only questions and no answers. Why a fire? And where?

I shake my head and tear the invite in half, then once more. Below, on the street, the argument has abated and everyone has left. I add the scraps to the ones already on the windowsill, shifting the washcloth out of the way. The motion causes a drop of water to fall. It lands on the word

FIRE and makes the ink run red, pulling forth a memory long forgotten, of someone hurt.

Hugh. He was the keeper of a list.

More memories bubble up, of a different life—one where I was called Scott. A life where I tried hard to find a brand, worried about rank, about being kicked out into the cold.

I sigh with contentment. Everything's better now. I'm not alone—I will never again be alone. I will always have Number One. I'm Two—closest to Number One, but the numbers beyond one are just for identification purposes, not a ranking. My job in the warehouse is to help distribute provisions—an equitable portion for each person of chocolate bars or oranges, and a lending system for unique items. I've contributed my copy of The Seattle Times and my bike to be shared with others.

A quick motion of my fingers sends the paper scraps, with their disconcerting remainder of a life best forgotten, off the windowsill and onto the street. The industrious sparrow will pick them up. Rolling the window closed, I give it a final wipe down, then head out, grabbing the remaining item on my dresser: a snow globe, which now has no more paper it needs to weigh down. I'll take it with me to the warehouse.

Today not being my day to use the bike, I'm on foot. The dome-town where I live is a cocoon warmed by the morning sun, and I spin the globe from one hand to the other as I walk. It too is a memory of someone...but it's no use. The name will not come. No matter. I spin it again and watch the plastic snowflakes tumble as if they're living things.

But my hands are clumsy and the globe falls. It shatters on the pavement and the snowflakes spill, escape. On the ground is an emptied shell, sunlight dancing in its fragments like flame. It's an illusion—which is a good thing, as inside the Dome a genuine flame brings the danger of an out-of-control fire sending everyone out the gates...

An emptied shell...

I remember.

Acknowledgments

Some books come easy. This one took me to writing places I never explored before—some felt like mountain vistas, others had a more of a lost-in-a-dark-cave-for-endless-days mood to them. I'm both exhilarated and thankful to be at journey's end, a book in hand.

My thanks go out to everyone who kindly provided feedback on bits and pieces and various versions of the manuscript: Mary Alterman, John Baron, Anne Charnock, Jill Marsal, Angela Mitchell, Richard Ellis Preston, Jr., and Roberta Trahan. The book is all the better for the wisdom of its whiz trio of editors: Kristen Weber, Shannon Page, and Marti McKenna.

Grateful thanks go out to the Maslakovic and the Baron sides of the family for their encouragement and support.

Most of all they go out to my husband John and my son Dennis, my comrades-in-arms (along with a goldendoodle named Grif) in the mask-wearing, home-sitting, uphill sort of year that was 2020—may we not see another like it anytime soon.

About the Author

Neve Maslakovic is the author of five novels, starting with *Regarding Ducks and Universes* ("Inventive... a delight." — *Booklist*). Her science fiction leans towards cozy, with plenty of mystery twists and humor. Her life journey has taken her from Belgrade, Serbia to a PhD at Stanford University's STAR Lab to her dream-come-true job as a writer. She lives with her husband, son, and high-spirited goldendoodle in the Twin Cities.

Find out more and sign up for Neve's newsletter at www.nevemaslakovic.com

Also by Neve Maslakovic

Regarding Ducks and Universes

The Incident Series

The Far Time Incident

The Runestone Incident

The Bellbottom Incident

Prequel to the Incident series

The Feline Affair

www.ingramcontent.com/pod-product-compliance
Lightning Source LLC
Chambersburg PA
CBHW031615100726
47898CB00006B/1802